THE

DISSOLUTION OF

Unrequited

from the bestselling author of Sometimes Moments

LEN WEBSTER

The Dissolution of Unrequited
Copyright © 2019 Len Webster
Published by Len Webster

Published: Len Webster 2019
Editing: Jenny Sims
Cover & Interior Design: Qamber Designs & Media

BOOKS BY LEN WEBSTER

The First Touch of Sunlight
The Wait For You

The Sometimes Moments Collection

Sometimes Moments (Sometimes Moments #1)
Sometimes, Forever (Sometimes Moments #2)
Sometimes. Honestly? Always. (Sometimes Moments #3)
Coming Soon

Thirty-Eight Series

Thirty-Eight Days (Thirty-Eight #1)
Thirty-Eight Reasons (Thirty-Eight #2)
What We'll Leave Behind (Thirty-Eight #2.5)
What You Left Behind (Thirty-Eight #3)
All We Have (Thirty-Eight #4)
With The First Goodbye (Thirty-Eight #5)
With The Last Goodbye (Thirty-Eight #6)

The Science of Unrequited: The Story of AJ & Evan

The Theory of Unrequited (The Science of Unrequited #1)
The Solution to Unrequited (The Science of Unrequited #2)
The Results of Unrequited (The Science of Unrequited #3)
The Dissolution of Unrequited (The Science of Unrequited #4)

When We Say It's Forever (3.43)
-The McClymonts Ft. Ronan Keating

For those who wait and love.
Those who experience unrequited.
One day, not someday, you will be immersed in so much love.
But for every day and every breath until then and after,
Just be you.

PROLOGUE I
ALEX

*W*e tried.

No one could ever say we didn't try.

Because we did.

And sometimes, like aspects and moments in life, we failed.

Not every relationship ends the way it should, and not every relationship lives up to the expectations set by others.

And some relationships, well, some relationships never flourish.

How I ended up here, in this moment, is a long story.

Quite like the story of Evan and me.

It took us many years to get to here.

To get us staring at each other.

Me on one end of the room and him on the other.

Eyes are on us, and a silent conversation occurs between us.

Questions that haven't met the surface.

Questions that might take forever to answer.

But, today, only one question really matters.

A question for him.

And a question for me.

We took the long way with life.

And like life's many stories, it's time ours ended.

Because I will have many regrets in my life.

1

But not being his will be my biggest.
He'll be my only regret that matters.
Just him.
My best friend.
My Evan Gilmore.

PROLOGUE II
EVAN

*T*he greatest love stories were the ones that triumphed through the very worst.

Prevailed against the doubt and continued to grow and strengthen with time.

My greatest love story was Alexandra Louise Parker.

My greatest triumphs in life were with her.

My life was full with her in it.

I can't say I was perfect.

But I knew perfection because of her.

Because she was and is, in every way possible, perfect.

And I miss her.

She was and will always continue to be my everything.

We've barely said much in the past six months.

We've barely had a lifetime together.

But what we had was something no one could take from us.

We'll never truly be over.

She's my ending.

My home.

Because the final page of my life will have her name written all over it.

Even if it means I have to wait a little longer for her.

But AJ doesn't know that.

5

Someday, she will.

Someday, she'll know that I'll love her with every day that passes us ...

Because she is the oxygen I will always need.

76

Os

osmium

ALEX

Now

Alexandra Parker hadn't felt an accomplishment quite like this in a long time. She had done it. She had finally finished her research assignment given to her at the start of her employment with Dr. Vincent Rodahawe.

She tested the equation she had worked on for the past year in the simulator, and it appeared to work with Dr. Rodahawe's research. She hadn't intended to become his research partner in any sense. When she had started at the institute, she was his assistant, and that meant cataloguing a lot of his research. But when Alex noticed and pointed out a miscalculation in his equation, Dr. Rodahawe had asked her to join his team.

"Oh, my God, Alex," Brandon, Dr. Rodahawe's former assistant now turned researcher from Oxford University, said in awe.

Alex set down her notebook on her desk and took in the projection data on the screen. "It looks like it works. The velocity of the engine is exactly where we want it without stalling. This is ..."

"Incredible," Brandon breathed.

It *was* incredible.

All her late nights in the lab making sure her equation had

no flaws had paid off.

"This formula can help prove Vincent's research. You're a genius, and you did it before the end of the week like you promised." Sadness swept Brandon's face. He could never hide his emotions. They had become great friends during her time in Zürich, Switzerland. His lips suddenly curved into a smile in an attempt not to damper the already tense atmosphere. "Do you know how many airlines will want to scoop you up when they learn you formulated this equation? You're saving the industry millions while also proving how dangerous a shift in force can be to velocity."

Alex nodded. "So I guess coming here after I graduated from Duke was a great idea, then?"

Brandon laughed. "Definitely. You may have slashed our research time by months, if not years. You should show Vincent."

"I will," she said, pushing her chair back and getting up. Then she picked up her laptop and shot Brandon a smile. "I couldn't have done this without you, Brandon. Without everyone's input. This wasn't just me. It was the whole team."

"Swiss Airlines or American Airlines?" It was a game they played after each advancement they made in their research. It was a question of who Alex would accept employment from if she were approached.

She mulled it over and then smiled. "Neither."

"Neither?" Brandon asked, his brow arched. Curiosity shimmered in his blue eyes. With his English accent and strawberry blond hair, Brandon was cute. He had a dimple that deepened with every flawless smile he made. Though nerdy, underneath the sweaters and ties, he loved to swim during his free time, and as a result, he had a chiseled body. A body she saw for herself when they swam laps around the pool in their free time.

As sweet as Brandon was, she would never date him. It was strictly professional for Alex. She would not jeopardize their relationship, her employment, or their research.

Alex spun around and glanced over her shoulder. "I'm waiting for NASA," she teased, knowing full well that NASA was Brandon's dream employer and not hers. NASA, on paper, would be perfect for Alex, but she knew Washington wasn't her next step. The next step for her was one she had made months ago.

When Alex made it to Dr. Rodahawe's office on the other side of the institute, she knocked on his opened door and watched him turn away from the whiteboard. Smiling at her, he waved her to come in. He set the marker on the tray as Alex held her laptop steady and entered his office. Once inside, she approached his desk and took in the wall full of whiteboards. They were full of calculations, equations, and diagrams. Dr. Vincent Rodahawe was a genius. All his awards and the Nobel Prize for Physics were proof of that. For Alex, she was honored he had chosen her as his research assistant over the other applicants.

"Is it good news?" he asked, excitement flaring in his brown eyes. When Alex first met the doctor, she was nervous. She had expected him to be no-nonsense and serious, but he was a dedicated physicist who loved what he did. The way he saw and spoke of the world and science was enchanting and inspiring.

Alex set the laptop on his desk and turned it around so he could see the screen. "With all the parameters and variables, it's good news, Dr. Rodahawe. Velocity was within our desired target without causing a stall. Though we will need to have trained pilots with the NTSB and STSB in the cockpit simulator. We can have the Swiss Transport Safety Board recreate the simulation first before we approach NTSB and Boeing." She reached over and pointed at the screen. "It's flawless in my calculations, but we need to have it tested by pilots for human factors. Number-wise, your research is one step closer to being proven, but a catastrophic dive can happen. We need human risk and reaction data for the next part of your research—which I'm certain the STBS and NTSB will cooperate with."

Dr. Rodahawe's eyes followed the screen until he glanced over and took in his research on the whiteboards. "You are correct, Alexandra. A seasoned pilot can get a plane out of a nose dive within seconds, but a rookie wouldn't. Not with that kind of speed and G-force. We can increase speed but only by a fraction without causing a stall." He gazed back at her, his eyes sparkling with pride. "But with your equation, we're one step closer to ensuring that doesn't happen while still increasing efficiency and speed. I'm very proud of you, Alexandra. No research assistant has ever excelled the way you have."

"Thank you for not firing me and seeing my potential after I called you out on one of your calculation errors," she said, still slightly embarrassed that she had told a Nobel Prize recipient he had made a mistake.

Deep and carefree laughter burst from her mentor, then he reached over and closed the laptop before he let out a sigh. "Is there any way I can change your mind, Alexandra? Is there any way I can keep you here in Zürich for three more years? More money? More independence?" Guilt pooled in her stomach, making her feel sick. "I'm sorry, Dr. Rodahawe," she said, shaking her head. "It's not a decision I make lightly. When I applied to be your research assistant, my boyfriend broke my heart, and I didn't want to give up my dreams for him. When I agreed to come to Zürich, it was only for a year. I would want nothing more than to stay and experience three more years of working with and for the best. It has been an honor to work with you, and Brandon and Julia, and all the physicists. But it's three more years away from my family and friends ... It means three years away from Sebastian. I couldn't do that. I've missed two months with him. I can't miss anymore. You have to understand how much I miss him."

Dr. Rodahawe nodded. "I do, Alexandra. I do understand." Though he might, his sullen expression told her he was still disappointed with her decision. "It hasn't been the easiest six months for you. You never gave up on this research when you could have. And I am so thankful for your sacrifices and your commitment to me, the research, and this institution."

"It has been the hardest six months of my life, but it has also been the most rewarding. Being here was a dream I never thought I'd get to experience, but I think it's time someone else experienced their dreams, too."

"When this research is complete, your name will be in my acknowledgments," he promised. "I'm proud to have been your mentor, Alexandra."

His praise had her eyes stinging as she made her way around his desk and wrapped her arms around him. "Thank you, Dr. Rodahawe," she said once she ended their quick hug. "For all the opportunities you have given me. For trusting in me. For letting me go home two months ago. Thank you for letting me be a physicist and for believing some Duke graduate was good enough to be in your presence."

Dr. Rodahawe set a palm on her shoulder. "You are brilliant, Alexandra. You are what physics needs. Thank you for letting me mentor you. I will always be here for you if you ever need me."

Smiling, Alex knew she had tied up all her loose ends in Zürich.

She was ready.

Ready to start her new life.

She was ready to finally go home.

Back to Brookline, Massachusetts.

Her apartment was empty.

It had been for six months.

It was empty the moment he left for the States. He had taken every possession he owned with him. Her heart included. The only thing that was a piece of home was the picture frame on her dresser. When they had moved into their Zürich apartment, it had already been furnished. They had gone shopping to buy everything they could to make it as homey as possible. It had been one of her favorite memories of them together in Switzerland.

Now, all traces of them were gone.

Nothing but memories to hold on to.

Alex had packed the rest of her clothing and research books in her suitcase yesterday, ready for her flight back to America tomorrow morning. It was nearing midnight, and she had just returned from her farewell dinner where her co-workers and mentor spoke so highly of her, making her cry before they even had their last drink together.

The beeping from her laptop had her turning away from her suitcase and glancing over at her bed. She noticed the video chat request from her best friend. Smiling, Alex got up from the floor and sat on her bed, pulling the MacBook to her lap and accepting the call. Seconds later, a bright smile consumed her screen.

"Alex!" Savannah Peters, Alex's best friend and roommate from Duke, said.

"Hey, Sav."

"How was your final day? Brandon still trying to get you to fall in love with him?"

Alex brushed her hair back and shook her head with a laugh. "It was good. Pretty emotional. And Brandon and I are just friends. He knows that. How was work? Have you just finished?"

Savannah nodded. "I just got home. Traffic in Montpelier was a nightmare, but I had to work in the city, didn't I? Now, let's talk about what's really important. Packed and ready?"

"Almost," she said, glancing back at her dresser to see all the picture frames of her family and friends. One picture made her smile. It was of her and Savannah during their Duke graduation over a year and a half ago.

"What's left?"

15

"Just pictures," she answered as she looked back at the screen.

Savannah's brows furrowed. "You're nervous to come home," she stated.

She sighed. "I am."

"You're scared to find out if he's moved on?"

"Yeah," she admitted in a small voice. Savannah was the only person who knew her heart's true affections. Knew of her longing and desires. "But I'm also coming home for my family."

Her best friend's lips pressed into a small smile. "You gave up a three-year contract with the Rodahawe Institute, Alex."

"I know. But I miss home. And he gave up a year for me to be in Zürich. I can't believe I said yes to three more years when I shouldn't have."

"It's going to be okay. It'll work out. You look so tired. I see it still keeps you up at night. I'll let you finish packing so you can sleep, but you should know how excited I am that you're coming home. It means I don't have to take a stupid plane to see you. One week in Zürich was not four years at Duke. I've missed you, Alex."

Alex's heart warmed, knowing that she missed her best friend, too. "I've missed you, too, Sav. I'll come up to Montpelier to see you once I'm settled back in Massachusetts."

"You better. Bye, Alex. Make sure you text me when you land. Have a safe flight!"

"I will. Bye, Sav," Alex said. She closed her laptop and set it next to her on the mattress. Then she glanced down at her suitcase, got off her bed, and made her way to the dresser. The drawers were already empty, and she'd donated the clothes she didn't plan on bringing back with her. She had begun planning her return to Massachusetts two months ago. The moment she landed in Zürich after her last trip home, she knew she had left her heart behind.

Once she reached the dresser, Alex picked up the envelope that rested on the oak. The very envelope she received weeks after she had applied. It was another reason to return home but not her true reason.

Alex's thumb brushed against the logo, and she smiled.

Massachusetts Institute of Technology.

She had done it.

It had taken her many years, but she finally had her acceptance letter into MIT. It wasn't easy applying from Zürich, and she had feared rejection, but Dr. Rodahawe was adamant that she'd be accepted into MIT's physics doctorate program with or without his recommendation letter. Setting the envelope down, Alex picked up the framed picture of them.

The real reason she was going home.

It had been eight weeks since she last saw him.

Eight weeks since she last told him she loved him and meant it.

Eight weeks felt like a lifetime.

But Alex knew longer.

She knew what a lifetime really entailed.

And it was full of misery.

^{77}Ir

iridium

ALEX

Sophomore year of college

I t didn't feel right.
To stand in front of someone she loved and not feel anything.

It didn't feel right that she didn't feel that love.

The love she knew she felt for him.

She was sure of it.

But at that moment, Alexandra Parker felt no love for her ex-boyfriend, Landon Carmichael. She was still hurt that he had chosen the NBA over her. Still angry that he had denied their relationship in a magazine. Lied to the world about her. About them. And lied to her about the teams interested in him.

Alex's time in Massachusetts wasn't long enough. It wasn't the space she had needed so desperately because while she was home, she was with Evan Gilmore—her former best friend and first love. Being with Evan reminded her of what she had lost while she was with Landon. She had been Landon Carmichael's girlfriend for so long that she lost track of where her dreams lay. Evan made it his mission to bring her back. To remind her that MIT was her dream.

That she was *AJ* Parker.

And during her time with Evan, she realized that she still

19

loved him and had kissed him. Parts of her still wanted to be with him, but it wasn't the time. Her heart wasn't his to have; it was her ex-boyfriend's. The very same ex-boyfriend standing outside her dorm room with a bouquet of different colored tulips in his hand, apologizing and pleading for her.

"Please, Alex. Please forgive me," he begged.

She didn't know what to say.

He had broken them up.

He ended them when the truth came out.

Landon stepped forward, closing the distance between them, pressuring her for an answer. "Please take me back. I was an idiot. I didn't see what was in front of me. It's you I want. I don't care about Phoenix. I want to be with you. Please take me back. Please."

Her heart ached.

She wanted to hear him say those words. Words she now had to refuse because she knew that she would go back to him. She'd lose track of who she was once more. She'd lose her dreams for him to keep his.

"Landon," she said in a tight voice. It was all she could say for fear she'd commit her heart to him again.

Evan Gilmore had just brought her back.

He'd worked so hard to show her his love and her dreams.

She couldn't do that to him.

Not when she knew she still loved him.

But that was the problem. She also still loved Landon.

"Please, can we just talk?"

Alex nodded, knowing that she would give Landon more than he had given her. Because that was the power of her love for him. "Okay," she agreed as she dug her hand into her purse and pulled out her keys. Just as she reached behind to grab the suitcase handle, Landon stepped forward and took it from her.

"I've got it," Landon said, causing Alex to step aside. She opened her mouth to object, but he shook his head. "I fucked up. I know I did. It doesn't mean I'll continue to hurt you. I want to ... no, I *need* to treat you right. I need to treat you better."

A crack developed in her heart as she remained quiet and headed to her dorm. She inserted the key, twisted it, and opened the door. Though she knew her roommate was at work, Alex couldn't help but wish Savannah was inside. She needed Savannah as a source of strength against Landon. Because she knew it wouldn't take him much to work his way back into her heart.

She had to remember he hurt her.

He hurt them.

He put his dreams ahead of hers without any thought or discussion.

Stepping inside, she made her way toward her bed and dropped her purse on it. Alex clenched her eyelids shut and inhaled deep breaths, telling herself that she could be strong. She had to be strong and fight for her dreams. When she felt confident enough to face him, she spun around to find Landon closing the door and then setting the flowers on her desk.

"Baby—"

Alex shook her head. "I am not your baby, Landon. You made that clear a week ago when you walked out that door."

Her voice broke.

She wasn't stronger.

She had kept her emotions in, but now they were bursting at the seams.

His chin dipped slightly as she noticed the shame and pain flash in his once bright blue eyes. In the entirety of their relationship, the only fight they'd had before their breakup was when he almost left her in Brookline. It was Landon who always did the leaving, and it was Alex who always did the fighting ... until last week.

"I know," he said in a small voice.

The Landon Carmichael before her had let himself go in the week since they broke up. He had dark circles under his eyes, and he hadn't shaved, a shadow of hair prickled his jaw. He might be sad, but he left her devastated when he ended them. At that moment, Alex knew she would always be the one sacrificing her dreams for him. Just as she had for everyone else. She needed Landon to understand what she would do for him. Understand that she had chosen him and loved him over Evan Gilmore and MIT. Landon had to understand that she still loved him more.

"You hurt me," she said, gaining his attention. His distraught blue eyes caused the tightening in her chest, taking her breath away.

"I know," he repeated.

Alex shook her head, fighting and begging her tears to stay away. "You don't know. You took my love for granted. I shouted in the middle of the street that I loved you after you used Evan's childhood nickname against me. That hurt, Landon. You have never hurt me more than that night because it made me realize that you doubted my love for you. My loyalty to you. You think I wouldn't join you in Phoenix? That I wouldn't have made it work?"

His jaw clenched as she saw his eyes gleam over with

unshed tears. "Alex ..."

She took a step forward, closing the space between them. "I would have," she revealed. "I would have followed you to Phoenix. To San Antonio. To whatever city you got drafted to because I love you, Landon Carmichael." Her tears ran freely down her cheeks. "And it angers me that you didn't even consider there being an us after you graduate. It breaks my heart that I'm not right for you. That my image hinders you. I hate how in love I am with you when I know you chose a future without me. Don't you get how much I love you?"

As if he couldn't take it anymore, Landon reached up and cupped her face, his thumbs gently brushing away her tears. "I'm sorry. I'm so sorry, Alex. I didn't mean it. Any of it. I don't want the NBA if it means I lose you. I don't want to lose you. I can't. I love you, baby. I love you."

She believed him.

But she hated that it took losing her for him to realize her love and her worth.

"That's not enough," she whispered as she pulled away from his touch. "It's not, Landon. Because then I'm the bad guy who held you back and ended your NBA career. I don't want to be that person to you. I can't be. I refuse to be."

Landon shook his head, desperation etching his face as he grasped her hands. "I can't lose you, Alex. I can't. Please give us another shot. You still love me. I still love you. Couples fight all the time. Just give us another chance. Let me take you to dinner. Let me fix this. I made a mistake. I love you, Alex. I'm still him. Let me be the guy you fell madly in love with."

It all broke away.

The strength she had accumulated was gone.

Because Landon was right.

He was the guy she had fallen madly in love with.

"Please have dinner with me?" he begged.

"Okay," Alex whispered, conceding defeat. "Just dinner."

He nodded as relief flashed in his blue eyes, and his shoulders fell from their stiff position. It seemed even his touch had relaxed. "Thank you. I won't ever let you down again. I won't. Never again," he promised.

She believed him.

Believed he was honest and he would try.

Then he tugged her to his hard chest and wrapped his arms around her, whispering promises in her ear as she closed her eyes and inhaled him. His woodsy cologne was so familiar, reminding her of how safe she felt in his arms. It was the opposite to how she should truly feel in her ex-boyfriend's arms. She was still hurt and needed space from him, so Alex pressed her palms to his waist and created the distance she desperately needed.

"I'm tired," she admitted. "I've had a long day. I'll see you tomorrow."

He nodded. "Okay." Then he bent his knees and lowered his face to hers.

Alex's breath hitched as he inched his lips closer to hers.

Anxiety raced through her as her eyes searched his.

She wasn't ready to kiss him.

She wasn't ready to wipe Evan's kiss away with Landon's.

Then he did the unexpected and pressed his lips to her cheek before he stepped back. "Good night, Alex." His eyes bore into hers.

She saw it.

His weakness and his fear. He was scared to lose her again. It didn't give her any pleasure knowing that she caused him as much pain as he did to her.

"Good night, Landon." She watched him press his lips into a tight smile and then make his way out of her dorm, leaving her even more confused than before.

Alex had hoped she wouldn't see him for a few days. She had hoped she could settle back at Duke and go over her conflicting feelings before she saw her ex-boyfriend again. But he ambushed her. And there wasn't much she could do but agree to dinner. At least it would be tomorrow night, and she'd have some time to herself before then.

The ringing of her phone had Alex blinking at her door and then glancing down at her purse. Sitting on her bed, Alex opened her purse and pulled out her phone to find Evan calling her. She chewed her lip as her thumb hovered over her screen. She took a deep breath, peeked at the door to make sure it was locked, and then answered his call, pressing her phone to her ear.

"AJ?" His voice was soft, almost as if it were full of fear.

"Hey," she replied.

She heard him hum before they sat in silence.

For minutes, they didn't say a word.

On and on did time pass them.

Their silence spoke volumes as Alex lifted her legs up onto her bed and pressed her back against the cold brick wall. She could hear the traffic from his end and knew he was still driving to Massachusetts. Not liking the way her stomach knotted, Alex decided that she should break their silence.

"Evan?"

"Yes, AJ?"

She inhaled sharply and exhaled in one short huff. "Landon was outside my dorm."

"Are you okay? Did he hurt you?" Evan asked, worry pitched in his voice.

"No," she strongly assured. "He didn't. He begged me to take him back."

Evan once again fell silent before he asked, "And did you?"

Alex shook her head even though she knew he couldn't see. "No. I'm going to dinner with him tomorrow night." She paused. "I have to be sure, Evan."

"I understand," he said, truth simmered in his voice.

She let out a sigh of relief, only just realizing how tense she had been. "Thank you."

"I'm scared," Evan admitted.

"I know. I am, too."

"I don't want you to pick him."

Her eyes fell closed, hating how small his voice was. "I love him, Evan. A week ago, he was my boyfriend, and I hadn't spoken to you in months."

"And you lost yourself for almost a year," he pointed out.

He was right.

Alex knew it.

She opened her eyes and took a deep breath. "You're not making this easy," she confessed.

"I don't mean to make it difficult, AJ. He doesn't know you the way I do. But I know you love him, so I can't force your hand right now. I promised I would be your best friend. And that's what I'll be if you call me tomorrow night and tell me it's him. I'll be your best friend. The best friend you've always needed and deserved. I better hang up and let you—"

"Wait," she said quickly, remembering their drive from Brookline to Duke. Remembering why her heart wanted and had chosen Evan during their road trip. And most importantly, she remembered what she left behind.

"What's wrong?"

"Thank you," she whispered.

"You don't have to thank me."

"But I do," she replied with a small smile to her lips. "You gave me answers I never thought I'd ever have. You made me understand you and your choices. Evan, you let my heart beat properly and freely for the first time in forever. In that car with you, I chose you because you gave me *me* again, so I left behind something for you."

Evan was silent as if he was scared to break the spell between them by speaking. "What did you leave for me?"

She bit her lip for a moment before she released it. "Do you remember that gift I gave you?"

"I do."

"I bought you that gift when I thought I had you. That I was yours. Then you broke my heart and I put the box away and never thought I'd see you again."

"I never thought I'd see you again either."

Alex felt a smile twitch at her lips. "You brought me back. I told you to trust me and not to open it until I trusted you. I trust you, Evan. I left the gift tag I wrote you on the passenger seat. I want you to have it. I want you to have my words and my trust."

She heard some rustling sound before he asked, "You trust me?"

27

"I do," she said in a small voice.

"Then trust me."

She flinched. "What?"

"Trust me, AJ. I won't read these words or open your present until I have your heart and you back. Until I see you and know you truly want me and not him, I'll wait for you. I'll wait until I see you and I'm with you to open your gift and read the tag."

Her heart clenched.

It was all she had ever wanted from Evan.

His hope for them was stronger than any promise he had ever given her.

"I don't know when I'll see you."

He exhaled. "I know. I'll wait. I'll always wait." She smiled at his words as he continued, "I'll let you get some sleep. You've had a long day. I'm gonna find a hotel and stay the night. I'll call you later?"

"Yeah," she agreed, not knowing what more she could say to him. "Call me tomorrow before your flight but let me know when you've checked in so I know you're okay."

"I will," he promised.

"Good. Good night, Evan."

"Good night." Just as she was about to hang up, he quickly said, "Hey, AJ?"

She stilled. "Yes?"

He inhaled a deep breath. "I love you. And I know that's not fair of me to say right now, but I do. I have, and I always will. Just in case I lose you and don't ever get to tell you. I love you, Alexandra."

She could say it.

Say three words and pretend it was no big deal.

But it was.

And she couldn't give him hope with three words.

"And to be fair to you, Evan, I can only say good night. I don't want to make promises to anyone right now—especially to you. I don't want a repeat of what happened last time we made promises. It can't be like that again."

"I know. It won't. Good night, AJ. For real, good night."

A smile finally spread across her lips. "Good night for real, Evan."

It was easy.

So easy to fall in love with Landon Carmichael.

To fall victim to his charm and his bright blue eyes.

To laugh along with his jokes.

To forget he destroyed her heart for an NBA career.

But it happened.

As Alex sat opposite him in a fancy French restaurant in Durham, she found herself loving everything about him. She gave him the chance at a clean slate, and he took it. He appeared at her door on time and dressed the part. He wore a white dress shirt and black slacks with polished leather shoes to match. He texted her to dress up, and she was glad she listened. When she opened the door wearing the simple, tight black dress, she was breathless at the hope in his blue eyes.

For a moment, she was disappointed the short beard that made him look even sexier was gone, but she loved the clean-shaven captain of the men's Duke basketball team more. And before her, he was it. The man she fell in love with. For their entire dinner, it felt as if nothing had come between them. That a week hadn't separated them. That Evan hadn't come back into her life and pieced together her dreams and future for her. That Evan Gilmore hadn't told her the truth behind his actions.

Landon reached over and grasped her hand after she finished eating the final bite of her ratatouille. Alex glanced up to see the soft smile on his face, causing her heart to ache. Confusion thumped at her temples. She loved Landon. There was no denying it. She felt it in her bones as they laughed and talked as if nothing had changed the position of their world around the sun. It felt so natural and real. They felt like them again, but the small voice in her head told her otherwise. It told her to guard her foolish heart and to be wary. And her heart had no intention of listening, still madly in love with Landon Carmichael.

Her ex-boyfriend squeezed her hand. "I'm sorry, Alex. For the article. For what I said. For making you think I didn't love you enough. I love you, baby. I was stupid and made a mistake. I don't want fame if it means I lose you. I'll work hard to earn your trust back, just don't give up on us. Believe me, Alex, I love you so much."

She felt it.

Every spoken word made her heart clench.

She believed him, and the determination to win her heart back and the love in his eyes were clear.

"Can we please try again?"

It was a loaded question—a heartbreaking question—

but her heart yearned to try. Even though her brain knew otherwise. He would still want the NBA. He was still a senior on track to graduate. They still had issues. Issues she wanted to work through.

"If you promise to be honest about the NBA and draft prospects with me. If that's a promise you can make and honor, then we can try again," she offered, hating the speck of insecurity that shimmered in her chest.

His large smile had her almost laughing. The little doubt in her fading. "I promise, I'll be honest. From now on, no more interviews, and if I have one, I won't lie about you and us. Never again will I lie about how much I love—"

A cough interrupted them, and Alex glanced over to find their waiter, a member she recognized from the school band, standing by their table. "Can I get you both the dessert menu?"

Alex felt Landon's eyes on her, and she shook her head. "No. Just the check, please. We're leaving."

"Of course," the waiter said before he left them alone.

"We're leaving?" Landon asked, getting her attention.

She swung her focus back on him and smiled. "Yeah. Don't we normally end each date at your apartment with ice cream? Unless ... Walt and Chase are home?"

He shook his head. "They aren't home."

"So your place?"

Landon nodded. "My place."

Alex wasn't that girl.

The girl who went back to a guy's place after a date.

She wasn't.

But this was Landon.

And she had agreed to try again with him.

It was a strange feeling to be back in her ex-boyfriend's apartment. Throughout the drive back to his place, Alex couldn't get herself to remove the ex from his title. Something was off. But the moment he smiled at her, and she saw the love bright in his blue eyes, that doubt fizzled away. She agreed to try again, and she was a woman of her word.

"Are you okay?" Landon asked as he turned away from the hallway table where he had just set his keys.

She stared at him, wondering how they found themselves here. They had been so perfect, and now she was questioning every decision she made. There was no doubt she still loved him. She felt it in her chest and each heartbeat. She needed to know the strength of her love for Landon Carmichael.

Nodding, Alex stepped forward, set her purse on the table on her left, and pressed her palms to his jaw. Confusion was the victor in her heart. She loved him, she was so sure of it, but she was also sure of the heartbreak he inflicted. The pain he'd left her reeling in. The confidence he'd stripped her of.

But Alex loved him.

So she kissed her ex-boyfriend.

The spark reignited instantaneously. The love a tidal wave. Her pain an earthquake. Kissing him confused her and liberated her. But that spark lacked intensity …

Lacked Evan Gilmore's touch.

Alex missed a beat in their kiss at the reminder of Evan. Her breathing faltered as she tried to shake his grasp from her.

32

Luckily, Landon didn't notice as he pulled back and grasped her hand. He led her to his bedroom door, pushed it opened, and yanked her inside.

The moment the door closed, something in her broke.

Something in them broke.

They kissed and touched as if they couldn't stand not to touch each other. Then clothes were torn away, and she found herself naked in his bed. As his lips fluttered over hers, her heart had had enough.

It wasn't enough for her.

Evan.

Memories of him hit her with such force.

At Blue Jay's.

In Boston.

Him giving her the truth.

Alex kissing him at Fenway.

Evan giving her back her necklace.

And finally, Evan telling her he loved her in the Duke car park.

Flashes of Evan Gilmore denied her intimacy with her boyfriend. They had been so close. Landon almost pressing into her, but she couldn't.

Everything felt wrong and off.

Because Landon's validation and love weren't what she wanted.

Alex Parker wanted a different kind.

And it wasn't Evan Gilmore's she wanted either.

I want to love myself.

I want my own validation.

Not Landon's or Evan's.

"Alex?" Landon's voice was tight with fear.

I want to be proud of myself.

This isn't it.

You won't support my dreams.

Tears began to form as she pushed him away. "I'm sorry, Landon," she whispered as she covered her face with her palms, sobbing into them. She felt so stupid for believing she needed his love when she really needed to love herself more.

Landon grasped her wrists and pulled her palms away. The light from the parted shades was enough to see the agony on his face. She wished she could take it away, but she couldn't. "Baby?"

Alex sat up, pressed her back against the headboard and shook her head. "I can't, Landon. I'm not ready to give up on myself and my dreams. I'm not ready for you to be ashamed of me."

"I'm not," he said as he got on his knees and cradled her jaw. "I'm not ashamed of you."

"You were. It's the only way to explain that article. It's the only way to explain why you chose your image over us."

"Alex, that article was a mistake. I love you." His face tightened with the desperation that flashed in his eyes.

Alex inhaled a deep breath, knowing what she wanted.

She was as sure as she was when she left Evan Gilmore and Stanford.

It was why she chose Duke.

I have to pick me.

"Landon," she breathed as she pulled his palms from her face. She stared in his blue eyes and saw how vulnerable he was in them. "I know you love me. I don't doubt that."

A smile peeked at his lips.

But she would take it away.

Just for now.

Just until she learned to love herself first.

"But I have doubts about our future together."

He flinched. "What?"

Licking her lips, she grasped his hand in hers and let out a sigh. "I need time, Landon. I need time to figure out me. I need to put me first. That's why I came to Duke, and it's what I need right now. You have basketball, and I have science. Let us sort those parts of our lives first. I'm still so hurt by your actions, and I need time. Because if I don't, I don't know if I'll ever forgive you. Can you give me that? Can you give me more time?"

Landon gazed down at her hands covering his. He clenched his eyes shut before he opened them and stared at her. "I can do that." Then he leaned forward and pressed a kiss on her forehead before he pulled his hand from hers and got out of bed.

Alex watched as he went to his closet and returned with one of his jerseys in his hand. He climbed on the bed and held it up for her. She stared at his jersey, and her heart clenched in her chest. She knew she shouldn't, but a part of her was so supportive of him and his dreams. And that piece of her had Alex raising her arms for her ex-boyfriend to slip the jersey over her naked body.

"Will you still stay with me tonight?"

"Yes," she whispered as he laid down.

Only for tonight.

In the morning, I'll leave and be everything I deserve by choosing me.

35

Alex laid down next to him as Landon pulled her into his arms and whispered, "I love you so much, Alex. I'm so sorry. I'll wait. I'll wait for as long as you want me to."

Maybe it was her vulnerable heart, but she believed him.

As she fell asleep in his arms, a piece of her forgave him ...

And continued to love him.

The morning light had Alex's eyelids fluttering as she let out a soft groan. She snuggled into her pillow, loving the way the arm around her tightened. Suddenly, voices had her slowly opening her eyes to find Landon asleep next to her. Alex smiled at the sight of him and reached up and pressed her fingers to his chiseled jaw. She couldn't deny that she had missed him in the week they had been apart.

Suddenly, last night came to her. It hadn't gone exactly the way she or Landon had planned, but she couldn't commit to being intimate with him. The touching. The tears. The I love you. And most importantly, Alex wanting time apart. Needed time to find herself. She and Landon had been so close; Landon was almost pressing inside her. But when the flashes of Evan Gilmore started, she knew she couldn't be intimate with Landon, and for that, she was thankful.

Sex would have complicated everything, so she was glad it didn't happen. She was glad he respected her desire for time apart and appreciated the truth in the words he whispered to her before she fell asleep.

Alex brushed her fingers against his jaw and then slowly

pulled his arm from her. Then she got out of bed and picked her panties up from the floor. After slipping them on, she decided she'd make them breakfast. Spinning around, she made her way to the door. She opened it gently before she stepped out, not closing the door completely behind her. She swept her hair behind her ear as she focused on the voices coming from the kitchen.

She recognized them as Walt and Chase, Landon's roommates. Alex hadn't seen them in so long and wanted to make them breakfast. Her breakup with Landon wasn't easy for them, and she wanted to make things right. Just as she was about to make her way toward the kitchen, their conversation grew louder.

"Is Lan up yet?" Chase asked, unaware that she was staring at their backs.

"Nah," Walt said. "Alex is over."

Chase tensed. "Did they have sex?"

"I heard moaning from Lan's room."

"Shit," Chase cursed.

"What?" Walt asked as he headed over to the fridge. "I'm glad she's back. Lan was a miserable fucker."

"Fuck, we have to make sure he checks to see if he used a condom."

Alex flinched.

What?

"Why? Why do you suddenly care about their sex lives?"

Alex didn't move, curious and desperate to hear Chase's answer.

Chase sighed. "I care about Alex, okay?"

Walt laughed. "You're a junior. Wait until Lan graduates.

37

I'm pretty sure he's only with her because she's a sure thing. So care about her when he leaves Duke for the NBA. She'll be heartbroken and an easy lay."

"That's not what I care about, dude, and she's more than that. I care about her health."

My health?

"Her health? What does that—*fuck!* He didn't … did he?"

Chase shook his head. "He told me Alex is on birth control. That means they would have had unprotected sex last night."

"But did he? While she was gone?"

Her heart dipped, anticipation threatening to choke her.

And then Chase confirmed it. "Yeah. Brought some blonde back from the bar the other night. Saw them come into the apartment and then I heard moaning. He was supposed to get tested today."

"Oh, my God," Alex gasped, causing Chase and Walt to turn around, horror written all over their faces.

Suddenly, she heard the door behind her creak and felt Landon's hands on her shoulders. "Morning, baby."

She ignored him, staring at Chase and Walt. "Is it true?"

Landon's fingers twitched. "What's going on?"

"Is it true, Chase?" she demanded. Her voice louder, causing Landon's roommate to flinch.

He was hesitant as he stared over her shoulder before he nodded. "It's true, Alex."

Landon had sex with someone else.

Last night, he hadn't mentioned it. They almost had unprotected sex. He was one flex away from being inside her without a condom. She trusted him, and he was willing to put her body at risk. Anger prickled her skin as she tried to keep it together.

Spinning around, she decided she'd give Landon a chance to explain. To prove to her that Chase was lying. When her eyes landed on him, she saw the shame and truth simmer in his eyes.

Oh, God.

"Tell me it's not true," she said in a small voice, terrified that if it were any louder, she'd hear the break in her voice.

"I-I," he stuttered.

Alex stepped back, wanting to be away from his touch. "Oh, my God. You had sex with someone else, and you didn't think you should tell me?"

"I can't remember, Alex." Landon reached for her, but Alex shook her head. "Baby, I was drunk. I can't even remember if I did."

"You can't remember? You stupid, selfish bastard!" she shouted, her body heated with anger and frustration. "You were really going to risk my health last night? I could have contracted an STD because I trusted you to be honest with me. You said you were done with the lies. That's worse than you lying about our relationship because once again, you didn't respect me. I should be hurt that you slept with someone, but I'm more hurt that you weren't going to tell me you had unprotected sex. I'm an idiot. I'm such an idiot. You're a liar!"

"Alex, I swear. I was going to tell you."

"When?" she demanded, pushing at his chest. "When you were inside me? Not once did you mention a need for a condom. Not once did you have that conversation with me."

"I'll get tested. I'll ask her if we did—"

Alex shook her head unbelievably at him. She had been so

39

LEN WEBSTER

blinded by him and her love for him that she didn't even think
he could have sex with someone else. "We're done." Then she
pushed past him, entered his room, and headed over to her bra.

"Baby, please," Landon begged as she ripped his jersey
off her with disgust and slipped on her bra and clasped it.

She ignored him as she swiped her dress from the floor
and put it on. Alex freed her hair before she picked up her
heels that were by his bed. She scanned his room, satisfied that
she had collected all her belongings. Alex didn't dare look at
Landon; she was so angry with him. She had never felt this
humiliated in her life.

As she passed him on her way out of his room, Landon
wrapped his fingers around her wrist and stopped her. Alex
spun around and pulled her arm free from his clutches.

"I loved you," she said, completely dumbfounded at how
irresponsible he had been while she was away, grieving their
broken relationship. "I loved you enough to take you back,
and this is what I get? I am disgusted with you. I am angry
with you. I am hurt because of you. And if I don't leave, I will
find myself hating you. We're done, Landon. We're over. You
go screw whomever the hell you want. I thought last night
was a pivotal moment for us, but I was wrong. I'm not your
sure thing anymore. I had no idea that was why you were in a
relationship with me."

Alex ignored the wounded expression on his face as she
spun around and made her way out of his bedroom. As she
headed toward the apartment door, she glanced over at Chase
and shot him a small smile.

"Thanks, Chase," she said before she headed down the
hallway, collected her purse from the table, and left the

40

apartment with fool written on her forehead and the need to cry clawing at her chest.

It was over.

They were over.

For good.

There was no way she'd ever trust Landon Carmichael again.

Not with her time.

Or affections.

Or even her heart.

And most importantly, she didn't trust him with her future.

Because that was hers, and it took heartbreak after heartbreak for her to understand that.

⁷⁸

Pt

platinum

ALEX

Now

F or eight in the morning, Zürich Airport was already bustling with travelers. Their movements made her dizzy. Only one Swiss Air flight was bound for Boston, Massachusetts, today, and it meant Alex had to leave her apartment early to avoid the morning traffic so she could check in on time.

"You didn't have to drive me all the way to the airport, Dr. Rodahawe," Alex said to her now former mentor.

Dr. Rodahawe smiled as he set down his cup. After Alex checked in, he insisted that they have coffee together before she went through security. However, pre-flight jitters meant she was too nervous to stomach caffeine so early in the morning, so she opted for a bottle of water instead.

"Nonsense, Alexandra. It would be wrong of me not to see my favorite research assistant off," he praised, causing Alex to smile.

"Well, I appreciate it. Thank you, Dr. Rodahawe. For driving me to the airport and letting me be your assistant at your institute. It's been an invaluable experience that I will never take for granted," Alex said wholeheartedly, afraid she might cry. They had done all the crying last night at her farewell celebration.

"You'll be phenomenal at MIT, Alexandra."

She pressed her lips together in a tight smile. "I'm so nervous. My Ph.D. at MIT is all I've ever wanted, so thank you for the recommendation letter. I don't think I would have gotten accepted without you."

"You deserve MIT. You've worked so hard. I did nothing but tell MIT the truth."

"Well, I'm thankful, nonetheless. So you promise to make time for me if and when you're in Massachusetts?"

Dr. Rodahawe smiled as he leaned across the table. "So long as you promise you'll come back to the institute if you're ever in Europe. I expect to see you published."

She rolled her eyes. Graduating with her Ph.D. was seven years away and being a published academic would take even longer, but she appreciated his belief in her. "I'll try my best to make you proud."

He reached over and grasped her hand in his. He reminded her so much of her father with that glint of pride in his eyes. "You already did the moment you turned down three years at the institute to follow your dreams. You're going to be a remarkable physicist."

Suddenly, her phone vibrating on the table caught her attention. She smiled at the doctor and pulled away to pick it up, seeing the message from her father. She knew it was one in the morning back in Brookline and that he was probably making sure she got to the airport safely.

Dad: Good morning, Alexandra. Just checking in. Did you make it to the airport okay?

Alex: I did. I've checked in. Just having coffee with Dr. Rodahawe before I go through security.

Flight leaves in a couple of hours. Are you still picking me up at the airport? I don't want you to have to leave work. I can take a cab back to Brookline.

Dad: My daughter is coming home after a year and a half in Switzerland. There's no way I'm not picking you up. Seb is coming, too, so pretend to be surprised.

Alex: Oh, God. I've missed him. I miss you, too, Dad. But, you know, Seb is the love of my life. Is Mum going to be at the airport?

Dad: No, I'm sorry, my love. She has an important meeting with her publisher in New York. She's so sorry, but she'll be home later tonight. I'll see you in twelve hours, Alexandra. I love you so much.

Alex: I love you, too, Dad. See you at Logan!

Three hours into her flight to Boston, Massachusetts, the plane hit turbulence, waking Alex from her sleep with the frantic whispers of the other passengers and the seat belt indicator coming on. She gazed out the window to find the sky dark and see a flash of lightning in the distance. At takeoff, it was nothing but clear skies. Alex turned away from the window and reached down to pull on her seat belt, ensuring it was tightly in place.

The plane vibrated violently, and her breathing thinned. Nausea roiled through her as she clutched her stomach.

"Oh, God," she whispered as she gazed up to find the seat belt light still switched on, desperately hoping the turbulence would ease.

"Ladies and gentlemen, the captain has switched on the seat belt sign. We are experiencing some heavy turbulence that will continue for some time. We apologize. Please remain in your seats with your seat belts fastened until the captain turns off the seat belt sign," a flight attendant paged through the cabin, not easing Alex's anxiety one bit.

She had never had a fear of flying, but she had never experienced turbulence like this. Suddenly, the plane dropped, and her stomach jumped, causing her nausea to rise. Alex flung forward, searching through the seat pocket for the airsickness bag. Once she found it, she desperately opened it and threw up in the paper bag.

"Oh, dear," the elderly lady said next to her.

"I'm so sorry," Alex said as she removed her face from the bag and closed it. She wiped her mouth with the back of her hand as the woman set her palm on Alex's shoulder.

"It's all right. You're not looking very well," she pointed out.

Alex attempted a smile as she pressed her palm back to her stomach. "Airsickness."

Then she felt it. Another wave of vomit forced its way up her throat as she slapped a hand to her mouth and turned away from the old lady with silver eyes. She tried to force it down until she could make it to the bathroom, but the plane's vibrations were making her feel worse. All she could do was attempt to get her body under control with each breath she took. But they weren't deep breaths. She was heaving, struggling to fight against the sickness, and she was losing. So Alex opened the sickness bag once more and was hit by the smell of vomit and tears formed.

"Here," the lady next to her said.

Alex craned her neck to find the passenger offering her a new sickness bag. She scrunched her used bag closed and took the new one from her savior. Once the bag was opened, Alex turned away and threw up for the second time just as the plane began to level out. To her relief, the seat belt light turned off just as she finished throwing up.

"Thank God," Alex whimpered as she sat herself up and scrunched the second bag closed. Then she turned to the lady next to her. "I'm so sorry you had to see all that. But thank you."

The elderly lady smiled as she unbuckled her belt and got out of her seat. "It's all right, dear. I'll let you go to the bathroom."

In her weak state, she managed to unclasp her belt and get up from her seat. A stewardess with a sympathetic and worried-filled expression walked toward her.

"Miss, are you okay?" she asked as Alex shuffled out of her row.

She nodded. "I'm fine. Just airsickness. I'm sorry, I'll throw these out."

The stewardess with her perfect makeup and slicked back blond bun shook her head. "I'll do that. And here," she said, handing Alex a small toothbrush and toothpaste. "I wanted to come over earlier, but the turbulence kept me in my seat as per protocol." Then she reached in her pocket and pulled out a small plastic bag.

Alex smiled her appreciation and dumped the used sickness bags into the trash bag. The stewardess stepped into an empty aisle and allowed Alex to walk to the bathroom. Once inside, she slid the lock in place and set the toothbrush and toothpaste on the small counter and gave herself a moment just in case she needed to throw up again. After a minute passed, she pressed her hand to her stomach and knew that the nausea had passed. She looked at her reflection in the mirror and sighed. The passenger seated next to her was correct. Alex was pale, and it wasn't a pretty sight.

Sighing once more, she reached over and picked up the toothbrush. Ripping the plastic off, she picked up the small tube of toothpaste. Just as she was about to run the brush under the water faucet, a knock on the door had her pausing. She spun around and slid the lock back to find the same stewardess with a bottle of water in her hand.

"Here," she said as Alex took the bottle from her. "The bottled water will be better for you."

"Thank you," Alex said with much appreciation before she closed the door and locked it. Then she set the toothpaste down and uncapped the bottle. A deep breath later, she poured the water over the brush, added the minty toothpaste, and then brushed away the gross taste in her mouth. When she finished, she dumped everything in the trash and made her way out of the bathroom and returned to her seat.

When she reached her row, the old lady smiled and got up, allowing Alex to return to her seat by the window. As Alex sat down, she could see the storm clouds had vanished, leaving behind clear blue skies. Setting her palm back on her stomach, she let out a sigh, hoping she could make it back to the States without being sick again.

As she buckled her belt, a packet of crackers caught her eye. She turned her attention to the old lady and furrowed her brows in confusion. Humor gleamed in her silver eyes as she said, "Don't worry. You'll make a great mother."

Her heart dipped, as did her stomach, and she was fearful that sickness would roil through her once more.

"You can tell?" Alex asked, dumbfounded.

The old lady laughed as she reached over, pulled out Alex's tray, and set the crackers on it. "Dear, I've had a few in my lifetime. I even have some grandbabies. How far along are you?"

Alex glanced down at her palm clutching her stomach and then back at the passenger. "Eight weeks."

It was true.

Alex was eight weeks pregnant.

She found out two weeks before she left Zürich to return home.

"Morning sickness is only going to get worse. I'm Ester, by the way."

"I'm Alex. I'm sorry, but how did you know I'm pregnant?"

Ester took the crackers from Alex's tray and opened them. "I saw you examining your food. You looked at the cheese and pushed it away. You only ate the bread. You changed your mind about coffee and settled for juice ... then you threw up. These crackers from the stewardess should help."

Alex took the crackers from her with an appreciative smile. "Thank you. I barely know what to eat. I stupidly packed my pregnancy books in my suitcase and didn't see one at the airport bookshop. Do you have any tips on what other foods I should avoid on this flight, if you don't mind me asking?"

"Not at all."

Relief filtered through her veins. Alex was scared she might eat something on the plane that wouldn't be good for her baby. "Do you mind if I take some notes?"

Ester shook her head. Alex stowed away her tray table and reached under the seat in front of her to pull out her tote bag. She raked through it and retrieved her notebook and a pen before she pushed her bag under the seat with her foot. Then she pulled out her tray, opened her notebook, and set it and the crackers down.

"Oh, my," Ester said, leaning closer to Alex and taking in the equations on the pages. "That's impressive. My husband used to be a high school math teacher. I see formulas he would probably know. Are you a math student?"

"I'm a physics TA at MIT … well, I'm supposed to be. I think my current situation might just alter that."

Ester blinked, seeming confused. "Do you live in Switzerland?"

Alex shook her head. "I worked at the Rodahawe Institute."

"Is the baby's father Swiss?"

"Ah, no," Alex said as her palm gently rubbed her stomach. "He's American. He's back home in the States."

The old lady smiled. "Now you eat. I'll give you all the pregnancy tips I can think of, but I'll save some for your mama to teach you."

Her mother.

Oh, God.

Alex hadn't told her parents—let alone her baby's father—

that she was, in fact, with child. But for now, thousands of feet in the air, she would concentrate on learning about what to expect from an unexpected friend, and it was definitely appreciated.

Ester Nightingale was a saint. It was the only way Alex could put it.

The old lady from outside of Providence, Rhode Island, gave her so many tips on pregnancy and motherhood. By the end of the flight, Alex promised to update Ester on how she and the baby were through email. Alex also found out that Ester and her husband had moved to Providence after living in Maine their whole lives to be closer to their daughter. When Alex asked her if she spent much time in Boston, Ester shook her head and said she only went to Boston so she could fly to Zürich to visit her son who now lived there.

To Alex's relief, Ester didn't seem to recognize her as Little Miss Red Sox. At the mere mention of the Red Sox, Ester said she'd rather knit than watch sports. It was one less worry for her. Alex was out of the media spotlight for over three years. Once Kyle proposed to Angie Fisher, Little Miss Red Sox was old news, which suited Alex just fine. It meant she could breathe easier when she was in Boston. But news of her pregnancy might just bring the spotlight back on her, and she didn't want that.

"Welcome home, ma'am," the US Customs officer said as he allowed her to pass.

"Thank you," Alex said, pulling her suitcase to find Ester waiting for her on the other side of the exit.

"I was starting to get worried," Ester expressed.

Alex laughed. "My bags were searched. I have a lot of textbooks and notebooks full of formulas. They were just making sure I didn't have anything deemed too sensitive."

"Do you have family picking you up, Alex?" Ester asked as they made their way to the terminal.

"I do. My dad said he'd be picking me up," she explained as they walked through the doors and to a terminal packed with waiting people. Alex moved away from the doors and stopped to reach into her purse. Pulling out a card, she handed it to Ester. "If you and your husband or even your family are in Boston and want someplace to have a nice dinner."

Ester grasped the card. "The Little Restaurant in Boston? I've heard so much about this restaurant. My daughter says they're always booked out for months."

Alex nodded, knowing her mother hated to turn patrons away, but the restaurant was booked full every night. "I know, but don't worry about it. My mother owns the restaurant. Just let them know who you are and that I sent you, and my mother will make room. And it's on me. So don't even think about eating there with the intention of paying."

"I don't know what to say," Ester said, her eyelids fluttering as if she were about to cry.

"That you'll go and tell me your thoughts on my mother's restaurant. She also has a bakery I'd love to show you, so please let me know when you're in Boston next."

Ester let go of her suitcase handle to hug Alex tightly. When she stepped back, she brushed away a tear. "You'll make a wonderful mother, Alex. You have such a kind heart. And please do let me know how the father takes the news."

"I will," Alex promised.

"Mom!" a woman shouted, and Alex and Ester glanced over at the woman with flowers in her hands.

"That's my daughter," Ester announced.

"It was lovely meeting you, Ester. Thank you for the tips and for taking care of me while I was sick on the plane."

"Of course, dear. Now you keep me updated on your pregnancy. Safe journey home, Alex."

"And safe journey back to Providence," Alex said before Ester walked over to her daughter.

Alex grasped her suitcase handle and scanned the terminal. She couldn't see her father or Seb anywhere. She walked away from the doors and began to search through the mass of people.

"Alexandra!" she heard someone shout to her left.

When Alex turned, the last person she expected to see at the airport waiting for her greeted her. Tears threatened as a wave of emotions overwhelmed her.

They were happy tears.

Tears of disbelief that he was here.

Tears proving she had missed him so.

Alex almost ran to him. The moment she reached him, his arms wrapped around her.

Warm.

Safe.

He felt like home.

A home set on fire a long time ago.

She hated the way doubt and misery chiseled their way into her heart. So she ignored what she felt and memorized his long embrace. An embrace she had assumed would be swift but wasn't. He held her as if they had all the time in the world. He held her as if he knew her heart needed him and this moment.

"Welcome home, AJ," he whispered as he squeezed her just that little bit more—almost as if he couldn't believe she was home.

A tear threatened, and she let it escape.

She should have held it back, but she couldn't.

She didn't want to hide her true feelings.

Not at this one perfect moment.

His arms unwound from around her, and she saw those light browns that she had missed so much. Then she noticed the sign in his hand that read: *Welcome home, AJ!*

She smiled at it, loving it completely.

"I would have made it fancier, but I was at Fenway and all they had were markers and poster paper for me to steal," he explained, holding it up properly in his hands.

Alex laughed. "It's perfect. Are my dad and Seb here?"

Evan Gilmore shook his head. "No, I'm sorry. Your dad didn't say why, but he asked me to pick you up. Is that all right?"

The plea in his eyes had her breathless.

They had so much left unsaid between them.

But she knew, no matter what happened, he would always be her best friend.

"More than all right," Alex confirmed.

Evan grasped her suitcase handle, pulled on it, and arched his brow at her, amusement clear on his face. "Just one suitcase and it weighs a ton."

Alex rolled her eyes. "It's all my books, some of my research, and notebooks."

"Jesus, AJ. Did you bring home any of your clothes?" he asked as he spun around, wheeling her suitcase along as they made their way out of the terminal.

"I brought home some."

And the pictures of us.

But she didn't say it out loud.

No, she kept that secret to herself.

"Ready to go home?"

Alex craned her neck to discover him staring at her. Then she nodded. It had been long overdue, but she was ready. And as much as working at the Rodahawe Institute for three years sounded like a dream, she had other dreams and ambitions she wanted to truly pursue.

"I'm ready to go home."

The moment Evan parked the car by the curb, she glanced over at her family home. It hadn't changed in the two months since she was last home. Her stay had only lasted days, but she still held on to those days with regretful longing. The purple tulips her father had planted for her mother in front of the house had yet to bloom, but she knew when they finally did, they would be vibrant and so beautiful. She knew her mother loved coming home to the tulips he had planted for her—a gift of his love always on display when in bloom.

"My dad's car isn't in the driveway. He must not be

home," Alex said, taking in the freshly shoveled path that led to the front door. She couldn't help but be disappointed that her parents and Seb hadn't been at the airport to pick her up, but she was thankful Evan was.

Evan.

Evan Gilmore.

Her best friend.

It had been years of wrong and right between them.

But she still loved and cared for him all the same.

Alex turned her attention back to her best friend to find him smiling at her. She wondered if he ever thought of her while she was in Switzerland. Wondered if he ever missed her the way she had missed him. She wondered how his life had been. And she had to know. Before she entered her house, she had to know.

"Evan?"

That smile of his faded. "Yeah, AJ?"

She took a deep breath as nausea decided it would be a great time to resurface. She swallowed hard, hoping to keep the sickness at bay so she could ask. "Are you happy with your life?"

He stilled as fear and uncertainty darkened his brown eyes. "What?"

Alex reached over and unbuckled her belt so she could face him properly. "With your life right now, are you happy? With how it all happened and ended? Are you happy right now?"

Evan blinked at her. He stared at her for a moment before he said, "I'm happy right now."

Her heart dropped, causing her chest to strain at its emptiness.

He's happy.

And that alone was enough.

"I'm happy with how my life is at the moment."

Alex smiled; although it hurt, she was happy for him.

"Hey, do you have your spare key? I haven't needed one for the house in over a year, and Dad isn't home," she said, changing the subject before her thoughts and her broken heart could do more damage.

"I do," he confirmed as he unclicked his belt.

Alex bent down and picked up her purse before she opened the door and slid out of Evan's BMW sedan. She made her way to the trunk to find that Evan had already opened it and pulled out her suitcase. He set it down and closed the trunk, taking in her childhood home with her.

"Crazy how it looks like it hasn't changed, but you know it has," Evan said. Then he pushed her suitcase toward her house.

He had no idea how right his words were.

How his words kept her by the curb staring and remembering all the memories in the house that hadn't changed but those inside it had.

"AJ!"

She lifted her chin, not realizing that she had been staring at her stomach. Alex had changed. Her life had already changed. A baby wasn't what she had planned before her Ph.D., but she was happy. Who knew where her life would be after seven years at MIT. Maybe she might miss her chance at motherhood, and this was it. And if this was her one and only chance, she was taking it because her life had changed for the better.

Alex smiled before she followed Evan up the path and

climbed the short steps until she stood outside the front door. She watched as Evan pulled out his keys, then inserted her parents' house key in the lock, twisted it, and nudged the door slightly open.

"You go in first. I've got your suitcase," Evan encouraged.

She pressed her palm against the door and pushed it, swinging the door open. It was strange to see the house so dark. Normally, someone was home, and it never felt this cold. As Alex stepped inside, she was suddenly blinded by lights.

"Surprise!" rang in her ears as she flinched in shock.

Alex blinked and saw the faces of those she loved. Her friends and family surrounded her. Even some of her mother's staff from the restaurant and bakery filled the hallway.

"Welcome home, Alexandra," her father said before her.

She succumbed to her tears. It was all a trick, and it had worked. She was surprised. Alex smiled at those who had been in on the surprise as she made her way to her father—who stood by the staircase next to her grandparents.

Alex dropped her purse, walked over to her father, and wrapped her arms around him. He chuckled at her earnest embrace, but she couldn't help it. She had missed him while she was in Switzerland. Missed his smiles and unconditional love. "I've missed you so much," she whispered into his shoulder and then pulled back. She glanced to her right to see her grandmother and grandfather. "You guys flew out all this way?"

"Of course, sweetheart," Grandma Louise said as she reached up and brushed her tears away. "We couldn't miss you coming home."

Stepping away from her father, she furrowed her brows. "Wait. Where's Seb?"

"Right here," her mother said.

She spun around to find her neighbors giving her mother room to enter the hallway. Alex made her way over to her mother who now stood next to Evan. When she reached them, her heart throbbed in her chest. For the first time in months, she felt love in her chest and not pain. "Hello, baby brother," Alex cooed to avoid waking him. She looked up to see her mother's eyes gleam with unshed tears. "Can I hold him?"

Carefully, her mother handed her the two-month-old. In Alex's arms was the most beautiful baby boy she had ever seen. "Welcome home, my love. I'm sorry your dad tricked you. We wanted to surprise you," her mother said and then kissed Alex's temple.

"It's okay. Thanks, Mum," she said and glanced over at all the guests. "Thank you all so much for welcoming me home. I promise to thank you all in just a minute. I want to hold Seb for a little longer."

"You all heard the woman of the hour," Alex heard her uncle Julian shout. "*Vamos!* Into the kitchen! Let's eat and drink and celebrate Little Parker coming home."

"That's not even French, Julian," Aunt Stevie said before everyone dispersed from the hallway and into the living room and dining room, leaving Alex alone in the hallway with Evan.

"He's so perfect," she said in awe. "He's grown up so much in two months."

"He's pretty incredible," Evan agreed.

She softly brushed her brother's fair hair back. "You are pretty incredible, Sebastian."

"Hey, AJ?"

"Hmm?"

59

"Can I hold him?" His question had her blinking in surprise.

Her heart raced in her chest as she glanced up at him through her lashes. "Okay."

Slowly, she placed Seb in Evan's arms. She had expected Sebastian to cry or stir. Instead, he seemed to cuddle into Evan's chest.

"Hey, little guy," Evan whispered. "I think you're almost as perfect as your sister, Seb."

And right at that moment, her heart damn near exploded at the sight of Evan Gilmore gently rocking the two-month-old she loved so much.

Tears consumed her.

Tears fell.

When she felt her phone vibrate, she brushed her tears away and reached into her jacket pocket. She pulled out her phone and unlocked it to find a new message.

Landon: Welcome home, Massachusetts.

Her chest tightened.

It had been months since she last saw him in the UK.

Since he surprised her when she had accompanied Dr. Rodahawe and Brandon at their seminar at Oxford University in England.

Alex: Thank you.

Nerves had her nauseous all over again as she typed once more.

Alex: Landon, we really need to talk.

79

Au

gold

ALEX

Sophomore year of college

T he vibrating of her phone on the wooden library table she sat at with her roommate had Alex clenching her jaw. The last thing she needed was more distraction. She needed to stay focused. Though most of her papers and reports were done, she still had a few to work on before she started preparing for her finals. She did not need any more setbacks. Unlike today's visit to the campus clinic, which was a necessity. She couldn't trust her ex-boyfriend. If he couldn't remember if he had sex with someone else, she couldn't trust him to remember to have used contraception either. When she left Landon's apartment, she had gone straight to her dorm room, showered long past the time her fingers had pruned, and then sat on her bed with a towel wrapped around her, thinking about how stupid she had been. Savannah had woken up and asked her what happened, and Alex—in disbelief—told her what her ex-boyfriend had done.

Landon had slept with someone else.

They were over at the time, but Alex was still grieving them. Was still loving him. She couldn't even kiss Evan Gilmore without guilt because she still loved Landon. But loving him couldn't excuse him. They almost had sex after he had slept with someone else without protection. The love she had for him twisted. The trust she held so tightly broke. She had always believed he would be honest with her, but she was wrong. They might have been over, but that didn't mean it didn't hurt her. How could he sleep with someone so soon after they had ended?

Because you're not right for him. He said so himself, her thoughts yelled.

You went to Boston to find yourself, her heart assured.

You found Evan again, her soul reminded.

It didn't matter that Landon slept with someone else. What mattered was he didn't tell her and risked exposing her to an STD. That alone was not love. The Landon she fell in love with would have never done that to her. The Landon who lied to her was not the man she kissed for the first time under the blue and white confetti. But the man who risked her health had her going to the clinic, not trusting his empty promises. It was risky to be seen getting tested. Anyone who recognized her could sell pictures and make some quick and dirty money. But even with the media distracted by Kyle and Angie, Alex couldn't risk having the spotlight back on her.

"That's like the twentieth time he's called since we got to the library," Savannah said, lifting her head from the management and communications textbook she'd been studying. Her blue eyes glanced from the phone to Alex.

Alex sighed. "He called nonstop during lab. I felt bad for Mika. Each time he tried to go over our experiment, Landon's calls would interrupt him."

"He won't stop, will he?"

"No," Alex said with a shake of her head. "I don't think

he will. He hasn't stopped calling since I walked out of his apartment yesterday."

Savannah's lips pressed into a tight line. "And you don't want to talk to him?"

"No … Yes? I seriously don't know. I wish I was angrier. I wish I yelled louder and hurt him, but I just couldn't do it. I wanted to, but … I was just tired. Tired of being disappointed and hurt by someone I love. Someone I never thought could do that to me. I thought he loved me. His messages while I was gone make me question whether it was love or guilt that had him texting me. He slept with someone else … or he didn't. I don't know what or who to believe anymore. Landon says one thing, and his roommate says another. Why would Chase lie?"

Savannah bit her lip. Then she released it and shook her head. "Chase has no reason to lie."

"Exactly. Even if Landon didn't sleep with her, he brought her to the bed we've been together in. I was miserable in Massachusetts when he was here getting drunk and taking other girls home." Alex closed her laptop and frowned at her best friend. "Landon broke my heart and trust, Sav, and I hate that I still love him. Even with everything he's done, I still love him."

Suddenly, a throat clearing had Alex and Savannah craning their necks to find a blonde with hesitation and fear on her beautiful face. "Excuse me?" the stranger interrupted.

"Yeah?" Savannah said, eyes roaming up and down the blonde wearing a Duke basketball sweatshirt.

"I'm Kelly."

Alex blinked at her, confused. "Uh, hi, Kelly. What can we do for you?"

Kelly chewed her lip. "You're Alex Parker, right?"

"Yeah, she's Alex Parker. Why are you asking?" Savannah asked, who now glared at Kelly.

Guilt consumed Kelly's face as her eyes gleamed over, almost as if she were about to cry. "I'm so sorry, Alex. I had no idea. I am so sorry. I was tipsy, and I went home with him. But I swear, we didn't have sex."

Oh, God.

Bile rose up her throat.

This was the woman Landon took home while she was in Boston.

"I'm not that girl," Kelly insisted. "I went home with him, and I forgot all sense. But I swear, we didn't have sex. Landon called me and told me what happened. I promise, we didn't have sex. He told me how much he loves you. You can be together. I'll get tested and show—"

"No need," Alex said, stopping her. "Look, Kelly, you seem nice, but you hooked up and went home with my ex-boyfriend days after we broke up. Sure, I'm hurt and angry, but I don't have a right to be because Landon and I were over. So if you're attracted to him, he's all yours. I appreciate your explanation, but I didn't need one. I'm never getting back together with Landon."

I'm never going back to Landon.

Alex felt the finality in her words. She was never going back to him. Landon Carmichael might have been the perfect boyfriend, but it didn't excuse his actions. Because it wasn't just him taking another girl home. It wasn't just him not being honest with her when it came to them almost having unprotected sex.

When it came down to it, they just weren't right for each other anymore. Their dreams differed. He would go on to play NBA, and she'd go to MIT. She was never going back to Landon Carmichael. And though she was happy with her decision, it did make her sad. He was her first boyfriend. She would never forget how good it was when she was his … until it all ended.

A small smile tugged at Kelly's lips as relief flashed in her blue eyes. "Thanks, Alex. I feel so guilty that I had to find you and clear that up. Landon's worried—"

"Stop," Alex ordered. "You don't have to worry about Landon and me. Like I said, we're over. Landon is free to date whomever he wants." *Because I'm not his sure thing anymore.* What Walt said last night resurfaced in her memory. Alex clenched her jaw. No, she was sure Landon loved her. He tried, but it wasn't enough for them to work. "If it's okay with you, my roommate and I would like to get back to studying."

Kelly took a step back. "Of course. I'm so sorry. I'll let you get back to your studying. And again, I'm so sorry about Landon, Alex." And with that, the woman Landon had taken home last week left the library with Alex staring at her back as she walked away.

"Wow," Savannah breathed, catching Alex's attention. "You have to admit, the girl had some guilt on her face. You were amazing. She didn't deserve your kindness. You were the bigger person, and I'm proud."

Alex lifted her laptop screen, ready to concentrate on her paper rather than her ex-boyfriend and his hookup. "I appreciate that, but she didn't do anything wrong. Neither did Landon until he was dishonest with me. Because of his actions, I had to get an STD test this morning. Now, you need to concentrate on studying. Management and communications is the class you struggle with the most."

Savannah rolled her eyes. "But after this study session, you are buying me ice cream to cheer me up before my shift."

"Sure," she said with a laugh before she picked up her cell phone, ignored all her missed calls and unopened text messages, and switched it off, ready to focus on her paper rather than her persistent ex-boyfriend.

Humming along to the song playing through her earbuds, Alex kicked her dorm room door closed behind her, walked over to her bed, and dropped her backpack on the mattress. Alex pulled her earbuds out, unplugged them from her phone, and set her phone on her bed. After she had finished studying with Savannah and treated her to ice cream, Alex went to the gym and ran on the treadmill, hoping it would clear her mind of Landon. It didn't work, and the music on her playlist caused her to miss him. So she listened to a few science podcasts for almost ten miles before she slowed down to a walking pace and changed over to some music.

Reaching up, she grasped the tie around her hair and slowly pulled it out, freeing her brunette locks. She was about to get ready to shower when her phone rang. Alex glanced down, saw Evan's name, and a small smile tugged at her lips. She picked up her phone and answered his call.

"Hey," she said as she sat down on her bed. She hadn't

spoken to Evan since before her dinner with Landon yesterday. He wished her luck before his flight back to California, and she told him she'd call him in the morning. It was almost six p.m., and she had prolonged her call to him all day, but she was glad he had called instead.

"Hey, AJ. Are you all right?"

She let out a breath of air. "Yeah, I was just at the gym. Had to run off my worries."

"Why? Is everything okay?" The concern was thick in his voice, causing her heart to stretch in her chest.

"Yeah," she assured as she shuffled back until her back pressed against the cold concrete wall. "I haven't had the easiest twenty-four hours."

"Want to talk about it?" he asked with a softness in his voice she missed.

Alex ran a hand through her hair, deciding that she had to be honest with her best friend. "I broke up with Landon ... for good this time. During dinner, it was like nothing happened. I realized all the things I loved about him, and it was so easy to pick him ... I *did* pick him. I thought that's what I wanted. I thought he was who I wanted ..."

"Oh," Evan breathed before he cleared his throat. He was silent for a moment. "That's okay. I promised I'd be your best friend even if you picked him. I'm okay as long as you're happy."

"I'm not happy," she confessed.

"You're not?" The hint of relief and surprise in his tone had her smiling.

"No," she said. "Evan, I chose Landon because it felt easier to be with him. Because well, I love him, but it *wasn't* easy. Being with you in Brookline was all the truth I needed.

When I kissed him and tried to be with him, I couldn't. I kept thinking of you and what you did for me. You protected my image at the sacrifice of your place in my heart and life. Landon would never do that for me. He would never choose me over his wants and needs. He didn't."

"AJ," Evan murmured. "What did he do?"

For a moment last night, she chose a man who could selfishly hurt her over someone who had been so selfless when it came to her life and happiness. The realization had her chin dipping with shame. "He brought some girl back home with him while I was in Massachusetts. We were almost intimate last night, and he didn't say anything. He wasn't going to say anything, but we didn't have sex because I realized I didn't want to be with him because of you. I overheard his roommates talking about him being with another girl."

"AJ ..." He paused. "Are you telling me he almost risked your health?"

Alex sighed. "Yeah, but they didn't have sex. She approached me while I was in the library and told me the truth. But don't worry, I went to the clinic this morning and got tested just in case."

"I'm gonna—"

"You're not going to do anything, Evan. It's over. For good. Forever. He abused and betrayed my trust. There's no way I can forgive him for something like that." Alex uncrossed her legs and straightened them, feeling them ache and plead for comfort after her run.

Evan was silent. After a few moments, he asked, "So what happens now?"

"We're seriously going to have this conversation now?

You just got back to Stanford this morning." She let out a soft laugh. "Don't you have class?"

"I just left my study group. I'm done for the day before practice. So can we have this talk?"

Alex sighed. "Evan, you know I love you."

"I love you, too—"

She pressed her back harder into the concrete. "But while I was at the gym, I was thinking. Right now, I can't. It wouldn't be fair to either of us if we start something. And it wouldn't be fair to my relationship with Landon, either. And I know you're going to say that Landon and I are over, but I want to look back and know that I did right by that relationship."

"I understand."

"Evan …"

"Yes, AJ."

Alex felt her heart hammer in her chest. She knew who she wanted, but she also knew what she needed. And that was time. If it was ever going to work with Evan someday, he had to give her time. "You know what I need."

"I do," he said in a soft voice. "Please ask me for it."

She froze, shocked that Evan wanted her to ask him for time. Her heart stopped before it clenched hard. He began to chisel the name of another's from her heart so that he could replace it with his own someday.

Or maybe he's chiseling it away to find his name still engraved within.

Alex swallowed hard. If Evan continued to search for his place in her heart, he'd find it in time. And she knew he would wait until she was ready to heal the scars and bruises he left on her soul.

71

"I need to be alone for a while. I need to focus on me. I need to focus on classes before summer break. This isn't me choosing him or you. This is me choosing *me*. I want to love myself. I want my own validation. I want to be proud of my choices. I want my dreams. You gave up so much for me to have a normal college experience, and I want that. I want to honor what you sacrificed for me because I never really experienced it on my own. I was always the captain of the basketball team's girlfriend. I want to be so much more than that." Alex glanced over at the photo of her and her ex-boyfriend from his championship game. A pang erupted in her chest, and she knew that she needed time to get over him and not just be known as his girlfriend.

She was sick of being a label.

Sick of being known as someone else's.

Little Miss Red Sox.

Landon Carmichael's girlfriend.

She was ready to be the Alexandra Parker she owed not only Evan but also herself.

"And I'll give you that," Evan announced. "All of it. I'll wait."

"No, Evan, you don't have to—"

"I need to," he added. "I need to. I'll give you space and time. But I need and want to wait for you, AJ."

Alex felt a new sensation consume her chest, just where her heart once beat with Landon's name. The part of her that missed Evan Gilmore rose, doubling and taking space another once took. "How about we make a pact? A best friend pact. Not like the promises we made on your steps last time."

"Okay," he said, sounding hopeful.

She inhaled a deep breath and released it slowly. "We'll try during summer break. When we're back home in Brookline and don't have the pressure of being in two different states, we'll try. We'll start new and forget everything else. Just you and me. What do you say?"

He was silent.

For a long time, all Alex could hear was his soft breathing.

"Yes," he whispered. "Yes, summer. I'll meet you back home. The next few months will be good for us. But I have one request about this pact."

Her brows furrowed, skeptical of what was to come. "Umm, okay?"

"No silence," he declared.

"No silence?"

Evan hummed. "Yes, no silence between us. Last time, it was my fault, and I'm so sorry. But this time, I'm in it forever. For a spot in your life. But I can't do this if we have silence. We have to talk to each other. We have to communicate. I've missed you, AJ. I miss talking to you. I miss you just being with me. I miss all of you, and I want to talk to you about your day every single day until summer. Until I can see you again."

Her heart clenched as butterflies swarmed her stomach. It could be possible to be with Evan someday, but she knew today wasn't that day. She'd be his best friend until they saw each other back in Brookline and decided where they went from there.

So Alex gave herself a second to think it through.

To see if doubt would cause her to hesitate.

It didn't.

"Every single day, I want to talk to you about your day,

Evan," she agreed with so much hope that maybe this time, it might be possible for them to work.

"I can't wait for every single day with you, AJ."

Me, too, her heart whispered.

On Saturday night, the captain of the Duke lacrosse team hosted a party at his house off campus, and it was already in full swing. The music thumped as Alex sipped her beer. It wasn't the most appetizing drink on the menu, but now that she wasn't the captain of the basketball team's girlfriend, special drinks weren't available to her. Alex was just another sophomore, and she didn't mind. She had no intentions of getting drunk, but the beer in her hand was enough to take off the edge of being at a party without Landon. But so far, it hadn't worked. Her discomfort at the party worsened when several guys from different Duke sports teams approached her and asked for a dance or to go talk outside. Alex refused every single one of them. According to Savannah, Alex was quite the prize to a lot of the jocks—there were even rumors of a bet to see who she'd rebound with. Alex rolled her eyes when Savannah told her that; she would not be pulled into such childish games because right now, dating was off the table.

"You need another one?" Savannah asked from next to her.

Alex shook her head and set the red Solo cup on the kitchen counter. "No, I'm good."

"I can get you something else to drink," Dean, the captain of the men's lacrosse team, offered.

"No, that's okay. I'm set for the night," she assured him.

Savannah raised her cup, and announced, "Incoming. One of Duke basketball's defenders is approaching."

Alex spun around to find Chase approaching her, beer in his hand and discomfort on his face. "Hey, Chase."

"Hey, Alex," he said once he reached her. His posture was tense. "Enjoying the party?"

In all her time with Landon, Chase had always seemed uncomfortable around her, though she was grateful to him for telling her the truth about her ex-boyfriend's activities while she was away. "So far, so good. How are things? How was the game?"

Chase's lips pressed into a fine line. "Things are awkward. It's been a rough three days since you left. He blames me for what happened, and I feel like a shit friend. But at least we won tonight."

"That's great that you guys won." Alex shook her head at him. "And no, Chase, it's not your fault. You did me a favor. Landon wasn't honest with me. He was probably never going to be honest with me about Kelly."

"You knew it was with Kelly?" He sounded surprised.

"Yeah. She approached me at the library the next day and said they didn't sleep together," she explained.

Chase raised his brow. "And you believe her?"

She shrugged. "Doesn't matter. I'd already gotten checked earlier that day."

"Clean bill of health?"

"Yup. Clean bill of health. Hey, listen, seriously, it's not your fault, Chase. If I could make it less awkward between you guys, I would, but I can't. I wish he didn't have to lose you and your friendship, but I don't want to be with Landon after that. I'm sorry."

He smiled at her. "It's all right. Landon will just have to deal with it—"

"You fuckin' asshole!" She heard shouted from her right, and Alex turned to find her ex-boyfriend launching himself at his teammate, shoving him into the counter.

"Landon!" she shrieked, grasping his shirt and trying to pull him off Chase.

Punches were thrown.

And she heard Chase groan.

"Lan, stop!" Chase ordered, taking Landon's hit.

Alex pulled on her ex-boyfriend's shirt once more, desperate to stop his assault on his teammate. Landon swung his arm too far back, hitting her in the jaw and causing Alex to stumble back into someone else's arms. She let out a harrumph as she looked up to find that the arms keeping her safe were Walt's.

"That's enough!" Walt growled. He turned her and inspected her jaw. "You all right, Alex?"

Where Landon's elbow connected to her skin ached, but she'd be okay. She reached up and pressed her palm to her injury and then nodded. "Thanks, Walt. I'll be fine."

"Baby, I'm so sorry—"

Alex spun around and pushed Landon away, taking in Chase and his bloody face. Her ex-boyfriend had shown a side of himself that Alex had never thought was possible. "I'm so sorry, Chase."

He finally got himself up and wiped the blood from his mouth, shaking his head at her. "I'm fine, but are you all right, Alex?"

"Don't ask her that!" Landon hissed.

She swung her furious gaze at him. "What is wrong with you? He's your teammate!"

"Who has always had a thing for you! He's the reason we're over," Landon argued. One look at his gleaming eyes, and she knew he was drunk.

"We broke up because you lied to me! You were dishonest. This has nothing to do with Chase. You hooked up with someone else days after I left for Boston. You kept calling and telling me you missed me, but then you took someone home with you. That's not loving and missing me," she argued, her tears now making an appearance. She didn't want Landon to see them and think they were for him. She was frustrated and angry that he ruined her night.

"Alex, are you okay?" Savannah asked.

"Dude, you're dripping blood all over my floor," Dean complained.

She glanced down to see the droplets of Chase's blood on the white tile floor and her ex-boyfriend's bloody fists. Exhausted, she gazed up to see the pleading in Landon's eyes. "Come on. I'll help you clean yourself up," Alex said.

Landon reached out for her hand, but she pulled away and then spun around. She didn't wait for him. She pushed past the people who witnessed the fight, ignoring their whispers. When she made it down the clear hallway, Landon gripped her arm and spun her around.

"Alex," he begged.

She pulled her arm free in disgust. "The Landon I fell in love with would never do that to his teammate and one of his best friends. What has gotten into you?"

"I miss you."

"No, you don't. Because if you did, you wouldn't have attacked Chase. He's done nothing wrong. You're the one who lied," she said, raising her voice.

Landon winced. "He likes you."

"And I loved you! I don't care for Chase in that way. You're all I cared about, and you showed me a side of you I am so disgusted with. You can't dictate who I talk to. I'm not your possession, Landon."

"No, but you're my girlfriend." Sadness consumed his bright blue eyes.

Alex shook her head. "They're not the same thing. I am not your possession or your girlfriend."

"But I love you."

She pressed her lips tightly together, refusing to admit that she still loved him. She didn't want him to know, and he didn't deserve to know. Just as she was about to tell him that he can clean himself up so she can go home, he grasped her shoulder and yanked her into him. His lips collided with hers, taking her by surprise.

For a single moment, she got lost in that familiar feeling.

That familiar desire.

For a single moment, she felt hope for them.

But then Landon's tongue met hers, and she tasted the whiskey. He was drunk. She pulled back, breaking his kiss. Instead of backing away like she expected, Landon's hands cradled her jaw, causing her to wince in pain. His mouth attacked hers, causing her to squirm and try to fight him. To pull away from the Landon she didn't know.

It wasn't working.

It seemed with every heartbeat, he became rougher.

He became desperate for her.

"Landon, stop!" she begged, pulling away for single moment before he turned her and pushed her against the wall, his body colliding with hers. "Ow!"

"Alex," he moaned as his lips found the corner of her mouth.

"Landon, you're drunk. Get off me!" His palm pressed harder against her jaw. "You're hurting me!" Tears now fell down her face.

"LANDON!" a voice shouted.

Seconds later, her ex-boyfriend was yanked off her, and Alex blinked her tears away to find Walt and Savannah in the hallway with them. Savannah appeared horrified and shocked. Walt had nothing but rage flashing in his eyes.

"I'm sorry, Alex," Landon's roommate said.

Alex wiped her ex-boyfriend's abusive kiss from her lips, stepped forward, and finally slapped the self-entitled asshole across the face. "I loved you, Landon. How dare you do that to me!"

Landon flinched. He didn't even attempt to soothe her slap. "Why are you giving up on me? You're not my sure thing when you were always my everything. We were together for ten months, Alex. Are you really going to throw away everything because of one mistake? Wasn't I good to you? Why did you go back to Boston and not fight for us?"

"Not fight for us? *You* gave up on us. And everywhere I went at Duke, I was reminded of you. My heart couldn't take that. You were good to me. But this ..." She pointed at him swaying in front of her. "This isn't you. This isn't the Landon Carmichael who was nervous on our first date. You're

79

not the Landon Carmichael I loved and chose." She blinked her surprising tears away. "I loved a different you."

"He's drunk," Walt stated.

"That doesn't mean that's okay, Walt," Savannah hissed, pushing the men aside and carefully wiping Alex's tears from her face. "Let's go home."

Alex nodded as she saw Landon's eyelids fall, realizing just how intoxicated he was. So she directed her anger to Walt. "You tell him in the morning what he did tonight. That he forced himself on me. He hurt me. He hurt Chase. Most importantly, tell him I never want to see or speak to him again."

Sadness and understanding swirled in his eyes. He opened his mouth to say something, but he quickly shut it before he nodded. "I'll tell him."

"And tell Chase I'm so sorry," Alex said before she left her drunk ex-boyfriend in the hallway and returned to campus with her roommate.

80

Hg

mercury

ALEX

Now

"Happy to be home?" Uncle Rob asked, getting her attention. Robert Moors was one of her father's best friends. Having grown up in Melbourne with her father and mother, he was married to her mother's best friend, Allison, and had an adoptive son, Romeo, and a biological daughter, Rosie Melissa. Uncle Rob and Aunty Ally adopted Romeo when he was twelve and had their daughter four years later.

She smiled at her uncle who had been the Australian Men's Olympic coach for almost five years. He was even his son's coach throughout his ongoing Olympic career. "Very happy. How're Romeo and Rosie doing? I miss them."

Uncle Rob smiled, pride sweeping his light blue eyes. "Rosie's in her last year of high school, can you believe it? The kids miss you, too. Rosie and my wife wish they could've been here, but Allison doesn't like Rosie to be left alone. And Romeo would be here if he wasn't training in South Africa for Worlds."

"He's still on track to attempt three back-to-back gold medals?" Alex asked as she set her apple juice down on the dining table.

"He's gonna try. I don't see why not. Thirty-four and he's

83

still at his best. He'd have had four back-to-back gold medals had he not gotten injured at his second Olympics—"

"Rob, seriously?" her father interrupted, causing Alex to laugh.

Her father pressed his hand on her shoulder. "Rob, my daughter's too nice and loves you too much to tell you that all the row talk confuses her. She's a physics genius, not a sports reporter."

Alex rolled her eyes. "No, seriously, Uncle Rob. I'm just jet-lagged. I swear I'm interested. I find rowing fascinating from a scientific standpoint." Feeling her phone vibrate, she pulled it from the back pocket of her jeans. She took in Landon's name and then lowered her phone so her father wouldn't see. "I'm sorry, I have to take this."

"Sure thing," her father said as Uncle Rob nodded at her. She slipped out of the dining room and made her way into the hallway. Alex had texted him almost an hour ago.

Landon: Hey. I'm sorry, I was at a PR event. Can I call you?

Alex: It's more of a face-to-face conversation.

Landon: I'll be in NY for a meeting soon. I can come to Boston then.

Alex: Okay, great. I'll see you then.

"Hey," Evan said, causing Alex to lock her phone. She plastered a fake smile on her lips and gazed up at him. "You all right?"

She nodded. "Yeah, I'm okay."

Evan frowned. "You're tired. Come on, I'll bring your

suitcase to your room, and you can nap. I'll let your parents know. I think you've survived a lot longer than most of them expected."

The teasing in his voice was so familiar, and she missed it. She couldn't believe she'd gone so long without hearing it. "Sure. That would be great. Thanks, Evan."

"No worries, AJ," he said before she climbed the stairs, and Evan followed, lugging her suitcase along with him.

When they reached her bedroom, she pushed the door open and stepped inside for the first time in two months. She smiled at the little welcome home sign on her bed and the bright glittery balloon tied to her bedpost. She hadn't realized how much she missed her bedroom until just now. Alex made her way to her bed, pressing her palm on the comforter before sitting on it, and then she looked up at Evan. He wheeled her suitcase to the foot of the bed, laid it flat, and then sat on the mattress with her. It'd been a long time since they were both in her childhood room together.

Memories of them caused her tears to threaten. To show him the truth. But she quickly blinked them away, not wanting to tarnish today, his happiness, or make him regret his decisions.

"So you're home," Evan said in a low voice, sounding curious.

She craned her neck to find him smiling at her. "I'm home."

"And what are Alexandra Louise Parker's big plans?"

Alex smiled at the grin on his face as she pushed off the bed. She went to her suitcase, bent down, and entered her lock's combination. Unzipping it, she opened the suitcase and glanced down, noticing the pregnancy books she was supposed to have packed in her carry-on. Alex reached over and covered the books with her sweaters, feeling guilty for keeping her pregnancy from her best friend. But Evan couldn't know—no one could. Not just yet. Alex let the suitcase's lid rest against her bed so she could look for the envelope. Once she grasped it, Alex got up and returned to her spot next to Evan. She inhaled a deep breath before she handed it to him.

She watched as Evan glanced down, his furrowed brows eased as his thumb brushed against the MIT logo. He peeked at her for a single moment before he flipped the envelope over, opened it, and pulled out the letter. His eyes scanned it, and then he lifted his chin, blinking at her as a slow smile crossed his lips.

"You did it," he breathed in awe as he set the admission letter down next to him.

"Yeah," she confirmed in a low voice.

His soft brown eyes caused her heart to clench. Before she was able to say more, Evan wrapped his arms around her, embracing her tightly. She felt it. His pride for her. Alex closed her eyes and listened to his strong heartbeats. For a moment, she allowed her heart to have this. This embrace and intimacy. Because when they parted, that would be the end. Moments later and to her disappointment, Evan broke their hug first and gazed down at her.

"I'm so proud of you, AJ. You did it! You got into MIT." His eyes shone with unshed tears.

Her heart vibrated in her chest, wanting to tell him everything she had hidden from him during the time they had been apart. Instead, she took the cowardice way out and kept quiet. "I have to find my own apartment in Cambridge ... or as close to MIT as possible. I'm home, but I don't think my parents need me in the way with Seb."

"Alexandra," he said in a small voice, causing her fears to drive her heart's beats into a chaotic mess.

"Yeah?"

Evan bit his lip nervously, then revealed, "I sold the house."

Her heart dipped, falling out of place for what seemed like the hundredth time when it came to Evan Gilmore.

No.

"What?" she whispered as she pulled away, needing space as she wrapped her arms around her stomach, anticipating the very worst.

Sadness and grief consumed his face. "I got offered a job in LA."

"You're going back to California?"

Evan let out a sigh. "I'll help you find an apartment before I move," he promised.

Devastated that her best friend would be leaving to move to the other side of the country, Alex nodded to save her voice from projecting her heartbreak. She had only just come back after a year and a half of being in Europe.

Now he was leaving.

Evan reached behind her and pressed his palm to the back of her head, bringing her close to him and pressing his lips against her forehead. Her eyelids fluttered closed, memorizing the soft feel of his kiss. When she opened her eyes, he was staring at her as his thumb brushed along her cheek.

"I'll let you get some sleep," he said, then got off her bed.

Alex faked a smile as she watched him slip out of her

bedroom. Once her door clicked closed, she crawled across her bed to pick up her purse her mother had brought up after Evan held Seb. Grasping it firmly in her hand, she pressed her back against the pillows. Taking a deep breath, Alex opened her purse and retrieved what she was looking for before she set her purse back on the bed. Then she flipped the picture over and took in the small dot.

The most spectacular dot ever photographed.

It was her baby.

Alex pressed a palm to her stomach as her thumb brushed against the glossy sonogram. Now that she was home, she'd have to schedule an appointment with her doctor here. She'd have to figure out appointments and birthing classes. Though it was daunting to think about doing it alone, she was ready for what was next.

A smile tugged at her lips as she decided to forget about her worries and concentrate on the fact that her baby's father would love him or her no matter what.

Knowing what his love had been for her … she was sure of it.

Yawning, Alex rolled onto her back and took in the way the sun filtered through the curtains and brightened her cold room. She smiled at the thought that she had just woken for the very first time in Brookline and not in Zürich. Alex was glad to be home. Her baby meant more than three years in Switzerland. Digging her hand under the pillow, she pulled out the sonogram she had hid there yesterday. After she had taken a short power nap, she showered and joined the rest of the party. Kyle and Angie had stopped by, and even Jordan and Carter. Alex and Evan had attended their wedding the summer before their senior year of college.

"Good morning, Little Atom," Alex whispered as she glanced from the picture to her stomach. It was crazy how much she already loved it. She wasn't sure if it was a girl or a boy, but the pregnancy book she read last night said she wouldn't know her baby's gender for at least two more months.

For now, she'd stick to calling her baby "Little Atom."

"Let's go get some breakfast," she said before she gently slipped the sonogram back under her pillow and flung the blankets aside. Rubbing her eyes, she walked over to her door and removed her robe from the hook. Once she slipped it on, she tied the sash and opened the door. The mix of voices traveling to the second floor of the large house had her smiling. It'd been so long since she'd spent time with her whole family. Her parents had invited so many guests to her welcome home party, so they'd rented a house close by for some of her family who were visiting from Australia. Alex made her way down the stairs and into the kitchen, smiling at Lori and Reese who were already at the table.

"Morning," Alex said as she headed over to the table and sat next to Lori. "Hey, Lori, how is your senior year going?"

Her cousins had grown up since she last saw them, and Alex knew Uncle Alex was more worried about Lori than Reese. His concerns apparently grew when Lori became cheerleading captain and began to date the starting linebacker. According to Uncle Alex, Lori was growing up way too fast for his liking. Though Alex was certain Reese would give her father something to worry about because Reese was just as pretty as Lori. The girls shared the same glimmering brown eyes and sweet smile Alex was sure would have her uncle worrying about boys someday soon.

"It's going really well, Alexi," Lori said as she set down her mug.

"I bet you're acing being a senior."

Lori's smile was big and sweet. "I try. Dad is always on my case that I do too much." She rolled her eyes. "I'm captain, so I have to do a lot."

Alex nodded, understanding her cousin. Back in high school, Alex's friend was captain of their high school cheerleading team, and Jordan was always busy. "How about you, Reese? How is your freshman year going so far?"

Her youngest cousin squinted at her. "How is it going so far, Alexi? Well, first, Will leaves a legacy I can't escape, and my sister is a senior. OH! And said sister is also the captain of the cheerleading team. You do the math. I'm surprise you haven't noticed the big L on my forehead."

Lori shook her head. "You're so dramatic, Reese."

Reese grinned. It seemed as if Reese hadn't lost her humor during Alex's time in Switzerland. "Exactly what I'm going for. After all, I am in the drama club. I have to be *very* dramatic."

Alex's mother pressed a kiss on Alex's forehead before she set a plate of pancakes in front of her. "Good morning, my love. Coffee?"

The thought of coffee almost made her sick. Thankfully, today seemed to be one of those rare days when morning sickness didn't cripple her. "Just juice please. Where's Will?"

THE DISSOLUTION OF UNREQUITED

"Already went out for his run," Lori answered. "Oh, Grandpa James is coming tomorrow, Alexi."

She smiled. "That's great."

"Alexi," Reese said from across the table as Alex picked up her knife and fork.

"Yeah, Reese?"

"Why isn't Nan here—Ow, LORI!"

Alex felt the vibrations on the table, knowing that Lori had kicked her younger sister into silence. Her father walked into the kitchen, slowly rocking Seb in his arms and interrupting Reese's question. "Good morning."

"Morning, Uncle Noel," Lori and Reese said in unison.

"Everyone else still in bed?" her father asked as he sat down next to Alex.

Alex leaned over and pressed a soft kiss on her brother's head. He had that clean baby smell she loved. Then her father kissed her cheek when she sat back. "Morning, Dad."

"No coffee?" he queried.

She shook her head. "No coffee. It tastes weird with pancakes. It's not a combo I like."

"Uncle Noel, why isn't Nan here?" Reese asked once more.

Her father's green eyes widened. Alex hated that she'd kept it from her youngest cousin for so long. To give her father a reprieve, she decided to explain it as she turned to face Reese and her curious brown eyes.

"Reese, the truth is …"

"Yeah?"

She inhaled a short breath and felt nausea swirl in her stomach. She let out a groan, hoping it was just nerves rather than morning sickness.

"Gillian doesn't like me," she revealed.

"She doesn't?"

Alex shook her head. "She's never liked me."

"Why?"

She glanced over at her father and then at Lori. "You know I love science, right? That I went to Zürich to work at the best institute in the world?"

"I do," Reese said.

"Okay. Well, Gillian doesn't really approve of me and my life choices."

Reese's jaw dropped. "That's so unfair. I think you're amazing!"

That had Alex laughing as she heard a knock on the front door. "It's okay because I know for a fact she loves you."

"I'll get it," her mother said as she walked out of the dining room to answer the door.

"But why can't she love you?" Reese pressed.

Alex sighed. "I'm different. Not everybody loves different, Reese. You just gotta find those who love you and accept you as you are, and welcome them in your life."

"Alexandra," her mother said, getting her attention. "You have a visitor."

"I do?" she asked as she set her silverware down on the table and got up from her chair.

Suddenly, Savannah Peters stepped from behind Alex's mother shouting, "Surprise!"

Alex quickly went around the table, wrapping her arms around her best friend. Then she pulled back to see the smile on Savannah's face. It had been almost eight months since Savannah had visited her in Zürich.

"Welcome home, Alex." Then she brushed her blond hair behind her ear and waved at Alex's family sitting at the large table. "Looking good, Noel. Baby Seb suits you."

Her father laughed. "Nice to see you, Savannah."

"Would you like some breakfast, Savannah? You must be tired," her mother said.

Savannah sighed. "Yeah. I left Montpelier at like five a.m. to get here, so breakfast would be great."

"How long are you in town for?" Alex asked.

"Just till tonight. I have work in the morning. My stupid boss only gave me a day. Is that okay?" The guilt on Savannah's face had Alex laughing.

"I'm just happy you made it."

Savannah squinted at her and then glanced over at Alex's mother. "Clara, do I have permission to have Alex all day after breakfast?"

Her mother smiled. "Only if you promise she'll have a good time."

"Oh, most definitely," Savannah said with a large smile on her face.

Alex was officially exhausted from shopping. After she and Savannah had breakfast with her family, she left her best friend cradling her little brother and went upstairs to get ready. When she made it into her room, morning sickness conquered her, and Alex threw up her breakfast. She sat by the toilet for some time before she showered and brushed her teeth. After she dressed, she made her way downstairs and told Savannah she was ready to go. Her best friend had eyed her suspiciously before they said goodbye to everyone and got in Alex's car. Alex drove them into the city and stopped at where she knew were Savannah's favorite shops from the last time she was in Boston. They had shopped for a few hours before Savannah noticed Alex's eyelids drooping as jet lag took its toll on her, so she suggested they get something to eat at Della's.

"Okay, Alex," Savannah said as she set her phone down on the table. "We spent hours shopping and talking about me. It's time we talk about you."

Her stomach knotted. There wasn't much she could keep from Savannah and being pregnant was definitely one of them. If she was going to tell anyone first, it was Savannah.

"What's there to say?" Alex said as she picked up the menu and opened it, skimming the options. Deciding on something light to eat, she opted for the salad without cheese since she hadn't yet researched what cheeses she could eat. Then she gazed up at Savannah and smiled. "I'm back after a year and half of being in Zürich, and I spent hours watching you choose new work outfits."

"And you bought none," Savannah complained. "You're going to MIT, Alex. You're gonna be a TA. You need new clothes. You left most of them in Zürich."

"I have until September, Sav."

Her best friend rolled her eyes. "I thought you'd be more excited about attending MIT."

"I am," she assured as she set down the menu. She might be excited about MIT, but her main concerns weren't clothes. It was to raise her baby. "I'm just tired."

"Hello, ladies. Are you ready to order?" their waitress at Della's asked. Since her mother's restaurant was busy and Alex didn't want to inconvenience anyone, they went to Savannah's second favorite restaurant in Boston.

"I'll have the salmon special," Savannah said as she handed the menu over.

"And for you?"

Alex closed her menu, and said, "Just the garden salad without cheese and dressing on the side, please," as she gave the waitress her menu.

"No cheese?" Savannah asked once they were alone.

Her heartbeat picked up as she took in the worry on her best friend's face. "No cheese."

"Alex." She sighed. "Something's up with you. You've been acting strange since our video chat when you were in Zürich. What's with the no cheese and dressing on the side? You normally ask for extra dressing. Are you okay? I'm really worried."

Alex swallowed hard, knowing she couldn't keep it from Savannah any longer. Someone had to know, and at least it wouldn't be a stranger. It would be her best friend.

Taking a deep breath, she straightened her spine and balled her fist. Then, in a low voice, she announced, "Sav, I'm pregnant."

81

Tl

thallium

EVAN

Two months ago

*T*ick.
    Tick.
Tick.

The waiting room's clock seemed to pitch higher with every frustrating second that passed. Evan Gilmore sat in the same uncomfortable chair for what felt like forever. He was told to go home hours ago, but he couldn't. He had to be here just in case she didn't make it. Glancing up at the clock, he calculated the time in his head and knew she would have already landed.

He hoped and prayed she'd make it in time. Evan knew how upset she would be if she missed the birth. Her father had called her over twenty hours ago, and she rushed to the airport to catch the first flight she could get on.

Mrs. Parker had been in labor for close to a day now. Her husband told Evan to go home hours ago, but he couldn't. Not until he knew that Mr. and Mrs. Parker's daughter made it to the hospital. Suddenly, the loud rushing steps caught his attention, and he noticed a brunette rush to the desk.

Alexandra.

Evan got up from the chair. For a moment, he hesitated,

remembering the last time he saw her. He should wait till he saw her face, to see if they were okay, but missing her had him walking to her.

It had been four months.

Four long, torturous months, and Evan couldn't stand another minute away from her.

"My mother. She's in labor and—"

"AJ," he said, interrupting her.

She turned away from the nurse behind the desk, and the relief in her emerald eyes broke and mended his heart, turning his limbs to Jell-O. He had missed her for months. Loved her for even longer than that.

"Evan," she breathed. "Is she okay?"

Before he could answer, Evan wrapped his arms tightly around her, feeling how right it was to hold her once more. She smelled like honey and fresh flowers. A fragrance that always reminded him of her.

When he broke their embrace, he looked down at her and nodded. "Come on. Let's sit. Your dad is with her."

AJ followed him over to the waiting room seats, placing her suitcase on the ground before they sat down. He watched her sigh and saw the tiredness on her face.

"How was your flight?"

She brushed her brunette curls back and sighed. "*Flights.* I had to fly to Dublin, which was fine, but then the weather turned bad, and they canceled all the flights because of the snow. I was stuck in Dublin for over eight hours, but it doesn't matter anymore. I'm glad I'm finally here."

Then she smiled.

It was flawless.

And beautiful.

And a smile he missed and dreamed of.

They were all right.

He had been so stupid not to realize it earlier.

That he loved her.

Still loved her.

But time got away from them again.

Realizing he had been quiet for far too long, he smiled and grasped her hand in his. "I'm just happy you're here."

That smile of hers softened as if a hint of sadness found a place in her heart. "Thank you for being here while I was in Zürich."

Evan squeezed her hand. "Of course. Your mother is, and always will be, family to me."

AJ glanced down at their hands and then looked back up at him. Her green eyes gleamed over with a flash of pain. Almost like lightning in the night sky, it was bright, beautiful, and frightening. "I don't think we should be holding hands, Evan."

"I know we shouldn't," he said in a tight voice. "But I can't think of a reason that makes sense except for the fact that I miss you. A lot. I've missed you a lot, AJ."

Her eyelids fluttered as she breathed, "Evan."

He told his whimpering heart to stop.

To let its affections for her go.

That this wasn't the time for his needs and desperate pleas.

He took her in and realized where they sat.

She's in a hospital ... maybe she hasn't noticed just yet.

"Hey, AJ?"

She tilted her head at him. "Yeah?"

"You did it."

"Did what?" Her brows furrowed.

He laughed as he squeezed her hand. "You're in a hospital without looking like you're going to throw up right now."

AJ blinked at him, and her eyes scanned around the waiting room. Then her jaw dropped in awe. "I guess I was just so worried about my mum that I forgot. But now I'm totally aware of the smell and ..."

Worry tumbled through him as he searched her face for any tells. "I shouldn't have said anything. I'm just proud of you since this is the first time you've been in a hospital and haven't run out in a panic. Are you okay? Are you going to be sick?"

"I'm fine," she said in a small voice before she inhaled a deep breath and then slowly exhaled it. "You're right. This is the first time I haven't run out of a hospital. I want to be here. I have to be here to support my parents. I'll be okay. So have you just been waiting?"

Evan nodded. "Yeah. But while we wait, catch me up. How's Dr. Rodahawe and everyone? How's your research and your formula going?"

To his surprise, AJ reached up and pressed her palm softly against his cheek like she used to. Like he missed and dreamed of. "Zürich isn't the same since you left." She paused and bit her lip. "Evan, I miss you a lot, but we shouldn't hold hands."

She tried to pull away, but Evan tightened his grip, shaking his head at her. "I was your boyfriend for three years, Alexandra. Not holding your hand while you're right here next to me doesn't feel right. I shouldn't have left Zürich. I shouldn't have left you." Then he took a deep breath. "I—"

And just as he was about to tell her he still loved her, her father burst through the doors, and announced, "Evan, I have a son." Then Mr. Parker glanced over and noticed his daughter, and his tears ran down his face. "Alexandra, you're here. You have a brother, my love."

She pulled her hand from Evan's and got up from the chair. "Can I see him?"

"Of course," her father said.

Evan blinked at the chair she left vacant. He'd wait until the Parkers had their moment with the latest addition to their family before he returned home.

"You coming?"

He glanced over to find AJ smiling at him. "Can I?"

She nodded as she held out her hand. "Like you said, you were my boyfriend for three years, but you have been a part of our family for much longer. You can't miss this."

She was right. He couldn't miss meeting her little brother. Evan stood, grabbed her suitcase and purse, and placed his hand in hers, feeling a sense of home envelop him. He was home. With her, he had always been home. Mr. Parker smiled as he led them through the doors, down the hall, and into a room on their right.

As he set AJ's suitcase and purse on the floor, he saw Mrs. Parker—the woman who helped raise him—holding a baby boy in her arms. Her hair was slightly messy and sweat dotted her forehead. When she lifted her chin and smiled at them, he saw the tiredness and love on her face.

"Alexandra, you made it," her mother said softly.

She released his hand and made her way to her mother's side and kissed her temple. AJ smiled at her baby brother. "I'm so proud of you, Mum. He's so cute. Did you pick a name?"

Her mother smiled. "Sebastian Marcus Parker."

She glanced up at her mother. "Sebastian?"

"Danny's middle name. I had to name my son after him. He was the one who inspired me to become a chef, and he continues to inspire me. Besides your father and my brother, he has been the only man in my life who has made it better. Well, that's not true …"

"It's not?" AJ asked, sounding confused.

Mrs. Parker lifted her chin and smiled at Evan, causing him to still under her loving gaze. "The moment you came into my life, Evan, you made it better, too."

His heart clenched at Mrs. Parker's words. Words she had no idea meant the world to him. He had never really known his mother, but he knew a mother's love because of Clara Parker. She had no business loving and taking care of him, but she did. And Evan would never stop being thankful for her love.

Evan brushed his tears away as he watched AJ blink hers free. "You made my life better, too, Mrs. Parker. You gave me a family I love. Thank you."

"You'll always have a family with us," Mrs. Parker reminded. After his relationship with her daughter ended, Mrs. Parker had told him those very words when he returned home from Switzerland. "Alexandra?"

AJ stared at him before she pressed her lips together and glanced down at her mother. "Yes, Mum?"

"Would you like to hold your baby brother?"

She blinked in surprise, and her body tensed with uncertainty. "I wouldn't know how."

Her father set his hand on Evan's shoulder, tearing his focus from the sight before him. "Thank you, Evan, for being there for Clara when her water broke and for driving her to the hospital."

"Of course, Mr. Parker."

Then Mr. Parker let out a soft sigh. "And thank you for being there for my daughter. You were good to her even after the end."

His heart broke at her father's reminder, and he focused on his ex-girlfriend. He watched as she held her brother for the first time and the wonder exploded in her eyes as she whispered to him.

And at that moment, he saw it.

He had always known she was all he had ever wanted, but seeing her cradle Sebastian was all he needed to see.

He wanted it for himself.

Someday, he wanted it.

When she was ready. When the stars and their universe collided and brought them together again, and they were bonded atoms once more. One day, he wanted it all with her. He wanted this sight for himself.

Alexandra holding our son or daughter in her arms.

The sight almost brought him to tears as determination and hope flourished in his chest. But he would have to wait. Wait until Alexandra Parker finished living her dreams in Zürich without him. Wait until the day she was ready.

And wait until her heart was ready for him once again.

The soft knocks on his front door had Evan glancing up from his laptop. After Evan left Zürich, Mr. Parker had helped him find some small marketing and management consultation jobs while he applied for bigger firms. Evan's current client was a small stationery company that needed advice on a new business model. It had been countless nights of working through the model so he could a draft a report with his findings and recommendations. Just as Evan was about to ignore the late-night visitor, he heard several more knocks. Sighing, he saved his report and got up from the kitchen table where he was working.

Rubbing the kink in his shoulder, Evan made his way out of the kitchen, down the hall, and to the front door. Once he reached it, he flicked on the porch light and then opened the door, surprised to see his ex-girlfriend in pjs and a thick coat.

"Alexandra," he breathed, his eyebrows furrowing in concern. "It's late. Are you okay? Is Seb okay?"

She smiled and then nodded. "It's stupid, me being here. But ..." She sighed. "I have a flight back to Zürich in the morning, and I love Seb, but he keeps crying every two hours. And that would be okay, but Dr. Rodahawe has me on assignment as soon as I land. I'm so sorry, but can I sleep on your couch tonight?"

"Wait," he said, confused. "You just got here."

"Yeah, four days ago."

He shook his head in disbelief. "And you're already leaving?"

She chewed her bottom lip before she said, "Yeah. They need me back at the institute. Plus, I'm almost done with my formula."

And for the first time in their entire relationship, he asked, "Can't you stay?"

Her eyes widened. "I can't, Evan. I can't stay."

"So this is your last night?"

She nodded.

His heart broke into fragments that would never heal the right way ever again.

He was lost without her.

He'd somehow managed to survive four months without her.

Evan stepped forward, throwing his heart, reason, and restraint in the wind as he cupped her face in his palms. "I love you," he whispered. "I still love you. Please say you love me, too."

Her eyes glazed over. "I do love you, Evan."

It was all he needed as he crashed his lips to hers.

His ex-girlfriend threaded her fingers through his hair as he walked them back into his warm house, kissing her as if his life depended on it. And in sweet relief, she kissed him back with as much urgency, love, passion, and want.

"Evan," she moaned as she kicked the door closed.

"Stay," he begged as he pressed her body against the door. "Please, God, please stay."

His hands left her cheeks and gripped her coat, ripping it open. Once she shrugged it off, AJ grasped the hem of his T-shirt and lifted it over his head, dropping it on the floor.

He panted as he ended their kiss and stared into her beautiful green eyes. "Please, Alexandra. Please stay with me," he begged one last time.

She reached up and cupped his face, gently brushing her thumb across his cheek. "Just tonight, Evan. I can only stay for tonight."

His heart ached. But it was all he could have. All she'd

let him have.

He slipped his hand under her tank top and grasped her hip, pressing her body against him. "Just tonight," he agreed in a tight voice. Then his forehead met hers. "But just know I'll still love you after tonight."

Waking up to an empty bed hadn't been what Evan expected. Sure, he knew deep down that she'd leave, but he had hoped some time during their night together she would change her mind. He had hoped as he made love to her, she would realize that it was him. That she had to stay with him.

Be with him.

Have the life they had worked so hard to have.

But it was evident when he woke up alone that he hadn't done enough.

When he woke up, he sat on his bed and thought about their night over and over again. What he could have done to make her stay. What he could have said to change her mind. But it didn't matter. She was leaving. She was returning to Zürich and taking his heart with her. Taking in a deep breath of the cold morning air, he walked across the Parker's driveway and approached the front door to find AJ hugging her crying mother.

"I'll be home again soon," AJ promised as she wiped her mother's tears away, her father looking on as he held her baby brother.

"Hey, Evan," Mr. Parker greeted.

His ex-girlfriend turned and faced him, her sad smile crippling his heart. "Hey," she said in a soft voice. The horn from a cab echoed, and she glanced over at the car. "I better get going. Traffic to Logan is gonna be insane." Then she bent down and kissed her brother. "I'll see you soon, Seb. Don't grow too much while I'm away."

"Christmas?" her father asked.

She nodded. "Christmas." She glanced back at Evan and stepped toward him. The sadness in her eyes was so hard to look away from. She reached up and pressed her palm against his cheek like she did last night when he made love to her. "I love you, Evan. And I don't think I ever told you enough how much I loved you being my boyfriend. How much I appreciated you coming to Zürich for a year to be with me. I don't know when I'll be home again. I took the job."

He stilled. "Three more years …?"

"Yeah," she confirmed. "Three more years in Zürich at the institute. I won't be an assistant anymore but a researcher."

Broken.

Her news broke him.

But she was achieving her dreams.

And that was all he had ever wanted for her.

Suddenly, the horn from the cab erupted once more. This time, it rang longer and louder. At that moment, he saw the flash of the future in her eyes.

It's still there.

He'd seen it as he made love to her.

Saw the hope for their future together.

She got on her toes and pressed her lips against his. "I'll still love you after I leave." AJ pulled her hand away and then smiled at her family. "I'll call you both once I land in Zürich. I love you all."

Evan watched as the love of his life wheeled her small suitcase to the cab. The driver got out, then lifted the trunk and placed it inside. She made her way to the car, pulled on the door handle, and slipped inside. Once the door closed, he watched the cab drive away, taking her with it.

He stood there long after the cab had disappeared from his sight.

So did her parents.

Evan spun around and took in the sadness on Alexandra's father's face.

He cleared his throat and straightened his spine, ready to finally ask him.

"Mr. Parker, I think we need to have that talk."

82

Pb

lead

ALEX

Now

"Y-you're pregnant?" her best friend uttered. Her piercing blue eyes were wide with shock, amazement, and wonder. Savannah shook her head in disbelief, her lip trembling as if she were coming to terms with the news.

Alex nodded. "Yes. I am."

Savannah tensed. "Oh, my God!"

"Yeah?"

"It's Landon's, isn't it? You've been so tight-lipped about what happened between you and him while you were in England. I can't believe he's—"

"Savannah," Alex said, interrupting her best friend's quick assumptions. "It's *not* Landon's."

Alex didn't think it was possible, but Savannah's eyes widened even farther as her mouth gaped. "It's not ..." She leaned forward and whispered, "Brandon's, is it?"

To her surprise, Alex let out a light, amused laugh. "It's not Brandon's. We're friends. You know that."

"Your baby could have had an English accent, and a nice one, too." Savannah leaned back against her chair. "So if it's not Landon's, and it's not Brandon's ..." She pressed her lips tightly together as hope resonated in her eyes. "You know who

I'd want, but I'll let you tell me."

Alex licked her dry lips as nerves and fear consumed her. She knew she would have Savannah's support, but she wasn't sure how she would react to the news. Ever since their junior year of college, she had been clear as to who Alex's "One True Pair" was. It would be the first time Alex would ever say the father of her baby's name out loud. The thought induced her anxiety and excitement. Her desire to be able to finally be honest.

"Savannah."

"I'll be here for you. No matter what, you'll have me by your side. Aunt Sav will help," she said with a glint in her eyes.

Her best friend's support caused her heart to clench. A part of her knew she might be a single parent, but she knew she'd be okay. She had Savannah's support, and she knew when she told her parents, she'd have theirs, too.

"And I will love Little Parker so much," Savannah promised.

"Actually," Alex said, unclenching her fist on the table. Then she let out an exhale. "He or she will be a Little *Gilmore*."

"Oh, my God," Savannah whispered, shock filled her entire face. "Oh, my God! Is it? Please tell me it's his."

She pressed her lips into a tight smile, ready to confess the truth. "*Evan's* the father."

"When? How?" Savannah blurted out as their waiter returned to their table and set their meals down.

"Thank you," Alex said as she picked up her fork, moving the lettuce around in her bowl. Then she glanced up at her best friend's impatient expression. "Two months ago. When I was home for Seb's birth. I had to go back to Zürich earlier than planned because Dr. Rodahawe wanted me on an assignment as soon as I landed. And well, Seb would not stop crying every two hours, so I went to Evan's house. He asked me to stay and then he told me he still loved me, and ... it happened."

Savannah's eyes gleamed with unshed tears. "You and Evan are having a baby together." Those tears of hers slipped down her cheeks. "Alex, it's meant to be. It's always meant to be you and Evan. And now you're home. This is perfect." Savannah's smile faded. "But you don't look happy."

Alex inhaled a deep breath and then released it. "He asked me to stay, Sav. Two months ago, he asked me to stay, and I was so stupid to leave. I was scared. That night, when we were together, I was so scared to stay and have the life I always wanted with him. I was so scared to leave the comfort of my research assistantship. I was scared that maybe if we had a normal relationship, we'd—*I'd*—not be what and who he truly wanted."

"Alex, that's insane. Evan loves you. And two months ago, he was still in love with you. You're pregnant with his baby now, so I know he'll be excited to have you both in his life," Savannah said in a soft voice.

"He's moving to LA, Sav," Alex added as she set her fork down on the bowl and pressed her palm against her stomach.

"What?"

She nodded. "Yeah. He told me yesterday. I don't want him to stay here in Boston if his heart and future lie elsewhere."

Savannah reached over and grasped her hand. "Alex, I know you don't believe this, but his heart and future lie with you. I know you're a big believer in dreams, and that you think Evan is going to give up his dreams for you, but you out of all people should know that sometimes dreams wait."

Sometimes dreams wait.

"You're right," Alex said, realizing just how true her best friend's words were.

"There's a flicker of determination in your eyes. What are you thinking?"

Alex smiled, knowing what she had to do. "That if Evan wants to be part of our baby's life, I have to move to LA. Not just for him, but also for our child. I don't want him or her to grow up not knowing Evan just because we're no longer together."

Her best friend's lips slowly parted. "But your Ph.D.?"

Her heart dipped, and Alex pushed past the nausea that swirled in her stomach. "We both know that it wasn't really going to happen, Sav. I'm due the first week of the fall semester. There's no way I can juggle all of that. I want to be a good mum. And a good mum knows what's best, and right now, my Ph.D. isn't what's good for Evan's and my baby."

"MIT's your dream."

Alex pulled her hand away from Savannah's. "I know, but like you said, sometimes dreams wait. And my Ph.D. and MIT can wait—especially if I move to LA. I know a few professors at Caltech. It's only a twenty-minute drive from LA, so that's an option."

"You'd give up MIT for Evan and your child?"

"Yeah," Alex answered without a hint of hesitation. "It's not about me anymore. I'll get my Ph.D. someday. I'll figure it all out. Now, you called yourself Aunt Sav … that's for life, you know."

Her best friend grinned. "Absolutely. I'm going to love

Little Gilmore for my entire life. And I know he or she is going to be better than all right because he or she gets to have you as a mother."

And for the first time since her first ultrasound in Zürich, Alex began to cry, knowing she would be someone's mother soon.

"Seriously, why can't I come with you, Alexi?" Reese asked at the front door as Alex buttoned up her coat.

She smiled at her youngest cousin. "Because you're meeting Grandpa at the airport after you and Lori go shopping. My mum did say that you could have as many cupcakes at the bakery as you wanted."

Reese rolled her brown eyes. "But that stuff is boring. Why can't I come with you and Evan?"

Alex picked up her keys from the hallway table and stuffed them into her coat pocket. "Reese, I promise, we aren't doing anything fun. You're not missing out on anything."

"Oh, yeah?" Reese folded her arms over her chest. "So what are you both doing?"

"I'll only tell you if you promise not to tell anyone—especially my parents. Okay?"

She grinned. "I promise."

Laughing, Alex heard a knock on the front door and stepped around her cousin. She grasped and then twisted the handle, opening the door to find Evan standing before her with a smile on his face.

"Morning, AJ," he greeted.

Her heart squeezed at the sight of those beautiful brown eyes as she pressed her palm against her stomach, hoping another round of morning sickness didn't strike her. She had spent a good part of the morning hovering over the toilet and throwing up before she showered and skipped breakfast. She knew it wasn't good for the baby to skip a meal, but the smell of her mother's cooking made her queasy.

"So what are you and my cousin doing today, Evan?" Reese asked behind her.

Evan raised a brow at Alex. She nodded as she stepped back so that he could see Reese. "Hey, Reese. Well, what did your cousin say?"

Reese's cheeks peppered with a pink flush as she unfolded her arms and pursed her lips. Alex knew that Reese had always harbored a crush on her best friend. "Alexi said it was a secret. I'm not allowed to tell."

"That's right. You won't, right?"

"I promise," Reese said, her eyes shimmering at him.

Evan stepped closer and set his hand on Alex's shoulder, his thumb brushing her shoulder blade. "We're going to look at some apartments."

"You're moving out?"

Alex glanced over at Evan and then back at her cousin. "Yeah. It's a bit crowed right now, and I don't want to get in the way. But don't tell my parents—just in case we don't find anything today."

"I won't tell Aunty Clara and Uncle Noel," Reese promised as Evan's hand fell away from Alex.

Evan winked at Reese. "Great. We'll be back in a couple

of hours. Ready to go, AJ?"

"Yeah." She nodded. "I'm leaving. I'll be back home soon!" she yelled out to her parents who were still in the kitchen with the rest of her family. Then she gazed down at Reese. "Tell Grandpa I said hi when you pick him up. We'll be home soon. Enjoy your shopping trip, Reese."

"I will. Enjoy your day with Evan!" her cousin said with a smirk on her face.

"It's much nicer than the house we just saw on Henry Street," she pointed out as she stared out of the window.

"Yeah, but a thousand dollars more for one less room and one street closer to MIT," Evan retorted with displeasure as he stepped away from the extravagant kitchen and joined her by the living room window.

The apartment they were in was a few minutes' drive to MIT. It was ideal but expensive for a one-bedroom apartment. Alex had to think realistically. She needed two bedrooms. The apartment on Henry Street would have made do had it had an elevator. There was no way she could raise her baby in an apartment complex that didn't have one.

"This isn't it, AJ," Evan stated.

She turned away from the view and gazed up at him. He was right. She was paying for luxury and location. In theory, she would have to give up MIT, and she shouldn't be looking at apartments at all.

"I know," she admitted in defeat. They had spent the past

two hours looking at real estate, and so far, everything had either been out of her price range or didn't have what she needed. It wasn't just about her. She had to find an apartment that would be suitable to raise her baby in. It didn't help her stress levels that every place they visited, Evan found a fault.

"Are you sure you want to rent rather than buy, Miss Parker?" her real estate agent, Maureen, asked.

She spun around to find Maureen holding her tablet to her chest. "I'm sure. There's no way I can afford to buy in Cambridge."

Maureen pushed her glasses up the bridge of her nose and pursed her lips. "Well, how long will your Ph.D. take?"

"Depends. It'll probably be seven years before I graduate," she answered.

The real estate agent stepped closer and flipped the tablet around to show Alex some graphs and numbers. "In the long run, it's much more economical for you to buy rather than rent. There's a condo on Pearl Street that has been on the market for months. If it's something you like, we could negotiate on the price."

Alex nodded as she took in the tablet's screen, her heart plummeting at a figure she hadn't expected to see. "Maureen, is that correct? Five thousand dollars a month to buy that house on Pearl Street?"

Maureen's lips pressed into a hesitant smile. "In the long run, it'll be much better for you, Miss Parker. I know it's a little bit more than your budget, but I did my research. You're affiliated with the Red Sox, and you came into some money—"

"What?" Alex gasped in shock. Her estate agent had done her research on her. But clearly not enough if she thought Alex still had two million dollars in her pockets. She had donated all that money to different charities during her senior year of high school, refusing to allow dirty money from *The Daily Sportsourage* to sit in her account. "You *researched* me?"

"You're a high-priority client. I just wanted to make sure I had all the information—"

"To get a sale out of her?" Evan asked with a hint of rage in his voice.

Maureen averted her eyes from Alex to Evan and back to Alex. She appeared to be appealing for help or a reprieve. "I wanted to find Miss Parker the right home."

Alex closed her eyes tightly in frustration before she opened them. "I can't afford any of the apartments you've shown me, Maureen. I don't have two million dollars in my account. I haven't been officially affiliated with the Red Sox since my senior year of high school. Look, do you mind giving us a minute?"

"Of course, I'm sorry," Maureen said before she left Alex and Evan alone. Then the front door closing echoed throughout the small apartment.

Sighing, Alex made her way to the white leather couch and sat down, defeat crawling across her skin and causing her temples to throb. She hated that she couldn't afford to live in Cambridge. She could if she tapped into her trust funds, but she was adamant to keep them untouched to secure her baby's future. Alex had a full ride at Duke and had she not, it would have cost her parents a fortune for her to attend college. As Alex leaned back on the couch, Evan sat down next to her.

"I can't afford anything, Evan," she admitted in a small voice, staring at the large TV in front of them.

"Maybe a one bedroom?"

She shook her head. A one-bedroom apartment wasn't going to work for her. Not now, anyway. Alex peeked over at the concerned expression on Evan's face. He felt sorry for her. It was clear in his telling brown eyes. "Stop that."

"Stop what?"

Alex sat herself up and let out another sigh. "The 'you feel sorry for me' look on your face. I barely made any money working for Dr. Rodahawe. I could only afford that apartment in Zürich because of you. You paid for it. I brought home nothing in our relationship while we were in Switzerland. I have made no real money for myself since high school. I have about maybe thirty thousand dollars to my name. And I know that's more than what some people have, but right now, it doesn't seem like enough."

"Hey," Evan said as he reached over and grasped her hands in his. "The last thing I feel is sorry for you, AJ. I'm in awe of you. You were busy trying to work on a formula that could change physics. And we shared that apartment in Zürich because you were my girlfriend. The last thing I wanted was for you to worry about money. Alexandra, I have money. I can—"

"No," she blurted out, interrupting him. As much as her heart ached and loved everything he was saying, it was wrong. It was wrong for him to stay and wrong for her to hear. Evan had lived a life without her for the past six months. He had to go to California and not pay for her to live in Cambridge. "You're about to move to LA, Evan. That's not a cheap city to live in. You don't have to take care of me anymore." Alex blinked back her hot tears, pulled her hands free from his hold, and stood from the couch.

"AJ," Evan breathed. The hurt in his voice was heartbreaking. She didn't mean to bring up their past, but it was the only way to correct their position in life's plans for them. They didn't belong together anymore. Alex couldn't take advantage of him and reap the benefits of his generosity.

"I think I'm done apartment hunting. There's no reason for me to leave Brookline. It's close enough to MIT. Plus, I don't think my parents would want me to move out so soon. I haven't been home for long."

Evan stared at her for a moment before he nodded and got up from the couch. "All right. I'll take you home."

Home.

The idea of home with Evan Gilmore was an out of reach dream she'd had for so long.

A dream she couldn't truly have now that he was happy with a life without her.

Alex had been Dr. Livingston's patient since she'd turned thirteen, and Dr. Livingston was the only doctor Alex felt comfortable with knowing she was pregnant. It had been a day since she and Evan went to Cambridge to look at apartments, and a day since Alex had brought up their past. They were supposed to have moved on and be friends, but it was too hard for her. She tried not to admit it to herself, but every apartment she and Evan looked at, she thought of the life she could have had with him. But Evan had sacrificed his dreams for her. He'd put them on hold to follow her to Switzerland, so she owed him his happiness, and it was time she let him go. For her sake, his, and their son or daughter's.

"It's good to have you home, Alex," the doctor said as she sat behind the desk. "How long has it been since you were last home?"

Alex brushed her curls behind her ear and mulled it over. "I was home two months ago, but it's been a while. I think I saw your daughter the summer after we graduated from college and I came to see you about vaccinations before I went to Europe. How is Claudia?"

Dr. Livingston smiled, pride gleaming in her blue eyes. "She stayed in Chicago for an advertising job after she graduated from the School of Art Institute of Chicago. She's doing really well. Your mother said you were still living in Zürich."

"I was. I got an opportunity to work at the Rodahawe Institute for three more years, but I turned it down."

"I see." She nodded. "And congratulations on your baby brother. I saw Sebastian for his checkup last week. He's beautiful. Your parents make the most stunning children. It's still early, but my money is on him having green eyes."

Alex let out a small laugh. "I think he will, too."

"But I'm sure you didn't come in today for a chat." Her carefree smile turned professional, reminding Alex of when she visited her doctor after she had become sexually active. "How are you? Is everything okay?"

Alex's smile faded into a tight line. She cleared her throat and then straightened her spine. The nerves somehow numbed her fingertips as her heart pounded heavily in her chest.

She inhaled once.

Exhaled a second later.

Then she finally revealed, "I'm pregnant."

"Okay," Dr. Livingston said, squaring her shoulders. "Did you see a doctor while you were in Switzerland?"

Alex nodded. "I did. I found out while I was in Zürich, and he confirmed my pregnancy. I was already six weeks when we did the blood test and then we did an ultrasound."

"Good. I'd like to perform another ultrasound today to see how everything is going. How far along are you?" she asked as she set her fingertips to the keyboard and began to type.

"I'm almost nine weeks," Alex revealed.

The doctor nodded as she continued to type away. "Well, before we do an ultrasound ..." She stopped typing and faced Alex. "You have options. An unintended pregnancy happens. I can give you some information about abortions if—"

"No," Alex said immediately. "I want this baby. I'm not having an abortion."

"Okay. Before we do an ultrasound, I have to recommend you not fly often. I insist the father flies to the States if you wish to give birth here in Massachusetts instead of Zürich."

Alex's shoulders weakened as she shook her head. "That's not a problem, Dr. Livingston. The father isn't Swiss."

Surprise flashed on the doctor's face. "Oh, I'm sorry. I shouldn't have assumed."

"It's okay," Alex assured. She knew that whatever they discussed in this examination room would not leave it. "Dr. Livingston, I don't know if you ever knew, but Evan Gilmore and I were together for a long time."

The doctor's hand fell away from the keys as compassion flared in her blue eyes. "I had my suspicions. I saw you both together one summer, and you were holding hands. It was only for a moment. I've been hoping you've been with the right Gilmore brother all this time."

Her heart clenched at the doctor's hope. The hope she was about to crush. "Evan and I are no longer together."

"I'm sorry to hear that."

For a moment, she wondered if her doctor thought that Alex's baby wasn't Evan's. That she somehow cheated on him, and that was the reason they weren't together. Alex hoped not. Not once in their entire relationship did she ever desire, want, or need anyone the way she loved him.

It had been Evan Gilmore the moment he returned to her.

"Evan's the father, Dr. Livingston, but he doesn't know. Not yet, anyway. I haven't told him, and I'm not sure how he'll take it," Alex said in a small, vulnerable voice. The fear of Evan's rejection haunted her dreams. "But no matter what, I'm going to love our child enough for the both of us. I might not be the world's greatest mum, but I'm gonna try."

Dr. Livingston's eyes gleamed as a smile spread across her face. "How about we get you to the scanner? We should be able to hear your baby's heartbeat today."

Her heart raced in her chest as excitement and the unknown controlled it. She wasn't sure how she would react to hearing her baby's heartbeat for the first time. A sense of sadness washed over her at the thought of doing it alone and Evan not experiencing this exact moment for himself.

"Dr. Livingston?"

"Yes, Alex?"

"Is there any way we can record the heartbeat?"

"We can do that."

She swallowed the lump in her throat. "And can we make two copies of today's ultrasound?" Feeling as if she needed to give the doctor more of an explanation, she added, "I'd like Evan to have all of this if he decides he wants to be involved. To show him that I've considered his role in our baby's life since the start."

Her doctor nodded. "I'll make sure you leave here with two of everything. Let's go hear your baby's heartbeat."

What felt like a lifetime later, Alex was in another room lying down as the doctor squeezed the cool gel on her exposed stomach. Alex held her breath as the scanner pressed against her stomach.

"It's okay, Alex. Breathe. Everything's going to be okay," Dr. Livingston assured as she began to search for the baby.

Silence.

The eeriest silence she had ever heard.

But then she heard it.

The distinct sounds from the machine.

Whoosh. Whoosh. Whoosh.

Alex swung her gaze from her stomach to the ultrasound screen as Dr. Livingston pointed at it.

"And there's your baby, Alex. He or she has a strong heartbeat for nine weeks."

Tears welled in her eyes as she took in the dot that was the size of a small peanut. The sound of her baby's heartbeat had her tears falling.

It was the most beautiful sound Alex had ever heard in her life.

"Wow," she breathed.

All her fears about Evan and the future disappeared.

At that moment, it was just Alex and her baby.

She began to cry, never wanting to forget the feeling of her heart radiating with so much warmth and love.

"You'll be a wonderful mother, Alex," Dr. Livingston assured.

And Alex believed she might be.

She was determined to be.

Within her thoughts, she made her baby a promise.

A promise between mother and child.

I will love you more and more.

Tomorrow and tomorrow.

For always and forever.

And I promise, your father will feel just the same.

Just give him time, Little Atom.

83

Bi

bismuth

ALEX

Sophomore year of college

I t had been almost five weeks since the party at the lacrosse team captain's house. Between classes, lab, papers, and spring break spent on campus, Alex had decided to be less social and focus on school. It meant not going to Landon's games. She was no longer his girlfriend, so that obligation was one she didn't have to fulfill. She missed him in those five weeks, but she had seen a side to him she hated. Landon Carmichael had been perfect until the moment life made him choose. On those rare nights, she thought about him and how she should have worked harder, blaming herself for their failure. She should have seen his possessive traits sooner. But he had never been that way. In the beginning, he was perfect. He loved her hard and promised her a future she believed in.

But now that future would never include her.

It was over.

It had been for months.

Alex liked being by herself and experiencing college on her own. She didn't have to text him to plan coffee dates or ensure she got him lunch when he had skipped it for practice. Alex only had to care about herself, and for once, it was nice. But she wasn't lonely. Not completely. She stayed true to her pact with her childhood best friend, Evan Gilmore.

Every day without fail, they talked, alternating between text messages and calls. He knew her class schedule after she gave it to him and called when she was free. He never imposed or forced their relationship, so it was nice. It was familiar. She had her best friend back and all her once dormant feelings for him simmered in her chest, wanting to erupt into the all-consuming love she once had.

Alex broke the promise she had made with her father and was slowly starting to fall back in love with Evan all over again. Part of her knew she didn't make that promise with an honest heart because, deep down, her love for Evan Gilmore laid dormant.

Waiting.

Hoping.

But she didn't dare let her mind linger on the thought.

Not right now.

They couldn't be together.

They promised they would try during summer break when they were both back home in Brookline. For Alex, she'd be home in a matter of days. For Evan, it would be in a few weeks since Stanford finished later than Duke. Her phone vibrating halted her steps as she fished her phone from her shorts pocket. Her smile was instantaneous the second she saw Evan's name on her screen. She continued to walk toward Chino's as she unlocked her phone and read his text.

Evan: Have you told Sav yet?

Alex: Are you serious?

Evan: Why?

Alex: You know her. I'm not joking, Evan. She'd freak out!

Evan: Don't be chicken, AJ! Just tell her.

Alex groaned and lifted her head the moment she heard voices. She was just outside Brooks Field at Wallace Wade Stadium where the graduation commencement had taken place—where she knew her ex-boyfriend would be because he had graduated today. For so much of his senior year, they spoke about her being at his graduation. But she wasn't, and it was strange to know that she wouldn't see him on campus in the new school year. It made her sad to know she'd continue college without him. And it caused her chest to heave knowing their future no longer twisted perfectly together in an unbreakable knot. Not when the knot had slipped one too many times.

Evan's latest text message got her attention, causing her to shake her ex-boyfriend from her thoughts.

Evan: Seriously, just tell her.

Alex: Fine. I'll tell Savannah about moving into an apartment my parents are paying for once I get to Chino's to see her. Okay?

Evan: Definitely okay. I have a team meeting. I'll call you tonight.

"Alex!" She heard her name being called.

Alex searched the crowds of graduates and their loved ones to find her ex-boyfriend walking toward her. Slipping her phone back into her pocket, a small smile spread across her face. Her heartbeat spiked at the sight of him in his cap and gown. No trace of that possessive gleam in his light blue eyes remained, and specks of her love for him remained in her chest. Her weeks of solitude only made her miss him.

"Hey," she said once he reached her.

"Hey, Alex," Landon greeted. The softness in his voice reached his eyes. On the outside, Landon looked like his old self. Not the drunk version who had beat up his teammate and then tried to force himself on her. "How are you?"

She tried not to, but she found herself laughing at his question. "I'm good. Congratulations on graduating."

He grinned—large, bright, and so familiar—reminding her of the boy who wrote her study cards and quizzed her with them. The boy who was nervous on their first date. "I wouldn't have if it wasn't for you."

Alex's brows furrowed in confusion, deciding to concentrate on now rather than then. "What?"

Landon reached up and adjusted the cap on his head. "If it hadn't been for you and what you said at that party, I wouldn't have realized what I was doing. I thought the NBA was a sure thing and let my life collapse around me. I let my grades start to slip. I let the love of my life go. Seeing you cry at that party after I kissed you sobered me up. You forced me to look at myself, and I didn't like what I saw.

"I don't know how it happened, or how I changed so fast, but I didn't recognize myself. I hated how I treated you. I let being captain, the pressure, the expectations, and the NBA change everything. I wanted the NBA so badly, and when I was told you could get in the way of that, I folded. I listened to the wrong people. They kept telling me who to be if I wanted to be someone, and I should have listened to you. But

132

I realized I was wrong too late. So I began to be a better man after you ended it."

Oh God, Landon.

She cursed him. Hated that she felt sympathy even when she shouldn't. She hated that a small part of her still loved him. But not like before. Specks of love. The last little bit before she was completely over him. She was almost there. But memories of their good times always seemed to resurface at the wrong time.

And Landon standing in front of her was a hurdle for her own sobriety.

"You changed. You weren't the Landon I fell in love with. The Landon who was so good to me and loved me. Instead, you lied to me. Your idea of your dreams and future was actually hurting me. But that's all in the past. I'm glad you realized, and congratulations on being the number one pick in the conference. You're going to do so well with the Phoenix Suns," she said. She had always wanted the best for Landon. It was just a shame he wanted it on his own rather than with her.

A bittersweet smile sprawled across his lips as he stepped forward. "I will always love you, Alex," he began to say as his hand slipped beneath his gown. "And I know I screwed us over. I know I don't deserve a second chance. But a love like ours was amazing when it was good. I made so many mistakes, and I can't ever make them right, but I want to try." He pulled his hand from under the gown and held something out to her.

Alex took it from him and glanced down at the round-trip tickets to Phoenix, Arizona. Her jaw dropped in shock as she looked at him. "Landon," she said breathlessly.

LEN WEBSTER

He wanted her to go with him.

Landon wanted her in his life.

"I want you to come with me to Phoenix for the summer before you go back to Duke for your junior year. We never talked about our plans, and that was my fault. Spend the summer with me, and I'll show you how much I love you and want to be with you. Then you can go back to Duke, and we'll make it work. We'll make a long-distance relationship work, Alex. We would have been together for over a year, but I ruined that for us. On our anniversary, I sat in my apartment and thought of the rest of my life without you in it, and I couldn't breathe. I want anniversaries with you, Alex. I want a life with you, and I'm prepared to do whatever it takes to make that happen."

Her heart broke for him. He had thought about it. He truly wanted it to work for them.

"Landon," she whispered.

"And we'll make MIT work. My contract with the Suns is for two years, and then I can move to the Celtics. I can make this work for us," he pleaded.

Alex stepped forward, reached up, and pressed her palm to his cheek. She was proud of him for graduating, for being drafted by the Suns, and for living his dreams. She wanted that for herself someday, but she would never reach her dreams as Landon Carmichael's girlfriend.

She hindered him as much as he would hinder her.

"I loved you," she said in a soft voice. Her heart felt full and empty of her love for him. It was impossible, but she loved and didn't love him at that moment. "I did. I loved you so much. You were my first boyfriend, and I loved you so

134

much. I proved that so many times, but when I needed you to prove it to me, you didn't … until it was too late." Alex set the tickets in his free hand as her thumb brushed against his cheek. "I can't give you any hope for us, Landon. I can't follow you to Phoenix. I can't give up MIT for you because you were never gonna give up the NBA for me. Not that I ever wanted you to. You became possessive when all I did was love you. But if I want to grow and follow my dreams, I have to let you grow and follow yours."

"Don't do this," he begged.

Alex shook her head as she got on her tiptoes and pressed a kiss to his cheek. Then she stepped back and smiled at him. "Take Chase with you to Phoenix. Fix your friendship with him. It wasn't his fault, Landon. Don't throw away your friendship with Chase."

He nodded, appearing to concede to her wishes. "Okay. I'll take him to Phoenix. I'm leaving Duke for Arizona tomorrow, and I can't help but think I'm leaving behind the best thing that has ever happened to me," he said as he slipped the tickets back under the robe. He reached up and cupped her jaw in his hands. The perfect balance between his careful hold and his calloused palms. She saw the truth and the love radiating in his eyes. "If you ever need a friend, I'm only a phone call away. If there's ever a chance to be with you, if there's ever a chance you could forgive me and love me again, call me. I'll take the first flight to you, and I won't let you slip away. I'll always love you, Alex. Always."

He pressed his lips to her forehead. She believed he still loved her, that he'd always love her, but to be fair, she knew she couldn't return that love. Instead, she smiled, wished him the best in the NBA, and made her way to Chino's without looking back.

Their relationship deserved the very best goodbye, and that was it.

Because the moment she said goodbye, that final piece of her fell out of love with him.

Her heart was now free to love another.

And her heart knew who her true love really was.

It was Tuesday afternoon, four days since her ex-boyfriend's graduation, and Alex was going through her drawers to pack all the clothes she wouldn't be wearing for the rest of the week. The plan was to box all the things she would use her junior year and put it in storage before she went home to Massachusetts. What essentials she didn't mail home last week she would bring on the plane with her. As the music continued to play through her wireless speakers, Alex pulled out more clothes and placed them in the box. Just as she was about to open the next drawer, her phone rang.

Thinking it was her parents wanting the details of the flight she had yet to book, Alex got up from the floor and made her way to her desk. When she reached it, she picked up her phone to find that it was Evan calling. She answered his call, unpaired her phone from the speaker, and then made her way back to her drawers, pressing her phone to her ear.

"Hey," she greeted as she pulled out another sweater from the drawer.

"Hey, AJ."

Once she refolded the orange sweater, she placed it in the box, and asked, "What's up?"

Evan hummed, and she heard different voices from his end. She knew it must be early for him in California. "Nothing much. Just on my way to the library to meet my study group."

"Your finals aren't for a while, right?" she asked as she gave up on her packing responsibilities to talk to her best friend.

"Not for a few weeks but it's been hard to study when I have baseball."

Alex frowned, a little disappointed that he wouldn't be home when she would. "So when will you be back in Boston?"

"Not for a while. I still have a few more games to finish the season," he answered as she heard a knock on her door.

"Hang on," she said as she got up and made her way toward the door. "It's probably Sav. She messaged earlier saying she forgot her key and would be by on her lunch break. She rushed out to go to work early. It's her final shift at Chino's before summer break."

"That's okay. Answer it," Evan encouraged.

Alex reached the door, wrapped her hand around the handle, and twisted it before she yanked it open. Her heart threw itself against her chest at the sight of him.

"*Evan*," she said breathlessly.

He smiled at her. "Hey, AJ."

At that moment, everything aligned.

Him, her heart whispered.

Him, her head agreed.

Only him, her soul testified.

Unable to help herself, Alex threw her arms around his neck and pressed her lips to his. It was the first time in months since she had felt Evan's kiss. Felt that perfect balance of firm and soft in his lips.

It had been months since she felt whole.

Evan had winced as if she shocked him before he caught up and kissed her back. His hands found her hips as he pressed her body to his, causing her to moan. It was desperate. The way they kissed with need was how she felt. She had dreamed of this for months, and now that Landon had left Duke, there was no guilt. This was perfection. Nirvana. Sheer bliss. This was how it was always supposed to be.

Evan's hands left her hips to cup her cheeks. Then he pulled her back, ending the passionate way they communicated how much they had longed for each other. He panted as his brown eyes sparkled. But that smile on his face was what truly made her breathless. His eyes roamed her face as if he couldn't believe she had kissed him. That she had thrown herself at him. It was impulsive. It was need. It was natural.

"What are you doing here?" she managed to ask between her heavy panting.

His thumb brushed along her cheek as his smile stretched farther. "I couldn't wait anymore. I had to see you."

Alex's eyes widened as she shook her head. "You're supposed to be studying for your finals. You're supposed to be concentrating on baseball. You said you had a study group."

He let out a soft laugh. "I couldn't concentrate. I had to see you. And I lied about meeting my study group."

"What?" she asked as she pulled away and stepped back. "Why?"

Evan entered her dorm room and closed the door behind him. "I wanted to surprise you, but Sav was busy at work. I was too impatient and decided to just come to your dorm. That's why Sav sent you that message so you'd think it was her at the door. One of the girls leaving was nice enough to let me in after I helped her with one of her boxes. It took me forever to find your dorm. The fake meeting was to buy me some time." Then he stepped closer and wrapped his arms around her lower back. "I didn't think you'd kiss me."

Alex tilted her head as she gazed up at him and pressed her palms to his chest, mystified as to why she broke when she saw him. But she knew the truth. She couldn't wait for summer. "I never imagined you'd be standing outside my dorm. You flew all this way to see me? Have you already packed?" she asked as she noticed he had no belongings on him.

"Not yet. I'm putting stuff in storage in California once Milos and I find an apartment."

"So you didn't bring any clothes with you?"

Evan laughed. "They're outside your door."

She pulled away from him. "Someone might steal your things. Grab them."

He shook his head. "I can always buy new clothes. I can't ever have this moment with you again after it ends, so I have to take it and make it count ..."

"What's wrong?" she asked once he paused.

Evan turned, grasped the handle, and opened the door. Alex watched him bend, then he turned and closed the door with his duffle bag in one hand. "I don't care about my clothes, but I do care about what's in my bag."

"Okay," she said, slightly confused.

Evan smiled as he opened his bag and pulled out a silver box. Her heart stopped, recognizing it immediately.

He dropped his bag and grasped the present she got him two Christmases ago in his hand. She stared at the cardinal ribbon and noticed the gift tag she had left in his car many months ago taped on the box.

"I never read it," he revealed.

Alex lifted her eyes from the present to him. "You didn't?"

He smiled. "I wanted you to read it to me, remember?" His gaze dropped to the box in his hands and then back at her. "Will you read it to me, Alexandra?"

Nodding, Alex stepped forward and removed the tag from the present. She bit her lip as she unfolded the tag and inhaled a deep breath. Alex knew every word she wrote by heart because she had stared at it long enough. Wrote each word with every heartbeat singing his name. She didn't need to read the words to recite them.

"To Evan," she said, staring into his eyes. Then she smiled, knowing how true her next words would be. "I love you here."

He inhaled a sharp breath, his eyes wide with disbelief.

Alex pressed her palm on his chest, feeling his wince and his strong heartbeats. "I love you there. I love you with over two thousand miles between us." Her forefinger tapped his chest as she said, "But right here … right now … I'm home because I'm with you."

"*AJ*," he whispered.

And that name from his lips brought her tears to life as she slid her palm over his collarbone and settled it on the back of his neck. She couldn't take it anymore. Nothing was going to stop her. With a true and full heart, she whispered, "You're my home, Evan Gilmore." She inched his lips to hers. "Merry Christmas." A kiss, a breath away. "Love, Alexandra."

"I had these words for months?"

"You did."

He closed his eyes tightly and pressed his forehead to hers. "Sometimes, I wish ..." He opened his eyes, regret staring back at her.

Alex nodded. "I know. I meant every word."

"Do you mean it now?"

She settled her palm on his hip. "Kiss me and find out," she said in a low voice.

Evan pulled back, then reached over and set the present on the dresser by the door. He took the note from her and set it next to the present. Then he moved his hands to her hips and held her in place. She thought he'd finally kiss her.

Instead, he stared at her as if he were memorizing her and this moment.

As if he couldn't believe that they were together again.

"When I kiss you ..." He squeezed her hips. "I want you to believe I can be your home again."

Alex reached up and pressed her fingertips to his jaw. "You *are* my home, Evan Gilmore."

His chest fell as if the weight had been lifted from him. "And you are mine, Alexandra," he replied in a soft voice before he ducked down and finally pressed his lips firmly on hers, sealing their love into a hopeful promise.

Alex felt her heart beat with every flutter of his lips and every graze of his teeth. Her heart soared when his tongue traced her lips before she parted them and allowed his tongue to find hers. Their kiss was an explosion of time, longing, missed opportunities, and pain. Their kiss was forgiveness and hope. Their kiss was an oath of forever as his lips pressed at the corner of hers and then trailed to her jaw and down her neck.

"Evan," she softly moaned.

"I miss you between all your calls," he muttered against her pulse as she walked him back to her bed. The need within her was suffocating, and she was desperate for his touch and his love. "I long for you with every word you send me." They fell onto her mattress as his lips pressed against the swell of her breast. "But I'm desperate for your smile, AJ." Evan propped himself up on his palms, gazing down at her. The adoration in his eyes had her sitting up, Evan following her.

Alex reached up and brushed his hair back. "It's okay to say it now."

Surprise darkened his brown eyes. "It is?"

She nodded with a smile. "I said goodbye to him a few days ago. He left for Phoenix. When I said goodbye, my heart did, too. Not a single piece of me loves him anymore. So it's okay to say it. I hear your struggle in every call. I can hear how desperate you are to say it. I know you've held back because you were respecting my need for time, but you don't have to hold back anymore."

Evan grasped her wrists and lowered them from his face. Then he cupped her jaw, his eyes locked on her as he said, "I love you, AJ."

Her heart gave up, consumed with love for him.

It was Alex's turn to remove his hands from his face as she reached down, grasped the hem of her shirt, and pulled it from her. She threw it on the floor and wrapped her hand around her necklace. "I love you, too, Evan."

"I love you so much," he whispered before he pressed a lingering kiss to her lips.

When he pulled back, Alex grasped his shirt and lifted it over his head, discarding it on the floor. Evan got off the bed, and Alex turned and grasped his belt. They didn't take their eyes off each other as she unbuckled his belt and then unsnapped his pants. Evan toed off his shoes and peeled off his socks before he pushed his pants and boxer briefs down until he could step out of them.

It had been a long time since she saw Evan naked.

It almost felt as if it were the first time.

Her memories did him no justice.

In fact, in the time they had spent apart, Evan's body was tighter. His muscles and abs were more defined. He had worked out and trained more, and his efforts definitely showed.

"Eager much?" she teased.

A glint of excitement and adoration sparkled in his eyes as he climbed on the bed, and Alex laid back down. There was no pressure to make this moment romantic.

It was just them.

Just AJ and Evan again.

Best friends who found each other again.

Who found *love* again.

Evan hovered over her. "You have no idea," he said as his fingers traced along the silver necklace, his touch causing her to shiver.

Alex sat up just a fraction and reached behind her, unclasping her simple black bra. She pulled the straps away and let it join the rest of their clothing on the floor. She'd expected Evan to glance down at her naked breasts, but his

143

eyes remained on her. She wondered what his thoughts were. If she was still as beautiful to him as she was their first time. To Alex, Evan was even more beautiful as she took him in.

She gazed at the bridge of his nose, noticing a faint freckle as she shifted her focus to his jaw to find a small scar. Alex reached up and pressed her fingers to it. "When did this happen?"

His fingers trailed down the middle of her breasts and down her stomach, causing her chest to heave in anticipation.

"Freshman year. I was running to third and collided with a Rice player. Don't even remember it happening. He got me in the jaw, and I remember waking up in the hospital with some stitches and a concussion," he explained as his hand dipped under the front of her yoga pants, cupping her between her legs and causing her breathing to hitch.

"Wh-why didn't—" She moaned when his finger brushed along the crotch of her cotton panties. "*Jesus*." Her hands grasped his shoulders as his fingers ran up and down her covered center.

"Why didn't anyone tell you I was in the hospital?" Evan asked in a hoarse voice.

She nodded, trying to hold back another moan as his fingers spun circles, and she felt her thighs tremble.

"Because I asked them not to," he explained as he moved her underwear aside and touched her, feeling how wet she was. "Christ, AJ," he cursed when his finger slowly entered her. Heat consumed her as that finger retreated and plunged back in.

"Oh!" She gasped as his thumb returned to where it ached the most, spinning circles and causing her to moan his name.

Her back arched as her eyes slammed shut. "Evan, oh my, God. Evan, I'm ... oh ... I'm close."

His fingers stopped, and he pulled his hand away. Alex opened her eyes and felt a tugging sensation. She glanced down to find him pulling her pants and panties down. Once they were discarded, she parted her legs, expecting him to settle between them. Instead, he crawled between them as his breath hit her damp skin, causing her to sigh. She hated to compare her sexual partners, but Evan was by far the better lover when it came to oral sex. With Landon, she always felt too exposed.

Evan's arms curled around her thighs as he parted them wider. His tongue flicked against her clit, and she let out a moan as her fingers dug into his hair.

Once.

Twice.

Three times did he flick against her before he flattened his tongue to intensify the pleasure, causing her hips to buck, desperately seeking detonation.

"I was scared," he said before he sucked on her clit.

"Oh! You ... Oh, God. Right. There ... Scared?"

It was getting harder to think.

Harder to stop herself from falling off the edge. From falling into the euphoria she knew would consume her with pleasure.

"Yeah," Evan said, giving her some mercy to catch her breath as he kissed the inside of her thigh. Then she felt his finger nudge her opening before slipping inside. He pulled out before he thrust two fingers inside, stretching her. Her heavy breathing turned into gasps as his other hand reached up and gently squeezed her breast. Alex grasped his hair, pulling at it as she moved her hips to meet each thrust.

"Evan," she warned as her body tightened.

He doubled his efforts, his fingers thrusting deeper.

Harder.

Then his tongue massaged her sensitive clit as his fingers found her G-spot.

Her legs trembled as she felt her insides clench.

She wasn't going to last any longer, and she gave up, allowing the pleasure to build.

And build.

And build.

Until Evan whispered, "Let go, AJ. Come for me."

He thrust once more before a wave of pleasure captured her and encased her in white-hot satisfaction.

She fell back on her pillows, gasping for air as she trembled. Evan made his way up her body and kissed her softly. He kissed her lovingly and slowly as if they had all the time in the world.

"You're so beautiful," he mumbled against her lips, causing her to laugh. She reached for his waist and pulled him to her, his hardness pressing against her stomach. "I've missed you so much, AJ."

"I've missed you, too," she said, truthfully.

Evan's thumb brushed against her bottom lip as she removed a hand from his waist and grasped his hardness between them.

"AJ," he groaned.

"Why were you scared?" she asked as she stroked him from base to tip.

He inhaled a deep breath as he glanced down at where they connected, and whispered, "Shit, AJ," before his eyes searched hers, and a smile tug at his lips. "I was scared that you might visit me."

Her hand stopped stroking him. "What?"

Evan bent down and kissed her deeply. He brushed her hand away from his erection, and she broke their kiss to peek down. Need blossomed within her as she watched him wrap his fist around his hard length and guide himself between her legs.

Then she felt him *there*.

His tip pressed against her opening as his eyes found hers. An unspoken question hung between them.

"I haven't been with anyone since him. I'm clean," she clarified.

He nodded. "I haven't been with anyone since you. I'm clean, too. But …"

"But?"

Fear etched his face. "I don't think I'm going to last very long."

A smile broke out on her lips as she cupped his face and spread her legs wider for him. "It's okay. We have all afternoon to make up for it."

Evan made a small nod as he slowly pushed himself inside her, Alex feeling and loving that familiar stretching sensation. She watched enchanted as Evan's lips parted and a silent moan escaped him. Moving one hand to the back of his neck and the other to his chest, she felt his fast heartbeat against her palm.

She loved him.

Loved his heart.

And his smile.

She had loved him all her life—even when she wasn't supposed to.

"Tell me why you were scared," she asked.

Evan panted, and she watched the muscles in his throat work as he swallowed hard. "I was scared because ..." He pressed farther into her, causing her chest to heave. "I wouldn't have let you go back to him, and I was sure that would have hurt you." And then he thrust his hips and filled her completely.

To the hilt.

And she was full.

Evan Gilmore was inside her.

They were making love for the first time in over a year.

It had been him all along.

Her heart swelled at his reason.

"You let me love him longer?"

Evan nodded, his chest heaving. "Because I knew it would make you happy."

She couldn't take it anymore as she brought his head down, and his lips met hers. They kissed slowly, in time with his soft strokes. Alex whimpered as his pubic bone brushed against her most sensitive part.

"It's you," he mumbled against her mouth as his hips drove into her harder.

Longer.

With thrust after thrust, he kissed her jaw and her neck, caressing her skin with his breath. Alex threaded her fingers through his hair as she wound her legs around his waist, feeling him even deeper.

"*Oh,*" she moaned as she met his thrusts.

"Fuck, Alexandra," he whispered by her ear. "It's always been you. I have always loved you."

"Evan," she begged as his slick chest slid across her breasts with each flex of his hips.

On and on.

He entered her.

He pulled out of her, causing a needy ache to fill her.

"I love you, please." She pulled his head up so that she could kiss him.

"Okay," he agreed, and he drove into her with fast and hard strokes.

That familiar lick of pleasure at her spine came back.

And she knew she was close.

She could feel it.

Her orgasm was on the edge.

"I love you," he confessed before she felt him stiffen. His erection throbbed, and he jerked inside her, spilling himself.

His orgasm set off hers, and Alex came, moaning his name.

Evan's sweaty body fell on hers as his ear pressed against her breasts, no doubt hearing her rapid heartbeats.

"It has always been you, Evan," she whispered.

"Always you," he breathed, tracing the curve of her breast.

And a soft kiss sealed his commitment on her skin moments later.

^{84} Po

polonium

ALEX

Now

"Oh, God," she groaned after she threw up for what felt like the millionth time this morning. The second she woke, nausea had hit her, and Alex bolted to her bathroom and puked her guts out. Unlike her other mornings, today's morning sickness made her lightheaded, feeling as if she had lost all her strength. It was undoubtedly the worst moment of her pregnancy so far.

"AJ?" She heard Evan calling out her name from the other side of her bathroom door.

Christ.

She attempted to lift her head from the toilet seat, but she couldn't. Instead, she closed her eyes and hoped to God he'd leave.

"Hey, you missed our appointment with—*Shit.* AJ, are you all right?" She felt his hand on her arm. "Hey, AJ, open your eyes."

She slowly opened her eyes and saw the concern bright in his brown eyes. "We had an appointment?" she asked, groggy.

Evan reached up and brushed her messy hair from her face. "Yeah. But it's okay. Maureen said we could reschedule. She'll do some more digging for apartments near MIT."

"I'm so sorry."

He shook his head. "Don't be. You should have called. I haven't spoken to you in two days, and I should have known you weren't feeling well."

Alex blinked at him. It had been two days since they last looked at apartments together. His offer to help was pointless since she couldn't afford any of the apartments they had seen. Yesterday, she saw her doctor for a checkup, and their baby—not that Evan knew just yet—was healthy and on track to be born the second week of September, meaning MIT was a question mark in the grand scheme of things.

"It was the burrito I got last night. Lori wanted Mexican at midnight, but it didn't ..." Alex gave up on her excuse, too tired to commit to it.

"Is Lori okay?"

She nodded as she pressed her palm on the seat and attempted to stand, only slumping back down against the toilet. "Yeah, she's okay. She got the tacos."

Lori doesn't have morning sickness.

"Here," he said as he pulled on her arm and somehow managed to lift her. In a swift move, she was in his arms. The thought of how he managed to do so with such ease had her stomach roiling. So she closed her eyes and snuggled into his chest, lost in the familiar scent of him.

The cure for her morning sickness seemed to be the smell of him.

Do you like the way Daddy smells, Little Atom?

"Who is Little Atom?"

She prayed her mind conjured that question. That she hadn't mentioned any hint of her pregnancy to him. She wasn't ready to tell him about their child just yet. Then she felt him set her down on her soft bed and cover her with the blanket.

"Get some rest, AJ. I'll come by to check on you later. Don't worry about helping me pack today. You need to rest. If you feel better, then we'll go to the Red Sox Gala." Evan pressed his lips against her forehead before he slipped out of her room, and her door clicked closed.

Alex opened her eyes and groaned, seeing the ceiling spin.

Evan hadn't pressed her to know who Little Atom was. He might have thought she was speaking gibberish, and Alex felt like she was. She had to tell him soon.

Maybe tonight after the gala Kyle invited them to.

Alex pressed her palms to her stomach as her thumbs softly brushed against her shirt. "I promise, it'll be special. So when you ask us, we'll have a good moment, a good story to tell you, Little Atom."

"Wow, Alex, look at you," Red Sox Operations Director Carl Nelson said as Alex handed Safia, his assistant, the invitation she received yesterday.

"Thank you, Mr. Nelson," Alex replied as she reached down and grasped her emerald silk dress. She lifted it up from the floor so she could walk into the large function room inside Fenway Park that held a lot of the official social engagements for the Red Sox.

For first-timers, many would think this was extravagant—the guests, the live band, the players, and celebrities—but it wasn't. Not for Alex. She had grown numb to it all. She had been invited to many Red Sox parties since she was sixteen.

"Good evening, Miss Parker," a waitress said once she had approached Alex. She wasn't surprised that the waitress knew her name. All the staff who worked at Fenway Park were expected to know all those associated with the players or the board.

"Good evening," Alex said as she pressed her fingers into her emerald rhinestone covered clutch. The expensive dress she wore was a loan from a designer Angie, Kyle's fiancée, had recommended. When Alex received her invitation yesterday, she had messaged Angie for help, and Angie had set up an appointment for her to see a designer in Boston. Trying on dresses was intimate for Alex, and she was happy that the pieces Balthazar Waynecraft had her try weren't too form fitting. She couldn't disagree with Balthazar when he said that the silk gown was made for her. It matched her eyes and made her brunette locks appear deeper in color.

"Champagne?"

Alex shook her head. "No, thank you. Do you have any sparkling water?"

The waitress glanced down at her silver tray and then shook her head. "I'm sorry, I don't. But I can grab you a glass."

"That would be great, but only after you're done making your rounds. I'm in no hurry." Alex stepped around the waitress and made her way farther into the party. Being at a gala was the last place she wanted to be, but Kyle had invited her. She couldn't let him down, and she wanted to see the players and staff who treated her like family. It had been so long since she was last at Fenway.

"Alexandra Parker?"

She came to a stop at the call of her name. Alex spun around and came face to face with a very familiar and handsome man. Not surprising, his tailored suit was impeccable. And as always, he wore the flag of Boston on one lapel on his jacket and a Red Sox pin on the other.

The mayor of Boston was still a very handsome man who exuded power and sex appeal. She had never been one of the women who fawned over him, but Alex wasn't blind. He was definitely one of the most attractive politicians she had ever met.

"Mayor Easton, how are you?"

He grinned, pleased that she remembered him. It was hard not to. "Ah, it's just Devon, remember?"

"Of course. I apologize. And it's just Alex. How is the office, *Devon*?" She didn't mean the flirty tone in her voice, but Alex was returning to her old social life and the role of Little Miss Red Sox. It was to appease Kyle and those who had welcomed her into their Red Sox family. It would also make life in Boston easier if the Red Sox fans continued to love her.

"Good. It's election year. Will you be in town to vote?"

Alex smiled. "Actually, I will be. I'll be at MIT for my Ph.D. this fall."

The mayor nodded, appearing impressed by her. "I love your love for the city of Boston, Alex."

"Thank you. I really do love this city," Alex said honestly.

"That's why I actually had to approach you the minute I saw you walk in. I was wondering if you would care to join me for dinner one evening?"

Alex blinked at him, shocked that he was asking her out.

America's favorite politician who was rumored to become the future president had asked her to dinner. Unable to answer him right away, she glanced around, trying to find someone who might interrupt them and save her from rejecting a very powerful man.

Then her eyes landed on the worst possible sight imaginable.

Evan was smiling at a woman Alex had never met. He was caressing her elbow as they talked and laughed.

Her heart sank.

Suddenly, she felt sick at the sight.

He was happy.

And maybe he had found love that made him so happy.

Alex felt hot all over as she fought against her tears. Her poor heart whimpered, wishing it had never seen him cup that woman's elbow. Alex turned away, not wanting to see if he would kiss her.

It would kill her.

She deserved it, of course, but it would still hurt her.

Her dream that maybe they could be a family would never be.

It was now clear that it wouldn't.

"Alex?" Devon said, getting her attention. "Are you okay? You look pale."

She nodded, swallowing hard to fight her tears. "I'm sorry. I'm still a little jet-lagged from my flight from Zürich," she lied. "What were you saying?"

His laugh was deep and intimidating. "I was asking you to—"

"Alexi, you're here," Kyle interrupted and cementing his

156

place as her hero of the night.

She shot the mayor an apologetic smile as he stood next to them. "Hey, Kyle," she greeted with relief.

"Good to have you home, kid." He turned to acknowledge the mayor. "Devon."

Annoyance flared in Devon's dark eyes as he glanced back at Alex and reached into his suit jacket, pulling out a card. He stepped closer and held out the card to her. "It's my *personal* number," he clarified as she took the card from him to be polite. "I've always found you to be incredibly smart, intriguing, and downright beautiful, Alex. It's just dinner. No strings or expectations. I hope to hear from you soon." Then he left, not even saying goodbye to Kyle who stood right next to her.

"What was that?" Kyle asked; the layer of protectiveness in his voice was strong.

Alex laughed as she opened her clutch and slipped the card inside. Though she wouldn't be going on a date with the mayor of Boston, she knew he wouldn't appreciate it if his personal number was released to the public.

"He was just asking me to dinner."

Kyle's nostrils flared with disgust. "I don't approve."

"I know. But you don't have to worry. I'm not going on a date with him."

He sighed in relief as he turned to stand next to her, gazing out at the guests. She watched him wince, and she glanced over to see that he was staring at Evan and the unidentified woman. It made her heart weep to see Evan smile that way. A long time ago, he used to look at her as if she were it. His entire life and heart. Now, he could barely look at her.

"You still love him," Kyle said.

Alex didn't have to look his way to know that Kyle was staring at her. A small smile contorted her lips as she finally tore her eyes away from Evan and stared at the man who had once thought he was in love with her. "Yeah, I do. But Evan hasn't loved me for a long time. Zürich made him miserable, Kyle. There was no way he would have stayed for three more years. He had to leave Switzerland before it truly destroyed us. He's happy here. Do you know her?"

"No, but I'm pretty sure I heard her say she works in LA."

LA.

Where Evan was moving to.

Was he moving there to be with her?

Alex understood it now.

And it broke her heart knowing that she had lost him.

That she had come home too late.

That being a family was out of reach for her and their baby.

She couldn't find the words to speak.

To her relief, "Kyle!" was shouted, and they both turned to find Angie waving him over.

"You better go," she said.

Kyle sighed. "All right, but don't go too far. We need to catch up, kid."

Alex nodded. "I won't be too far away," she promised.

She watched as Kyle walked away and headed over to his fiancée. When people began to block him from her sight, she gazed over to find Evan still with his mystery woman. It hurt to see him moving on. To see him smiling and happy. To see that he had always had a life without her.

At that moment, she made a choice.

She spun around and confirmed that choice.

She didn't feel like Little Miss Red Sox anymore.

They had all moved on.

Now, she felt like an annoyance in all their lives.

An annoyance in his heart and life.

Because she was no longer AJ.

She was just a girl in a green dress, trying to keep her broken heart from evaporating into the air.

So Alex left the gala and made her way to the elevator. Once inside, she pressed for the floor above. She tried not to listen to her burdening thoughts as the elevator moved. When the doors parted, she walked the length of Fenway Park until she made it to the entrance and found the night guard at his position by the turnstiles. Alex walked up to him, and he smiled at her.

"Alex, good to see you, child."

"Hey, Reggie. It's good to see you."

He smiled. He had lost a lot of weight since she last saw him. Reggie appeared healthier and happy. "Welcome home, by the way. Fenway hasn't had its true heart for a while now. But she's returned. *Sweet Alexandra.*"

She blushed at the song title change he referenced. "I know I don't have my pass with me since I just got home, but do you think I could go up to my seat? I haven't sat in it for a long time. I can give you my ID and phone. You can use it as collateral if you need to."

He chuckled at her. "Nah. You're all right. You go on up and take all the time you want. I'll make sure no one disturbs you who shouldn't."

"Thanks, Reggie," she said thankfully before she turned

and made her way up through the tunnel and into the stands.

Each step she took was like coming home.

The Red Sox, Fenway Park, and the city of Boston had always been her home.

And as she took in the perfect green ballpark, she almost broke down in tears. Because although she had lost Evan Gilmore a long time ago, she would raise his child with the same undying love he had for her when he was in love with her.

Alex stood by the barrier next to the row of her season seat and pressed her palm against her stomach.

"Welcome to Fenway Park, Little Atom. Your dad and I spent many years here watching your uncle become a legend," she whispered as her tears made the field blurry. She quickly blinked, holding them at bay. Then she walked down the row and to her seat.

When she reached it, Alex sat down and took a deep breath, her eyes roaming the lit stadium. Then she glanced over at the bleachers, and her heart clenched at the memory of the times she and Evan had been in that part of Fenway.

Alex gazed down at her palm still on her stomach. "I didn't know it, but I fell in love with your father here in Fenway during a game against the Rockies, wearing away baseball caps and surrounded by thousands of fans. I, along with everyone at that game, was unaware that I was in love with Evan Gilmore." She let out a low exhale. "That I'm still in love with your father."

"AJ?" Evan's voice was like a whisper. She turned her head in his direction to find him at the end of the row.

"Hey," she said in a small voice as he made his way to her and sat in his old seat. He stared at her with his eyes full of concern. He had let her go six months ago, so there was no need for any concern. "It's crazy how this is the quietest I've ever heard Fenway."

"Are you okay?"

Her heart clenched at his question. Heat consumed it, but she breathed through the pain. She should have let Evan go. However, she had promised to love him forever. But it was time she grew up. She had to. She was going to be a mother. And she might have to do it alone, but she would be okay. Because it had to be about his dreams now.

Los Angeles.

A new life.

A new love.

A whole future without her.

"AJ, you haven't seemed like yourself lately. Are you sure you're okay?"

"I'm okay," she said, her heart full of guilt. "I just needed air."

"In our old seats?"

She nodded. "Yeah."

Evan shook his head at her. Disbelief written all over his face. "Then why are you crying?"

Alex reached up and pressed her fingertips to her wet cheeks. He was right. She was crying. "Because I'm scared," she confessed.

"Of?" His voice was full of his own fear. She heard it as

loud as it rung in her ears.

"The years we'll spend apart the moment you leave for LA."

Pain contorted his face. "AJ," he said.

She shook her head to stop him. It would be a night of confession and goodbyes for the last time. "And I hate that I came home for you too late. That I should have never left. You asked me to stay, and I didn't."

"You came home for me?" His voice was tight, and she heard the sadness that pleaded to be freed.

"I started to plan my return the moment I landed back in Zürich. But I couldn't let Dr. Rodahawe or the team down. I gave myself two months to finish the equation, and if I didn't, I'd know I tried my best. I had to come home for you, but I was too late." A tear slipped down her cheek, and Evan reached up and brushed it away. "I have a question I need to ask you."

"Okay," he encouraged.

Alex pulled away from his touch and squared her shoulders. "Can I buy your season ticket from you?"

Evan flinched in shock. "You want to buy my season ticket?"

"Yes," she confirmed. "Whatever you want for it. I'll even use some of my trust fund money. I was once offered over two hundred thousand dollars to rent it while I was in Zürich. I'll offer you anything."

It was irresponsible of her to promise him that kind of money, but if she was going to give her child something of Evan's, it would be his seat at Fenway Park.

But Alex wasn't stupid; she knew the real reason.

She couldn't sit in memories with someone else.

"What? Why would you want to buy it from me?"

162

Alex licked her lips nervously as she allowed for the truth to be set free.

Because she fell in love with him in Fenway.

And he deserved the truth within the grounds where she had kissed him for the first time during her sophomore year of college.

"I can't stomach the idea of sitting here at Fenway with a complete stranger when I've shared all my best memories with you by my side. I don't want to share more moments of my life with someone who isn't you," she revealed. "It already breaks my heart knowing that you sold the house we spent our own Christmas in. It hurts my soul that you're going to LA. And I can't continue a normal life here if I have to pretend that the person sitting on my right isn't sitting where my best friend had once held my hand or cheered with me even when he didn't want to."

"No," Evan said, surprising her. She was stupid for expecting him to give up his season ticket. Kyle had gotten it for him, just as he had for her. Then Evan reached up and grasped her hands in his. "It's not happening, Alexandra. It's not happening because I plan on going to every Red Sox game here at Fenway Park with you."

Her heart had pieced itself together at his vow.

She knew she shouldn't get her hopes up, but she'd allow herself to have a little hope.

For her baby.

Their baby.

My baby.

His baby.

Our baby.

Sickness roiled in her stomach as she blinked at him, realizing that she had to tell him.

It was only right.

She couldn't take that right of making the decision of whether to be part of their baby's life from him.

That was his right.

Not hers.

Alex pulled her hands free and wiped her tears away with the back of her hands. She was thankful she was wearing waterproof mascara, and she didn't have panda eyes after examining her hand.

It was time.

He deserved to know.

Now before he leaves.

It might be the worst mistake or the best decision she would ever make.

Her heart clenched.

Her stomach flopped.

Her head became dizzy with guilt and hope.

So Alex took a deep breath, mentally told their child that it would be okay, and released that breath she had taken before she revealed to him the very truth she loved most about herself.

"Evan," she said in a soft voice, giving herself a single second to walk away, but she couldn't.

She couldn't do that to him.

To herself.

And most importantly, to their child.

"Evan, I'm pregnant."

85

At

astatine

ALEX

Sophomore year of college

"What time is it?" Alex asked as she stared at his strong jaw.

Evan reached over and turned the clock on her nightstand in their direction. "Just after four."

Sighing, she lifted herself from his hard chest and sat up, brushing her hair behind her shoulder. "Sav will be here in like an hour. She can't see us like this."

"Right," he said in sharp tone, causing Alex's brows to furrow as he sat up.

"You want my roommate to see us naked in my bed the moment she walks in?"

Evan shook his head. "No, I'm sorry. It just sounded like you're embarrassed to be seen with me."

Alex reached up and cradled his cheeks so that his eyes were firm on hers. Her thumb softly brushed along his skin. "That couldn't be further from the truth, Evan. Sav is optimistic when it comes to my love life. She'd approve too much, and I'd rather love you without the pressure of fulfilling everyone else's hopes for us—especially when we go home."

"And you feel nothing for him?" he asked as he wrapped his fingers around her wrists.

"I feel nothing for him," she admitted as she swung a leg over his lap and straddled him. Then she pressed a chaste kiss to his lips. "I don't love Landon like I used to. I love you, Evan. I've always loved you. You brought the real me back when I was home. You reminded me that my dreams are important, too. You gave me my best friend back, and I want to spend the entire summer with you and loving you."

Evan's hands left her wrist and captured her hips. "You know everyone will be home, right?"

She nodded. "I know."

"We can keep us a secret," he suggested.

Her heart twisted at his suggestion.

"A secret?"

A secret meant lying.

And lying about her love for Evan had been what she was good at for so many years.

This time, she didn't want to lie.

But she knew that if they wanted to be together without the pressure of everyone's expectation, they would have to remain a secret.

"We don't have to be. But I know Hunt, Carter, Jordan, and Addison are going to be home, then there's my brother and the Red Sox. We can't walk around Boston holding hands without being stopped and asked about it. You know the papers. They'll somehow write that we broke Kyle's heart even though he's madly in love with Angie."

Alex's hands fell from his face and rested on his shoulders. "And then there's my parents," she added. "Okay. Let's figure us out before we let people know. That way if we don't last the entire summer, we don't let anyone down."

Evan winced. "You don't think we'll last the entire summer?"

She let out a breath of air and gazed into those hopeful and fearful brown eyes. "I want us to. I know we can. I don't want to be with anyone else but you."

"And I couldn't imagine the rest of my life with anyone but you," Evan said in a soft voice as he leaned forward and kissed the tip of her nose. "Come on. We better dress before Sav comes back to the dorm. She might come back early."

"You're right," she agreed as she climbed off his lap and sat back down on the bed. "You can take a shower if you want. We have a private suite."

Evan nodded as he got out of the bed, then leaned down and pressed a kiss to her lips. "I'll grab your robe," he said before he went to her door and removed the silk robe.

"Wait," she said, taking in the present they ignored earlier on her dresser.

Alex was well aware of how in love she was with him. He promised to open it when she trusted him, and she did. She couldn't love anyone else more than Evan Gilmore, and it was time he knew that.

"Everything okay?"

She nodded and pointed at the present. "Can you also bring the present I got you to me?"

His eyes widened, understanding what it would mean for them. Evan grabbed the box from the dresser and returned to her. He handed her the robe first, and Alex slipped it on. Then he sat on the bed and looked at the present in his hands.

"I've been tempted to open it," he said as he gazed up at her.

"But you didn't."

He shook his head. "No, you told me to trust you, and I did. I do trust you, AJ."

"Open it," she encouraged. "I trust you. I trust the friendship you've given me. I trust the love you've offered me. I trust the life you've promised me. I trust you, Evan Gilmore. With my entire heart and soul, I trust you."

Evan set the box on the bed, reached up and set his hand on the base of her scalp, bringing her lips closer to his. "With my whole heart and soul, I love and trust you, Alexandra," he whispered before he softly kissed her. It was sweet. Innocent. Enough to feel his adoration and love. Then he pulled back and picked up the box. "Are you sure?"

She nodded with a laugh. "I'm sure," she said as she tucked her legs beneath her, excited and nervous for him to open her Christmas present. It wasn't the most expensive gift, but it was priceless and, most importantly, symbolic.

It represented her trust and her love.

Her hope and her belief in him.

She offered him her future to share with him.

He just had to be patient and want her enough.

And as he tore away the ribbon, she was sure he understood the power of this present for them. Evan was careful as he ripped away the silver paper, letting it land on her sheets. Then he removed the lid and set it down with the paper. Alex held her breath as he reached inside and pulled out the blue Duke cap. Evan held it in his hands, staring at it. Getting on her knees, she pushed the paper, ribbon, and box out of her way as she kneeled in front of him. Alex took the cap from him and stared at it with a small smile.

Her heart beat hard in her chest. She remembered the day

her eyes landed on the cap. What it felt to love him at that time. What it meant to her. Alex felt it all and more. She and Evan had grown so much since they parted ways the first time in Brookline.

Now, she was ready.

She had said goodbye to her past and was ready for her future. A future she took her time accepting, needing, and wanting.

Alex lifted her chin, her smile deepened as she took in Evan's soft brown eyes. She inhaled a deep breath and set the cap on his head. "You gave me an opposition's cap and told me to trust you, and I did. When I bought this cap, I wasn't just giving you an opposition's cap because that's what we did."

"You didn't?"

She shook her head as she cupped his jaw in her palms and straddled his lap. She glanced at his lips before she stared into his eyes. "I was sharing Duke with you."

His lips parted with wonder. "You were?"

"I was," Alex confirmed, her thumb brushing his scar. Had Kyle told her that he was in the hospital, she had no doubt she would have gone to see him to make sure that he was all right. She was sure she would as she was sure of her love for him. "I took Stanford away from us, Evan."

"Hey," he said, grasping her hips. "It was better this way. You're here. You're happy. You're your own person. It was for the best. You got to be you, AJ."

She nodded as he brushed her tears away. "I bought this cap because I wanted to share Duke with you. I hid it from you for so long, and I didn't want to do that anymore. I bought this cap intending to make it work between us. That when you were here at Duke, you were always here with me. That you could trust me to always keep you safe the way I trusted you to keep me safe with the Rockies fans. I wanted you here at Duke with me. I wanted to love you here. Trust you here. I wanted to share my life with you here at Duke."

"Do you still want all those things with me?"

Alex looked at the stitched Duke cap and nodded. "I want to love you here at Duke, Evan," she whispered, lowering her lips to his. "I want to trust you here." She pressed a kiss to his lips and grasped the brim of his cap so it wouldn't fall. "I want to share my life and Duke with you." Then she kissed him deeper, feeling all the love she withheld from him burst.

Evan pushed her onto her back and pressed his body to hers. "I want to share my life and Stanford with you. Thank you for this gift, Alexandra. I understand why you asked me to wait until you trusted me again, and it makes it worth so much more to me." He ducked down and kissed her.

Wrapping her arms around him, she knocked the cap from his head and laughed when it fell off the bed. "Sorry," she mumbled against his lips.

He laughed as he pulled back. Evan glanced over at the cap and then back at her. "Should I pick it up?"

"Leave it," she replied as she pulled him back to her.

"But ..."

Alex shook her head and peeked over at the time. "We have less than an hour before I can't have you like this. Just be with me."

He didn't fight her.

Instead, Evan Gilmore kissed her.

He touched her.

His lips left promises on her skin.

And most importantly, he whispered, "Eight protons. Eight neutrons," as he made love to her, but this time, he also added …

"Forever."

It was the final day of her sophomore year of college and Evan's second day at Duke. He had a ticket booked for later tonight to return to California from Massachusetts. As he promised, he would accompany her back to Boston where he would have dinner with her and her parents before he returned to Stanford for the rest of his sophomore year.

To keep their undefined and new relationship a secret, Evan slept on the floor to throw off her roommate's suspicions. When Savannah had asked what was going on between them, she had lied and said that she and Evan were just best friends again. That he only came to Duke to help her pack before they returned to Massachusetts. Alex could tell that Savannah didn't believe her, but it seemed she changed her mind when Evan laid down sheets on the rug and Alex handed him a pillow.

When Savannah left their dorm, they snuck quick kisses and whispered words. Then Alex showed Evan around campus, confident she wouldn't run into anyone on the basketball team. Most of the team had already left, and to her relief, no one stopped to ask her who Evan was. It was quite clear no one paid her any attention now that she wasn't the basketball team captain's girlfriend. The only person Evan met at Duke was Mika, her lab partner. Alex had introduced Evan as her best friend, and to her surprise, he seemed proud of the title. Mika was welcoming and friendly, and Evan had appeared to like him.

"Are you sure you don't want me to help you with the rest of your boxes, Sav?" Evan asked as he secured the fridge in the back of Savannah's truck.

Savannah smiled as she took the box from Alex and headed toward the back of the truck. "Y'all have a flight to catch. All the heavy things are already in the truck. The rest is stuff I haven't packed just yet. Seriously, y'all better get a move on. The cab will be here soon."

Alex smiled once Savannah set the box down and returned to her. "You better come to Boston this summer."

Savannah laughed. "Yeah, because besides your mother's restaurant—which I love that I can always get a table at because of you—Della's has the best garlic fries I've ever had. So yeah, y'all will be seeing me. Plus, I can't imagine going the whole summer without seeing my best friend."

"I can't imagine going the entire summer without you." Alex wrapped her arms around Savannah and held her tight. "I'll miss you."

"I'll miss you, too, Alex."

"AJ, the cab is here," Evan said, interrupting them.

Alex unwound her arms from around her best friend and brushed away the tear that had escaped. Out of all the people she had met at Duke, Savannah was by far the one Alex cherished and was thankful for the most. "Drive safely back to Vermont, okay? And if you need to stop in Brookline, please do. Oh, and if you need a place to stay in New York, call my uncle. I don't want you to stay the night anywhere else if you don't need to."

Savannah rolled her eyes. "Yes, Alex." Then she smiled at Evan. "She might be your best friend, but she's *mine* as well. You take care of her in Brookline."

"I will," Evan promised. "AJ, you forgot to tell her about the thing."

"Oh!" she said, surprised that she had forgotten. Her roommate swung her suspicious gaze over to Alex. "Sav, I know you hate the dorms in the morning. And you hate it at night when you come home and see people you don't want to see who stick their nose in your business. So I was thinking ..."

"What were you thinking?"

"I was thinking about moving off campus for junior year and wanted us to share an apartment together," Alex suggested.

Savannah's blue eyes widened. "Alex ..."

"I need more space than a dorm offers. Some of the best physicists started planning for their postgrads during their undergrad. That's what I have to start planning for, life after Duke."

A hesitant smile sprawled across Savannah's lips. "Alex, that's a great idea. But I can't afford rent *and* utilities. What I make at Chino's would never cover it. I won't be mad if you find another roommate who can afford to live with you. You'll want something nice, and I can't afford anything nice."

Brushing her hair behind her ear, Alex stepped forward and set her palm on Savannah's shoulder. "I don't want another roommate, Savannah. I want you."

"But I can't afford—"

"Neither can I," Alex said, cutting her off. "My parents

are covering it."

"No," Savannah said firmly. "Absolutely not. I am not letting your parents pay for my living expenses. That's not happening, Alex."

"Please, Sav? It's one of the only requests my mother has for letting me move off campus and away from Duke basketball. Please?"

Savannah glanced at Alex and then at Evan before she sighed. "Fine. On one condition."

"Okay?"

"I have to pay rent."

"That's non-negotiable. My father insists."

Savannah glared at her. "I am not a charity case, Alex."

"You're not a charity case, Sav. I want to live with you," Alex said as she reached into her jeans pocket and pulled out her phone. She unlocked it and dialed the last number she had called. It rang twice before her father picked up.

"Hello, Alexandra," he greeted.

"Hey, Dad."

"Is everything okay? Did your flight get canceled?"

Alex grinned at the horror on her roommate's face. "No, Dad. We're about to leave for the airport in a second, but I just asked Sav to move in with me and she insists on paying rent."

Her father laughed. "Can you put her on?"

She handed her roommate the phone. "He'd like to speak to you."

"I hate you," Savannah hissed as she snatched the phone from Alex and set it to her ear. "Hello, Noel ... Oh, yes. I understand. I know you care about my education and that college is expensive but ... You shouldn't have to worry about me. I love that you and Clara care, Noel ... Yes, Alex is my best friend, and I'd love to live with her, but ... No, I insist. I will fight you and your wife. Really? Pay whatever I can each month? That works for me. Thank you, Noel. Tell Clara I said thank you, too. I'll be sure to visit this summer. I'll speak to you soon. Bye." Then Savannah hung up and handed Alex back the phone. "Your dad would like me—if I want to and if it's possible—to work less at Chino's and study and experience college. He said college was some of his best years, so I shouldn't spend all of mine behind the counter making coffee. So I guess your hot father is persuasive."

Alex cringed. "Ew, Sav. That's my dad you just called hot."

Her best friend grinned. "You deserve it. Now, y'all should go. Have a great summer."

"Have a great summer, Sav," Alex said and hugged her once more.

When they pulled away, Savannah glanced over at Evan and whispered to her, "I approve of y'all being friends, but be careful. He might be your OTP but don't forget what he did to y'all."

The pang of guilt erupted in her chest. Right now, she was more than just Evan's friend. She was his secret lover, and she hated that she had to keep it from Savannah until she was sure she and Evan would work. That dreams and fantasies could be a reality for them.

Savannah walked over to Evan and gave him a hug. "Thanks for your help, Evan. Have a great summer."

Evan nodded at her with a smile. "You, too, Sav. We'll see you in Brookline."

"Definitely."

Alex turned around and walked over to her suitcase that had been by Savannah's truck. She grasped the handle and lifted it before she returned to Evan who had picked up his Stanford duffle bag. "Cab is over there," he said.

Once they reached the cab on the other side of the parking lot, the driver got out and asked, "Cab for Evan?"

"That's me," Evan said as he took Alex's suitcase from her. Then he followed the driver to the trunk, and the driver lifted the lid. Once her suitcase and Evan's duffle were inside, they got into the back seat and buckled their belts.

"Where we headed today?" their driver asked.

"The airport, please," Alex answered. She stared out the window and watched Duke pass her as the cab pulled out of the parking lot. Then she felt Evan grasp her hand, and she turned to smile at him.

"Ready to go home?"

Alex's smiled deepened. "I'm ready."

"I have faith that your brother will bounce back from last season's World Series loss," Burnley, their cab driver from New Orleans, said as he pulled up to Alex's parents' house. The first time she met Burnley was when he had driven her to Evan's house during Thanksgiving break and Evan had never shown up. It seemed like so long ago that she had waited for him on his doorstep. But she wouldn't tell him just how she had met the famous Red Sox cabbie. Their time together wasn't about reliving the pain of the past. They were moving on together. They were giving each other a fair chance at something real.

"The injuries after the Philly game didn't help the team. But Kyle's definitely stronger after he recovered from his ACL surgery," Evan said as he unbuckled his seat belt.

"Have you been able to see many games, Mr. Burnley?" Alex asked.

The cab driver turned in his seat and faced her. "I saw three full series last season, Miss Alex. Thank you for getting me those tickets. You didn't have to."

She smiled, happy that in her absence at Fenway Park, another had experienced it. "You don't have to thank me, Mr. Burnley." Alex leaned over and picked up her purse from the floor.

Just as she was about to open it to pay the cab driver, Evan leaned forward and handed the driver the fare. "Thank you for the ride, Mr. Burnley."

"You're very welcome, Mr. Evan," he said before he took the cash and then got out of the cab.

"I was going to pay," Alex complained.

Evan rolled his eyes at her and then slid across the back seat to her. He pressed a kiss to her cheek, enticing the silly grin on her face. Alex glanced around to find the trunk lid still up and no one on their street as she pressed her fingers to his jaw and kissed him full on the lips. She knew it was risky, but she didn't care.

They'd been careful for two days.

They needed a second of recklessness to take off the edge.

When she pulled away, she whispered, "I love you." Alex

lowered her hands from his jaw. "It's the first time in days that I've said it without feeling guilty for keeping it from Savannah."

"I love you, too, AJ. Dinner is going to be hard with your parents. I don't want to keep anything from them."

Alex let out a small groan. "I know. Me either, but they'd understand. Do you need to pack before dinner?"

"I hate that I have to leave you tonight to go back to Stanford," he said with a hint of sadness to his voice.

"It's okay," she assured. She reached over and squeezed his hand. "I'll drive you to the airport tonight. Go pack and don't worry about anything. We'll be okay."

"We'll be okay," he promised.

Alex smiled, hearing the truth in his promise. "I'll see you at my place after you're finished packing?"

He released her hand with a nod. "Yeah."

Alex grasped her purse in one hand and the car door handle in the other. She pulled on the handle, opening the door. Once she was out of the cab, Burnley stood next to her with her suitcase.

"Welcome home, Miss Alex," he said in a sweet tone as he removed Evan's bag from his shoulder and handed it to him. "You, too, Mr. Evan. Boston's missed y'all."

"It's good to be home," Evan said, surprising Alex. He had never been one to love or call Boston home. For so many years, the city had suffocated him. But she knew that this time, home was about being with her. "I'll see you soon, AJ."

She nodded. "Yeah, come over when you're finished."

"Okay," Evan said before she watched him walk toward his childhood home.

"Over a year ago, it was different," Burnley said, reminding her that she was not alone.

Alex craned her neck to find the cab driver also staring at Evan. "Yeah. Over a year ago, we were different people."

"And now?"

She mulled his question over. "We're almost there," she said as vaguely as possible.

Burnley pressed his lips together and nodded, his dark brown eyes twinkling. "I'm happy to see that beautiful smile of yours again, Miss Alex. If you ever need a ride back to Logan, all you have to do is call for me. And if that boy so much as hurt your feelings, I'll be second in line behind your daddy to beat his ass."

Alex laughed. "Thank you for the concern, Mr. Burnley, but I think this time I know better. And I'm sure my father would love to meet you after that statement. You drive safely back to the city, okay?"

"I will. Y'all have a good summer." And with that, Burnley got in his cab and drove away.

Spinning around, she took in her childhood home as she grasped her suitcase's handle. The house still looked warm and inviting. It still looked like a well-loved family called it home. Smiling, Alex rolled her suitcase up the path and to the front steps. Once she lifted the heavy suitcase up each step, she came to a stop at the front door and flipped open her purse. She raked around until she found her keys and inserted the key into the lock. With a twist, she unlocked the door, and pushed it open before she dragged her suitcase inside, noticing how quiet the house was with her parents at work. Then she closed the door behind her, too tired to haul her suitcase up the stairs, and headed to her room.

She entered her room to find flowers and a welcome home sign her parents had left on her desk. When she made it to her desk, she picked up the bright violets and smiled, knowing that was her father's choice. She had almost been named Violet as they were the flowers her father had brought to the delivery room for her mother after Alex was born. Her mother had suggested Alexandra after her uncle, and the rest was history.

Setting the bouquet down, Alex spun around and took in her bedroom. She felt different standing in it—as if she were a whole new person. She walked over to her bed and noticed that she had kept the framed picture of her ex-boyfriend and her in Southport on her nightstand.

Sitting on her bed, she reached over and picked up the silver frame, her heart clenching at the smiles on her and Landon's faces. She remembered that day. He had driven them to Savannah's hometown so she could deal with her mother. It had also been the day she had told him she loved him for the very first time. Her chest constricted at the memory of what followed. She had trusted him and loved him enough to be intimate with him. He had been the only guy Alex had been with after she had lost her virginity to Evan.

Suddenly, sobriety came to an end as tears slipped down her cheeks. She might not love Landon like she used to, but she was sad that those memories had to be forgotten. Landon Carmichael had loved her—to the best of his abilities he had—and she'd felt it. But life made him choose, made her choose, and they had come to an end.

Brushing away her tears with the back of her hands, Alex let out a deep breath and reached over and pulled the drawer open. Alex glanced down at the picture once last time, allowing her fingers to brush against his glass-covered face before she set the frame inside and closed the drawer.

Finally putting Landon, their memories, and their love away.

86

Rn

radon

EVAN

Now

"Evan, did you hear me?" his ex-girlfriend asked, her voice tight and full of fear.

He was in shock.

He had no idea how to answer her.

AJ's pregnant.

It made sense.

Why she wanted a bigger apartment.

Why he found her hunched over the toilet this morning.

It wasn't food poisoning.

It was morning sickness.

His best friend, the love of his life, his ex-girlfriend was pregnant.

Holy shit, AJ's pregnant.

A smile slowly spread across his face.

AJ's going to be a mom.

Mom.

She's going to be a mom.

Then it hit him. Realization sliced his chest and plunged deep inside him, stretching his ribs apart as his stomach dipped.

She spent time with him in the UK.

Mrs. Parker had told him that when he had lunch with her after he had picked her up from one of her parenting class. It had been when Mr. Parker's flight from New York had been delayed. She had taken him out to eat as her way of thanking him, though there had been no need to. He would do anything for Clara Parker. But that was the afternoon she had let slip that his ex-girlfriend had gone out with her ex-boyfriend.

The ex-boyfriend she had chosen over Evan the very first time. But AJ had yet to mention him since she returned to Brookline. She never indicated to Evan that she was back together with him.

That hope that maybe it could be his diminished.

She's pregnant with his baby ... She has to be.

For a single moment, the thought saddened him. Jealous that she had moved on while he had been in Boston after their breakup. He had missed her and spent every day hoping she'd come home and he'd beg for her forgiveness.

Those bright emerald greens of hers searched his, waiting for him to react.

She was pregnant.

It wasn't his.

But as he looked at her, he felt a sense of warmth replace the jealousy in his chest.

That baby would be half of her.

It's AJ's child.

She was the best person he knew. And he knew that he would love that child as much as he loved its mother. He'd be there for her and support them both. He'd step up if the famous NBA player wouldn't. He might not make millions, but he would give them his undying love.

Seeing her watery eyes, Evan stood. He watched her chin dip as her tears rolled down her cheeks. Then he got on one knee and grasped her hand in his.

He had to make her a promise.

A vow that he wasn't going to let her do it alone.

"Even though it's his, I promise I'll be there for you and this baby. It's half you, and that makes me want to love him or her with my entire being."

AJ cupped the side of his cheek, her thumb grazing his skin like he remembered. Her touch was as soft and as perfect as he recalled. "Evan," she whispered.

"Yeah, Alexandra?"

She inhaled a short breath as her jaw clenched. Her green eyes twinkled with the fear and adoration he had missed seeing. "It's yours."

It's ... mine?

"W-what?" he stammered as he got onto his knees, fearing he'd tumble over.

"You're the father, Evan," she revealed.

"I'm ... *Me?*"

His heart beat so fast he was terrified that it would give out.

He couldn't breathe.

His head spun at the revelation.

At the truth he had wanted.

He was going to be a father.

Better yet, the mother of his baby was his best friend.

"I never slept with him when I was in England. We went to dinner, and that was it. That was three months ago. I'm eight weeks pregnant. It's yours, Evan. You're the only man I've been with in almost four years." Her eyes never broke away from his.

His smile returned. "I'm going to be a dad?"

AJ bit her lip as she pulled her hands from him and stood, staring down at him. "Yes, but you don't have to be. I don't expect you to—"

He shot up onto his feet, shaking his head at her. "No," he begged. "I want to be a father. I want this baby with you."

"Evan, I won't let you not go to LA. You were excited. You even sold your house. Besides this baby, you have no roots here anymore. You're ready to move on with your life. And I won't let our son or daughter be the reason you stay here. Boston has never truly been your home."

My home was with you.

But I ruined that.

I'm trying to make up for that.

But you don't know that.

"Look, we should talk. But not here in Fenway Park. Let's go for a drive. We'll talk all of this through. We'll make this work, Alexandra," he said.

So we can be a family.

She shook her head. "I'm tired. Right now, I'd rather go home. I know you mean that, us working this out, but you haven't thought it through. This baby, if you choose to really be a part of his or her life, will change yours and alter your happiness. I don't want you to conform to fit in my life, Evan. Not again. And not anymore. I want you to be happy."

He understood what she meant. He knew why she would doubt his commitment. He had left her in Zürich. Evan had been the one to give up on her. So he understood why she was cautious when it came to their baby.

Our baby.

188

AJ and I are having a baby together.

His heart swelled with love.

He would have to prove to her that he wasn't going to give up on her.

Prove to her that he still loved her.

"Okay. Let me drive you home," he said.

"No," she declined. "I'm sure you had plans tonight. I can grab a cab—"

"Alexandra."

Her bottom lip trembled. "Yeah?"

"You're the mother of my unborn child," he stated.

"I am," she breathed as if she were only now truly coming to terms with the revelation. And that soft, beautiful smile of hers spread across her lips. "Yes, you can take me home."

Turning off the ignition of his BMW, he let out a sigh and glanced over to find AJ staring out the passenger side window. She had been quiet during the entire trip. He wanted to talk to her and had planned to drive to Rhode Island like they used to and talk through where they went forward in their lives.

They were having a baby.

The baby he thought wasn't his but had desperately wanted to be a part of its life. But he was the father. He was going to be the father of Alexandra Louise Parker's baby. It would be half her. His heart throbbed at the thought once more.

She was the mother of his unborn child.

"My parents don't know," AJ finally said as she craned her

neck to face him, frowning. "With all of my family coming in from Australia and New York, and them busy with Seb, I haven't had the chance to tell them that they're going to be grandparents."

His heart stalled at what she just said. Mr. and Mrs. Parker, AJ's parents—the very couple who had helped raised Evan—were going to be his child's grandparents. His eyes stung at the thought. He couldn't think of a pair more perfect to be his child's grandparents. They would love him or her just as much as he and AJ would love their child.

"I won't say anything to them until you're ready," he promised.

She smiled with appreciation as she unclicked her belt. "Thank you."

"I'll walk you to your door," he said as he freed himself of the seat belt and pulled on the handle to open the car door. Once he slipped out and shut the door, he walked around the car to her as she opened her door. Evan grasped the handle and opened it wider for her.

"Thank you," AJ said before she got out of the car and fixed her beautiful silk dress that matched the color of her eyes. She had drawn him to her the moment she entered the party. Had he not been talking to one of the newest MLB executives, he would have gone to her immediately.

Side by side and step by step, they walked toward AJ's front door. Once they had climbed the short steps and stood under the porch light, she let out a sigh and faced him. She offered him a small smile as she brushed her hair behind her ear. Her bright green eyes gleamed at him.

"It's okay if you don't want to be part of our baby's life.

It might not be for you right now. I can do this on my own. I will never stop you from wanting to meet or be a part of his or her life later on." She paused to take a breath. "You can pursue your dreams in LA. It's about your dreams now. You came to Zürich to be with me, and you weren't happy, but I won't stop you from going to California. We'll make it work if that's what you want."

He knew that whatever he said right now, she would not believe. She wanted him to think it over, but he didn't need time. She did. Evan knew what he wanted. It was his baby and the love of his life. But he would have to prove to her how true he was to his dreams of them being a family. A dream he had always wanted but never voiced out loud.

"Okay. I'll think about it. Good night, AJ."

"Good night, Evan," she said as she turned to open the front door.

Once she opened the door, Evan made his way down the steps and toward his car. He slipped into the driver's seat and started the ignition. Evan peeked back at her house to find that she was staring at him. She must have expected him to go to his house next door, but he didn't. He had gone straight into his car, ready to drive to Cambridge to meet someone who would change his life.

Throughout the ride into Cambridge, he thought about Alexandra. Of her stomach swelling as their baby grew. The thought of her giving birth and cradling their child. He thought of the life he'd live with her as his partner and not just his best friend. Thoughts of her and their future with their child consumed him during the ten-minute drive. Evan wanted it all, and he was determined to have it all. He just had to work harder than ever before.

He needed to prove to AJ that he was in it forever.

For more than promised words.

He wanted a life with her and their baby.

A happy one, no less.

As he pulled into the short driveway, he smiled at himself. He was going to be a father. He should be scared, but he wasn't. It felt right. It was what he had always wanted with AJ someday.

And that someday had come.

It might not have been the way he had planned, but he wouldn't change it for the world. As Evan turned off the engine, he stared at the house. That sense of rightness glowed in his chest because he now knew the choices he'd made since he got back from Zürich were the right ones.

Pulling on the handle, Evan got out of the car, closed the door, and made his way to the red painted wooden front door. He inhaled a deep breath, grasped the doorknob, and twisted it, knowing that it would be unlocked. He let himself into the warm house and set his keys on the hallway table. He went down the hall and into the kitchen as he combed his hair back before he stepped into the living room.

"What do you think of our home?" he asked, desperately wanting approval.

"It's perfect, Evan."

"You think so?"

192

He smiled, pride filling his chest as he watched Mr. Parker, AJ's father, turn around to face him. "I do, and I think she will, too."

Evan sighed in relief. "She always did want to live on a street like this one."

"You kept all the original features. It has three bedrooms, and it's close to MIT. My daughter will love this house," Mr. Parker said.

Evan headed over to the kitchen and pulled on the stainless steel fridge door. Retrieving two bottles of beer, he closed the door and headed over to AJ's father. "Thanks for looking at what's been done so far. I know with your house being full that this was the only time you could come over without raising suspicion."

Mr. Parker took the beer from him with a smile. "I left the spare key on the hallway table. I also sent Clara some pictures, and she agrees that Alexandra will love it. When you bought this house four weeks ago, we weren't sure, but after seeing what you've done, it's amazing."

"I still have a lot of painting to do. The room I picked out for Alexandra's office still needs the carpenters to come in and build her bookcases," he said as he led Mr. Parker toward the dark gray couch he had picked out a week ago. It was comfortable and large enough for several people to sit on. When he lived with AJ in Zürich, he learned early on that she was a woman of comfort rather than design when it came to furnishings.

"Can you still afford the rest of the renovations? I know you wanted to replace the floorboards. Clara and I can add to your funds," Mr. Parker offered.

Evan shook his head. "Nah. I'm good. Kyle gave me more than enough for the family house so he and Angie can settle down. Plus, I still have money from my parents that I never used. This house will be done. You know she's been looking for apartments in Cambridge."

"Has she found any she likes?"

"No. She couldn't afford the ones with more than one room. Plus, I made sure I pointed out all the faults of each apartment so she didn't fall in love with them. The moment I drove past this a month after she went back to Zürich, I knew it was perfect for her ... Perfect for us."

"And what if she doesn't want this house?" Mr. Parker asked, his brow raised.

Evan took in all the renovations he had done in the past month—all his hard work that she might not have wanted done in the first place—but he remembered when they were kids and she pointed at the houses in Cambridge from her parents' car. She used to point and say, "I want a house like that one." She had even asked him to buy her one similar to the one he had purchased for them.

"Then she doesn't want a house together. I won't force her to stay," Evan said. "But if she's ready for a life together in this house, then she knows I was committed from the start."

Mr. Parker took a pull of his beer and set it to rest on his thigh. He stared at him as if he were trying to find the answers on Evan's face. "You still want to be with my daughter?" There was no hiccup in his voice. His question was serious.

"You and I both know she wanted to stay in Zürich for those three extra years. You should have seen her, Mr. Parker. She was amazing at that institute. I was just the boyfriend she'd come home to and go out of her way to give attention to even though she was tired." Evan reached out and set his beer on the coffee table he had assembled two days ago. "She wanted to stay. I saw it in her eyes, but I was holding her back. Even though I vowed never to do that to her, I was. So when I came home, I prepared for her eventual return."

"So you bought her a house."

Evan nodded. "MIT is still her dream, so I knew someday she'd come home."

Mr. Parker nodded and then stared at his beer on his thigh. "You didn't answer my previous question, Evan."

He took a deep breath. "Yes. I long to be with your daughter. I long to make her happy. To make her smile. To be a part of her life. To have a life with her here. But I couldn't live with myself if she didn't stay in Zürich and achieve her dreams. She had never been happier than when she worked at the Rodahawe Institute, and I was just getting in the way." Evan stared at Alexandra's father. His baby's grandfather. Mr. Parker didn't know it yet, but in eight months' time, he would have a grandchild.

In eight months' time, Evan would have a son or daughter.

In eight months' time, he'd be a father.

And two months ago, Evan had asked Mr. Parker a simple question.

It was time they spoke about that talk they had after they said goodbye to AJ before she returned to Switzerland when Seb was born.

Digging his hand in his pants pocket, he grasped the velvet object that felt as if it had been burning a hole in his pocket all night. When Alexandra had revealed that she was pregnant, all he wanted to do was ask.

"Mr. Parker?"

Alexandra's father lifted his chin. "Yes, Evan."

As much as Evan would love to tell him that he and AJ were expecting a child together, he couldn't. He couldn't take that away from Alexandra. And right now, he had no idea how Mr. Parker would react. All Evan knew was that he had to assure Mr. Parker how committed he was to Alexandra and their baby.

Evan pulled out the box, stared at it for a moment, and then opened it. The green diamond and rose gold engagement ring twinkled in the light. Sixteen small diamonds surrounded the circular green diamond.

Eight protons.

Eight neutrons.

Just as he had designed.

It wasn't the largest diamond engagement ring, but Evan thought it was perfect for her. She hated to wear flashy jewelry and wouldn't feel comfortable wearing a large diamond on her finger.

"Can I see it?" Mr. Parker asked.

He handed it over, hoping for Alexandra's father's approval. "I'm sorry it's not bigger, but I couldn't get them to find a larger green diamond in time. And although it isn't as green as her eyes, it matches her eye color when they soften and she's lost in thought or she tells me she loves me. It's this rare moment when instead of her green eyes darkening, they actually soften. And that's the color of that green diamond."

"It's perfect, Evan," Mr. Parker said with a gentle smile.

Evan cleared his throat. "Mr. Parker, two months ago I

asked you for your blessing to ask your daughter to marry me. You told me I had to wait three years to ask her. She's home now. And I know I never deserved your daughter, but I believe in the depths of my heart that I am the only person who will ever love her right or die trying. I'd like to ask you again."

Mr. Parker's eyes widened before he nodded. "Okay, son."

Son.

He had no idea how much hearing him call Evan son meant. All his life, he wished for a father like Nolan Parker, and he had raised Evan with more love than Evan's actual father.

"Mr. Parker, for over three years, I was your daughter's boyfriend. After we graduated, I followed her to Switzerland where I loved her more and discovered just how in love I was with her. Six months ago, I made the horrible—but right—decision to leave her in Zürich so she could continue with her career and make a name for herself. I shouldn't have left her, but I wanted her to experience those three years at the Rodahawe Institute. I wanted her to concentrate on her research, and she did. She finished her formula that will help Dr. Rodahawe's research. Two months ago, I asked your daughter to stay with me. To my horror, she made me proud by saying no and taking the job in Zürich. She stopped making sure I was all right to chase her dreams after I had hindered her for so long.

"A month ago, I drove and drove after she didn't come home for Christmas and New Year's after a snowstorm in Zürich canceled all flights. We used to go on long drives, and I drove all the way to Watch Hill in the snow so I could feel closer to her. I sat on that beach for hours. Instead of going straight home after I drove back, I drove to MIT for her and came across this house, knowing instantly it was perfect. The next morning, I bought it for her. It needed work, but as you can see, I've spent the past month updating all the old features of this house."

"And you've done a great job," Mr. Parker praised.

Evan smiled. "Thank you. When Alexandra and I were young, she used to tell me about her perfect house. It would be old. It would have scars that needed fixing. It would have a wooden staircase. It would have windows that had stained-glass features so that when the light shined through, it'd paint the floorboards with beautiful colors from the sun. The kitchen had to be the heart of the house because she was raised in one that was just the same. And her bedroom had to be facing the morning sun so she could feel it on her skin when she woke up. When I saw this house, I knew it was hers. It had it all. Scars and all. I want the rest of my life with your daughter.

"I'm not him. I'm not her ex-boyfriend. I'm not a famous NBA player who makes millions a year. I gave up my baseball career because Alexandra's happiness was more important to me. Baseball never made me as happy as being with her. I'm not going anywhere. I go where she goes. I'm not going to LA. I was offered the job but never wanted it. The Red Sox offered me a permanent position in their operations department, so I can provide for your daughter. I want to stay here in Massachusetts and love and support her. I want to come home to her after she spends her day at MIT as she earns her Ph.D. I want her to tell me about her day and every day for the rest of our lives. I love your daughter, Mr. Parker. I will always love Alexandra, and I want to spend my life by her side as her husband."

"Well," Alexandra's father said as he shut the ring box and handed it back to him, "I've always considered you a son. For over three years, you made my daughter happy. No one understands her the way you have and do. As I said two months ago, I'm honored to give you my blessing to ask my daughter to marry you, Evan."

"Thank you, Mr. Parker," Evan uttered with so much joy that his voice almost cracked. Then he returned the ring box in his pocket, wrapped his arms around his maybe future father-in-law and held him tight before Mr. Parker let out a soft laugh and broke them apart. Mr. Parker set his beer on the coffee table and stood from the couch, Evan doing the same.

"It's up to my daughter, you know. I may have given you my blessing, but it's up to her to give you an answer." Mr. Parker held out his hand. "And I think it's time you called me Noel, Evan."

Evan firmly shook Alexandra's father's hand. "Thank you, *Noel*."

"I better get back to my beautiful wife and amazing kids. Thanks for the beer and for letting me see this place. I know you'll take care of my daughter. I'll let myself out. Good night, Evan."

"Good night, Noel," Evan said, then watched Mr. Parker walk down the hall toward the front door. When the door opened and shut, he let out a heavy breath. A pressure had been lifted from his shoulders. Evan had been worried that Alexandra's father would change his mind about his blessing to ask for his daughter's hand in marriage.

Evan glanced at his beer and decided he needed to do more to the house tonight and not return to the gala. He had made his way upstairs and picked up his toolbox in the hallway before he entered the last room on the left. It was a room he had no idea what to do with. But as he stood inside it, he knew exactly what room it was for.

It was their baby's nursery.

It faced the direction of the rising sun, and he or she would experience exactly what Alexandra wanted in the morning.

Evan walked over to the windowsill, crouched down, and set his toolbox down. Then he pulled the ring box out of his pocket, opened it, and set it on the wooden ledge. If he ever got distracted or frustrated when it came to fixing up the old Cambridge house, he would just look over at the ring and be reminded of what he was working toward.

To give Alexandra a home.

To give his baby a loving home.

To promise Alexandra a life.

A life they would share with their child.

This morning's heavy snowfall made it a little difficult to drive. The traffic out of Cambridge to Brookline was clear compared to the traffic coming into the city. Evan had spent last night sanding back the walls and painting them white. He had managed two coats before he picked up AJ's ring and went back downstairs to sleep on the couch. He should have driven back to his old place, but he was too tired. Once he returned to his childhood home, Evan had showered and changed before he walked across the driveways and up to Mr.

and Mrs. Parker's front door. He had brushed the soles of his shoes on the doormat, shook his hair of the snowflakes, and then knocked on the door.

Evan glanced down at the bouquet of violets he'd picked up on his way home. Throughout the night, he replayed her words. Over and over again, they gave him comfort and a sense of panic.

He had to do better.

Be better for AJ and the baby.

Proposing to her right away would have looked drastic and completely irresponsible. For now, he'd be there for her and tell how much he wanted to be a part of their baby's life.

He was ready to become a father.

"Oh, good morning, Evan," AJ's mother said once she opened the door with that stunning smile of hers.

"Good morning, Mrs. Parker."

Mrs. Parker frowned. "My husband told me that he asked you to call him Noel. I think it's time you call me Clara, Evan."

Evan smiled as she stepped aside. "If you don't mind, I'd like to continue to call you both Mr. and Mrs. Parker for a little while longer."

"That's more than fine," she said as she closed the door. "I like the bouquet. Alexandra is upstairs. You can go up and see her. Everyone else is asleep, and I'm making breakfast. Would you like to join us? It's been a while."

"I'd love to join you," Evan said before he climbed up the stairs and made his way to AJ's room. As he stood in front of her door, his heart raced in his chest as his palms sweated. He was nervous. He was anxious. He had no idea how she'd take his news. She might have changed her mind about his

201

involvement in their baby's life.

Evan hoped and prayed she hadn't.

That she wouldn't use his past mistakes against him.

Inhaling a deep breath and then slowly exhaling the air, he formed a loose fist and knocked on her door. "AJ, it's me."

"Come in," she said.

Evan pushed the door open to find her still in bed, reading a pregnancy book. She glanced over at him and lowered the book with a small smile to her lips as he walked toward her. Once he reached her bed, he sat down on the mattress and handed her the violets.

"Thank you," she said as she peeked down at the purple flowers. Then she set them on her nightstand and faced him. "Morning."

Unable to help himself, he cupped the side of her face with one hand as he brushed her hair back with the other. Those bright green eyes softened, reminding him of the color of the engagement ring he had designed for her. Evan took a deep breath, released it seconds later, and then cradled her face with his other hand. "Good morning, Alexandra."

"Are you okay?"

He nodded, and whispered, "I want this baby with you. I want to be a father. I want to be the father of the child you're carrying, not just by DNA, but by helping you raise him or her. I want us to be a family."

His heart boomed.

His breathing became impossible as his lungs squeezed in anticipation.

He lost sensation in parts of his body as her lips slowly parted and that awe in her eyes was a sight he would never forget.

And at that moment, he let his desire and want for commitment speak for him. "I love you, Alexandra."

He sealed his love with a soft kiss.

Her lips were how he remembered them.

Remembered their last kiss before she returned to Zürich.

Remembered how heartbreaking it felt in his bones.

This time, he felt love and hope.

When AJ pulled back, her eyes gazed into his. Just when he thought she might say that she loved him, she grasped his elbows and lowered his hands from her face and dug her hand under the pillow.

Evan watched as she pulled out a picture and set it in his palm, and said, "I love you, too, Evan Gilmore."

He lifted his chin to see that small, vulnerable smile of hers. The one that told him she meant it. That she was afraid her love wouldn't be enough. But she had no idea that it was all he ever needed.

Her love.

Their love.

The love for their child.

Evan looked down to find she had set the sonogram in his hand. He grasped it and stared at the dot.

That dot was their baby.

They had created that dot.

It became a blur.

That dot became lost in his teary gaze, and all he could do to find it was blink.

"We're going to be parents," he mumbled as he felt AJ press her palm to his cheek, wiping away his tears.

"Yeah," she said as his eyes found hers.

And that moment, in her bedroom, on her bed with the pregnancy book by her lap and the violets just visible to his left, was perfect.

She was perfect.

Their baby dot was perfect.

"I love you, AJ," he said in a low voice and just for them as he pressed his forehead to hers. "Thank you."

It was all he could say.

Thank you for her.

Thank you for coming back.

Thank you for still loving him.

Thank you for having their child.

Thank you, thank you, thank you.

⁸⁷**Fr**

francium

87

Fr

francium

ALEX

Summer before junior year of college

Alex tied the ribbon and then slid the box across the counter. "Have a nice day."

The male customer who ordered a dozen red velvet cupcakes smiled and slipped a few bills in the tip jar. "You, too."

Sighing once she saw the line she spent so long serving had ended, she took in the packed bakery. Customers filled the booths and tables, enjoying her mother's cupcakes. Alex knew that this was the quiet period before the lunch crowd came in for the savory cupcakes and pastries The Little Bakery in Boston offered. Alex reached into her apron pocket and pulled out her phone. She had felt it vibrate earlier but ignored it to help out as much as she could before she took a break.

Though she loved working at her mother's bakery, she had spent a lot of the summer with Evan Gilmore. It was hard keeping them a secret, and it was torture pretending he was just her best friend and nothing more. The only time they could really be together was when her parents were at work. The afternoon they had returned from Duke, they had made love in her bed before her parents came home. It was risky, but she only had hours with him before he returned to California. As she dressed, she realized it had been the first time she had ever been intimate with someone in her bed. Alex had never slept with her ex-boyfriend in her bedroom. When they were alone together, it was always in the guest room.

Alex tried not think of why that was. She tried to leave her ex-boyfriend in the past. Her summer belonged to Evan, and she knew that being with him again was right. Before he returned to Stanford, they decided they weren't ready for her parents or Kyle to know. They wanted to be sure of their relationship before they came clean, especially with Evan returning to California. When she dropped him off at the airport, a sense of déjà vu washed over her. Evan kissed her and promised it wouldn't be like last time.

And it wasn't.

He called her the moment he landed.

Evan called and messaged her every day until his sophomore year at Stanford ended. Alex was there for him and was disappointed for him when the Cardinals didn't make the play-offs. The moment he completed his finals, he said goodbye to his teammates and friends and returned to her.

Evan was right.

It wasn't like last time.

Because this time, he came back to her and surprised her when he appeared at her front door. There was nothing to say as she pulled him into her empty house and kissed him. In that reuniting kiss, she felt all the promises he had yet to make. She tasted their future together and was sure of her choice. Their weeks apart after he came to Duke were what they needed.

It gave her relativity.

Time.

And most importantly, clarity.

THE DISSOLUTION OF UNREQUITED

She was sure loving Evan Gilmore was the right choice.

But of course, loving him wasn't easy, especially with keeping that love a secret, but they made it work. Alex snuck over to his house and would spend the night or see him early in the morning. She was sure her parents had their suspicions, but she assured them that they were best friends just spending the summer hanging out.

As Alex unlocked her phone, she smiled at Evan's message.

Evan: Hey, AJ. How's work? I've barely seen you this week. Can I see you tonight?

Alex: Busy period just ended. Mum and Dad are heading over to New York to see Lori and Reese later tonight. That means we have the next few days of uninterrupted bliss.

Evan: Perfect. So dinner at my place after they leave?

Alex: Sounds great.

Evan: Want me to pick you up since you rode into the city with your dad this morning?

Alex: That would be great. I'll see you later this afternoon.

Evan: Hey, AJ?

His question had her brows meeting.

Alex: Yes, Evan?

Evan: I miss you. I see you, but I haven't been able to really see you.

Her heart swelled in her chest.

Alex: I know what you mean. I miss you, too. I love you, Evan.

Evan: I love you, too.

"You all right, my love?" her mother asked, interrupting her intimate exchange with Evan.

Alex locked her phone and tucked it back into her pocket. She smiled at her mother who was walking out of the kitchen with a tray of brownie cupcakes. "Yeah. Just texting Sav. Are you and Dad still going to New York tonight?"

Her mother began to arrange the cupcakes in the display case and nodded. "Yes. Lori asked me to bake for the cheer team's summer party. Are you going to be okay? You know you can come with us."

Any other time, she would have.

But this summer was about her and Evan.

"I have to catch up on some science journals. I'm a little behind. Plus, I might email Mr. Miller and see if he has any extra material to read that he has come across recently." It wasn't a complete lie. They were things she did plan to do besides be with Evan.

Her mother stood and laughed. "Alexandra, it's summer."

"Which means I get to read freely."

"Well, spend some time actually relaxing while we're gone. Didn't you say Jordan and Addison are home for the summer? You should see them," her mother encouraged.

"I will," Alex said, hearing the bell echo in the bakery. She glanced over as a very familiar face walked through the bakery doors.

210

"I'll put the next batch in the oven. Tell him I said hi," her mother said before she disappeared into the kitchen.

Alex nodded and turned her attention to the green eyes glinting at her. "Welcome home, Hunter."

He grinned at her. "It's good to be home, though later than I anticipated. You look really good, Alex." His smile stretched wider. "Really good."

"Thanks, Hunter. You stayed in California for most of the summer?"

"Stayed in Santa Cruz. Heard the whole gang is back in town, though, so I had to come home."

"You want any cupcakes? They're on the house."

Hunter peeked over at the glass display and then back at her. "Only if you sit down and catch up with me. I haven't heard from you since high school."

Alex laughed awkwardly. He wasn't wrong. Once she left for Duke, she cut all ties with her past. Reaching behind her, she unknotted her apron, took it off, and set it on the counter. "Mum, I'm taking a break. Need some help up front!" she yelled as she picked up a plate from the stack. "So what'll it be?"

"Surprise me," he insisted.

"Sure thing." Alex grabbed the tongs, reached over, and picked up the Irish whiskey cupcake. Setting the cupcake on a plate, she put the tongs down, walked around the counter and found a free booth. She slid down in it and pushed the plate toward him once he sat opposite her. "It's the Irish whiskey cupcake. I'm pretty sure it was your favorite."

He grinned at her. "It is. God, I haven't had one of these since the last time I was home. Your mother's cupcakes are way better than anything I eat in California."

"I'll pass on the praise. How is UCLA?"

"Still loving it. I heard you were dating the number one NBA draft pick."

Alex winced—surprised that Hunter would mention her ex-boyfriend. "Uhh, yeah, I was. How did you know that?"

Hunter chuckled. "Alex, you might not be in Red Sox articles anymore, but you're in ones concerning NBA draftees. I read the articles about you two."

"Yeah, well, Landon and I are over. Have been for a while now. He's in Phoenix, and I'll be going back to Duke after summer."

He picked up the cupcake, peeled the paper back, and took a bite. She watched him close his eyes as he let out a soft moan of satisfaction. "Goddamn, this is amazing," he said once he set the cupcake down and swallowed his bite. "As much as I love this cupcake, I came to ask you something."

Her brow raised. "You did?"

"I did," he confirmed. "I'm having a party at my place tomorrow night. You should come and celebrate the fact that we're all back home."

"Hey, AJ!" she heard Evan call out as he walked through the bakery doors, getting her attention.

"Evan?" Her brows furrowed. "What are you doing here? I thought you were stopping by later?"

Evan glanced down, surprised to see Hunter sitting opposite her. "Hey, Hunt. I didn't know you were home."

"Just got home yesterday. I was just mentioning the party I'm having tomorrow night," he said as he got out of the booth. "You both should come. I better get going. Got a lot to do. It's nice to see you two are best friends again." And with that, he picked up his cupcake, bid them goodbye, and left her mother's bakery.

"What was that about?" Evan asked as he gazed down at her.

"He just stopped by. I thought you were coming by later."

Evan combed his fingers through his hair. "Kyle asked me to stop by Fenway for some Red Sox family stuff. It's not for a while, so I thought I'd see if you wanted to grab some lunch."

"Lunch sounds good," she said, getting out of the booth. "The rush is over for a bit, so I'm sure Mum and everyone won't miss me. Follow me to the office?"

"Sure," he said as she led him away from the booth and toward the back of the bakery.

As they passed the second entrance to the kitchen, she yelled, "Mum, I'm going to lunch with Evan."

"All right, Alexandra!" her mother shouted back.

When they made it to her mother's office, she opened the door and let him enter the office first. Alex closed the door, and just as she spun around, Evan cradled her cheeks and his lips collided with hers. He kissed her deeply and with passion as he pressed her against the office door. His hands left her cheeks and captured her waist.

"Evan," she moaned, moving her head away from his lips. "We can't."

He panted as his forehead pressed to hers. "I know."

She rubbed her lips together as she peeked up at him through her lashes. "Not in Mum's office. I promise, as soon as they leave for New York, we can spend hours together."

"I honestly can't wait," he admitted.

Alex reached up, cupped his jaw, and pressed a soft kiss to his lips. "I love you; you know that."

He nodded. "God, I love you."

"This shit is revolting," Candy, one of their high school classmates, said as she coughed. "Jesus! You'd think the starting batter for the Bruins could afford better shit."

"You don't have to drink it, Candy," Addison remarked.

Willow, who Hunter dated during high school, laughed as she snapped a picture of Candy's contorted face taking another shot from the bottle. "Alex, you are not catching up on the numbers here. You're three behind."

Alex set down her red Solo cup, feeling the sweet haze of the two drinks she had consumed in quick succession. "My head is already spinning, Willow."

"I think you definitely have had enough," Jordan said.

The party at Hunter Jamison's parents' penthouse apartment was loud and hot. The music was a mix of old school rap and party anthems. To keep their relationship a secret, Alex and Evan had gone to the party together but went their separate ways soon after they arrived at the party. They had said hi to each other and spoke of how much they missed each other when they were pouring drinks. Besides those secret moments, they had barely spent any time together. He was busy with his high school baseball teammates, and Alex was with the girls from the cheerleading team. It was awkward being around Addison, the girl Evan took to prom, but Evan had told Alex what Addison had done the night he found her at Blue Jay's, so she decided to put the past behind her.

"Hey, girls," Hunter said as he stood in front of them. "Having fun?"

"Shit drinks, Hunt!" Candy said.

He glared at her. "You just have a shit palate, Can. Alex, how are you doing?"

"Fine," she replied.

"Do you need anything?" Hunter asked, his green eyes sparkling at her. His caramel skin the perfect canvas for his eyes. It was no surprise that he was still so beautiful two years after high school.

She felt the girls' eyes on her, but she ignored them as she shook her head at Hunter. "I'm good."

"Well, find me if you do," Hunter said with a wink before he returned to his group of friends. Hollers boomed over the music as a game of beer pong began in front of them.

Addison, Willow, and Candy scurried to the empty drinks table, leaving Alex and Jordan alone. "If I didn't know any better, I'd say Evan Gilmore is looking at you as if he can't stand being away from you for another second."

Alex glanced over to find Evan looking at her. He had a small smile on his lips before he glanced away. "I doubt that," she said, trying to play it off.

Jordan's laugh echoed her tipsy state. "Oh, Alex. I wish you'd open your eyes. Look, he's on his way."

She watched as Evan approached them and stopped in front of her. "Hey, Jordan, you mind if I borrow AJ for a second?"

"I don't mind at all," Jordan said as she opened her purse and pulled out her phone. "I have to call Carter. I wish he hadn't gone back to Notre Dame for the weekend."

Evan stepped closer and grasped Alex's hand, pulling her away from Jordan and toward the balcony. They had to squeeze past many of the partiers and drunks. Someone had spilled their drink on their shoes, and Evan held her hand tight to hold her up so she wouldn't slip.

Once they reached the sliding door, he slid it open, and they stepped out into the dark night. He slid the door close, giving them some privacy from the rest of the party and the world. Just her and Evan on a balcony with the warm Boston air ghosting along their skin.

He led her to the railing and faced her. His face showed no hint of emotion as if he was keeping all his cards carefully to his chest.

"What's wrong?"

Evan inhaled a deep breath. "Do you know how many guys were eyeing you?"

Although she was tipsy, she rolled her eyes and then gazed out at the twinkling city. "Quite the view."

"You are," Evan said.

Alex peeked over to find him staring at her. "I meant the city," she corrected as she turned to face him.

"And I still mean you."

She swayed slightly as a small smile touched her lips. Then she wrapped her arms around his neck, thankful that the darkness kept prying eyes away from their intimacy. "Evan?"

"Yes, AJ?"

She tightened her arms around him. "Summer's going to end soon."

He sighed. "I know."

"I go back to North Carolina, and you go back to

California." Alex pressed her lips tightly together. "What happens when we go back to college?"

"I want to be with you." His hands found her waist. "I love you, AJ. I truly and unbelievably want to be with you."

Her heart fluttered in her chest, loving his declaration. "So we're together? Like really together? Like I'm your girlfriend, and you're my boyfriend?"

Evan let out a soft laugh as he inched his face closer to hers. "Yes. If that's what you want. I'll fly to Duke whenever I'm not playing. You can come to Stanford whenever you can. And on breaks, we'll come back to Massachusetts."

"We're really going to do this?" she asked. Her heart clenched with hope.

"I really want us to do this. We can do this. We can make this work. I promise, we'll make this work," Evan said with so much assurance in his voice.

"I love you, Evan Gilmore." Alex got on her toes and pressed her lips to Evan's.

Correction—she pressed her lips to her *boyfriend's.*

And somewhere between each kiss and moan, he whispered, "Eight protons. Eight neutrons."

In two weeks, summer break would end.

Two weeks.

That was all the time she had left with Evan before they had to fly back to North Carolina. Alex's parents wouldn't be making the trip to Duke this time since her father had to fly to

Hong Kong for work and her mother was joining him. Because Alex had a lot of her things already in storage, she wouldn't have to drive the almost eleven-hour trip to Durham. Instead, she and Evan would fly to Duke to set up her new apartment before they flew to Stanford in California a few days later to help Evan and Milos move into their apartment off campus.

"Evan," Alex said from his bed as she watched him button his shirt. "Relax, okay?"

He lifted his chin and eyed her. "Seriously, AJ? You want me to relax?"

She got up from his bed and walked toward him, taking over as she buttoned his white long-sleeve dress shirt. "It's just dinner."

"With your parents."

"Which you've done plenty of times before," she reminded as she peeked up at him through her lashes. The fear and anxiety flashed in his eyes.

Evan sighed as he collected her hands with his and shook his head. "Yeah, as their daughter's best friend. Not as their daughter's *boyfriend*."

Alex smiled. It made her heart flutter that he was so nervous, but he didn't need to be. Tonight, they were going to reveal to her parents that they were finally together. It had been almost a month since Hunter Jamison's party. Almost a month since they started officially dating. "You'll be okay, Evan. I'll be right there with you."

"What if your parents don't want us together? AJ, I don't have the best track record with them—especially with Molly," Evan said, his voice tight.

Pulling her hands free from his, Alex reached behind her

and unclasped her necklace. She glanced at the silver atoms and smiled as she got on her toes and wrapped the necklace around his neck. She fixed it into place, and it rested against his chest. Then Alex tucked it under his shirt and let out a breath of air. "There."

"You're letting me wear your necklace?"

She nodded as she placed her palm over it, feeling it against his shirt. "Because after dinner with my parents, you're going to take it off." Then she grabbed his hands and pressed them to the sides of her neck. "And these hands will clasp it back around my neck as you whisper you love me and promise me that whatever happens next, we'll be together. You told me that you wore it so you'd have a piece of me with you. You have all of me. But if you're afraid of whatever my parents will say tonight, go back. Think back to Christmas when you gave me that necklace and told me you loved me for the first time. I'm not going anywhere, Evan."

"Promise?"

"Promise," she said as she slid her palm up his neck and to the back of his head, bringing his lips closer to hers. "I'll be right beside you."

Evan ensured their kiss exploded by sealing his lips over hers. If they had more time, she'd kiss him with more passion, but her parents would be waiting at her mother's restaurant, and they couldn't be late. Not if they were going to reveal that they were finally together. She couldn't let Evan know that she was nervous. Sure, her father now knew why he had chosen Molly, but Alex was sure he only approved of their friendship.

His approval of their love was another question altogether.

Ending their kiss before they lost control, she pulled back

and pressed her lips together. Then she lowered her thumb and wiped away the traces of her pale pink lipstick from his lips. "I love you. No matter what." Her boyfriend smiled that flawless, breathtaking smile as she stepped back. "Now, I'll let you finish up, and we'll leave when you're ready."

Just as she made her way to his bedroom door, he called out, "Alexandra?"

She spun around. "Yeah?"

"I love your parents, and it would hurt if they didn't approve," he admitted. "But not being with you would kill me. I can live with them never thinking I'd be good enough for you because it's true, but I can't imagine being with anyone but you. It's always been you." Then he closed the distance, cupped her face in his palms, and pressed his lips to her forehead in a soft, sweet kiss. "You're oxygen in my lungs. Every atom in me loves you. Eight protons. Eight neutrons, Alexandra."

And at that moment, it all fell into place.

No hint of doubt in her mind.

They would make it.

"I believe you," she whispered, "Just like you're the oxygen with each breath I take. I love you, Evan Gilmore."

It had taken them a half an hour with the city traffic to make it to her mother's restaurant. As always, they avoided waiting in line outside and walked straight into The Little Restaurant in Boston where everyone knew their names. Danny Fletcher,

her mother's former mentor and current head chef at the restaurant, had stepped out of the kitchen to walk them to their table where her parents were waiting for them. He asked how they were before he returned to the kitchen.

"I'm sorry. The traffic was crazy," Alex said as her father got out of his chair and pulled out hers. "Thanks, Dad."

Evan sat down next to her, and she could see his hands shake. She understood why he was nervous because she was, too. "Mrs. Parker, you look lovely this evening."

Her mother smiled. "Thank you, Evan."

"Mr. Parker, how was work?"

Hearing the tightness in his voice, Alex grasped his hand under the table and squeezed it in reassurance.

"Hectic," her father replied with a sigh as he reached over and picked up his glass of wine. He took a sip before he set it back down and smiled. "But that's only because my boss wants everything done so I can concentrate on the management issues in Hong Kong. It's been twenty years since I helped expand that office, and there's still problems."

"It's because Danford left when Gregson was still partner," her mother said.

"Yeah, Gregson treated my best manager like crap. Thank God Mercer owns the entire company now. All right, enough about work. How's the summer training going, Evan?"

Evan released her hand and cleared his throat. "Good. Kyle insisted I train with the Red Sox batting coaches, so I've also been training with him. He's the best pitcher in the Major League, so it only makes sense that I practice my batting against him."

"That's great. You had an unbelievable season. You could

221

go pro," her father pointed out.

Alex glanced over to discover Evan's tense posture. He was almost still. "Dad, Evan's just about to start his junior year."

Her father nodded. "Right. But Kyle was a first-round selection after his senior year of high school. There's no reason Evan can't be drafted, too. He's just as good."

"Mr. Parker." Evan turned his face, and she saw the pleading in his eyes. He didn't want to tell her father that he didn't want to go pro in the MBL after he graduated from college. And she was sure that her father didn't want to hear that right before they told him they were together. So Alex nodded at the silent pleading.

It's now or never.

"Dad," Alex said, getting his attention. "Mum."

Their eyes focused on her, and she saw the fear on their faces. The same fear she felt. "Yes, Alexandra?" her mother said.

Alex took a deep breath and looked over to see the anxiety written all over Evan's face. He was expecting the worst reaction from her parents. Alex knew that they might not be too pleased, but they would accept them. It might take some time, but she knew her parents would come around. They loved her, and they loved Evan.

She reached out and grasped Evan's hand, and said, "Evan and I are together."

"*Together?*" Her father's voice held no emotion to it, and she felt Evan wince.

"Yes, sir. I'm in love with your daughter," Evan replied.

Her father nodded, but it didn't feel reassuring. "When?"

"Dad, it doesn't—"

"When, Alexandra?" he demanded in a raised voice.

222

Alex winced. "When what, Dad? Because that question is very vague."

"When did you get together?"

"I flew out to Duke just before summer started," Evan answered.

Her mother smiled. "So not when Alexandra was with Landon?"

Alex understood her parents' concern, but how she and Evan ended up together wasn't wrong. She and her ex-boyfriend had been over. "No, Mum. Not when I was with Landon. I hadn't even seen Evan for months until I came home after the breakup. And before you even rush into more questions, we didn't start anything until Landon graduated and left for Phoenix. And we didn't become a couple until this summer. I know we shouldn't have kept it from you, but we wanted to be sure. We didn't want to get your hopes up if it ended in disaster. We just wanted to be sure."

"I understand, Alexandra," her mother said.

"I swear, Mr. and Mrs. Parker, I wouldn't have gone after your daughter if she was still in love with him or was with him. That's why I stayed away for so long."

Her father seemed to ignore what Evan had said and looked at her. She saw the disappointment flare in his green eyes as he asked, "Do you love him, Alexandra?"

"I do, Dad. I'm in love with him," she declared, not taking her eyes from her father. "We want your approval."

"No," her father said before he stood. "Excuse me."

"Nolan!" her mother shouted as Alex's father left their table.

Alex sat there in shock, not believing what just happened. For the first time in her life, she didn't have her father's approval. She was so sure that her father would approve. He had helped raise Evan. "Oh, my God," she whispered.

"I'll go talk to him," Evan said, but Alex shook her head.

She pulled her hand away from her boyfriend's and stood. "I'll go. Mum, if you feel the same way as Dad does, I'm sorry to disappoint you. I'm in love with Evan, and I'm not going to stop. You've known for years how much I love him."

Her mother's brown eyes gleamed with unshed tears. "I know, my love. I approve of your relationship. Honestly, I've known about you two all summer. But you're your father's little girl, Alexandra. His *only* little girl. When it's someone like Evan, he's just scared to see you get hurt."

"I won't hurt Alexandra," Evan promised.

"I know you won't, Evan, but you're not a father. You don't quite understand how much my husband feels. He takes our daughter's pain, sadness, and heartbreak personally. Alexandra, go after your father. Just know that deep down he loves you, both of you. He'll come around. I'll keep Evan company."

"Wait, AJ," Evan said as he got out of his chair. He reached for his coat hanging on his chair and covered her shoulders with it. "You left yours in the car, remember? It's cool outside."

She smiled. "Thank you. I won't be too long." Then she reached up and pressed her palm to her necklace that was under his shirt. "Nothing changes, okay?"

He nodded and then pressed a kiss to her hair. "Nothing changes."

Alex then stepped away from the table, smiling at some of her mother's staff as she walked to the front of the restaurant and pushed the door open once she reached it. Stepping onto the sidewalk, she turned to find her father standing by the windows, staring at the French restaurant across the street. She brushed her hair behind her ear and made her way toward him.

"I remember the day we were at the Smithsonian," her father said once she reached him. "You held my hand as you listened to that MIT professor talk about physics. I had no idea what he was saying, but I looked down to find you with wide eyes, staring at him as if he spoke of the universe's secrets to you. That little girl is the pride of my life."

"And what about the girl who told you she finally ended up with the boy she's loved her entire life? Is she still the pride of your life?" she asked in a tight voice, her heart clenching, terrified her father would say no.

Her father faced her, the sorrow bright in his green eyes. "Yeah," he breathed. "She still is, and she always will be."

"Then why don't you approve? Do you know how guilty Evan feels? I know we kept it from you, but that was all me because I was scared. I was scared of how I felt. I was scared that after years of wanting to be with him, I would be let down, but I was wrong. I was wrong to doubt what I felt. And I was wrong to be scared because I'm not anymore, Dad. I feel free."

"Did you not feel free with Landon?"

Alex shook her head, hating that her ex-boyfriend entered their conversation. "Not completely. Not when it came time to choosing. Do you not approve of Evan because you thought Landon was it for me?"

"No," he said strongly. "I had hopes that Landon would treat you right and better, but I always knew you still loved Evan. You're just … young, Alexandra."

She let out an unbelievable laugh. *"Young?* Dad, I'm twenty. Mum was my age when she married you. She left Australia to come here to be with you."

"Exactly! You're too young."

And then it hit her. He was scared to let her go. "Dad, I am not marrying Evan, okay? I'm *dating* him. I am not moving to California to be with him, either. If you had just stayed and not freaked out, you'd know our plan. We're going to do this long distance. I'm returning to Duke, and he's going back to Stanford at the end of summer. I love Duke. And no, it's not MIT, but it's so much better because I have Sav and all my friends. I can't leave them. I love Evan, but I don't belong at Stanford. I never did. So I'll visit him when I can, and he'll visit me when he can. Then when it's break, we'll come home and spend time here in Massachusetts. We'll make it work. I'm so committed to making this work. I love him, Dad, and I know he loves me."

"I just ..." He sighed. "I raised Evan. And each time he broke your heart or made you cry, he hurt me and your mother. I know you've said it's not his fault and that he never knew, but I kept questioning the kind of man he'd be. The kind of man I helped raise. I'm scared he'll hurt you again. I'm scared you'll give up more of your dreams to make him happy. As your father, don't I have a right to care about my daughter's happiness?"

Her heart clenched in her chest as she stepped forward and wrapped her arms around her father, holding him tight. After a long embrace, she stepped back, and said, "You have every right to care about my happiness. I'm happy, Dad. Whatever has happened with us in the past, that's on me and Evan. Never you. And if anything happens this time, it's not on you, Dad. It's *never* been on you."

"You raised me right, Mr. Parker," Evan said behind her, startling her and her father.

She spun around to find her boyfriend walking toward them. "I thought you were with my mum."

He smiled as he reached her. Once they faced her father, he threaded his fingers through hers, holding her hand. "She told me I should have my say while she went to the kitchen to give Danny and everyone a hand. So I'm here to have my say." He squeezed her hand and then swung his gaze to her father. "Mr. Parker, you raised me right. My actions aren't a reflection of you. I made those mistakes on my own. I was young and took Alexandra's love and heart for granted, but I'm not that guy anymore. I will never, ever hurt your daughter like that again. I know you don't approve, and I shouldn't be surprised. Alexandra is your only daughter, so I can understand why you wouldn't want her dating someone like me—someone who made her shed tears and broke her heart and trust. But besides all of that, you know me.

"You've raised me. You know that I am the only person who would ever love and understand your daughter and her dreams. That I am the only person who understands why she loves science. The only person who understands why she can't breathe in Boston. I'm the only person she has ever truly opened her heart to. I am the only person who was able to bring her real self back. I'll do right by her. I promise, I'll be that guy. I love Alexandra. And I regret not realizing that earlier, but I can't change that. I can only embrace my love for her and prove to you, every single day, that I am worthy of her love."

Her father's jaw tensed. Then he sighed, his shoulders sagging. "If you mean everything you say, then I have some questions."

"Of course," Evan said.

"You won't put pressure on my daughter to come to Stanford?"

Evan shook his head. "Like I told Alexandra, only when she can."

"You won't let my daughter give up on MIT?"

"No. Her dreams are my dreams. So my dreams are for her to go to MIT. For her to be everything she wants and needs in life. And I'm not giving up until I live and experience her dreams with her."

A smile finally spread across her father's face. "You will go to Duke to see her. There are no ifs or buts, Evan."

Evan let out a soft laugh. "I already have plans to see her at Duke."

"You will make my daughter happy?"

"It's my life's purpose."

Her heart threw itself against her chest as she glanced up at him. She knew from the seriousness on his face that he meant it. That he was sure of it.

"You won't ever hurt my daughter again." It was an order rather than a question.

"Mr. Parker, months ago I told you the reason I hurt your daughter. I was trying to protect her. I know I did it wrong, and then she fell in love with someone else. The pain of someone else hurting her is a hurt that I never want to experience again. And to know that I have hurt her worse than that makes me sick. I won't ever hurt Alexandra."

"And you love my daughter?"

"Entirely."

Her father nodded. He inhaled a deep breath before saying, "I approve of you dating my daughter. And I apologize for how I reacted in there. You have to understand that I'm her father, and she's my entire world. So when Alexandra told me you two were together, I saw flashbacks of my little girl crying, and that had me saying no. But I know you, Evan, and you're not that guy anymore. But I swear to God, I will never let you see her again if you repeat yourself. You might have my daughter's heart, but I'm her father. I will *always* be her father. So long as you treat my daughter right, love her completely, encourage her, and support her, I approve of you and my daughter being together."

Alex released Evan's hand, stepped forward, and hugged her father. "Thank you," she said into his chest as he cupped the back of her head, holding her. She felt like a small child again in his safe and loving embrace. She felt like no one could ever hurt her when her father held her. "I love you, Dad."

Her father pulled her back and smiled down at her. "And I love you, Alexandra. I always will. So long as you're happy, and he makes you happy, then you have my approval. Now, come on. Let's go celebrate that you two have finally found your way before your mother decides she wants to work in that kitchen for the rest of the dinner service." Her father stepped around her, and Alex spun to see him shaking Evan's hand. "I'm proud of you, Evan, for standing up to me and for standing up for her. And for finally becoming the man I knew you could always be. I'll see you both inside."

When her father returned to the restaurant, Alex grasped Evan's arm and turned him to face her. "You meant all that?" she asked. Her heart was close to exploding from the warmth and love that filled her chest.

"Every word."

Her hands trailed up his arms and settled on the nape of his neck. "You have my father's approval."

He nodded. "That doesn't mean I give up on proving to him, your mother, and you that I love you. I'll continue to do that."

"I love you, Evan Gilmore," she announced.

Her boyfriend's eyes swept around them. "We're in the middle of Boston."

She smiled. "It's about time Boston found out which Gilmore brother I was and am truly in love with," she said, and then she kissed him.

⁸⁸ Ra

radium

ALEX

Now

I love you, AJ.

Alex repeated his words in her head as she watched him continue to stare at the sonogram of their baby. It was a picture from her six-week scan. She had the one from the scan a few days ago, but she would show him that later. She wanted to show him the very first image she saw of their child. Their Little Atom had grown in almost three weeks. According to her doctor, Alex was on track to give birth in early September, which meant her spot at MIT was not looking so secure. But she'd handle that hurdle when she saw the dean of admissions. But make no mistake, Alex would give up her Ph.D. for her child.

It was that simple.

As much as her heart soared that he still loved her, his love came with doubt, and she wondered the truth of it. He might only love her because she was carrying his child, so she wouldn't let her heart hope for more. It was too risky. She couldn't risk her baby losing its father because she was stupid enough to think they could be together again. Alex had to be smarter than that. He had broken up with her, and he was happier without her. She couldn't just jump back into a relationship with Evan Gilmore. For now, she was content

233

with knowing that her baby had two parents who would love him or her with all their hearts. That was what Alex wanted the most. Her heart could remain bloody, scarred, and torn, but her baby deserved the very best and that meant having a loving father.

A long time ago, she had dreamed of being married to Evan and having his children. Now, she had half that dream. Being with Evan was a dream she couldn't have. Not if it could harm her baby's relationship with him. So for the first time in almost four years, her love for him would find itself in an unrequited state once more.

She was back where they started.

Back to unrequited.

And she would have to find a way to be satisfied with her life being that way. Now that Evan wanted to be a part of their baby's life, he deserved more than just a photo. He had every right to be a part of the pregnancy. Disregarding the memory of his lips on hers for the first time in two months, Alex pulled away the blanket and got out of bed. She made her way to her desk, opened the drawer, and pulled out the DVD. Once she closed the drawer, she picked up her laptop and returned to her bed. She sat down and leaned back against the headboard as Evan gazed up from the sonogram. Alex set the laptop on her thighs, lifted the screen, and logged in.

"I have something I want to show you, if you'd like," she said as she opened the DVD case and popped out the disc.

"What is it?" Evan asked, scooting closer to her.

The feel of his body touching hers caused her heart to make those crazy, needy beats. The same beats it made two months ago when he asked her to stay.

Alex cleared her throat and stretched her lips into a smile as she pushed the DVD into the drive. "I had an ultrasound a few days ago, and it's recorded on this DVD. Do you want to hear our baby's heartbeat?"

"I want to hear *our* baby's heartbeat."

Reaching over, she opened her nightstand drawer and pulled out her earbuds. She plugged it into the side of her laptop and handed them to him. "You don't want to hear?" he asked.

"I've already heard it."

Evan handed her one earbud. "Listen with me."

"Evan, you should—"

He shook his head. "I want to hear my baby's heartbeat with the woman who's carrying him or her."

My baby's heartbeat.

God, it sounds so good hearing him claiming our baby.

Alex put in the earbud just as Evan did, and then she pressed play on the menu and watched as his eyes fixated on the screen. Watched as his eyes widened when the beats of their baby's heart boomed. Watched as his lips parted in awe. When he turned and set his palm on her stomach, Alex winced at his touch, overwhelmed by tears. She hadn't meant to be this emotional, but she was. He was touching her stomach as if the ultrasound was live.

When he reached over and paused the DVD, Alex pulled the earbud from her ear. Evan Gilmore had never been more beautiful than at this moment. His eyes were soft with a beautiful gleam to them thanks to his unshed tears. The awe on his face made her breathless. He pulled his earbud from his ear and faced her. His palm softly returned to her stomach.

"That was the most beautiful sound I have ever heard in my life, Alexandra."

"I agree," she said as she used her hand on her pillow to lift herself up, then press a kiss on his temple. His hand slipped away from her stomach. "You can listen to it again if you'd like while I take a shower."

"You don't mind?"

Alex picked up the earbuds and set them in his palm before she set the laptop on the bed. "Not at all. I listened to it all night after I got home. You can keep this copy. It's yours." She got off the bed and smiled at him, relieved that he loved and was awed by their baby. "Would you like to stay for breakfast? I'm sure my mother won't mind."

Evan smiled at her, his eyes still holding that glint. "She already asked. I said yes."

"Okay. I won't be long," Alex said before she made her way to her bathroom. When she reached the door, she glanced over to find Evan straightening his legs and setting her laptop on his thighs. He put in her earbuds and pressed play on her laptop. She smiled, loving that he wanted to listen to their baby's heartbeats again.

But then Evan Gilmore did something unexpected—an act that tore her heart to shreds—because it made her fall in love with him all over again. He reached over, picked up her pregnancy book she had been reading, opened it, and began to read. Alex stood there for a moment and watched him, completely captivated by him.

She still loved him.

And as she stood there, pressing her palm to her stomach, Evan glanced over at her and smiled. They might not be together, but she knew he would make an amazing father. *I'm sure of it.*

After breakfast, Alex and Evan spent time with her family. Lori and Reese caught Evan up on school, and the two sisters fought for his attention. And true to Evan's good nature, he sat and listened to Granddad Marcus and Grandpa James discuss Australian Rules Football. Grandma Louise had put an end to Alex's grandfathers' argument on which team was better. According to Grandma Louise, it was not an appropriate conversation topic if it meant Alex's cousins were exposed to family bickering. After Aunt Stevie, Uncle Julian, and Uncle Rob came over, Alex and Evan said their hellos, then went to his house.

Evan had tried to argue with her, but she told him that a promise was a promise, and even though it would hurt her, she would help him pack up the rest of his house for his move. *Los Angeles.* The elephant in the room. The elephant she was too scared to discuss.

After she had showered and dressed, she joined Evan on her bed and thought about how they'd work. He hadn't said anything about staying in Massachusetts, and she knew it wasn't fair for her to ask him to. Alex knew that she would more than likely have to move to California. She decided that once she helped Evan pack all his belongings, she would go home and search for apartments close to LA.

She probably couldn't afford to live in the city, but she'd

try her best to find something appropriate since there was no way she'd find a job with benefits. She had enough money for rent for a little while and enough to buy some of the things she would need for their baby, but she knew she'd have to access her trust funds sooner than she would have liked. There was enough to pay for their child's future, but she didn't want to use too much of it.

Alex did have one job prospect, and that was tutoring. She had her science degree from graduating at the top of her class at Duke. She could tutor high school and college students in all the major science and math fields. It wouldn't be the most lucrative job, but it would be income. Once she found an apartment and was settled, she'd run ads and get in touch with people she knew. Some might judge her fall from grace, but she was about to become a mother. Her pride had no say. She was happy to go from working at the best research institute in the world to tutoring students if it meant her baby's needs were met.

Alexandra Louise Parker had gone from MIT Ph.D. student to tutor. But at least she would still be using her knowledge and education. It was still a plan. And hopefully, she would have enough students sign up to tutor.

"I got more boxes," Evan said as he entered his bedroom.

Alex had been sitting on his bed when he went to the garage to grab more boxes. He had told her that most of the furniture had already been sold with some of it staying at his brother's request. Alex didn't like that he had sold the house, but there was no point in Evan keeping up its maintenance if he was moving to California. Alex smiled as she got off his bed and took the flat box from him.

"Is it just your room that needs packing?" Alex asked as she began to build the box. Once he built the one he was working on, he traded, giving her the already constructed box and taking hers.

"Yeah," he said as he constructed another box. "When you were sick the day of the gala, I got everything mostly packed. Are you sure you're feeling okay to help? I can do it on my own, AJ."

"You don't have to worry. I'm feeling okay today." Alex scanned his room. It was as if it were frozen in time. Other than his missing baseball jerseys and posters from the walls, it was still the same. "So where would you like to start?"

Evan frowned. "Umm, the closet?"

"Sure." Alex made her way to the closet, set her box down, and flicked the light switch. Evan joined her and set his box next to hers. "I don't know what you want to keep. Maybe you should decide, and I'll just pack?"

"That works for me. I'll pull down the boxes from the top shelves, and you can look at the ones on the bottom."

Alex stepped over the empty boxes, sat on the ground, and pulled a box to her. She lifted the flaps and peeked inside. They were all his old board games they used to play. She laughed at the memories of him beating her at almost every game they used to play.

"What's so funny?" he asked as he set down the box he pulled from the top shelf and sat next to her.

"They're all your board games. What do you want me to do with them?"

Evan hummed. "You can have them if you want."

"You want me to keep them? They're not baby appropriate games."

That had him laughing. "No, they're not. We'll make a not sure pile and decide later."

Nodding, Alex pushed her box to the side and reached over and grabbed another. She set it in front of her and opened it, her heart dipping when she noticed what box it was. Alex reached inside and pulled out *The Chronicle*, Duke's student newspaper. The paper did a highlight on her as a future physicist and she was on the front page with her professor. Evan kept it after all this time.

"AJ, you okay?"

"Yeah," she said in a small voice as she set the newspaper back inside. "It's all the newspapers and magazines I was in while I was at Duke. We'll throw—"

"No," he said, reaching over her and pulling the box from her.

"Why?"

Evan sighed. "I want to keep them."

She shook her head. "It's okay, Evan. My parents already have all of these."

"No, AJ. I want to keep them for our son or daughter to read someday. You were inspired by the achievements of physicists, and I want our child to someday look at those articles of you and be inspired by all your achievements."

She had no words as a tear slipped down her cheek, completely taken aback by his reason to keep all the newspapers and magazines. Alex reached up and brushed her tear away. "Okay," she finally said and cleared her throat, hating that got her so choked up. "What's in that box?"

Evan looked down, reached inside, and pulled out old pictures. Then he handed her a stack. "They're photos from our senior year of high school."

Alex laughed the moment she came across Hunter Jamison in the water dunking booth he volunteered to sit in for charity. She flipped to the next photo of Evan. It was his official high school baseball team picture. She showed it to him, and he rolled his eyes.

When she came across a picture of him at prom, a lump formed in her throat. It was of him and Addison. The date he chose over Alex. They were dancing, and they had smiles on their faces. Prom had been the night she thought Evan had chosen her. She had gotten a dress in New York and had her hair and makeup done so that she was the perfect date. But after he had taken pictures with her for her parents, he told her he was choosing Addison to please his coach. It was the night she realized that Evan would never see her as more. He had broken her heart that night, and she had chosen Duke instead of Stanford.

Alex continued to look through the stack and came across pictures from their senior homecoming. No one had asked her, so she didn't attend. But in the pictures, she saw that Evan had indeed lied to her—though, she asked him to. Homecoming looked amazing. And in the next picture, he was holding Addison in a sway. She wasn't sure why she suddenly felt so hurt, but she was. Alex hadn't meant to cry, but it was happening.

"AJ?" She lowered the pictures so that he could see. "*Oh.*"

All the pain she suffered came back to her. Every heartbreak he put her through made those tears fall. And what hurt the most was that she was packing away their memories.

If not in this box, there'd be ruminates of them in another.

They would be thrown out.

There would be nothing left of them.

"We never got a dance," she said in a small voice.

"No, we didn't." He sounded as sad as she felt.

Alex brushed her tears from her cheeks and looked at him. "We're never going to have a first dance," she realized out loud. "I'm never going to know what that's like with you."

Evan dropped his pictures in his box. "Alexandra ..."

"I can't do this," she revealed in a sob as she stood. "I can't pack up memories of us because I know that means we're done. I told you I'm pregnant, and you're moving on with your life. I don't know why I expected you to stay, but you're not going to, and it isn't fair to just come back into your life and expect you to drop everything for me and this baby. But please, I can't do this. I can't pack away pieces of our lives together because that hurts, Evan. It's torture. I'm sorry, but I can't do this." Then she stepped over her box and made her way out of his closet.

Before she could reach his bedroom door, Evan raced after her, gripped her hand, and caused her to come to a stop. "AJ, please."

Letting out a strangled breath, she spun around. "How do we do this? Do I move to LA to make this work? Is that what you want? Because I can do that." Tears streamed down her face. "But then I'm just the mother of your child who followed you so that our child can be part of your life."

"I love you," he whispered.

Alex's bottom lip trembled as her heart clenched at the sorrow in his eyes. The truth gleamed in them, giving her the answer. "But just as the mother of your child, right? I need you to figure out what that I love you means now. If you're saying it because I told you I'm pregnant with your child or if it's because you still truly love me. I won't be mad if you say it's because I'm the mother of your child. I just need to know so I know my place in your heart and in your life. If you've met someone, love someone, that's okay, too."

His eyes widened in disbelief. "Met someone?"

She nodded. "At the gala. If you love her, that's okay."

"I don't love her. I barely know her. She's from the MLB, a new executive who is visiting some of the teams. I had to be nice to her." He exhaled a heavy breath. Relief filled her lungs and chest at the revelation of who that woman at the gala was. But it didn't rid her of the anxiety that whispered her deepest fears. "I-I love you..."

"You hesitated," she stated, her heart weeping. "You've never once hesitated to tell me you love me. You used to say, 'Eight protons. Eight neutrons.'" She forced the smile on her lips and wiped her tears away. "I'll start searching for places near LA. Just let me know where you're moving to, and I'll find a place that's not too close. I'll have Dr. Livingston recommend some doctors. I'm sorry I can't help you pack. I just can't, Evan."

Alex spun around, twisted the doorknob, and opened the door. As she walked out of his bedroom, she left behind her heart as her tears continued to roll. She didn't want to move to California, but she had to. For him and the baby. When she made it to the stairs, she heard Evan rush out of his room.

"Alexandra!" he shouted, causing her to stop. "And how do you love me? As the father of your child or ...?"

She didn't hesitate.

What she felt was true.

It had always been true.

"I love you. You're the love of my life, Evan Gilmore. Always have been. Always will be. I'll bring your copy of the heartbeat you left in my room over later tonight."

And that was all that was needed to be said.

It was all she could manage to say as she made her way downstairs and out of his house. When she shut the door behind her, she shivered. The snow had picked up since this morning. Folding her arms over her chest for warmth, she felt her phone vibrate in her pocket. Alex walked down the steps and pulled it out of her pocket as she made her way toward her parents' house.

Tonight, she had to do some research. If she could find an apartment that was cheap, she'd have one of her father's connections at the LA office check it out for her. When she made it to her front door, she unlocked her phone to find a new text message. Guilt ran hot through her heart as she read his name.

Landon: Hey, Massachusetts. I'll be in Boston tomorrow afternoon. I'll see you then?

Oh, no.

She clenched her eyes shut for a moment before she replied. In England, he reminded her of how true his love for her had once been. But his love wasn't the one she had desperately wished to speak volumes by a staircase. Alex was stupid for wanting declarations from Evan. She knew she should have protected her heart better. Kept her lips tightly shut and saved herself from the brutality.

It was just a dinner that gave Landon too much hope and

left her with so much guilt.

She wished Dr. Rodahawe hadn't insisted she accompanied him to England.

She should have known better.

Alex: Tomorrow is perfect. I'll see you then.

At 10:37 a.m., Alex stood outside The Polion restaurant. She thought about meeting her ex-boyfriend at her mother's restaurant, but there was no way she could hide that she was having breakfast with Landon Carmichael from Evan or her mother. The restaurant that specialized in home cooking had been ranked the second-best restaurant in Boston for the past few years—behind The Little Restaurant in Boston. Her mother even knew and was friends with the head chef. But for what she was about to do, she needed privacy away from anyone connected to her.

She had meant to meet Landon seven minutes ago, but she hesitated. Alex had stood outside of the restaurant and felt sick. It wasn't morning sickness that made her want to throw up. It was facing the mistake she had made three months ago. The mistake that wouldn't leave her. And that was giving Landon Carmichael hope. Hope that there was a chance at a future.

Taking a deep breath, she knew she couldn't delay it any longer. She had to see him. Tell him that they weren't possible. Not now or ever. Alex released the breath she had inhaled and walked toward the restaurant's front door. Once she grasped the handle, she pulled it open and stepped inside, feeling the warmth the winter conditions outside had neglected her of. She shook her head of any snowflakes and made her way to the podium.

"Hello, Alex," the waitress greeted.

Alex shouldn't be so surprised, but she was. Throughout college and her time in Switzerland, she forgot what it was like to live in a city where everyone knew her name. Her return and appearance at the gala the other night had already hit the magazines. Reports claimed she returned home just when the Red Sox needed her the most.

But she wasn't home for them or to assume her former title of Little Miss Red Sox.

She was only home for Evan Gilmore.

Yesterday, she walked out of his old house in tears, realizing that his love for her wasn't the love she had once known. For the very first time since their first I love you to each other, Evan Gilmore had hesitated.

His I love you didn't feel right anymore.

Alex saw it in his eyes.

The fear.

He didn't love her the way he used to. He loved her as the mother of his child. It should be more than enough, considering he had left her six months ago, but it wasn't. She still loved him. Still hoped and waited for him. But it wasn't about her or her heart anymore.

It had to be about their baby.

"Alex?"

She blinked, realizing that she had been quiet for too long. "I, umm, sorry. Hi. I have a table."

The waitress smiled and nodded as she stepped away from

the podium. "Your guest is already at your table. As requested, we've sat you both toward the back of the restaurant and away from the windows."

"Thank you. I appreciate that a lot," Alex said as she followed the waitress through the restaurant and toward the back.

Alex kept her head down, hoping that no one noticed her. The last thing she needed was to be photographed with Landon. She only now wondered why she didn't just go to his hotel. Or better yet, why she didn't just go to New York to see him. In New York, she could get lost. Her name was only known to Yankees fans there.

When Alex reached the table, she noticed Landon staring at his phone. She couldn't believe it had been three months since she last saw him. Before that, she hadn't seen him in years.

"Here we are. I'll let you both have some time together, and I'll grab you some water," the waitress said as Alex sat across from Landon.

When they were alone, Landon smiled at her as he placed his phone on the table. "Hey, Massachusetts."

His nickname for her was still said with so much adoration. So much sweetness and warmth.

"Hey, Landon," she replied, not wanting to say Connecticut for fear that it might bring up old feelings and memories she didn't want to revisit.

"How are you?"

Small talk. She could do small talk.

Suddenly feeling warm, Alex reached for the button on her coat and popped it free. She continued to unbutton until she could pull her coat from her and hang it behind her chair.

"I'm good. Just settling back to life here in the States."

"How was Zürich?" he asked, his phone lighting up. He picked it up and then turned it over so that it was face down on the table. "Sorry."

Alex shook her head. "Don't be. Zürich was amazing. I miss my apartment, my work desk, the institute, and everyone, but I have missed home more. How are you? How's the Hot Spurs?"

He grinned. It had been over a year since he transferred from the Phoenix Suns to the Hot Spurs. It was his dream team. They had reportedly paid millions to have him on their team. He had exceeded expectations when he became the number one draft pick. "I'm doing great. Better now that I get to see you. You're even more beautiful than the last time I sat in front of you."

"Landon," she breathed, hating how her stupid heart clenched at the sweet memories of them. The memories that snuck up on her.

Her ex-boyfriend reached out and covered her hand with his. "I still love you. I can make it work."

She shook her head. "Landon—"

"Excuse me, are you Landon Carmichael?"

Alex flinched and pulled her hand away, hating the flash of hurt in his light blue eyes. But he hid it well as he spread his lips and turned to their interrupter. It was a woman, holding a pen and a napkin.

"That's me. Hi," he confirmed.

"My boyfriend and I are big fans. I can't believe you're here in Boston. Can I get your autograph and a picture? He'll never believe I met you. We were at the Lakers game last season, and he was just blown away," the fan said.

Landon smiled as he took the napkin from her. "What's your name and your boyfriend's name?"

"I'm Britt. My boyfriend's name is Johnny."

Alex watched as Landon nodded and scribbled out two different names, a message, and signed the napkin. "There you go."

"Can we take a photo together?"

Landon hesitated as he glanced over at her, but Alex offered a reassuring smile. She was happy to wait. This was his life now. He was living his dream right before her.

"Sure thing, Britt," Landon agreed.

Him saying her name had the fan's cheeks turning bright pink. "Oh my, God," she breathed in awe as she held out her phone to Alex. "Do you mind?"

Alex shook her head as she took the phone from her. "Not at all." Then she got out of her chair just as Landon had. As he stood next to the fan and wrapped an arm around her, Alex held the phone steady. "One. Two. Three."

Then she took the photo and another two to be sure before she handed it back to her.

"Thank you so much," Britt said as she looked at her phone. When it appeared she was happy, she lifted her chin and smiled. Then Alex saw it, curiosity and recognition in her brown eyes. "I know you ... Aren't you famous? I swear, I've seen you in a modeling spread or something."

Alex shook her head, slightly relieved that she didn't recognize her as Little Miss Red Sox. Her Texan accent was enough for Alex to relax. "I'm neither."

Her nose crinkled. "I know you. I swear, I do."

She glanced over at Landon and eyed him for help.

"Sorry, Britt. It was lovely to meet you. Hope you don't mind if we get back to our table. Tell Johnny I said hi," Landon said, coming to her rescue.

The fan mumbled something, but Alex had already sat back down in her chair, still reeling at the idea of being discovered at a restaurant with her ex-boyfriend.

"I'm so sorry about that, Alex," Landon expressed with so much sorrow that she shook her head at him.

"It's okay," she reassured. "I was scared she'd figure out who I was. I'm not used to it all just yet. I guess my anonymity while at college and in Zürich spoiled me."

Landon's brows pulled as his lips pressed a fine line. "You're scared they'll see us together?"

Her pulse quickened.

The air in her lungs thinned.

The collision would soon find them.

Alex nodded. "I am," she said honestly. "For almost four years, I was no longer in the tabloids about the Red Sox. I was no longer Little Miss Red Sox. For the past year and a half, I've been in science magazines and papers because I got to work with Dr. Rodahawe. I don't miss my old life in the spotlight, Landon. I'd rather never be in it ever again."

"I understand." Then he sighed. "It's probably why you were more comfortable with me in England than right now."

She inhaled a deep breath, releasing it slowly to calm her nerves. But it didn't work. She knew what she had to say wasn't easy, but she had to. For his sake and hers. "Landon, that's what I want to talk to you about."

His hand covered hers in an instant. The features of his face were taut with concern, and those light blue eyes pierced into her, heat consuming her chest. "Okay."

"Landon, I can't," she answered the question she had thought about for the past three months. "I can't be with you."

His face was emotionless. His posture was tight. "You ... *can't?*"

Alex shook her head as she pulled her hand free from his. "Landon, I'm sorry. I shouldn't have let you leave with the impression that there could be hope for us. We ended in college. You were the one who ended us."

"Alex," he choked out. "I was a dumb college kid. I was so stupid. I've grown since then. I know who my true friends are and who truly loved me. You were both. You're still both."

"I can't be both, Landon," she said more firmly, hating that she put them in this situation. "You're everything I can't have or want or need or love. Not anymore. Maybe back in college if you had said it all when we were ending in my dorm room. But no. You let me go to Boston after we broke up. You said you were sorry and left. I came back and forgave you, and we almost had unprotected sex without you telling me you had almost been with someone else. Nothing in our lives meet. England was ..." She sighed. "An anomaly. We shouldn't have been there at the same time. We can't be together. We're so different but still in the same situation. Your dreams don't complement mine."

"What is so bad about having someone who is a professional athlete love you, Alex? Huh? What is so bad about me loving you? Taking care of you? What is so bad about you loving me?"

Her heart ached at the way his voice broke. She couldn't do this any longer. "Everything, Landon. Because I'm not your soul mate. I was just some girl in college who brushed you off at a frat party during her freshman year. We had it right for so long until it wasn't anymore."

"You're not making any sense."

Alex eyes closed, knowing what she had to do. What she had to say. When she opened her eyes, she stared into those desperate light blues and knew what she had to say would break his heart, but it was what he needed. What they both needed. Their futures were never in sync—except for their time at Duke.

"Landon."

"Yes, Alex."

Inhale.

Exhale.

Count to three.

One.

Two.

Three.

"I'm pregnant."

Her ex-boyfriend's lip trembled as shock filled his wide eyes. "Is it ... *his*?" He gulped. "It is his?"

Alex dropped her hand and pressed it to her stomach. "Is it Evan Gilmore's baby?"

He nodded, the agony on his face caused her heart to clench, hating that she was hurting him. She saw how hard it was for him to accept that she was pregnant with another man's baby. The man who had her heart before she had even met Landon Carmichael.

"Evan's the father."

His eyes gleamed with unshed tears. It was as if he realized that there was no future for them. "Were you ... when we were in England?"

"No," she said. "I went back home a month a later. I'm sorry, Landon. But it's not fair to you, or him, or my child if we tried."

"Are you with him?"

To her surprise, a tear ran down her cheek as she shook her head. "No. We've been over for six months."

Landon's posture didn't relax as he licked his lips. "I can help."

Alex winced. "What? Help?"

"I can help you with your baby. If he isn't stepping up—"

"He is," she said, stopping his assumptions. "Evan's going to be the father of his child, Landon. I didn't want to see you so I could ask you to raise my child. Your mother and sister would freak out. You, the father of some other man's child? No. Even if Evan didn't, I wouldn't want that for you. I'd do it alone. But he is. I appreciate how much you care, but we'll raise our son or daughter in California and—"

"What?"

Crap.

She shouldn't have mentioned California.

"California?"

"Yeah. LA is next."

Disbelief was written all over his face. "No. *Here* is next. MIT is next. Alex, what are you doing?"

She sighed, hating that she understood why he was angry. She had made it clear throughout their relationship that her Ph.D. at MIT was the next stop in her life. "It had been. But my life has changed, Landon. It's not about me anymore.

253

I'm going to be a mother. And I can't stay in Boston when he's going to be in LA. I'm not going to be with him. I know we're over. Part of me still wishes we weren't, but it's been six months, and just because I'm pregnant doesn't mean we're right for each other anymore. I'm moving for my child."

"You don't belong in LA, Alex. You belong here. You belong at MIT."

Her heart fluttered at his belief in her, but she knew it was only temporary. "MIT was a dream. Things change. I'm going to be a mum first and a physicist second. That means I go where I need to go. And Caltech is a great school."

Landon stared at her. His silence was deafening. Then she saw the flash in his eyes, and she wondered what was going through his thoughts. He reached over and grasped her hand in his hands. His eyes softened as he let out a breath. "I understand, Alex. I can see it in your eyes that you will never love me the way you love him. I'm sure you did once … until I destroyed that. If you ever need a friend, and I mean friend, I'll be here for you."

"Thank you," she said with a smile. Because she believed him. She believed that he understood her decisions. "And I'm sorry if you came to Boston expecting more with me. I just don't love you like I used to and never the way I love him."

He nodded, the pain remaining etched on his face. "I'll never stop being grateful to have loved you, too, Alex. And though I hate that you're giving up on MIT, I do understand why. You'll make an amazing mother, Massachusetts."

At that moment, Alex knew she had no more skeletons.

No more shame.

She had finally settled all the bridges that led to Landon

Carmichael.

89
Ac
actinium

ALEX

Junior year of college

The excitement that ran through Alex was incredible. For the remaining weeks of summer, she spent every single second with Evan. She had been worried her father would change his mind about his approval of their relationship, but he seemed to be okay. She had even caught him smiling at them at the dinner table when her mother had cooked Evan his favorite meal, the famous Parker family lasagna. It felt like old times—when Evan was welcomed in her family home as if he lived there.

Her parents treated him as if nothing had changed between them at all. She was sure it was uncomfortable to watch Evan kiss her the first time. They were at the front door after they had spent the day in Rhode Island. He was kissing her goodbye when her parents opened the front door and caught them. It had been awkward for everyone, but they kept their displays of affection private—mainly at his house and in the bedroom. They had kissed outside of her mother's restaurant after they told her parents about their relationship, but decided that since no one spotted them, they would remain private. Their relationship was still theirs and no one else's to mess with. They were safe from Boston having any judgment of them and being in the magazines. They protected their relationship with their secrecy.

Now they were back in Durham walking toward the apartment her parents were renting for her and Savannah. She had flown out of Boston early this morning with Evan, and they planned to spend a few days setting up her new apartment. Her roommate and best friend, Savannah Peters, would be driving to North Carolina from Vermont tomorrow, giving Alex and Evan the day together. The only time they could ever be together was when her parents were at work. And to avoid any accidental walk-ins, they ensured that anything physical stayed in his bedroom and not hers. But they had a day to be lost in each other and not have to rush to get to dressed and pretend as if they weren't together.

"Do you want to be the one to open the door to your apartment for the first time?" her boyfriend asked once they reached 6A of the Infinity Warehouse Apartments.

Alex stopped next to him and smiled. She reached into her purse and pulled out her key. Her parents had surprised her with the three-bedroom apartment, and they were allowing Savannah to live with her almost rent-free. The only condition they had for her best friend was that if Savannah wanted to pay rent, she paid whatever she could afford and concentrated on school. Savannah countered the offer by adding that she had to drive Alex to campus and pick up all their belongings from storage tomorrow.

Evan rolled her suitcase away from the door, giving her room to insert her key. With a smile, she twisted it and heard the door unlock. Alex pushed the door open and glanced over at her boyfriend.

He had a large smile on his face. "You should go in first."

"Okay," she said. She removed the key and took a large step inside, greeted by the short hallway and the sight of the living room ahead of her. Then she spun around and grinned at Evan. "Oh, my God. I'm standing in my very first apartment."

Evan reached over and grasped the handle of her suitcase, wheeling both of their luggage inside and leaving them by the wall. He took in the brightly lit apartment. "Wow, your parents did well."

Alex nodded. "One of my dad's clients makes frequent trips to Durham. So when he heard that Dad was looking for an apartment for me and Sav, his client did some scouting and found this place. It's a five-minute drive to Duke, and it's close to everything I could possibly need. He made sure a new fridge, washer, dryer, and the TVs were installed."

"He did?" he asked once he closed the door.

She closed the distance and grabbed her boyfriend's hand, saying, "He did," as she led him down the hall and to the open plan living room and kitchen. "Wow."

"Your dad's client obviously appreciates your father doing his accounting because holy shit, AJ, this view!"

Letting go of Evan's hand, she walked to the kitchen counter and set her key and purse on the marble top before she headed to the large floor-to-ceiling windows to take in the view from her apartment. She could see Duke from where she stood. "I don't want curtains."

"I wouldn't either," Evan agreed as he stood next to her.

"This is so crazy," she admitted as she shifted to face him. "Summer ended so quickly, and now we're here. In two days, we fly to California and then we have two days at Stanford before I have to come back here."

"I know," he said in a small voice.

"I don't feel like we had enough time."

Evan stepped closer, capturing her cheeks with his palms. "I didn't think I would even get to have the summer with you. We'll make it work, okay?"

She nodded. "This is the only time I wish I was at Stanford rather than Duke."

"Other way around, AJ. I wish I was going to Duke." Then he ducked his head and pressed his lips to hers, kissing her. His lips smooth and perfect against hers. He kissed her softly. He kissed her as if today was the very last day he'd see her. He kissed her as if he loved her.

Alex pulled away, afraid that they were skipping a conversation they should really be having. "No repeats, okay? No repeats of everything we got wrong before I came home. We have to talk. We have to be honest with each other. We have to see each other."

"I already have a plane ticket to see you in three weeks," he revealed.

"Really?" She was shocked.

Evan's thumb brushed against her bottom lip. "Really. I checked with my coach. We won't have preseason training yet."

Alex smiled as she grasped his shirt, whispered, "I love you so much," then pulled on his shirt so that his lips returned to hers.

This time, she kissed him with desire.

Her body hummed with need.

She ached to feel his touch.

"AJ," he muttered into her mouth as her hands released his

shirt and her arms wound around his neck, pressing herself to him, feeling his hardness against her stomach.

"Please," she moaned softly. "Please, Evan."

He broke their kiss and glanced over her. "Which one's your room?"

Alex gazed over her shoulder and noticed that the bedroom doors were closed. "The master bedroom."

Evan bent his knees, his palms finding the back of her thighs, and lifted her so that her legs wrapped around his waist. "I assume it's this one," he said. He walked to the door on the right as Alex peppered his lips, cheek, and jaw with kisses.

When they reached the door, he whispered, "Hold on tight, baby," before one palm left her leg to open the door. Alex squeezed her thighs as he stepped inside, carrying her. She glanced over to her left to find her bed and a new mattress with its plastic still on. Evan set her down, and she turned to find that the view from her bed was stunning. Their corner apartment came with perks.

"A set of brand-new sheets are on that chair," Evan pointed out.

Alex glanced over to find him picking up a sheet set and tearing away the plastic seal. He pulled out the yellow sheet and walked over to her brand-new bed. Evan laid it down over the plastic covered mattress and then returned to her.

"Should we just make your bed now?"

She let out a laugh and then shook her head. "No way," she said as she grasped his hand and walked them toward her bed.

When the mattress hit the back of her knees, she stopped, and Evan said, "Sit down for me."

Alex did as instructed, her eyes never leaving his as she

lowered herself down, feeling the soft sheet against her skin. As Evan got on his knees, he pressed his lips against her neck, her breath hitching in her throat as his tongue traced unrecognizable patterns. Her pulse quickened as his palm settled on her bare knee. Unable to stop her fidgeting hands, she threaded her fingers through his hair, desperately needing to touch him.

"Alexandra," he whispered as his kisses moved to her collarbone and then to her cleavage exposed by the dip of her short-sleeve, V-neck summer floral dress.

"Please, Evan," she begged, his hand trailing up her thigh.

His hand left her leg and returned to unbuttoning her dress. He had managed to get three undone, revealing her black lace bra. Evan pushed the dress apart and tugged at her bra, exposing her naked breast to him. His thumb gently swiped across her nipple, hardening it. She ached so badly to have him. He leaned forward, his breath was a soft whisper against her skin before his tongue licked across her hardened bud.

A soft moan escaped her as she pressed her palm to the mattress, offering more of herself to him. Evan used one hand to pull on her bra while the other returned to her leg. Trailing up until his thumb brushed along the top of her lace covered core, he caused Alex to gasp.

"Evan, please, I need you." It was a plea. She should be embarrassed, but she wasn't. Her body was hot, needy for the release her beautiful boyfriend could give her.

"Unbutton the rest of your dress for me, baby," he ordered in a hoarse voice, his light brown eyes darkened with lust and desire.

Alex bit her lip as she reached down and unbuttoned the

remaining buttons, leaving her exposed in only her bra and panties. She was about to shove the dress off her shoulders when Evan shook his head.

His palm settled on her stomach as he said, "Lie back."

Once she did, she felt his breath on her core, causing Alex to widen her legs farther, her message clear.

She needed him to touch her.

To put her out of her misery.

And she knew he was torturing her. She sensed it as his thumb brushed along her mound, just missing where she ached to be touched the most.

She got on her elbows, looking down at her boyfriend between her legs. He had gone down on her many times this summer, but right now, it felt different. It was different because they were in no rush. They could savor the moment and get lost in their pleasure like they truly wanted to. His eyes met hers as his fingers dug into the sides of her panties. For a second, he didn't move as she panted. Then he watched as he pulled her underwear down her hips and along her legs until they reached her ankles. He yanked them off before he grasped her ankles and lifted her feet onto the mattress, spreading her so he could see her. All of her.

Evan scooted closer, his arms cradling her thighs as he leaned forward. She had expected him to continue his teasing game, but to her sheer relief, he ran his tongue along her wet slit, causing Alex to fall onto her back, consumed by the feel of his warm tongue on her.

He continued his soft, lazy licks.

Up and down, generating hot heat between her legs.

Alex reached down and grasped his head, angling her

hips a little higher to get more friction. Understanding what she really needed, Evan flattened his tongue on her clit and stroked, alternating between soft circles and licks.

"Oh, God, Evan," she cried as her pleasure built.

She felt her body tense.

Her chest heaved as she gulped for air.

He didn't let up as her hips bucked for more.

To reach the crescendo she knew Evan could give her.

"AJ," he murmured against her, the vibrations causing her to jerk with pleasure.

"Evan, please. Please, I'm so close," she begged. He pulled her clit between his lips and sucked, causing Alex to let out a moan. "Evan," she whimpered before she pressed her lips together to stifle her cries.

"That's it, baby."

His thumb now spun circles. As his tongue found her entrance, she could have sworn she heard a door close. Alex's froze, her hips off the bed as she tried to listen for more movement. Evan was too lost in giving her pleasure that he continued his tongue's stroke on her. When she didn't hear anything, she turned her head away from the door and concentrated on her boyfriend.

He licked.

Nipped.

Softly bit.

And sucked.

His tongue thrust.

His tongue stroked.

On and on.

Hard and soft.

Close.

So close.

"Evan," she whispered her warning. "I'm going to—"

And just before she could finally explode into euphoria, her door swung open, and her roommate screamed, "Surprise— *Oh my, God!*"

Alex squealed as she covered her breasts with her dress, her impending orgasm dwindling as Evan stopped all movement to cover the lower half of her with the rest of her clothing.

"I am so sorry," Savannah mumbled as she scrambled out of Alex's bedroom.

Once the door clicked close, Alex covered her face with her palms, horrified that her roommate had caught her with a man between her legs.

And it wasn't just any man who was giving her pleasure.

It was Evan Gilmore.

To Savannah, he was Alex's best friend.

And best friends didn't have oral sex in the middle of the day.

Alex lowered her hands the moment she felt Evan sit on the bed next to her. "I can't believe that just happened," she said in horror and embarrassment as she sat up. Then she glanced over to see the amusement on his face. "It's not funny, Evan. That was definitely not how I wanted Sav to find out about us."

The humor faded from his face as he brushed his hair back. "How did she even get in? I thought she was coming tomorrow."

"You heard her. She yelled surprise. My parents must have sent her a key." Alex sighed. "I have to go talk to her. If we pretend it didn't happen, it'll be weird."

"Okay," Evan said as he got off the mattress and held out his hand. Alex set her palm in his as he helped her up from the bed.

Alex bent down, picked up her panties and slipped them on. She didn't bother with her ballet flats that had fallen on the floor as she buttoned up her dress. Once she ran her fingers through her hair, she made her way to the door and opened it. Alex stepped out to find her best friend in the kitchen, staring out the large windows.

Sheepishly, Alex approached the kitchen counter with a lot of caution. Savannah might lash out at her. She might tell her she was an idiot for getting involved with Evan Gilmore. Hell, Savannah might not even want to be her roommate after walking in on Alex and Evan. She was sure it wasn't the kind of housewarming Savannah was expecting.

"I am so sorry, Sav. I thought we were alone. I didn't know you'd be home," Alex said once she reached the counter.

Savannah shook her head. "It's called a surprise for a reason, Alex."

"I'm so sorry," Alex repeated, voice tight with guilt. "That's not how I wanted you to find out about us."

Her roommate finally turned and faced her. She squinted as if she were trying to understand Alex. Then she yelled out, "Evan!" Moments later, Evan walked out of Alex's bedroom. "Right." Savannah pushed off the marble countertop and faced them once Evan stood next to Alex. Savannah's face was serious. Taut and unrevealing. Alex was expecting the worst. To hear Savannah's wrath and disapproval of them. "I KNEW IT!" she declared.

Alex flinched in surprise. "What?"

Savannah let out a laugh. "I knew something was happening between y'all during the summer. I'm not an idiot. I must admit, when I walked into my apartment for the very first time, I did not expect Evan Gilmore between my best friend's … y'all know what you were doing. Hot, of course, but I'm scarred. I saw bits of you, Alex, that I'm not supposed to. Lucky I didn't interrupt y'all having sex."

Alex's fast heart rate eased. "So you're okay with us?"

"Are y'all fuck buddies?"

"*No!*" Alex and Evan said in unison, causing Savannah to flinch.

Alex sighed as she reached down and grasped Evan's hand with hers. "We're together, Sav. As in *really* together. Evan's my boyfriend."

A smile spread across Savannah's lips. "And this is … love?"

"I'm in love with AJ, yes," Evan announced.

"And you, Alex?"

Alex looked over at the way Evan stared at her with those light brown eyes. Soft and absolutely beautiful. She knew in her heart what she felt. "I love him, too."

"That's all I need to know." Savannah began to walk out of the kitchen, causing Alex to pull her hand from Evan's and chase after her roommate. Savannah picked up her purse next to Alex's suitcase as Alex came to a stop.

"Sav, do you … do you not approve?"

Her roommate winced. Then she spun around, annoyance flared in her eyes. "Seriously, Alex?" She let out a laugh. "Of course, I approve. I'll just let y'all finish. I'm gonna pick up some groceries and maybe a few beanbags to sit on."

Relief poured into her chest and relaxed her tense limbs.

Her parents approved.

And now Savannah.

Then she smiled. "Seriously, I will definitely not approve if y'all don't get back in that bedroom and finish what y'all started. Text me when y'all are sated and hungry." And before Alex could even reply, Savannah was out the door.

Spinning around, Alex made her way back to the kitchen, grasped her boyfriend's arm, and led him to her bedroom.

"AJ?" Evan asked, amusement in his voice.

Once they were in her room, he kicked the door shut, and Alex threw herself at him, kissing him and promising him that everything would be okay.

Because she knew deep down that it would be.

That *they* would be all right.

"I love you," he murmured as he laid her down on her bed, his body covering hers.

"I love you, too," Alex said as she reached down and grasped the hem of his shirt, wanting him naked. "I'd love you more if you didn't have clothes on right now."

Laughing, Evan brushed her cheek, and whispered, "I'd love you even more if you were finally out of this dress."

"I'm sure, Mum," Alex said as she continued to type her physics report. Satisfied with her conclusion so far, she grasped her phone from between her shoulder and ear, easing her neck cramp. She had been on the phone with her mother since Savannah set Alex's cup of tea down several minutes ago. Alex had decided to work at Chino's coffeehouse for a while before she went out to dinner with Savannah after her shift.

"Are you really sure you'll be here tomorrow?" The concern in her mother's voice had Alex laughing.

"Mum, I assure you, I'll be home tomorrow. I checked in for my flight before my last class."

Her mother sighed in relief. "I just don't want you to miss Kyle's surprise party."

Alex leaned back against her seat and pressed her lips together. "I won't miss his party, Mum. I'm landing before Evan, so I'll wait at Logan, and we'll grab a cab back to Brookline. That should give us plenty of time to help you set up. Are all the players coming over?"

"Yes. Your father and Uncle Alex have been busy setting up all the chairs and table. I hope we have enough room. We checked with Evan, and he says it's okay to use his place if we need to."

"Seriously? Why didn't we just have it at Fenway? They have the facilities for it."

"I know. But it's only a worst-case scenario. If you have any problems with your flight, please call your father or me. We can't have you or Evan missing. You're both so important to him," her mother said.

Alex cringed. She hated that she and Evan hadn't told Kyle that they were officially together even though she knew it wouldn't matter. He was so in love with his girlfriend, Angie. But Evan and Alex had both agreed to tell him together.

"I know, Mum. If Evan and I didn't have classes, you know we would have been there already. I better go. If I don't finish this report, I'll be stressing over it all weekend. I'll call you tomorrow, okay? I'll even call you when I get to the airport so you won't stress out so much."

"That would be nice. I'm sorry I'm stressing about all of this. It's his first birthday with you and Evan finally talking to each other," her mother clarified.

She smiled. She and Evan were finally talking. They were also finally together. They had been for months. In the days since college started, they spoke every day on the phone. Just last weekend, she had flown to California to spend the weekend with him. They had also spent a whole day searching for the perfect present for his older brother. Evan had mentioned he was nervous because Kyle Gilmore was the last person they truly needed approval from. They had her parents and Savannah's, so Kyle was the very last.

"I better go. Bye, Mum. Tell Dad I said hi."

"Bye, my love. I'll see you tomorrow."

"See you tomorrow," Alex said before she hung up and set her phone on the table. Rubbing the kink in her neck, she returned her attention to her report and began to read it over. She already had a few other papers due in the coming weeks, but this was her major assignment. So long as she had the basics down, she would be able to enjoy her weekend in Massachusetts.

"Alex?" she heard someone say.

Turning away from her laptop screen, she found the brand-new captain of the Duke men's basketball team standing next to her.

She smiled. "Hey, Chase. How are you?"

Chase Anderson grinned, pleased to see her. Alex wasn't

going to lie. She had avoided anything that included the basketball team because she couldn't face them. Alex had become friends with a lot of the players and their girlfriends, but that was when she was dating Landon. Now that they had been over for almost eight months, she had no business including herself in their social activities. Most of her time was spent in the library, the lab, with Savannah, on the phone with her boyfriend, or in California. Sometimes it felt as if Alex was always in a rush, but she didn't care. Her long-distance relationship with Evan was perfect.

"I'm good. Mind if I sit with you?"

Alex shook her head. She had always liked Chase and appreciated that he told her the truth about what her ex-boyfriend had done while she was in Boston. "Not at all."

Chase sat in the free seat across from her. He was wearing a Duke basketball sweatshirt. His hazel eyes weren't as bright as her ex-boyfriend's, but they still sparkled at her. "I've barely seen you around campus. How are you?"

"I'm doing really great, Chase. How was your summer?"

"It was amazing. I went to Phoenix with Landon. He told me that he wanted you to go with him, but you told him to take me instead. I just wanted to thank you for that. And I'm not saying thank you for letting me have the chance to meet NBA players and staff, but because Landon and I repaired our friendship," he said.

Relief warmed her chest. She had always felt awful that Chase suffered when it came to her and Landon's relationship ending. He was only telling her the truth, and Landon had mistaken it for a betrayal.

"Well, I'm glad you went." Her smile faded as curiosity

filled her heart. Curiosity she knew she shouldn't let get the better of her. "How is he?"

Chase pressed his lips together. "Heartbroken."

"It's been months, Chase. He knows that, right?"

He nodded. "He knows he ruined everything. So how was your summer? I never see you around campus."

Alex brushed her ponytail over her shoulder and straightened her spine. "I spent the summer in Massachusetts. It was great. Sav and I moved into an apartment off campus. Plus, with it being my junior year and physics being so competitive, I've been focusing on applications for internships and job opportunities."

Surprise sparkled in his face. "You're far ahead of any senior I know. I barely look at the syllabus. You should come to a game."

"Chase ..." Alex felt a wave of guilt hit her, making her cringe in her seat.

"The team misses you and so do the girls."

She pressed her lips into a tight line and nodded. "I'll try." It wasn't a promise. Alex knew she didn't belong in that stadium anymore.

Not when she was Evan Gilmore's girlfriend.

That part of her life had ended months ago.

"The team and I would like that." Then a flash of anxiety washed over Chase's face. She had never seen him so nervous in the time she had known him. "Alex?"

"Yeah, Chase?"

He let out a hesitant laugh and combed back his blond hair. "I was wondering ... I know this is kind of going behind Landon's back and everything but ..."

Alex stilled, her heart kicking into overdrive. Worry pumped through her veins with every breath she took. "But?"

"Would you like to go out to dinner with me sometime?"

Oh, God.

She had always thought Chase was being nice to her because she was his best friend's girlfriend, not because he was interested in her. She felt like an idiot. She should have seen it earlier. Alex had always ignored Chase's interest in Little Miss Red Sox when she had first met him, but when she was with Landon, she was blind to him. Only cared for her ex-boyfriend. And she knew the best way to let him down was to tell him the truth.

I have a boyfriend, Chase.

But she couldn't. She knew he'd tell Landon, and it was none of Landon's business that she had a boyfriend. That she was in love with someone else.

"Chase," she began, "I think you're amazing. And you're going to write your own name in Duke and NCAA history. But I don't think it'd be right if we went on a date. I'm sorry. I just want to concentrate on school. I hope you can understand that."

Sorrow dulled his hazel eyes. "No, I completely understand. I'm sorry. I just … I just thought … I'm sorry, Alex."

Alex sighed, hating to disappoint him, but she felt nothing for him. And most importantly, nothing for Landon. She only loved Evan. "I'm sorry, Chase. I tried dating and was happy being with Landon, then it kinda just fell apart the moment life made us choose. It wouldn't work with us. You're a senior, and I'm a junior. You'd have to think seriously about your future while I'm still at Duke. I think you're great, but I could never do that to Landon. And I could never do that to you either."

Chase nodded as he got out of his seat. "You really did love him."

"I did," she confirmed.

"Wow," he breathed. "I feel like a shit friend. I saw you sitting here, and I thought it was time someone treated you right. And I guess I wasn't that someone the moment I asked you out. Because that would hurt you. I'm sorry, Alex. I hope we can be friends and that you come to a game."

"Thanks, Chase. I appreciate that. And yeah, I'll try my best to come to a game."

He nodded, the shame still on his face. "I'll see you around."

Alex watched Chase walk out of Chino's in disbelief. She knew she hadn't handled it properly, but she hoped she let Chase down as kindly as possible. She liked him. They could be great friends someday, but she wouldn't get his hopes up. She knew no one would snatch her heart from Evan Gilmore's clutches.

"What was that about?" Savannah asked, surprising Alex and almost making her jump out of her seat. Alex glanced over to find Savannah setting a new teacup on her table. "You haven't touched your other one, so I assumed it was cold. So what was that?"

"Thank you," Alex said, reaching over and picking up the teacup. "Chase just asked me out to dinner."

Savannah's brow arched. "Seriously?" Alex nodded. "But you said no, right?"

"Correct."

"You told him you have a boyfriend?" Savannah lowered her voice.

Alex shook her head. "He'd tell Landon."

"And you think Landon will get angry?"

She shrugged her shoulder. "I think he'd say something. Right now, I'm happy. Evan and I are happy. Keeping us a secret is just easier than having to be scared that someone or something will ruin us."

Her best friend smiled. "Good thinking. I just gotta clean up my mess and then we can head to dinner. Mexican or Italian?"

Alex laughed. "Whatever you want, Sav."

"Let's go Southern since you're going back to New England tomorrow."

The party her mother had set up for Kyle was stunning. She had managed to get a tent set up in the backyard with red and white twinkle lights wrapped around the frame. The food she had spent the past few days making was incredible. And all the guests were reeling after shouting surprise when Kyle had walked out, expecting a small barbecue with the Parkers. The guests invited were his teammates, his close friends, and some of the management staff. It was a smaller event. And Kyle's girlfriend, Angie, had been in on it.

As Alex watched them laugh and talk, she knew he had finally found the one in Angie. She didn't meet Angie while she was dating Landon, but when Alex finally did during summer break, Angie always looked at her as if she was in the wrong. It was a weird feeling, so Alex finally asked her if she had done anything wrong. Angie had apologized profusely and admitted that it was hard for her to like her, considering Alex had hurt Evan by not picking him. Alex understood and asked if they could start over, telling Angie that she and Evan were best friends again. Alex could tell that she didn't believe her, but she hoped she wouldn't tell Kyle her suspicions.

She and Evan hadn't been ready to come clean then.

But they were now.

And after Alex landed, Evan had surprised her by waiting outside her gate when she stepped off the plane. He had taken an earlier flight that landed an hour before hers did. He had kissed her and whispered how much he missed her before they walked out of the terminal with their carry-on luggage and hailed a cab.

During the ride back to Brookline, he caught her up on all the things he had wanted to tell her in person, and she had done the same—even telling him about Chase asking her out. Evan didn't seem to worry about Chase and said he was confident in her love for him. His belief in her and their love warmed her heart, and she had kissed him. Although it was hard when they were apart, it was perfect and real when they were together. Their long-distance relationship was working.

"Have you got any tips for my daughter, Alex?" assistant batting coach Archer Reynolds asked.

Alex turned her attention back on the coach and smiled. "Apply for as many schools as she can. I applied for eight."

"And what was your success rate?"

"One hundred percent. I got into five Ivy League schools, NYU, Stanford, and Duke. If Dawn wants a tour of Duke, have her call me. If she needs help with her college essays,

I'm happy to help. Don't worry, Coach. She's going to get into a great school with her GPA. I'm pretty sure I still have my guidebooks that helped me through my applications. I can find them later and let you take them home to her."

Relief poured into his gray eyes. "Thanks, Alex. I appreciate that—"

"Hey, Coach," Evan said, interrupting them. "You mind if I borrow my gir—best friend for a moment?"

"Not at all. Thanks, Alex. I'll grab those books before I leave tonight." Then the coach was off to join the rest of the party.

"Books?" Evan asked as he stood in front of her.

Alex set her glass of Coke down and smiled, wishing she could freely wrap her arms around him and kiss him. But she couldn't because too many people around them only knew them as best friends. People they knew would keep their secret from the public. But not just yet.

"Dawn's a senior this year. Coach Reynolds wanted some advice for her."

Evan stepped a little closer, his eyes twinkling with the red and white lights above them. "You did get into eight of the best schools in the country."

"And you got into the best schools on the West Coast."

He chuckled, shaking his head. "But I didn't get into five Ivy League schools. It was smart of Coach Reynolds to talk to you about college applications." Evan reached for her hand and grasped it.

She glanced around to find people unaware of their touch. "Evan," she warned, afraid someone would suddenly see.

"We have to tell him," Evan said.

Her jaw clenched, and she nodded, knowing they had to. She pulled her hand from his. "Let's go now before he gets too drunk or something."

"Or *we* make him drunk."

"You don't think he'll take us being together well?"

Evan frowned. "I honestly don't know, AJ. But we're okay if he doesn't, right?"

Alex nodded. "More than okay."

"All right. Let's go." Then Evan led her toward Kyle and Angie. Her parents weren't too far away, and she could see her mother's concerned expression. She offered a reassuring smile as she walked past them and stood next to Evan once they reached Kyle.

"Hey, you two," Angie said with a smile. "Alex, your parents did a great job."

"They did," she agreed.

"Yeah, Alexi. Noel and Clara did amazing. I don't know how you all kept it from me. This is the best birthday I've had in a long time," Kyle stated.

Alex glanced over to see Evan's tense expression, and she knew that hostility would find them within moments.

"Kyle, can we talk to you for a moment? Sorry, Angie. Nothing personal," Evan said.

"Oh, of course. I'll be with Alex's parents if you need me."

Once Angie was gone, Kyle squinted at Alex and then at Evan. "What's going on?"

"Kyle, you know we love you," Alex began.

The captain of the Red Sox's eyes widened. "Is this about Angie? You don't like her."

Alex shook her head. "No, Kyle. I love Angie."

"Then what's this—" Kyle stopped talking the moment Evan grasped her hand and linked his fingers with hers.

"Kyle," Evan said in a soft voice. "AJ and I are together."

Kyle was silent.

Too silent as he glanced back and forth between them.

Alex couldn't read the emotion on his face.

Evan squeezed her hand in reassurance but seeing Kyle so quiet made her even more nervous than when they told her parents or when Savannah found out.

This was Kyle Gilmore—the very Kyle Gilmore who begged her to love him instead of Evan—so his approval meant everything.

Without it, she wasn't sure if she'd ever see Kyle again.

"As in ...?"

"Yes," Alex answered as she tilted her chin and assured Evan with a smile. Then she swung her focus to see the emotion she understood in his eyes. It was pain. "As in we're really together, Kyle."

He shook his head and then a smile finally formed on his lips. "I'm happy for you both."

"You don't look happy," Evan pointed out.

Kyle let out a soft laugh. "Had you both told me this almost four years ago, I'd have told you both that I'm not. But I am. I'm happy, so please don't think I'm not. I love Angie. Old feelings just came back for a minute."

Alex released Evan's hand and stepped closer to Kyle. "So you're okay with me dating Evan?"

"So long as your happy, Alexi. Then, yeah, I'm okay."

Her heart squeezed in her chest. "And you and Evan

are going to be okay? Us being together won't change your relationship with him?"

He shook his head. "He's my brother, Alexi. I'm happy he has you."

"Thank you," Alex said before she got on her toes and pressed a kiss on his cheek.

"So how are you two not all over each other now?" Kyle asked, the curiosity thick in his voice.

Alex turned and stared at her boyfriend who only shook his head and said, "We can't go public for a while."

"Why not?"

She took a step toward Evan and pressed her hand on his arm. "I'm sorry we can't."

"It's okay, AJ," Evan said.

"It's not." Then she turned around and faced the confusion on Kyle's face. "I just don't want the pressure of everyone's expectations to destroy us. If that makes sense."

Kyle nodded, his brown eyes dilating. "I understand. I do."

"So we didn't ruin your birthday?" Alex asked in a small voice.

He laughed. "Not at all. I can actually stop worrying about you two now. For over a year, I worried about you, Evan. Your loneliness and your heartbreak scared me. But I can see how truly happy you are. You both have given me the best birthday. If you both will excuse me, I have to go tell my girlfriend how in love with her I am."

When Kyle left them to find Angie, Evan grabbed her hand and led her out of the tent and back toward her house. He opened the side door, stepped inside, and then he led her up the stairs and into her bedroom, kicking the door shut behind them.

In the darkness of her bedroom, he whispered, "I love you," as he cupped her face.

"Even though we have to hide?"

Evan pressed his lips to her forehead, and Alex was just able to see his face from the lights breaking through the parted curtains. "The rest of the world can wait to know how much I love you."

"Evan," she breathed, completely in awe of his declaration.

"I'm serious, Alexandra. The rest of the world can wait. Just you and me."

"Okay," she agreed. "Lock the door."

She felt him wince. "Are you sure?"

Alex nodded. "Yes. It's okay. My parents are busy being hosts. Make love to me. Please."

Evan left her, and she heard the click of her door locking. He returned to her, sweeping her into his arms before he set her on her bed.

Clothes were removed.

Touches intimately enhanced by the darkness.

Moans deafened her ears.

Her heart pounded in her chest as her boyfriend pressed at her entrance.

"I love you, Alexandra," Evan whispered as he slowly entered her.

In the dark, with the rest of the world outside her bedroom window blissfully unaware, Evan Gilmore made love to her.

And somewhere between his thrusts and her moans, her tears fell.

Because he was right.

The rest of the world would have to wait because they were too busy falling further in love with each other.

They were safe.

Their love stayed pure.

They owed the rest of the world nothing.

And owed each other everything.

90

Th

thorium

ALEX

Now

"Thank you," Alex said once she gave her cab driver the fare. She smiled and then pulled on the handle, opening the car door and stepping out. Once she was out, she closed the door behind her and pulled her coat tighter, trying to keep the cold winter air from touching her skin, but it was no use. She shivered as the wind assaulted her, causing her hair to fly wildly.

Sighing, she made her way up the path. She climbed the steps, reached the front door, and turned the handle, knowing that it would be unlocked. But her home wasn't empty. She had family waiting for her. She hadn't told them that her ex-boyfriend was in town. All she said was that she was going to the city to run some errands. The mention of Landon would have brought up questions and caused more trouble than she needed before she saw him and ended all ties.

As she sat and ate breakfast with him, she knew that friendship could be possible, but she didn't want it. She wasn't sure if Landon was capable of it. So she had said goodbye with no more promises. He promised to keep in touch and made sure she was okay as he held the cab door for her. Landon had kissed her cheek, and she had smiled before she slipped into the cab and he shut the door. Alex didn't look back as the cab pulled away from the curb. She refused to give him an ounce of hope.

As she pushed the door open, she yelled out, "I'm home!"

She stepped inside her house and closed the door behind her. Alex made her way over to the hallway table and set her purse down. After untangling her scarf and unbuttoning her coat, she spun around and hung both on a hook. Once she toed off her ankle boots, she headed down the hall, realizing just how quiet her house was. Her parents should be home, along with her grandparents, aunts, uncles, and cousins. They weren't all going home for a few days, so her house shouldn't be quiet.

When Alex entered the living room, she halted at the sight of Evan sitting on the couch staring at his hands. She couldn't see his face. It had been a day since she walked out of his home, revealing to him that he was the love of her life. They had left things unresolved between them.

"Evan," she said in a wary voice, stepping farther into the living room.

"How could you?" he said, his rough voice had her stopping.

"What?"

Evan turned his head and glared at her. The rage in his eyes had her wincing. He got up from the couch and turned to face her. "I don't understand you, AJ. I don't understand a lot of things you do. I don't understand why you would do this to me."

Alex shook her head. "I don't know what you're talking about, Evan."

He glanced down at his phone in his hand. *"Landon Carmichael spotted with college sweetheart in Boston."* Then he swiped at the screen. *"Little Miss Red Sox and Hottie Hot Spur photographed reigniting college romance."*

"Evan," she said, hating the pain in his voice and on his face.

Her heart ached as he continued to read articles.

Articles that had just gone live.

She had just come home from seeing Landon.

There would be pictures.

Witnesses.

And Evan had found it.

"Breaking news: Landon Carmichael spotted telling college sweetheart he loves her. NBA's hottest bachelor seems to be off the market," Evan read out loud.

"Stop it," Alex begged.

"No," he growled. *"Landon Carmichael reported to be making Celtic move to be with girlfriend."*

"Evan," she cried, clutching her chest. "Stop! It's not like that."

Evan lifted his chin. "Not like what, AJ? Not like a picture says a thousand words?" He turned his phone, showing her the screen. It was a picture of Landon holding her hand with a smile on his face. To her horror, there was a smile on her face, too.

Her heart broke.

Her stomach churned.

She understood his rage.

She was disgusted in herself.

Alex's eyes stung as tears succumbed her. "Evan, it's not what you think."

"Did you plan this? Did you plan to see him?"

She clenched her eyes shut, nodding her head. Alex opened her eyes, and the tears quickly returned. "I did."

"When? When did you plan all of this?" he demanded.

"After you and I got home from the airport. He messaged me … I needed to see him."

Evan stumbled back. "Needed to see him?" Then he composed himself, closing the distance. His heartbroken glare killing her inside. "Have you been sleeping with him?"

A small gasp escaped her. "No. I've only been with you since college. It's only been you."

Evan shook his head. "That's a goddamn lie, Alexandra. I know this because it has never only been just me. You chose him. I asked you, and you chose him!"

"I didn't choose him. I met up with him because—"

"Because you want it with him, don't you? You want the famous NBA player. I gave up a career in the Major League to follow you to Switzerland. I gave up what he couldn't for you. I loved you! You want a family with him, then go! Be with him. But he is not raising my—"

Alex stepped forward and slapped him across the face, Evan immediately cupping his cheek as tears ran down her face. "You, Evan Gilmore, you're the love of my life! I've only wanted you. My entire life, it has been you."

"Yet you go see your ex-boyfriend. Yeah, you treat the love of your life, the father of your child, some way!"

"I wanted that part of my life over!" she screamed, finally losing it.

"Yeah?" Evan wondered. "Well, this part is, too."

No.

288

A tortured whimper escaped her. "You don't want to …?" She couldn't finish her question.

Sorrow flashed in his brown eyes. "I don't know what I want right now. I'm angry with you, AJ. I'm angry that these pictures and titles exist. I am so angry with you that I can't even look at you."

Alex blinked her tears away as her other hand covered her stomach, protecting their baby from verbal harm. "So you in my life, that's over?"

Her chest ached.

It was a question that would end it all with one answer.

Evan didn't answer right away.

"Because if that's true, I … I can't follow you to LA."

"I know." Evan glanced away. "I'm leaving for LA tonight. I have to go before I start my new job. I came over to tell you."

He didn't say he'd stay.

That he wanted to be part of their baby's life even if they were truly over.

Alex reached up and brushed her tears from her cheeks. "Okay."

Evan stepped around her and made his way out of the living room. It felt over even though she didn't want it to be. That dream of them together, raising their child was a stupid fantasy that broke her heart, but she couldn't let her pain affect their son or daughter. So Alex spun around, hating that he was walking away and believed the lies in papers and not her.

"Evan!" she called out. He stopped for a moment before he turned and faced her. The heartbreak in his eyes illuminated. "I have my twelve-week scan in three weeks. If you're back in Massachusetts, I'd like you to be at the scan with me. Only if you're home." Alex clenched her hands into fists, fighting back her tears. "I'm sorry. I know you don't understand, but I had to see him. I had to end his hope for us. I made a mistake by going to dinner with him in Oxford. I was trying to fix it. I was trying to ... It doesn't matter. Like you said, this part of my life with you is ... over."

He said nothing.

Instead, Evan nodded, spun around, and walked out of her house and more than likely out of her life. Alex stood there in shock with tears falling down her cheeks. She was stupid for thinking that her seeing Landon would stay a secret. A sob broke free from her chest. She had crossed a bridge but burned the land surrounding her.

She lost Evan.

Her baby lost its father.

And most of all, she lost her heart through her own foolishness.

Mum: Alexandra, if you have any issues with Seb, please call me. I'm so sorry to just leave you with him so I can deal with this emergency at the restaurant.

Alex: It's okay, Mum. Seb and I have got this. Plus, now that everyone's gone back home, we can spend some time together.

Satisfied with her reply to her mother, Alex set her phone on the table and took in her baby brother lying in his port-a-

290

crib. It had been four days since Evan left for Los Angeles, and she hadn't heard from him. She had hoped maybe he'd call and tell her that he realized he was being unreasonable for not listening to her side of the story, but he never did.

It felt as if she couldn't stop crying when she was alone. She kept replaying Evan's words. Evan's anguish. She couldn't stop the pain that sliced every part of her heart. She kept thinking of her baby's future, and Alex hated that she said she wouldn't follow him to LA. She regretted it the moment it left her lips.

She couldn't take it back.

As much as she wanted to, she couldn't.

He had walked out of her house before she could really come to terms with what was happening around her. She had no one else to blame besides herself. There were so many things Alex should have done differently, and how she confronted Landon Carmichael was at the top of her list.

"You're so perfect, Seb," Alex whispered as she watched his arms move.

Just as she was about to lean over the crib and pick her little brother up, nausea swept through her. Alex stood straight and slapped a palm over her mouth. She swallowed hard, hoping it was a false alarm. She hadn't had morning sickness for the past two days. Alex knew it wouldn't last long, but she had hoped it wouldn't continue.

She was officially over the nine-week mark. And according to her many pregnancy books, she'd be able to find out the gender of her baby in another two months. That was one of her milestones she was looking forward to. The thought of having to experience it alone caused a strain in her chest.

Evan had been in California for four days and didn't look to be returning. A part of her knew she might have to do it alone. Alex knew that she could do it if Evan walked away, and it was beginning to look as if she might have to.

Her brother crying had Alex shaking her head, concentrating on him rather than her churning stomach. Alex reached down and picked him up. She held him to her chest and slowly rocked him, hoping he'd fall asleep. She had no idea why he was screaming because she had just changed and fed him moments ago.

Alex glanced around the living room, trying to find his blue elephant. It was a small toy that played a soft lullaby that helped him sleep. But she couldn't see where her father had put it before he left for work this morning.

She groaned as her head suddenly felt heavy with irritating thumps. Gently rocking her brother, he cried louder. Alex began to panic, not knowing what her brother wanted. She had barely spent any time with him and didn't understand his cries. It made her realize how little she knew about babies. Tears of frustrations came and left as she felt her stomach flip.

"Oh, God," she said as she carefully set her brother back in his crib. She needed to make it to the bathroom and pronto. But as she spun around to rush to the bathroom, Alex felt the contents of her stomach rise, and she fell to her knees, throwing up on the floor.

Alex clutched her stomach, hoping that it was it.

But as she tried to stand, the dizziness clouded her vision and her arms gave out. Alex fell cheek first into her own vomit. The thumps in her head boomed, causing her to wince in pain. Seb's scream pitched higher, and the dizziness made it hard for her to open her eyes. Somewhere in the distance, she heard a door open and then footsteps.

Alex pressed her palms to the floor, trying to push herself up. "Seb, I'm sorry," she said in a weak voice. "I'm so sorry. I'm trying."

Tears rolled down her cheeks.

She couldn't do it.

There was no way she could be a good mother if she couldn't even take care of her two-month-old sibling.

"AJ?" She could have sworn she heard Evan's voice. Then hands gripped her arms and slowly lifted her. "Jesus, AJ."

Alex pried her eyes open to find Evan cradling her to his chest, her vomit ruining his shirt. "Evan?" she mumbled out before her eyes fell closed once again.

She felt herself being carried. Then she was laid down on the couch, and she slowly drifted to sleep. The crying became a soft lull as the pressure in her head eased.

It felt like a lifetime later when she felt arms around her, and she mumbled, "Evan?" She opened her eyes to see him. If she didn't feel so nauseous, she'd feel the relief in her chest bloom. "Wh-what? You're supposed to be in LA."

His lips curved into a small, bittersweet smile that was wrapped with so much sorrow that she wanted to close her eyes to be free of it. But she couldn't look away—even in her groggy, disgusting state.

"I came home because I realized what a mistake I made. I'm here to take care of the woman carrying my child. The woman I let down because I believed the stupid articles. I didn't even let you speak. I let my jealousy and hurt take over. I'm so sorry, AJ."

"I'm sorry, too," she whispered as she snuggled into his chest, allowing her heavy eyelids to fall shut with his strong arms wrapped around her.

The soft lullaby she heard had Alex slowly opening her eyes and cringing at the bright room she found herself in. She blinked hard several times before she discovered she was staring at her bedroom door. She had no recollection of how she ended up in bed. The last thing she remembered was Seb crying and being on the living room floor covered in her own vomit. Her morning sickness had hit an all-time worst. It had never been so bad that she had passed out.

Seb ... Shit!

She jolted up, realizing that she must have left him alone. Her head instantly throbbed, but she didn't care. Ready to pull the blanket from her, she noticed Evan sitting on her window seat. She froze, seeing her baby brother in one arm and Evan reading her pregnancy book as he softly rocked him. Next to her ex-boyfriend was Seb's blue elephant, playing the lullaby that filled her bedroom.

Glancing down, Alex saw she was dressed in one of her old Stanford shirts and a pair of pj shorts instead of the jeans and sweater she'd worn this morning. Her heart ached when she realized that it was one of Evan's old baseball shirts. He must have carried her to bed and cleaned her up because Alex was sure she fell into her own vomit.

She lifted her chin and saw the concern consume his

brown eyes. "Hey," he whispered, "how are you feeling?"

Alex brushed her hair back and then dragged her palms over her face just in case Evan hadn't cleaned her up and she still had vomit on her face. "Better," she said as she pulled the blanket back and got out of bed. She walked over to him and picked up her brother's blue elephant before she sat on the window seat. She smiled at the sleeping baby in Evan's arm.

Evan lowered the book and set it next to her. "That's good."

"How long have I been out?"

"A couple of hours," Evan answered. "I just fed Seb so he'll be out for a while." Then she watched as Evan slowly stood and set her brother in his basinet. He must have brought it from the nursery while she was passed out.

"You're really good with him," Alex stated, envious. "He only cries with me."

Evan sat back down next to her. "He was just hungry."

Alex nodded, digging her teeth into her lip to stop herself from crying. "I should know that." Her voice was tight. Her tears dragged down her face to her bitter disappointment. "I'm supposed to know when a baby is hungry."

"Hey," Evan said, getting her attention from her sleeping brother to him. "It's okay, AJ."

"It's not. You're better at this. Seb has spent more time with you in his life than he has with me. I spent his first two months in Zürich, so he doesn't know me. He cries. I'm supposed to know why he cries and how to fix it. Instead, I pass out on him." Alex got up from the window seat and turned the blue elephant over and pulled on the string to restart the lullaby. Then she set it next to her baby brother. He was so beautiful when he slept. It surprised her how such a little baby had such a pair of lungs on him. "I didn't mean it, Evan," she said in a small voice.

"Didn't mean what?"

She turned, and her heart plunged at those anguished brown eyes of his. "When I said I wouldn't move to LA for you and this baby. I didn't mean it. I'll still move if that's what you want. To be in his or her life. I promise, I'm moving so that you can be closer to our child and nothing else."

"AJ," he breathed.

Alex blinked her tears free as she attempted to muster a smile. But her broken heart ensured that didn't happen. Instead, a sob escaped her. "I swear. I swear we're over. Just like you wanted four days ago." She wiped away her tears and tried to control her emotions. "The part of my life I share with you is over. I shouldn't have hid seeing Landon from you. I was trying to fix a mistake, and I didn't mean to hurt you." Then she glanced down at her clothes and sighed. "And thank you for cleaning me up. I should probably get downstairs and clean—"

He shook his head. "I already cleaned up your morning sickness from the carpet."

"Thanks," Alex said, feeling awkward around him.

Evan Gilmore was just the father of her child.

That was all he wanted to be.

And she had to respect him and his decision.

"Can you sit back down for a second?" Evan asked.

Alex nodded and sat on the window seat that held so many years' worth of memories for them. It made her sad knowing that those memories would never be retold so fondly again.

She had held a tiny thread of hope when they had ended so long ago.

But as she looked into Evan's eyes, she knew that thread would snap.

Severing them.

Ending their ties.

To her surprise, Evan reached over and grasped her hand, causing her to flinch at his touch. "You'll make a great mom, Alexandra," he assured in a soft voice. "And I'll be by your side. I'll *always* be by your side."

She believed him.

She hated that she did.

Her belief met with love that shouldn't exist.

"I appreciate that," Alex said.

Evan took a deep breath and released it. His brown eyes darkened as she noticed his lip twitch. "And I wanted to say ..."

"Yes?"

"I'm sorry, Alexandra."

Alex winced. "What?"

He sighed, shame contorting the features of his face. "For accusing you of wanting him to raise our child. For telling you the part of your life with me in it was over. For accusing you of wanting to be with him. For not believing you when you cried and told me that I was the love of your life. When I saw those pictures, I couldn't think straight. I was jealous. I was angry. I hated that you didn't tell me. That maybe I took too long, and you went back to him. And I'm sorry I told you I gave up a career in the Major League for you as if I made the wrong decision. I'd pick Zürich with you over and over again. I'm sorry, Alexandra. I'm so sorry. I was angry because

I wasn't allowed to be angry. I'm not your boyfriend anymore, but I reacted as if I was."

She squeezed his hand. "I'm sorry, too. I should have just told you. I didn't think, and I'm sorry. I had no idea we'd been photographed. I swear, I was ending his hope. He knows that I will never want him or love him the way I loved you."

"Does he know you're pregnant?"

Alex nodded. "He does. He knows you're the father, and he knows I'm never going to be with him." Then she pulled her hand from his, realizing that if she said any more, she'd confess she loved him. That she was willing to have her love go unrequited to have him in her life. But instead, she changed the subject. "How was LA? I didn't think you'd be back so soon."

"I actually came back for a reason."

"You did?"

Evan nodded.

Hope flourished in her chest.

Me.

Us.

Our baby.

Our family.

But Alex pushed those traitorous thoughts from latching onto her heart. She knew the truth. There was no true future with Evan Gilmore.

Evan inhaled a deep breath and scooted closer to her. "I came back for you," he revealed. Alex's eyes widened in shock. "I came back to take care of the woman who is carrying my child. The woman who I haven't stopped loving. The woman who I'll always be in love with. I came back to ask if we could try again."

She winced.

Her breathing stalled.

"Try again?"

Fear flared in his eyes as a smile curved his lips. "Yes. Not for the baby. For us. I want us to try again. I wanted to try again the moment I left Zürich. So will you go on a date with me?"

"A date?" she breathed.

An amused laugh escaped him. "A date. A real date."

"You're asking me on a date after you cleaned up my morning sickness? I looked disgusting."

Evan reached up and cradled her face in his palm. "You're beautiful. You have always been beautiful." He kissed her forehead, and her chest tightened with longing and sweet memories of them.

"But why are you asking me on a date?" she asked once he pulled back, her eyes searching his.

He was silent for a moment as he stared at her as if he were memorizing this moment to tell someday. A heartbeat later, he inhaled a deep breath, exhaled, and said, "I'm asking because you're the love of my life, AJ. You always have been."

Alex's lips parted when she saw the vulnerability flash in his eyes.

She believed him.

"You always will be," he declared.

Her heart soared with relief and love.

Alexandra Parker was still the love of Evan Gilmore's life.

Six months after he left her, he was asking her to try again.

And her answer was a whispered, "*Yes.*"

⁹¹ Pa

protactinium

ALEX

Senior year of college

"I'm so sorry!" Alex yelled as she slammed the apartment door shut and ran down the hall to find her roommate in the kitchen. Her eyebrow was raised and humor shone bright in her blue eyes.

"You are so lucky I love you," Savannah said as she set her water bottle on the counter.

Alex sighed as she rushed over to the dining table and dropped all her books and bag on it. "I know. I lost track of time at the lab with my research. I'm so, so sorry, Sav. I promise as soon as I get back from Stanford, I will spend the entire day shopping for graduation dresses with you."

"We were supposed to go today before your flight."

"I know. And I know you've been looking forward to it. If I didn't finish this research that is due on Monday, I wouldn't be able to spend the whole weekend in California with Evan guilt-free."

Savannah's lip twitched as she crossed her arms over her chest. "And did you submit your paper?"

"I did."

"Then good."

"Are you mad?"

301

Her roommate laughed. "No. I'm not mad, Alex. It's your boyfriend's last play-off series game as a senior and captain of the Stanford baseball team. Are your parents going?"

Alex shook her head as she unzipped her bag and pulled out her purse. "No. Work and everything. But if Stanford wins the play-offs, they'll be at the championship game for sure. Oh God, is that the time?" Alex asked, noticing the clock on the wall. Her flight was boarding in less than three hours, and she hadn't even packed. With so many of her final papers due in the past few weeks, she'd been all over the place trying to finish them and juggle the internship applications in Massachusetts for after graduation.

"You go pack, and I'll drive you to the airport," Savannah ordered.

"Right. I swear, I'll be five minutes."

Savannah let out an unbelievable laugh. "Seriously, Alex? Five minutes to pack for a weekend with your boyfriend?"

Alex set her purse on the table and smiled. "I have a lot of my stuff already at his apartment. I just need to pack the new dress and shoes he wanted for dinner, then I'll be ready to go to the airport. I'll be right back." She spun around and bolted to her bedroom. Once she was inside, she went to her closet and pulled her small suitcase from the top shelf and set it on the floor.

She was thankful that during their junior year of college, Evan had her leave some of her clothes at his apartment he shared with Milos. It made last-minute flights to California to see him much easier. It went the same way for her boyfriend. In her closet, he'd left several of his shirts, sweaters, a few shorts, pants, pairs of socks, and underwear in a drawer. Alex stood, removed the brand-new black dress she bought from the hanger and laid it flat in her suitcase. Then she grabbed a few extra shirts, a pair of jeans, her Converse, a pair of black heels to go with her dress, and a pair of ballet flats. She even included the lingerie set she had bought to surprise her boyfriend. It was an impulse buy while she had been shopping with Savannah a few weeks ago.

Alex glanced down at the Duke sweater and blue skinny jeans she wore. She didn't have time to change and what she wore would be more comfortable for her flight. Just before she zipped up her suitcase, she packed Evan's Stanford sweater to change into once she got off the plane so she could ditch Duke's colors for her boyfriend's.

In the almost two years since they started dating, they had managed to keep their long-distance relationship thriving. It wasn't easy. It included a lot of back and forth between California, North Carolina, and Massachusetts, but they had made it work. When Evan played at a school close by to Duke, she always found a way to attend his games. And Evan, vice-versa when he had a week off or it was the off-season. The most they had ever spent apart was three weeks. Never allowing months to separate them. And when junior year ended, Alex surprised him by going to Stanford early. She had spent the few weeks helping him study for his finals before they went back home to Brookline.

Their almost two years together had been amazing. Evan was still not fond of flying, but he managed through every flight. He always told her that seeing her was worth the anxiety of flying. The little arguments they had seemed to go away the moment they were in each other's arms. They made it work.

And when senior year finished, they would finally have a normal relationship in Massachusetts. Alex hadn't found a job just yet, but she was trying. Her decision to delay her Ph.D. was purely so that she had the work experience in the lab, guaranteeing she was a better candidate for a place at MIT.

"Alex! Come on!" Savannah yelled from the kitchen.

Alex zipped up and locked her suitcase before she walked out of her closet, picked up her jacket from her bed, and then exited her bedroom. Once she returned to the dining table, she picked up her purse, opening it to ensure she had her driver's license to board the plane.

"Have you already checked in online?" Savannah asked as Alex shoved her purse and some of her text books into her backpack and zipped it up.

"Yeah, before I left Mika at the lab. I have my boarding pass on my phone," Alex replied as she slung the backpack on and grasped the handle of her small suitcase. "I'm ready to go."

"Great," Savannah said as she swiped her keys from the kitchen counter. "Oh, you got some letters today."

Alex wheeled her suitcase to the kitchen and took the bunch of envelopes from her roommate. She flipped through several different letters and decided they could wait until she returned to Duke on Monday morning. But just as she was about to set the envelopes down, she came across a logo that made her heart stop. Her hands shook as she dropped the other letters on the counter and held the large envelope in her hands. She stared at the logo and read the name over and over again.

The Rodahawe Institute.

"Oh, my God," she breathed.

"What is it?" Savannah asked.

Alex shook her head. "It's a letter from the Rodahawe Institute."

"The Roda-what?"

She glanced up at the confused expression on Savannah's face. "The Rodahawe Institute. It's one of the best research institutes in the world."

"And you applied?"

Alex flipped the envelope over, ready to tear it open. "I completely forgot I did. It was back when I was a sophomore, and I was dating Landon. One of my professors suggested I apply. I wasn't going to, but then Landon broke up with me, and I applied. I forgot that I even sent in my application. I even had to do a video interview for it."

"Well, open it!" Savannah encouraged, her voice full of excitement.

With shaky hands, Alex ripped the envelope open and pulled out the contents. She expected a single piece of paper, but there was a thick pamphlet underneath a letter. Readying her heart for rejection, she took a deep breath and read the letter in her head.

Dear Miss Parker,

It is with my sincere pleasure to offer you the position as my research assistant in classical mechanics. I have chosen you from thousands of applicants from around the world. Not only for your knowledge in your specialized field of physics, but also for your desire and determination to learn more as evident in your video interview.

Miss Parker, your recommendation letters exceed any other applicant, and I would be honored to have you be a part of the team here in Zürich, Switzerland. The Rodahawe Institute is one of the finest research facilities in the world, and I believe it could be the very institute that will hone your skills, knowledge, and expertise.

Please find included all the information you will need to start your research assistantship.

I look forward to meeting you in person.

Regards,

Dr. Vincent Rodahawe.

Founder.

The Rodahawe Institute.

Zürich, Switzerland.

Alex finished reading her letter. It didn't feel real. She should feel happy. The Rodahawe Institute was the institute every scientist wanted to work at. It would be the pinnacle of any scientist's career. To start her academic career at the very best would be a dream come true, and the fact that she had been chosen by Dr. Rodahawe as his assistant out of thousands of applicants was proof that she deserved the position.

"Alex?"

She peeked up to find Savannah's furrowed brows. "I'm sorry. Let's go to the airport."

Savannah shook her head and stepped closer, taking the letter and pamphlet from Alex. "Let me read it." Her jaw dropped. "Alex, you got offered a position at the best institute in the world. How are you not happy right now?"

"It's in Zürich, Switzerland, Sav."

"Oh," her best friend breathed.

Alex took the letter and booklet from Savannah, removed a strap from her shoulder and flipped her backpack to her stomach. She unzipped it and shoved the letter and booklet inside. Then she gripped her suitcase handle and nodded.

"Yeah. It's in Europe."

"And you won't go?"

"I don't know," Alex admitted. "I can't believe I got in. But it means I have to go to Switzerland, and that's not part of the plan. Evan and I are supposed to go back to Massachusetts after graduation. He had plans to get an apartment close to MIT and a job in the city. We're supposed to finally be together."

Savannah frowned. "Are you really going to turn down the position?"

"Yes," Alex said, not hesitating. "It might sound like I'm giving up a dream for him, but the almost two years I've had being with Evan have been the best of my life. I don't want to give him up. The Rodahawe Institute wasn't the dream. It was MIT."

"You really do love him."

"I do," Alex said with an honest smile. "Now, can we go to the airport? I can't miss this flight. I really miss Evan right now."

Savannah laughed. "Yeah, let's get you on that flight."

307

Almost nine hours later, Alex stood in the terminal, looking for her boyfriend. She had planned to spend the six-hour flight working on one of her research papers, but she had spent it staring at her acceptance letter from the Rodahawe Institute. Her heart wanted it. Wanted to work with a Nobel Prize winning physicist. She wanted to assist him, learn from him. She wanted it. Over two years ago, she had applied purely out of heartbreak, but now, she wanted it. She loved the idea of working with and alongside a man of such importance as Dr. Rodahawe.

But the pros of working at one of the best institutes didn't outweigh the cons. She couldn't leave Evan. She couldn't stomach the idea of spending another year away from him. When her plane landed in San Francisco, her decision had been made. She would turn down the offer. There was no way Alex was going to leave Evan. Not after everything they had been through. She wasn't going to throw almost two years away.

Hiking her backpack higher on her shoulders, she got on her tiptoes, trying to find him. The crowds after a deplane were always hectic. She watched people find their loved ones as she continued to search for her very own.

"AJ!" she heard Evan shout.

She turned in the direction of his voice and watched him make his way past several people, smiling at her. Alex ran toward him, and the moment they reached each other, she dropped the handle of her suitcase and wrapped her arms around him. Evan lifted her up, and Alex wrapped her legs around him, not caring that they were on display.

Alex let out a soft laugh and pressed a kiss on his lips. "God, I've missed you."

"I've missed you, too, AJ." He kissed her back, peppering the corner of her mouth and her cheeks with kisses. Then he set her down and cupped her face. "I can't wait until we graduate, and we don't have to spend so many weeks apart again."

Guilt had her chest clenching, but she shouldn't feel guilty. She was turning the Rodahawe Institute down for a life with Evan. Alex knew she was making the right decision for them.

"Me, too," she whispered.

Evan let go of her face and grabbed her suitcase. "Come on. Let's go eat before we drive back to my apartment. Do you want to eat in San Francisco or at Stanford?"

She smiled. "Like that's a real question. San Francisco, of course."

The party Alex and Evan found themselves attending was lively. After they had celebrated the Cardinals making it to the NCAA championship, Evan had taken her out for dinner—opting to celebrate his win with his girlfriend rather than his team. After their dinner at one of her favorite restaurants in Stanford, Evan had promised they'd only spend a few minutes celebrating with the rest of his teammates.

The fellow Cardinals chanted his name as the drinks were passed around. Alex stuck to vodka and Sprite rather than the warm beer the players were drinking. In the almost two years since they started dating, she had gotten to know his teammates and their girlfriends very well. It sucked that she couldn't attend all their social events since she was at

Duke, but she attended as many as she could. A few minutes of celebrating had turned into three drinks for Alex. Evan had stuck with his one beer as they danced and partied with the rest of the Stanford Cardinals.

"Another drink, Alex?" Chuck, the starting pitcher, asked.

Alex glanced down to find that the ice in her glass had melted away. "Oh."

Evan took her glass from her. "Are you okay? Do you want another?"

"I can do with one more but ..."

Her boyfriend grasped her hips and smiled at her. "AJ, I love you, but I'm too sore to clean up your vomit. I mean, I will, but I really don't want to."

She wrapped an arm around his neck, pressing her body close to his as she hummed. Another drink was most definitely not what she wanted at that moment. "Can we go home?"

"You want to go home?"

"I do," she whispered. "Really want to celebrate you winning. Just us. Alone."

"Just us?" Evan raised his brow. "*Alone?*"

She nodded, her body swaying. Yeah, she was tipsy, but she knew exactly what she wanted. "I'm wearing a present I picked out for you."

Her boyfriend glanced down at her little black dress, and his eyes found hers. "You did?"

"I did," she said as her other arm wrapped around his neck. "But we're wasting it just standing here."

He kissed her full on the lips and grabbed her hands from around his shoulder. "Chuck, we're leaving."

Chuck with his crooked nose grinned. His dirty blond hair

had been tousled by the girl he had attached to his hip since they arrived at the party. "Cardinals! The captain is leaving!"

"*O Captain! My Captain!*" the people in the room shouted, referencing Walt Whitman's poem.

Evan laughed as he grasped her hand and addressed his teammates. "Chuck's in charge. No trouble tonight. Don't let me down. We're so close to the championship."

"Bye, everyone!" Alex said with a hiccup.

"Laters, Duke!" someone called out, causing her to laugh.

Her boyfriend tugged on her hand. "Let's go home, baby."

In her state, she giggled. "Yes, Captain Gilmore, sir."

"God, we gotta get you home," he groaned.

"You're really giggly when you're tipsy," Evan pointed out as he pulled her into his apartment and then led her down the hall.

Alex pulled on his hand and stopped him from moving. Wrapping her arm around his shoulders, she leaned closer to him, her lips close to his. "I really, really want you."

Her boyfriend circled his arms around her waist. "Bedroom?"

"Please."

He pressed his lips to hers as her fingers glided into his hair. "AJ," he groaned when they heard the loud sounds of typing. "Milos is home."

She pulled away, frowning. "So not tonight?"

Evan shook his head. "It's still early. I forgot he has a programming assignment due."

311

Alex understood. "Okay. But can we go to bed now? I'm a little ..." And as if on cue, she swayed a little.

"Let's get you to bed." He walked her down the hall and into the living room where they found Milos by his monitors. "Hey, man," Evan said.

Milos turned in his seat and smiled at them. "Hey, guys. Saw the results. Congrats, Ev."

"Thanks, Milos."

Her boyfriend's roommate pushed his glasses up the bridge of his nose. "You guys want some coffee? I'm going to make some more."

Evan shook his head. "I'm going to get AJ in bed. She drank far more than she wanted. She's got a flight tomorrow. Night, Milos. Don't stay up too late, man."

"I won't. Night," Milos said before Evan took her to his bedroom and closed the door behind them.

Alex made her way to his bed and sat on it, her head suddenly spinning and making her feel sick. She pressed her palm to her temple and groaned. "Evan," she whispered.

"Yeah, AJ?" he said as he kneeled in front of her. "You're looking pretty pale. Are you okay?"

"I think I want to sleep." She reached behind her and tried to pull at the zipper on her dress.

Evan, noticing her struggles, reached behind her and pulled it down. Alex pushed the straps down and freed her arms. Then she stood and shimmied out of her dress, leaving her in the black lingerie that was about to go to waste. She had spent so much money on the lace set, but right now, she was definitely not in the mood.

Her boyfriend left her and made his way into his closet.

He returned seconds later with one of his Stanford Baseball shirts just as she stepped out of her black heels.

"Arms up," he instructed.

Though she was tipsy and feeling a little sick, she couldn't help but laugh as she raised her arms. Evan slipped the shirt over her body.

"Thank you," she said, loving that she was wearing one of his shirts to bed. "Do you have to do any work? Or can you come to bed?"

Evan pressed his palms to her cheeks and looked her in the eye. "Bed with my girlfriend is what I want right now."

She pressed a kiss to his chin. "I love you," she whispered as she pulled away. Evan stepped around her and pulled the blanket back for her. Alex climbed into bed and laid down. Then her boyfriend covered her with the blanket before she snuggled into the pillow.

"I'll just change," Evan said.

Alex nodded as she sat herself up. "Can you get me some Advil from my backpack? I'm not feeling really good."

"All right. I'll get you some water, too. Just lay back down and close your eyes."

"Okay," Alex said as she laid back down and closed her eyes. She heard Evan unzip her backpack and rake around inside.

Then, after a few moments, she heard nothing.

It was too quiet.

Alex opened her eyes and sat up to find Evan at her backpack with a letter in one hand and a booklet in another.

"Evan?" she said in a small voice. She could only see half of his face. Half of his anguished expression.

313

"Not once this weekend have you said anything about the Rodahawe Institute," he said as he craned his neck and faced her. She couldn't read the emotions in his face. She was too scared to know exactly which emotion was affecting him most.

Was it disappointment?

Betrayal?

Annoyance?

She pulled the blanket from her and scrambled to the edge of the bed. "I wasn't hiding it from you. Honest. I just forgot."

Evan stood, his nostrils flaring. "Were you going to tell me?"

Alex swallowed the sudden and large lump in her throat. "No."

He flinched. "Why?"

"I don't know," she said in a small voice. "I just got the letter before my flight. I haven't had a real chance to sit down and think clearly."

He glanced down at her acceptance letter and then back at her. "Are you considering Zürich?"

Alex wet her lips. Her head still pounded, and she swore she saw two Evans. "It's the Rodahawe Institute, Evan. Dr. Rodahawe chose me to be his research assistant out of thousands."

"When did you send in your application?" His grip on the letter tightened, crinkling it.

"Over two years ago," she said in a little voice. Her hands rubbing at each other out of nerves. "It was when I was home after Landon broke up with me. I wasn't going to apply, but I was so heartbroken that I couldn't think of anything else. I sent it off, and the next day you came to Blue Jay's and talked to me. I forgot about it until the other day when I got the letter."

Evan nodded as if he understood the truth she was telling. "But you're considering it."

Alex got off the bed and closed the distance. She took the letter and booklet from him and dropped it on the floor. "Evan..."

"You are," he stated, the hurt etched on his face. "I can see it in your eyes. Tell me the truth, AJ."

Part of her wanted to.

It would be a great opportunity for her career.

But a larger, needier part of her wanted to stay with Evan.

Continue to be with him and truly have a normal relationship.

But she couldn't deny herself this chance.

She swallowed hard, trying to relieve the tightening in her throat, but it didn't work. "It's a once-in-a-lifetime opportunity."

He winced, surprised by her statement. Evan pulled away from her touch and took a step back, distancing himself from her. "MIT and Massachusetts are next, AJ. Not goddamn Switzerland!"

"I know going back home was next for us. But—"

"It's a year, Alexandra! A goddamn year without you. Away from you. It's not just another state. It's another continent! You didn't even discuss it with me!"

Alex shook her head, realizing that she was suddenly hot all over. It wasn't a fight they should be having while she was intoxicated. She was barely putting it all together. She was afraid of what might slip from her lips. "There was nothing to discuss, Evan! I applied when we weren't talking. It was my choice. I got accepted into the best research institute in the

315

world. We both agreed that I'd take a year off before I applied for MIT. I can honestly say that when I got that letter, my answer was no."

"*Was?*"

She winced, realizing what she just said.

What she had implied.

That she wanted Zürich, Switzerland, over Massachusetts with Evan Gilmore.

"It's just a year," she said in a small voice.

Evan shook his head. "We've spent two years apart! You want to spend another year away from each other?"

Alex didn't answer right away.

She wanted to say that she didn't, that she wanted to be with him, but it wouldn't be the whole truth.

The academic in her wanted to go to Zürich.

Wanted to work with the man who had won a Nobel Prize in Physics.

When her silence had been enough for him, Evan stormed out of his room, leaving her in shock. Tears rolled down her cheeks. Evan had left. She was still tipsy, but she knew what she had said, what she had implied. Alex glanced down at the acceptance letter on the floor and then at the wide-open door. She heard the front door slam shut, and she fell to her knees, sobbing at how one letter had ruined them.

Alex hadn't slept.

All night, she sat on her boyfriend's bed and waited for

him, but he never returned. She had called and texted, but he never answered. Evan leaving her had sobered her up. Milos had checked on her and offered her coffee, but Alex had refused. She appreciated his generosity, but she was too upset, too worried over Evan's well-being to think of anything else. Alex glanced at the time on her phone and saw that her cab for the airport was twenty minutes away. Evan was supposed to drive her, but her boyfriend was currently MIA.

Her phone vibrated in her hand and her pulse raced, thinking it was Evan.

To her disappointment, it wasn't.

It was Savannah.

Sav: Did he come home?

She blinked away her hot, threatening tears and replied to her best friend.

Alex: No. I've called, but he doesn't pick up. I'm worried, Sav. You should have seen his face. I broke his heart.

Sav: I'm sure everything is going to be okay. Your flight's soon.

Alex: I know.

Locking her phone, she got off Evan's bed and spun around. She had made his bed and tidied up. She wasn't sure if he still wanted her clothes in his closet, so she had packed them all in her suitcase to take with her back to Duke. There was no point in keeping them in his closet. They would be graduating soon, and she'd have to take them home with her anyway. Picking up her backpack, she slung it on and pulled up the handle of her suitcase. She took in the folded Stanford shirt she'd worn on his bed. The one he'd put on her last night. And this morning, she had taken it off with so much heartbreak.

Alex couldn't believe how stupid she had been.

She should have been more sure.

She should have assured him more.

Alex had already emailed the Rodahawe Institute to video chat with Dr. Rodahawe. She wanted to personally thank him and decline his offer, but he was in Norway on assignment for a week, so she'd have to wait until then. Some in the science community might say that she was giving up a once-in-a-lifetime opportunity, but Alex knew she wasn't.

Evan was her once-in-a-lifetime opportunity.

She had made a mistake by bringing the letter with her, but just as she had decided back in Duke, she would not be going to Zürich when she graduated. Her plan—the plan she had made with her boyfriend—would remain. Alex would return to Massachusetts and finally be with Evan Gilmore the way they always should have.

Alex tucked her phone into her jacket pocket and made her way out of Evan's bedroom. Her boyfriend's roommate, Milos, was in the kitchen with a tight expression on his face.

"Any word?"

She shook her head. "No. But I have to leave for the airport. I stayed as late as possible, but I have to go. I really do want to stay, Milos, but I have classes. When he comes home, can you have him call me? I know he won't want to talk, but I just want him to let me know that he's okay."

Milos nodded. "I'll tell him, Alex."

"Thank you, Milos. Good luck on your programming assignment. I'll see you later." Alex gripped her suitcase handle, turned, and made her way toward the apartment's front door. She unlocked it, twisted the handle, and opened the door. She held it open with one hand as she pushed her suitcase into the hall. Then she stepped out and closed the door behind her.

She was about to make her way toward the elevator when she noticed him sitting on the floor by his front door. His hands were in his lap, his chin dipped so she couldn't see his face.

"Evan," she said in a careful tone.

"You're leaving?" There was no emotion in his voice.

Alex inhaled a short breath. "Yeah. My cab will be here soon. Did you just get home?"

He shook his head and then lifted his chin. "No. I never left. I've been sitting out here all night. Thinking."

"You stayed in this hallway all night? Evan, I waited for you to come home so we could talk," she said.

Evan stood, sadness filling his eyes. "I know. I just had to think. You were tipsy, and I wanted you to sleep."

Alex let go of her suitcase and stepped forward, pressing her palms to his neck. She felt him flinch at her touch. "I don't want Zürich, Evan," she cried.

"AJ—"

She shook her head at him, her tears slipping down her face. "I don't, okay? Sure, a part of me wants to, but my entire heart wants Massachusetts with you."

He froze, hesitation written all over his face. Evan reached up and wrapped his fingers around her wrist, pulling her hands from him. "You have a flight to catch. You should go."

Alex's eyes widened. He had never been so cold to her

during their entire romantic relationship. He must have sensed her anxiety as he captured her cheeks in his palms. Then he wiped her tears away. But his touch felt so foreign and unsure. His eyes softened but not with the love. It was still sadness she saw, and it made her chest tighten.

"Do you want to come downstairs? We should talk."

Evan pressed his lips into a very fake smile. "You'll miss your flight. Go. Call me when you land. I just need some time. We'll talk when you're back in North Carolina," he promised. Then he dipped his head, and his lips met hers.

His kiss was as cold as the way he acted toward her.

She tasted it.

His lips tasted of his heartbreak and disappointment.

And when he pulled away, she saw the anguish in his eyes. "Have a safe flight, AJ." He attempted another smile, and whispered, "I love you."

She believed him.

But she also believed the heartbreak on his face.

Holding back another set of tears, she said, "I love you, too. I'll call you when I land."

Somehow, over two years ago, she had gotten it all so wrong between them.

Now, she wished she had never sent that application.

Her triumph had become her downfall.

Foreshadowed the possible end of her relationship with Evan Gilmore.

^{92}U

uranium

ALEX

Now

A lex stared at her reflection in the mirror. She still looked the same. All the baggy clothes she wore hid her bump. She knew she'd only get bigger but was thankful that she was barely showing. Dressing for her date with her ex-boyfriend was hard to do. All the dresses she had in her closet were tight and definitely showed her pregnancy. But she had one emerald dress that flared at her hips, hiding her small bump. The long sleeves would keep her warm from the cold temperature. Paired with some black stockings and boots, she was sure it was dressy enough. All Alex could do was pray that Evan wasn't taking them anywhere fancy. Pressing her palms under the curve of her stomach, she turned slightly to see the small bump. At nine weeks, their baby was about an inch long. It was crazy to see the changes in her body, knowing how small her baby was.

Yesterday, Evan had helped her take care of her baby brother. She had also learned that when her mother and father needed someone to look after Seb, Evan was always close by to offer a hand. He knew exactly how to care for Alex's brother. She stood in awe as she watched him change Seb's diaper, feed him, burp him, and rock him. None of her pregnancy books warned her about how emotional it would be to watch the father of her child take care of a baby. Evan had thought he had upset her by knowing so much, but he hadn't. He only made her aware of what a wonderful father he would be.

He had stayed until her parents came home and even helped make dinner, but Alex had only eaten a couple of bites. She couldn't stomach food, and by the end of their meal, she was tired. She had blamed it on her jet lag, but she knew she could only use that excuse for a couple more days. If her mother and father weren't so consumed with her baby brother, they might have been more aware of her symptoms. Tonight at dinner, they would discuss their future and how they would raise their child together. Evan had come back for her, but she knew he had responsibilities. He would have to return to LA soon.

A knock on her door had Alex dropping her hands from her stomach and turning so she looked back at the mirror. She brushed her brunette curls behind her ear, checked over her makeup, and nodded at her reflection.

"Come in," she called out, brushing her palms over the bottom of her dress. She glanced over her shoulder to find her mother stepping into her bedroom.

"You look lovely, Alexandra."

"Thanks, Mum," she said, turning to face her. "Seb down for the night?"

Her mother walked over to Alex's bed and nodded. "Your father's reading him a story."

Alex stepped away from the mirror, pulled on her dress's hem, and headed to her desk. She picked up her silver atom necklace and stared at it. It meant so much to her. She had kept it long after Evan had left Zürich. At night, she would wrap a hand around it and think of him, think of them. And when she found out she was pregnant, she did the very same, but this time, her other palm pressed against her stomach. She thought of him with their child constantly. When she wasn't at the institute, he was all she had thought about for months. Pushing away the past and concentrating on the present, Alex clasped the necklace Evan Gilmore had given her and let the silver atom pendant rest against her chest.

"You're nervous," her mother pointed out.

"Yeah," Alex admitted in a small voice as she walked across her room and sat on her bed next to her mother. "It shows, huh?"

Her mother nodded. "It does. You keep fiddling with the hem of your dress." She reached over and grasped Alex's hand. "I'm sorry, Alexandra."

Her brows met with confusion. "What? Mum, why are you sorry?"

"Because you've been home for a while now, and we've barely spent any time together. You were away for over a year in Zürich, and you're finally home. Between Sebastian, the restaurant, and the bakery, I feel like I haven't given you enough time ... or love."

Alex smiled, shaking her head at her mother. "Mum, stop. It's okay. You have your hands full. You gave birth two months ago. Before Seb, the last time you had to change a diaper was over twenty years ago. Don't apologize. I didn't give you all enough time to adjust to me coming home."

"Actually," her mother said as she squeezed her hand. "I've been expecting you home every day since you left after Sebastian's birth. I didn't think you'd stay in Zürich for those three years, my love."

"You didn't?"

She shook her head. "No."

"How did you know that?"

"Because I wouldn't have been able to spend three years away from your father. Career or not, I knew you'd stay a little longer to finish your formula but not permanently. You love Evan too much."

"I do love him too much," Alex admitted. "He's kind of the reason I'm looking at an apartment in Los Angeles."

Her mother frowned. "Oh?"

She nodded. "Yeah."

"And MIT …?"

Alex removed her hand from her mother and shook her head. She couldn't tell her mother the truth just yet. That she and Evan were expecting a child together. She didn't want to get her mother's hopes up at the thought they could truly be a family. Tonight was just dinner. Alex had to prepare herself in case it didn't end the way she truly hoped it would.

"For six months, I lived a life without him. I have never known what being at MIT has felt like, and I survived, but I'm barely breathing without him. I was alone, and I couldn't stop hurting in Switzerland. I know that going to LA is going to disappoint you and Dad, but I want to go. I want a life with him. I want to be his again. I can't wake up alone again and wonder if he's met someone. Someone who is completely uncomplicated and gives him what I can't. MIT is worth nothing to me if I lose him for good. He's the love of my life, Mum. He's my soul mate. And if I never go to MIT, I'm content with that. I'll be happy with my life because I am going to get my Ph.D., and I don't need MIT to get it."

Her mother cupped Alex's cheeks in her hands, staring at her in awe. "They always said you were like your father, and they weren't wrong. You not only have his eyes, but you also have his heart. You're not disappointing me or him, Alexandra. We're so incredibly proud of you. We've only ever wanted you to be happy. I have always wanted you to be happy. That's why I came in to see you before your date. You haven't been yourself since your meeting with Landon ... well, since you got home."

The mention of her ex-boyfriend had her wanting to wrap her arms around her stomach, protecting herself and her baby, but she couldn't because her mother would know. Alex had been lucky enough to keep it a secret for as long as she had. She just needed to last a little bit longer. Landon wasn't a topic she particularly wanted to discuss, but if anyone understood why she saw him, her mother would. She had the moment she came home after the articles about Alex and Landon went live and Evan had left.

"It's just been a little harder to adjust to life back home. I'll be my old self soon."

"Do you want to talk about what happened with Evan? I know he was hurt."

Tears stung at Alex's eyes. "He was. He was so upset. I should have been honest about seeing Landon. I regret that part, but I am glad I saw him. It was the end for us. I felt it." The tension eased in her chest, knowing how true her statement was. "Mum, can I ask you something?"

Her mother dropped her hands from Alex's face. "You can ask me anything."

A smile touched her lips. "Mum, is Liam happy?"

Her mother's eyes shone with unshed tears at the mention

327

of her ex-fiancé. Then she nodded. "He's happy. It took him a while to find her, but when he did, he said it felt right. She makes him so happy."

Tears rolled down Alex's cheeks. "So Landon's going to find someone, too?"

"I have no doubt in my heart that he will. If Liam, who was so stubborn, can, then so can Landon. You don't have to worry about Landon anymore, Alexandra."

Alex felt a weight lifted from her as she broke into sudden tears.

Her mother was right.

I don't have to worry about Landon anymore.

"Thank you, Mum."

Her mother wrapped her arms tightly around Alex. "I know you've felt so guilty about seeing him," she said as she pulled away, "but you don't have to anymore. You can love Evan and never question your love for him. You let Landon go, my love. It's time you take what you have always wanted and deserved." She cupped Alex's jaw and pressed a kiss on her forehead. Then she smiled at her. "Don't ever feel as if you didn't love him right. You did. You owe him nothing and owe yourself your own happiness now."

"Thank you, Mum. Really. Thank you," Alex said with a small smile. "I'm gonna finish getting ready."

"Okay," her mother said before she dropped her hands from Alex's face and got up from the bed. Then her mother made her way to the bedroom door. Alex watched her pause at the door and turn to face her. "Alexandra?"

"Yeah, Mum?"

She pressed her lips into a soft smile. She had opened

her mouth to say something but closed it quickly. Then she drew in a short breath before saying, "Don't forget a coat. It's snowing out there."

"I won't," Alex promised.

"And Alexandra?"

"Yes, Mum?"

Emotion swept her mother's light brown eyes. "I'm so proud of the woman you are. I love you so much."

Her heart swelled at her mother's pride and love. "I love you, too, Mum."

Seb had fallen back to sleep before the knock on the front echoed in the house. Alex glanced up at the clock on the wall and saw that Evan was right on time.

"I'll get it," her mother said, and Alex returned her focus to the little boy in her arms.

Her father had shown her just how Seb liked to be held and rocked. She was much better with him today than she was yesterday when all he did was cry. But as she took in her baby brother, she knew that all his cries were worth it. She didn't even care that this was the first time he had ever let her rock him to sleep. In fact, she treasured this moment.

"It's crazy how much I love you," she whispered to her baby brother.

"Alexandra, Evan's here," her mother announced as she lifted her chin to find her ex-boyfriend with wide eyes, staring at her.

"Hey," she said in a low voice, not wanting to wake Seb. "Evan?"

The muscles in his throat worked as he swallowed hard. Then he pressed his lips together and nodded. "Yeah. Are you ready to go?"

She nodded. "Give me a second. I'll just put him in his crib."

"That's all right. I've got him," her father said as he got up from the armchair and stood in front of her to take Seb in his arms.

When Alex was sure that her brother was safely in her father's arms, she got up from the couch and brushed her hair behind her ear. "Thanks, Dad." Then she faced Evan. "My coat and purse are in the hallway." On her way out of the living room, she kissed her mother and father on the cheek and followed Evan toward the coat hook on the wall.

She watched as he took her blue coat from the hook and held it out for her. Smiling, she spun around and threaded her arms through her coat as Evan helped her into it. Just as the thick coat settled on her shoulders, her parents stepped into the hallway. She wasn't sure why they appeared so nervous. They had seen her and Evan together before. They had been a couple for over three years. But she understood the anxiety. This was their first date since they had broken up. It was the first time they would really spend time alone together since the night before she left for Zürich after her brother's birth.

"Evan," her father said as Alex buttoned up her coat, causing her to flinch.

"Yes, Mr. Parker?"

Her father glanced over at her mother and then back at Evan. "You're no longer my daughter's boyfriend."

Evan tensed next to her as her heart dipped. The truth in her father's words was like a hot iron rod through her chest and uncomfortable heat consumed her.

He wasn't her boyfriend.

Not anymore.

He hadn't been for six months.

This date was the decider.

"Dad," Alex said, hoping he understood the warning tone in her voice. The last thing she and Evan needed was pressure from her parents.

"No, AJ, it's okay." Evan took a step forward, grasped her purse from the hallway table and handed it to her. "I know I'm not your daughter's boyfriend, Mr. Parker, but I haven't stopped caring about her. I'll never stop. That's not a promise." He glanced over at her and smiled. "It's a commitment I first made when she made me hers."

"All right, Nolan," her mother said, humor layered her voice. "You two have a good night."

Alex turned away from Evan's promising brown eyes and nodded at her mother. "Good night," she said as she spun around. She led Evan away from the table and to the front door. She twisted the handle and pulled the door open.

Once she stepped outside, she shivered at the frosty night. She heard Evan join her on the porch before the door closed. He was by her side in seconds as she stared at his car parked on the curb rather than in his driveway.

"Evan?"

"Yeah, AJ?"

She tore her gaze from his BMW and focused on him under the porch light. "We're not going anywhere fancy, are we?"

His brows furrowed in confusion. "Why?"

"I'm not really dressed for fancy," she answered with a hint of embarrassment in her voice.

A smile graced his lips as he reached down and grasped her hand with his. "I know you, AJ. Fancy isn't you. There's somewhere I need to take you before we go to dinner."

She tilted her head at him. "There is?"

He nodded. "It's not too far away. Trust me?"

"Always, Evan," she said in a soft voice.

Because she did.

She trusted him even when she knew there was a chance it could all end in flames for them.

Fifteen minutes of driving through the light snow later, Alex found herself standing in front of MIT's Great Dome. Evan had surprised her. After begging that he tell her where he was taking her, she would have never guessed the college she had been accepted into for her Ph.D. would be where they currently stood. The last time she stood in this very spot was back in her sophomore year of college. Evan had made a pit stop during their drive back to Duke and took her to MIT to remind her of her dreams. It seemed as if he was doing the very same.

She was supposed to start her Ph.D. in September. She was also due in September, making it almost impossible for her to do her Ph.D. That, and she had already promised herself, Evan, and their baby that she'd move to LA. It was the only way they could be a family. And it wasn't as if Caltech wasn't a great school. It was. At the end of the day, MIT was just another American college. And that was what she told herself when she thought about not attending.

"Alexandra?"

She didn't take her eyes from the Great Dome. Those conflicting emotions had rendered her speechless. For her whole life, MIT had been her dream, yet she had said goodbye to it so many times. And when she finally got accepted, she had to say goodbye for good.

"I want you to have this," Evan said.

That had her swinging her gaze to find him staring at her. "Have what?"

Her ex-boyfriend inhaled a deep breath and expelled it seconds later. "I want you to have MIT."

Alex shook her head. "I already told you, Evan. I can make LA happen. I'll move."

"AJ," he whispered as he collected her hands and turned her. "I want you to have MIT. I can provide for you and our baby. You've already sacrificed MIT so many times for me. For us. It's time you have your Ph.D. at the school you've always wanted. You got in, AJ. I want this for you. I've always wanted this for you."

She shook her head in disbelief. "Do you have any idea what you're saying, Evan?"

He nodded. "I do."

Her heart dropped.

Spiraling down into the depths of pain she hadn't known in so long.

He wanted her to stay in Massachusetts. He would go to California.

They wouldn't raise their child together.

And Alex swallowed down the lump in her throat, hoping the pain would go away. It didn't. It illuminated and strengthened, almost causing her to throw up. But she braved the fake strength she hoped her face portrayed.

"Let's go to dinner and talk some more," Evan suggested.

She wanted to shake her head and tell him no.

That her heart couldn't take talking about a life apart.

But she had to.

She had to for their child.

"Okay." She pulled her hands from his and spun around, making her way through the snow and toward his car.

She finally got MIT.

But she lost Evan Gilmore.

The silence and tension between them during the car ride were almost suffocating. There was so much she wanted to say, but she couldn't. It didn't feel right for them to be on different sides of the country once again. It didn't seem right that they didn't raise their son or daughter together. But Alex was too hurt to speak.

He had given her MIT but took her future with him away from her. She hated that she was too shocked to fight for them. Alex knew he wanted to focus on his own career, but she thought he'd stay.

Part of her was happy for him.

That he didn't choose her for the sake of their child.

"We're here," Evan announced.

Alex blinked to find that they were on a suburban street. She hadn't been paying attention to where they were going because she just assumed they were going to eat in the city. But they were parked on a Cambridge street. Alex turned her head and took in the house. From what she could see of the dimly lit two-story house, it was stunning. It was from the Queen Anne period and had all its charm. The lights were on, and she wondered whose house it was.

"Come on," he said, opening his driver's side door.

She turned to face him. "What are we doing here, Evan?"

A smile twitched his lips. "This is where our date is."

"What?"

"Just trust me, AJ," he said as he slipped out of the car.

Confused, Alex unbuckled her belt and pulled on the car door handle. She grasped her purse from her lap and got out of the car. Closing the door behind her, she breathed in the cold air. Alex crossed her arms over her chest, hoping to keep her warm. She watched Evan climb the three steps and reach into his jacket pocket. Alex scanned the street to find it was empty and then rushed to Evan's side. He let out a shaky breath as he inserted a key into the lock.

"Evan, whose house is this?"

He twisted the key and pushed the door opened. He didn't answer as he stepped into the house. She glanced over her shoulder to make sure no one was watching them. They were possibly breaking and entering. She had no idea what Evan was thinking, but she had to make him leave the house. However stupid Evan was, she loved him enough to protect him from prison.

So Alex cautiously entered the house.

There were no immediate alarms, so either the owners hadn't set them or Evan knew the code.

But he has a key ...

The realization had her relaxing a fraction, knowing that maybe he was house-sitting for one of his friends or one of the Red Sox players. She knew a lot of them lived around Cambridge. Figuring that was the plausible explanation, Alex turned around and closed the door behind them. Once she twirled back around, she noticed that Evan wasn't in the hallway. Alex advanced down the hall to find the walls were bare. Evan stood in the middle of the living room, and it appeared as if it were in the midst of being decorated.

There was a couch and a coffee table. There was a unit for a TV. Plastic covered the floor, and she spotted a few paint cans. Alex was confused. She glanced over at the kitchen and saw a dining table. Draped with a white tablecloth, it was set with plates and silverware, and the candles decorating it were lit.

"Evan," she said as she faced him. "Whose house are we standing in?"

Evan inhaled a deep breath, straightened his spine, and she watched as a smile slowly spread across his lips. "It's ours."

"*Ours?*" she breathed.

"This is where I want us to raise our child together. In this house. Under this roof. On these floorboards. I want it all ... with you ... here ... in Massachusetts."

Tears consumed her eyes as she glanced around her.

It wasn't an apartment.

It was a home.

Their home.

"Say something," Evan said in a small voice.

She knew that voice. It was one laced with fear and self-doubt. One she knew for so many years. When he thought he was never good enough. It was the voice she had fallen in love with. Her eyes found him as she blinked her tears to fall freely down her cheeks.

"You bought us a house?"

Evan stepped closer to her and then nodded. "It's a ten-minute drive to MIT. It's not too far from Brookline, so you can see your parents and Seb as much as you want. The daycares around Cambridge are some of the best in the state. It's close to stores and the train line. And if you even wanted to walk to MIT, it's twenty-five minutes max."

"Why?" she found herself whispering.

He stepped forward and grasped her hand. "I'll show you why."

Her steps mirrored his as they made their way out of the living room and up the stairs. He walked her down the hall and stopped outside of a closed room. Evan grasped the door handle and twisted it, opening the door. He led her inside, and Alex took in the white painted room as Evan released her hand.

Above the window seat, she noticed the stained-glass panels. She had always wanted a house with them, but only Evan Gilmore knew that. She had always loved the idea of the colors mixing with the sun to reflect on the floor. It reminded her of her great granny's house in Australia. Great Granny Parker's home in wine country Victoria was filled with stained-glass window panels, and they were always so beautiful. Alex couldn't help but miss her great-grandmother at that moment. She had passed away when Alex was ten.

"I haven't finished his or her nursery yet. I just finished the window seat before I left for LA," Evan revealed.

"You made that?" she asked in awe. It resembled the one in her room, complete with a white cushion top.

He smiled. "Kyle helped."

"He did?"

"Yeah. It's been hard keeping this house a secret from you."

Alex walked around him and sat down on the window seat, taking in the room. It was perfect. She could imagine them in it with their baby. She could even visualize just where the crib would be.

"Who else knew you bought this house?" She watched as he made his way toward her and sat down.

"Your parents," he answered.

It hit her.

She understood why her parents were so curious when it came to her apartment hunting when she told them that she wanted to find a place closer to MIT. Evan had bought them a house.

Us.

He bought us a house.

He wants to raise our child together in this house.

"Evan," she breathed.

"Yeah, AJ?"

She inhaled a sharp breath. "What about LA?"

"I have a confession to make."

Alex stilled, seeing the nervous flash in his brown eyes. "Okay ..."

"I bought this house a month after you left." *What?* "I

bought this house for you because I knew someday, you'd come home. I was driving, and I thought of you. Like I did every day since I left Zürich. I missed you. I went to MIT, and I wanted it for you. As I was driving back to Brookline, I came across this house for sale and knew. I knew I wanted to grow old with you here. For the past month, I've been fixing it, and it's almost done. I have to get someone to install the new stained-glass panels I had made. That's why I went to LA. I had this talented glass artist make them. I had to go and check them out before he sent them. I'd have taken them with me, but they weren't finished."

"Stained-glass panels?"

He nodded with a grin. "I got some specially made for this room."

"You did?"

"I did. They're for that wall over there," he said, pointing at the bare wall on her right. "It's a series of different panels with atomic numbers on it. For example, there's a glass panel with the eighteenth element to represent the moment you told me you were pregnant. A panel with the nineteenth element to represent hearing his or hers heartbeat for the first time. I have a few dates and elements to give him, and they look amazing. I can't wait to show you the finished pieces."

Alex was in awe.

"Evan, I don't know what to say …"

He reached over and grasped her hand in his. "Tell me you want all of this with me. This house. MIT. Raising our baby together. A life together. If you don't, I understand."

"I want it," she assured with the full strength of her sure heartbeat. "But I want all of that with you in LA. It's your turn.

Your career—"

He shook his head. "I had a job offer in LA, but I've always had a better offer here in Boston."

She flinched. "You did?"

"I did," Evan confirmed. "I couldn't tell you until it was all finalized. I wanted you to understand that I wanted to stay here with you before you even told me you were pregnant. That I've wanted a life with you here in Boston even before you left for Zürich. That morning you left, I knew what I wanted, but I knew it wasn't the right time. So while I waited, I got started on this life I wanted with you."

Her heart warmed inside her chest. "You have a job here in Boston?"

"With the Red Sox."

Her eyes widened. Her stomach dropped. Her palms clammed. "No, Evan." She tried to pull her hand from his, but he held on tight.

"AJ, I want—"

"You've never wanted a career in baseball. Don't join them. Please."

One hand left hers as he reached up and pressed it gently on her cheek. She saw the flash of softness in his eyes. It was love. And her chest engulfed in flames. Because it was what she had wanted for months. "I'm not joining the Major League. I'm not playing for the Red Sox. I wouldn't do that to you or our child." He smiled as his thumb brushed her cheek. "I'm working in the operations department. I'm working at a desk. My job involves the running of Fenway Park rather than the team."

"So you're not …?"

Evan let out a soft laugh as he shook his head. He dropped her hand and captured her face in his palms. His eyes searching hers. "No," he breathed. "I'd rather be here in Massachusetts with my child and the love of my life. It's time I realize that Boston was always my home because it was where you always called home. And where you go, I go. My home has always been *you*, AJ. You've always been my home even when we were apart."

A tear escaped down her cheek and landed on his thumb. "You bought us a house."

He nodded.

"You waited for me."

Evan's lips pressed into a larger smile.

"You did all of this for us."

"I did because it was right."

Alex reached up and wrapped her fingers around his wrists, unable to hide it anymore. "I love you, Evan Gilmore. I'd have followed you to LA. I'd give up Zürich a thousand times and more to have you. I will never stop because you and this baby are my entire life."

Evan wiped her tears away as he whispered, "Eight protons. Eight neutrons."

"You love me, too," she stated.

He nodded. "I love you, too, Alexandra."

And a perfect kiss was all the confirmation she needed.

That he loved her.

That he loved their child.

That he loved the future they could have together.

A future that she fell in love with over and over again with every whisper of his love between each kiss.

It was true.

It was right.

They were right where they needed to be.

A forever in a house with a nursery that had stained-glass windows in Cambridge, Massachusetts.

93

Np

neptunium

ALEX

Senior year of college

The remaining weeks of her senior year of college at Duke University were a blur of excitement and utter heartbreak. Since her fight with Evan over the Rodahawe Institute acceptance letter, they barely talk. Actually, Alex did all the talking because Evan had shut himself off from her. He'd ask her how her day was and then when he got his answer, he'd tell her he loved her and had to go. She didn't feel his love. Not in his words or his touch. He never came back to Duke as promised. Instead, Alex had flown to Omaha, Nebraska, for his championship game. She was horrified to find how fake he was around her parents. He played the perfect boyfriend. For a moment, he was the old Evan, but after her parents had watched him win the NCAA tournament with the Cardinals and flown back to Boston, he returned to cold Evan Gilmore.

The Evan Gilmore who couldn't look her in the eye as he made love to her. But when he had whispered he loved her, she felt it. That was the only I love you she believed. When they finished, he rolled off her, and Alex let the dark room conceal her tears. Their fight had no resolution. As hard as Alex tried, he didn't want to talk.

He didn't even want to hear her tell him that she had spoken to Dr. Rodahawe. Just the mention of him had Evan wanting to end their calls and video calls. He didn't know that she had given up the position as Dr. Rodahawe's research assistant. He didn't know that she gave it all up to be with him. To love him. Alex had thought the moment she declined the offer, their relationship would return to normal.

It hadn't.

In fact, it got worse.

She hadn't heard from Evan in almost a week. She knew he had finals soon, but it felt as if he had finally given up on her, given up on them. And each night he didn't return her calls, Alex would lock herself in her room and cry, heartbroken that Evan didn't want to talk to her.

"He could still show," her best friend and roommate, Savannah, said as she fastened her earring on her lobe.

Alex sat on Savannah's bed and shook her head. "We both know that if he was going to be here today, he would already be here."

Savannah shook her head. "It's your graduation, Alex. He has to be here. He loves you. He's proud of you."

"Thanks, Sav. But since that fight about the Rodahawe Institute, we haven't been the same," Alex confessed as she fought back her tears so she wouldn't ruin the makeup Savannah had applied on her. "He won't look at me or talk to me. I hurt him really badly."

Her best friend quickly sat down next to Alex on the bed and wrapped an arm around her shoulders, bringing Alex close. "Hey, don't. You and Evan are fine. He's just not dealing. But he will. Y'all will make it work. You've done long distance.

What's another year?"

"Sav ..."

"No, you and Evan are somethin' special, Alex. It ain't going away—"

"I turned down the Rodahawe Institute. I'm going back to Massachusetts."

Savannah tensed, her arm falling from around Alex's shoulder. "You did?"

"Yeah," Alex confirmed as she got off Savannah's bed. "It's okay, though. I'd probably just be getting coffee. It's no big deal."

"Alex—"

"I'll let you finish getting ready. I'll be out in the living room."

Savannah nodded, the worry never leaving her face. "Okay."

Alex smiled as big as she could and made her way out of Savannah's room. She should be happy. She was graduating with high distinction from Duke after her thesis received unanimous support from the committee members. This should be one of the greatest days of her life, but Evan's distance had taken away the shine of today. Once Alex stepped out of Savannah's room and into the living room, she smiled at her parents, grandparents, and Savannah's father. Because her roommate only wanted her father at her graduation ceremony, she let Alex have her spare tickets so that her grandparents from Australia could attend. Her grandpa James was too unwell to make it to Duke from Australia. Alex had been upset, but she much rather her grandpa get better than risk him feeling worse with travel.

"Savannah almost ready?" Mr. Peters asked.

Alex nodded. "She is."

"Alexandra, come have some champagne," Grandma Louise said.

"Thanks, Grandma, but I need to make a phone call." She noticed her mother's concerned expression but ignored it. "I won't be long."

"All right," her grandma said as Alex turned and made her way to her room. Once inside, she closed the door behind her and clenched her eyes tight, forcing her tears away. When she was sure none would fall free, she opened her eyes and made her way to her bed. She sat down on the mattress, then reached over and picked up the picture frame of her and Evan. It was of them kissing at Watch Hill in Rhode Island. It was the first time they were there as a couple.

Her heart clenched at the memory of how sweet and true his love for her had been back then. Her chest ached at how different he loved her now. Alex set the frame back down on the nightstand and picked up her phone. She pressed the home button but found no missed calls or text messages from her boyfriend.

She wasn't going to lie—it hurt.

It hurt so damn much to see him not care.

It was her graduation day.

In a few weeks, she was supposed to be at Stanford to watch him graduate. She wasn't sure if he even wanted her there. Evan hadn't sent her a ticket. She had sent him one to her graduation almost a month ago.

Taking a deep breath, she unlocked her phone and pressed on her call history. All her outgoing calls were to him. He had called her once, and that conversation only lasted a few minutes. She heard the hurt in his voice he tried to hide from her. Alex pressed on his number and held the phone to her ear as it rang.

And rang.

And rang.

"Please pick up," she begged.

"Hey." Her heart's beats increased as relief consumed her. Just as she was about to tell him how happy she was to hear his voice, she heard, "You've reached Evan. Sorry I'm not here right now. Leave me a message."

Beep.

Alex let out a sigh.

She wanted to cry.

She wanted to yell.

But most of all, she felt foolish for thinking he'd pick up. So she'd leave him a final message and let him decide where they stood.

Gripping her phone tightly, she exhaled a heavy breath. "Hey, it's me. I know it's too late for you to be at Duke right now. If you were going to be here, you would have been by now. Something's not right with us, Evan. It hasn't been since that fight. You don't want to talk. Well, then maybe you'll just listen. I have to hope you'll listen. I don't want Zürich, Evan. I don't want to lose you. Not again. Not after everything. I spoke to Dr. Rodahawe after I came back to Duke and declined his offer. I want Massachusetts with you, and I am so sorry that I even considered Switzerland without you." Alex reached up and brushed her tears from under her eyes, not allowing them to fall down her cheeks. "Even though you won't be here to see me graduate, I'll pretend you're there in the crowd with my family. Call me when you can. I love you, Evan Gilmore. I love you so much. It'll always be you before anyone or anything else."

Alex hung up and set her hands in her lap, wondering how it all went wrong. If she had known over two years ago that the application she sent would affect them like this, she would have never sent it and avoided all of this. She'd have never hurt her boyfriend. She'd never experience him not being at her college graduation. A knock on the door had her lifting her chin to find her father stepping into the room. He had a careful smile on his face as if he were cautious of saying something wrong.

"Can we talk for a minute?"

Alex nodded as she set her phone back on her nightstand. "Sure."

Her father closed the door, crossed the room, and sat on her bed with her. "It's unbelievable to see how bare the apartment is now that you're graduating."

She took in the room and agreed with a nod. "I just have a few things left to pack before we head back to Massachusetts. And thank Mr. Marlon for us for finding this place. It's been incredible to live here for the past two years."

"I'll tell him," her father said as he slung an arm around her shoulder and brought her close. "I can't believe you're graduating college."

Alex laughed. "Yeah. I can't believe it either."

Her father squeezed her shoulder before he dropped his arm from around her. "I'm so proud of you, Alexandra."

"Thanks, Dad."

"Are you going to be okay if he doesn't show up?"

Alex faced her father to find him expressionless. It was as if he was hiding his true feelings from her. So to assure him that she would be, Alex smiled. "I'll be okay."

Her father sighed. "You would have been graduating from MIT had it—"

"No, Dad," she said, cutting him off. "We're long past blaming Evan for something stupid I did during my senior year of high school. I chose Duke. I love Duke. And I might not have been accepted into MIT either. It wasn't anyone's fault but my own. I made the decisions. I chose for me, and in the end, I got it right because my roommate became my best friend. I wouldn't have met Savannah had I gone to MIT."

He smiled. "Speaking of Savannah," he said as he got up from the bed and pulled something out of his pants pocket and then returned to the bed. He handed Alex the piece of paper.

Alex unfolded it to find that it was a check for her roommate. "Fifteen thousand dollars?" she breathed in disbelief.

"I thought I'd ask you first if it was okay. I didn't need Savannah to pay rent for this place, so I didn't touch the money she was sending me. She sent more than she should have. Plus, she drove you around and paid for groceries, too. I rounded it up a bit, but I just wanted to make sure you were okay with me giving Savannah back her money."

She let out an unbelievable laugh as she gave the check back to her father. "She'll say no, but I don't mind at all, Dad."

Her father's eyes softened as he pressed his lips in a tight line. "I'm sorry he's not here, my love."

"Me, too," Alex said. Her parents only knew snippets of her and Evan's fight. She didn't tell them about getting into the Rodahawe Institute. There was no point now that she had turned down the offer. They'd only be upset that she didn't take it.

She had her reason.

And he was back in California.

"Your mother and I don't have to go to his graduation at Stanford."

Alex shook her head. "No. He invited you both. Our rough patch shouldn't get in the way of you two seeing him graduate from college."

"You really do have a kind heart, Alexandra," her father said. He leaned forward, pressed a kiss on her forehead, and smiled down at her. "I'm so proud to be your father. I'll let you have a minute and meet you outside."

"Okay," Alex said before her father slipped out of her room, leaving her alone. She got off her bed and walked to her bathroom. Once she turned on the light, she approached the counter and took in her reflection in the mirror.

Alex ran her fingertip underneath her eye and fixed the small smudge of eyeliner. She sighed once more before she put her broken heart and disappointment in a box and locked it away for the day.

Only for today.

So she could enjoy the fact she was graduating from Duke.

Alex smiled as she took a photo with Tammy, a friend from one of her physics classes. Tammy had dated one of Alex's friends, Mika, during their junior year of college, but they had broken up the summer before senior year. The breakup was apparently mutual, and both had remained friends, making it a little easier for Alex to hang out with them when they weren't in class.

"We'll have to take another picture once the ceremony is over," Tammy said as she adjusted her graduation cap on her head. Her blond curls shifted, and she combed her fingers through them to get them back to the way she had styled them.

"Of course," Alex promised as Mika Newman walked up to them.

"Tam, you don't mind if I borrow Alex for a second?" he asked. Mika had started off as Alex's lab partner, but they became close friends. Besides Savannah, there was no one else she trusted more at Duke than Mika.

Tammy shook her head. "I'm gonna go take a photo with the others before we have to line up."

Alex turned and smiled at him as he walked her to his parents who she had met several times during their visits to Duke. "Hello, Mr. and Mrs. Newman."

"Hello, Alex," Mika's mother said. "You look lovely."

"Thank you, Mrs. Newman," she replied.

"You don't mind taking a picture with Mika? Just in case he runs off and we don't get one with you."

Alex shook her head. "No, of course, not. I don't mind at all," she said as she wrapped an arm around Mika's back and smiled at the camera his mother pointed at them. Spreading her lips into a smile, she watched Mrs. Newman take the picture and show her husband for his approval. He nodded, indicating that the photo was to his satisfaction.

Just as she was about to pull away from Mika, she heard a familiar voice say, "*Alex?*"

She froze.

Disbelief washed over her.

She couldn't believe he was here right now.

Turning away from her lab partner, she took him in. He was dressed the part of a guest in black dress pants and a white dress shirt. He even wore a Duke pin on his shirt. And in his hands was a bouquet of white tulips. Alex tore her eyes from the bouquet and looked at his light blue eyes.

"Landon," she breathed.

"Hey, Massachusetts," her ex-boyfriend greeted.

Alex wasn't going to lie.

She felt her heart burst at the sight of him.

Old memories flared in her chest.

Maybe it was the fact that Evan wasn't here to watch her graduate that made her feel grateful that Landon was standing in front of her.

"I'm so sorry," Alex said as she turned around and smiled apologetically at Mika and his parents for being so rude.

Mika glanced over at Landon and then back at her. His expression was tight as if he were uncomfortable with Landon in their presence. Mika didn't know the specifics of her rough patch with Evan, but she could tell he was not a fan of Landon's. "That's all right, Alex. I'll see you in there?"

"Yeah. I'll see you in a minute." Alex spun around and faced her ex-boyfriend. "What are you doing here?"

Landon smiled that flawless smile as he handed her the bouquet. "Congratulations on graduating, Alex."

Her heart foolishly squeezed at his sweet gesture. "Thank

you. But seriously, Landon. Why are you here?"

"Some of my old Duke teammates are graduating." His cheeks peppered with a blush as he scratched his head. "And, well, it was an excuse to see you graduate."

Alex was in utter disbelief. "You flew all the way from Phoenix to watch me graduate?"

He nodded. "Yeah. I'm incredibly proud of you. I know that had you followed me to Arizona, you wouldn't have graduated with Savannah and all your friends."

"How are you not mobbed by people right now?" She had no idea how the paparazzi or the other students didn't surround him. He was the NBA Rookie of the Year in his first season with the Phoenix Suns. He had exceeded all the expectations set for him.

His laugh was so warm and familiar. "People are too busy to notice. Listen, Alex, do you think we could go for a walk? For old time's sake?"

"Ahh ..." She hesitated. A small part of her wanted to. He had been such a big part of her life when they were together, and she still thought of some of their moments together so fondly, but that didn't mean she wanted to share her graduation with him. The one person she wanted to wasn't with her, but that didn't mean she couldn't go on a walk with Landon.

"Alexandra," she heard her father say behind her.

Her eyes widened, realizing they weren't alone. That it was definitely a bad idea to go for a walk with him. Alex shifted as her parents and her grandparents stood next to her. "Landon, you remember my family."

From the corner of her eye, she noticed Landon nod. Then he stepped forward and held out his hand to her father. "Of course. Hello, Noel."

And to her surprise, her father shook her ex-boyfriend's hand. "It's good to see you, Landon. How's the Suns?"

"Amazing. Clara, you look as beautiful as ever."

Her mother smiled. "Thank you, Landon."

Then Landon shook hands with her grandfather Marcus and kissed her grandmother Louise's cheek just as he had with her mother. "It's good to see you all again."

Alex handed her father her bouquet. "Landon and I need to talk. We won't be too long."

Concern washed over her mother's face bright as day. But Alex didn't have a rational reason as to why she wanted to catch up with him. It had been over two years since he broke up with her and chose his future. It had been over two years since she took him back and they almost had unprotected sex. But there was something gentle in his blue eyes. He wasn't the Landon Carmichael she had once loved. The Landon Carmichael who had broken her heart and faith in him.

He appeared as if he had changed.

As she looked at her mother, she saw the confusion and disappointment consume the features of her face. There was a message to that expression. And Alex knew it was, *"You have a boyfriend."*

She was very aware that she had a boyfriend. And her going for a walk with Landon Carmichael had nothing to do with Evan Gilmore breaking her heart by not showing up. It had nothing to do with him. No one understood the relationship she had with Landon.

It had been perfect … until it wasn't.

"I won't be too long," Alex promised. Then she smiled

at her family, assuring them that nothing would happen with Landon. It was just a walk.

For them to both say goodbye to Duke together.

They had nothing to worry about.

Because Landon Carmichael didn't have her heart anymore.

It was currently in Stanford.

Where it always belonged ...

With Evan Gilmore.

Other than the science department and the library, the Sarah P. Duke Gardens was one of Alex's favorite parts of Duke. However, it held too many memories of her ex-boyfriend for Alex to visit after they broke up, so she didn't. In the two and a half years since she and Landon had ended, Alex had never once visited the gardens. The last time she sat on this bench was with her ex-boyfriend. It was also the bench he had shown her when they had first taken a walk together during her freshman year of college. It was also the wooden bench that had hosted their first date.

Now, it was the wooden bench where they'd say goodbye.

She would be leaving Duke tomorrow once she finished packing her apartment.

Her next and final stop was her home in Massachusetts. In a couple of weeks, she was supposed to be in California. But she wasn't sure if Evan still wanted her at Stanford. She had to hope that he did, but Alex would be ready when Evan made the decision. To decide whether he wanted her at his graduation and whether he wanted a life with her after they finished college.

"Alex?"

She took her eyes from the tree she had been staring at and faced Landon. "Yeah?"

He frowned. "You look miserable sitting here with me."

Alex shook her head. "Sorry. I'm not. I'm just tired."

"I know when you're lying," Landon said as he reached over and grasped her hand. Alex flinched. It had been so long since he last touched her, but she remembered his touch. Remembered how gentle he could be. Then she remembered the night of the lacrosse captain's party. The night he had been so rough and forced his kisses on her.

She cleared her throat and shook the memories away. "You do?" Alex asked, surprised.

He nodded. "I was your boyfriend for almost a year, Alex. I know when you're miserable. Are you okay?"

A long time ago, she would have told him everything. But now, she couldn't. It wasn't right that she told him about her relationship with Evan. They were their issues, and Landon had no business getting involved. So Alex would lie.

"After hating Duke, I'm going to miss this place."

Landon laughed. "Yeah. I miss this place, too." He squeezed her hand. "But I only miss this place because I miss you."

Her stomach dropped as she pulled her hand free. "Landon…"

"I do miss you, Alex."

She swallowed the lump in her throat as she felt the

nervous tremors consume her. She saw the hope in his eyes and knew that she couldn't let it bloom. Alex had to be honest. "Landon, I'm seeing someone."

He flinched. The pain bright on his face. "Is it … is it serious?"

Alex nodded. "It is."

"As serious as when you and I were together?"

"I love him, Landon." She rested her hand in her lap, away from him.

Landon rubbed his lips together as he glanced out at the gardens. Then he finally faced her. "And he loves you?"

A small smile splayed on her lips. "He does."

"Is he here? Wait—" His eyes widened. "Are you dating Mika?"

To her surprise, a laugh slipped past her lips. "No, I'm not dating Mika. We're really good friends. But no, he's not here at Duke."

Disbelief darkened his blue eyes. "Your boyfriend isn't here to see you graduate?"

"He's busy." It was all she could offer.

Landon got up from the bench, shaking his head as fury consumed his face. "Why the hell isn't your boyfriend here? What kind of guy are you dating, Massachusetts?"

Alex sighed. "It's complicated."

"How is it complicated? This is one of the most important days of your life!"

She got off the bench and walked over to him, pressing her hands on his arms to get him to stop pacing. "Landon, I appreciate the concern, I really do. But what Evan and I—"

Oh, no.

"Evan?" Landon murmured, his face taut with pain. "You're dating *him*?"

"We've been together for almost two years," she admitted, slightly afraid of how her ex-boyfriend would react to the news.

Landon's chin dipped. "Almost two years?"

She could see him doing the math.

He wondered if she cheated on him.

"I know what you're thinking, but no, I didn't cheat on you. I was faithful. I was so in love with you. Evan and I got together during the summer before my junior year. He's not here because we had a fight. He found out I got into the Rodahawe Institute."

"The Rodahawe Institute," Landon breathed, pride now gleaming in his eyes. "You got in?"

Alex tilted her head. "You know about the Rodahawe Institute?"

"I know Dr. Rodahawe is your favorite living physicist. He wrote one of those journals you left at my apartment when we were dating."

A smile peeked at her lips as she let his arms go. "I can't believe you remember all that. But yeah, he has an institute in Zürich, and I was chosen to be his research assistant."

"That's why you and he are fighting? That's why he isn't here?"

"Yeah," Alex said as she attempted a smile. "But don't worry, okay? It's going to get better."

"How?" He sounded skeptical.

Alex felt her phone vibrate in her dress pocket. She realized it must be her parents, and that she had to get back to Brooks Fields for the graduation ceremony. "Look, we better go." She turned around and returned to the bench, picking up her graduation cap and dusting it clean.

Landon was by her side in seconds, gripping her wrist to stop her from leaving. "First, tell me how it's going to get better? I can't go back to Phoenix worrying about you, Alex. I care about you … I still love you."

Her poor heart squeezed, loving and hating that after all this time he still loved her.

"Landon," she said in a small voice, "I love Evan. I chose to return to Massachusetts instead of going to Zürich. He doesn't know this yet, but we'll work it out. We always do."

He pursed his lips and then let go of her wrist. "Are you happier with him?"

"I am," she admitted, knowing that it would hurt him to hear. "I love him, Landon. For a short time in my life, I loved you, too, but I've always loved Evan. He was always my soul mate."

"You love him enough to give up an opportunity of a lifetime to live and work in Zürich?"

She didn't have to think.

She didn't stutter as she replied, "I love him more than enough. Come on. Let's get back. I don't want to be late to my own graduation."

Landon nodded, and without saying another word, they walked out of the gardens and toward Brooks Fields. She felt awkward, like she should say something, but Alex had no idea what. They had said enough at the bench. In fact, Alex had said more than she should have, and Landon had reacted much better than she thought he would. It slipped from her. In some way, she had expected Landon to have found out years ago.

And it surprised her that he hadn't exploded in a fit of rage. He had surprised her. Landon had grown up a lot since they broke up.

When they made it outside of Brooks Fields and to the crowds of fellow graduates, Alex turned and faced her ex-boyfriend. Deciding this was the best time to finally say goodbye, she smiled at him.

"Thank you for flying all this way, Landon."

The hurt in his eyes had softened to the light blue gleam she missed. "I wouldn't miss it for the world. You were a beautiful part of my life, Alex." Then he bent down and pressed a kiss on her cheek. "I'll always love you, just know that. And I can't wait to watch you walk across that stage because I know I'm going to be so proud of you. Maybe we'll see each other again. Maybe had we ... Maybe if I ..."

"Hey," Alex whispered as he stepped back. "Don't do that to yourself, Landon. We're where we're both supposed to be. You should go see your teammates. My family's waiting for me. And thank you for the flowers."

"Hey, Landon!" someone shouted behind him.

Landon glanced over his shoulder, sighed, and then faced her. "Guess this is goodbye?"

Alex nodded. "Goodbye, Connecticut."

He laughed. "Goodbye, Massachusetts."

Then Alex watched him turn around and make his way to the graduating seniors on the basketball team. A sense of sadness washed over her, hating to see him walk away. She had said goodbye but talking about Evan to her ex-boyfriend left her emotions an utter mess. Sighing, Alex spun around to find her parents before she graduated. She wanted to assure them that nothing had happened with Landon. That a talk was a talk. Alex went on the search through the crowd to finally find her family's backs turned to her.

"Hey," Alex said as she put her cap back on.

As she reached them, her parents stepped apart and her heart almost burst through her chest. Tears stung her eyes as she broke into a run, not caring that he may or may not want her right now. Alex threw her arms around him, her cap toppling to the ground as she pressed her cheek into his hard chest.

His arms wrapped tightly around her. "I'm so sorry, AJ."

Alex shook her head, knowing that right now everything was okay. So long as she held him tight, everything would be okay. "You're here," she whispered, fighting back her tears.

Evan grasped her arms and pulled her back. His eyes flashed with an apology she accepted. "Take it," he urged strongly.

Her brows furrowed. "Take what?"

"The job in Zürich, AJ. Take it."

"What job in Zürich?" her mother asked behind her.

Alex shook her head as she pressed her palms to his chest. "No. I told you I want to go back to Massachusetts with you after we graduate. I mean, if you still want me to be at your graduation ..." Her voice lowered. "And if you still want to be with me."

Sadness swept his face. "Of course, I want to be with you. You're all I want. And I don't deserve it, but I want you at Stanford. I know the past few weeks have been hard on you, and it's my fault. I didn't take it well, I know. I'm so sorry, Alexandra. I was selfish. My flight got canceled this morning because of bad weather, so I had to take the next one, and I just got here. I'm so sorry I wasn't here earlier. I'm sorry I've been so selfish. You didn't deserve that. You didn't deserve my silence and my coldness."

Her heart expanded in her chest. He was being honest about his mistakes, and she had to be honest with hers. "I have to be honest with you."

He blinked slowly at her. "Okay."

"I just spoke to Landon," she revealed.

Evan's lips parted. "*Oh*," he breathed.

"I told him that we're together. That I love you."

"And how did he take it?"

Alex slid her palms up his chest to settle on his neck. "Maturely. He came to see me and his other teammates graduate."

Evan's chin dipped. "And as your boyfriend, I almost missed it."

"You're here now," Alex assured, lifting his chin higher. "I'm so happy you're here, Evan."

"I'm so sorry you thought I wouldn't be. And I'm sorry I walked out on you when I found that letter. I didn't mean it. Any of it. I'm sorry I made you feel like I wasn't proud of you because I was. And I am. When I read that letter, I thought you were outgrowing me. That you didn't tell me because you didn't want me to be a part of your dreams. And if you don't, I'm not mad. I don't deserve to be with how I acted. I do mean it when I say you should take the job as Dr. Rodahawe's research assistant."

Alex shook her head as she dropped her hands. "I don't want Zürich if I have to leave you, Evan. These past couple of weeks are proof that I can't spend another year without you."

He took a deep breath as he stepped closer and cupped her jaw in his palms. "If you'll let me, I'll follow you."

"Follow me?" she asked breathlessly.

Evan nodded. "I did some research. I need to apply for a foreign nationals without gainful employment visa, but we have time for that over the summer before you have to leave for Zürich."

Alex's jaw dropped. "You would seriously come and live in Zürich for a year?"

"For you?"

She nodded. "Yeah."

"I would, Alexandra." Then Evan leaned forward and pressed a kiss on her lips. "I will."

It was soft.

It wasn't like the others since he found the letter.

This was meaningful.

The way he kissed her was right.

They fit again.

She felt and tasted his love for her on his lips.

A cough had her pulling away, realizing this was the first time they had been so public in their displays of affections around her family. Alex glanced over her shoulder to find a smirk on her grandfather's face and her father looking away.

Alex spun around and faced her family. "Everyone who I wanted is here. Let's get this graduation started."

"Wait," her mother ordered. "Someone care to tell me what's going on? What job in Zürich?"

She glanced over at her parents and then at Evan. Alex inhaled a deep breath and knew she couldn't keep it from her parents any longer. She had received an email a few weeks ago from Dr. Rodahawe stating that the position would remain hers for a short amount of time if she happened to reconsider. She was never going to. Alex had chosen Evan, but her boyfriend had changed his mind. He wanted them to stay together, and he was going to follow her to Zürich to chase her dreams.

"A few weeks ago, I got a letter from Dr. Vincent Rodahawe from the Rodahawe Institute. He chose me to be his new research assistant at his institute in Switzerland."

Her father's eyes widened. "Switzerland?"

Alex nodded. "He's a Nobel Prize recipient. He's the world's leading expert on subatomic particles and velocity. He chose me to be part of his team, Dad."

"That's what you were fighting about?" her mother asked, eyebrow raised.

Evan nodded. "I didn't handle the news very well. But this is Alexandra's career and journey toward MIT."

"And you'll go with my daughter to Switzerland?"

Her boyfriend glanced over and smiled at her. "Yes, Mr. Parker. If that's what she wants. My life belongs next to hers. I love your daughter, so I'll go wherever I need to go. And for us to be together, our next stop is Zürich."

Her grandfather Marcus bent down and picked up her cap, handing it to Evan. "Well, then, son, you have the honors. It's time to see my beautiful granddaughter graduate from college."

Evan smiled as he stepped in front of her, pressed a kiss on her forehead, then placed the graduation cap on her head. "I am so proud of you, Alexandra."

"Thank you for being here."

"I wouldn't miss it for the world," he said as his palm ghosted down her arm and clasped her hand with his. "Eight protons. Eight neutrons."

Smiling, she whispered, "I love you, too, Evan Gilmore."

⁹⁴**Pu**

plutonium

ALEX

Now

"AJ," Evan whispered as he inched his lips from hers, sweeping her hair away from her face. The small, soft smile on his face had her heart filling with warmth.

Filling with belief.

To the absolute brim with love for him.

"So our lives are here now?"

He nodded. "In Massachusetts, yes."

"And us?" she asked in a small voice, needing him to confirm where they stood.

His thumb brushed along her cheek. "You're everything to me. I want us to be together again. I want us to raise our child together."

Alex reached up and wrapped her fingers around his wrists, pulling his palms from her face. Nerves suddenly rolled through her, making her palms sweaty. It was a question she didn't expect a positive answer to, but she just wanted the truth from him.

"And you're ready to become a father?" Alex shook her head, realizing how blunt she had been. "It's okay to say you're not one hundred percent ready because I'm not. I'm getting there, though."

Evan's face hardened. His serious expression had her straightening her spine, ready to hear the truth. "I don't think any expectant father or mother is completely ready, AJ. I'm going to be honest and admit that I wasn't expecting to be a father for some time. I mean, we're twenty-four." He reached over and grasped her hands as if he knew she was about to look away and wanted to stop the sting in her eyes from developing any sorts of tears. "But, AJ, you should know that when we were together, I wanted, dreamed, and looked forward to the moment you gave me my first child. I've always wanted you to be the mother of my child. And yeah, it was a surprise, but that doesn't mean I don't want him or her or you. I want him or her *and* you. I want to be the man you come home to. The man you plan and spend the rest of your life with. The man you raise your child with by your side." He inhaled a deep breath, squeezing her hands. "I want to be your boyfriend again."

He wants to be my boyfriend again.

Her heart swelled like it hadn't before.

"I want to be your girlfriend again, Evan," she said in a small voice. "I want everything in life with you."

The mega-watt smile on his face had her laughing as Evan got up from the window seat and pulled her up from it. "I have to show you something."

Alex tilted her head. "You do?"

"I do," he said before he led her out of their baby's nursery and down the hall to another door. His other hand grasped the brass knob, and he glanced over his shoulder at her. "It's not quite done like the rest of our house, but it will be."

Our house.

God, she loved the way it sounded from his lips.

The closest she had ever heard was *their* apartment.

Their home did so much more to her.

It made her feel complete.

For the first time in six months, she felt whole.

She and Evan were back together.

They still had a lot to work out, but she was sure they could do it together. She was positive that they would and could.

"Evan, I think the house is perfect."

He laughed. "AJ, it's a renovation mess. But I promise it'll be finished before the baby is born. It'll be complete, and we can move in."

Alex blinked at him, realizing that all this time he had been moving fifteen minutes away from the house he had grown up in. "Evan, why did you even sell your house? It's close enough to MIT, and it's huge."

Letting his hand drop from the brass doorknob, he spun and faced her. "I've never wanted to spend the rest of my life in that house. And I've never wanted you to spend the rest of our lives in that house either. Sure, you made it feel like a home when we were growing up, but each time you left, it felt cold. My parents left me alone in that house. So when they transferred the deed to me when I turned eighteen, I knew it wasn't my home. It was a place to crash at when I wasn't at Stanford. When I left Zürich and stayed in that room, I knew I had to get out. So I sold the house to Kyle after he told me he wanted to move out of the city with Angie."

Her eyes went wide with utter shock. "Kyle bought the house?"

"He did," Evan said as he reached behind him and opened the door, pulling her inside the dark room.

Alex felt his hand disappear from hers, and then she heard him flip a switch before the room brightened. It was larger than the nursery, and from what she could see from outside the window, this bedroom faced the backyard. Then she noticed the bed to her left and the doors that led to what she presumed was the bathroom and closet.

"Is this …?" she whispered.

"It's our bedroom," Evan confirmed. Then he stepped in front of her, a smile bright on his face. "I want this life with you. Only you. Well, that's not true."

"It's not?"

He shook his head as he stepped forward and pressed his palms on her stomach. "I want this life with you and him or her. Just the two of you. You're all I need." He glanced down at her small bump and then back at her, tears in his eyes. "I used to think that later in life, your children would call me 'Uncle Ev,' but I can't imagine it. It always felt a bit wrong. Your children were always meant to call me *dad*. Just like my children were always meant to call you *mom*."

Fighting against her tears, she pressed her hands against his cheeks. He was right. Her children were always meant to call Evan Gilmore dad. Her heart clenched when she noticed a tear fall down his cheek, and Alex brushed it away with her thumb.

"Evan," she said in a soft voice, staring at his glassy eyes through her lashes.

"Yeah, Alexandra?" His hands remained on her stomach.

"Our child is going to call me *mum*. I'm Australian, remember?"

He laughed as his palms shifted and grasped her hips. "I remember. You're the most Australian New Englander I know. But our child will also be American."

Alex pulled her hands from his face and then wrapped her arms around his neck. "She's going to call me *mum*, Evan."

Evan's brow raised. "*She?*"

"Or he. We won't know for about two more months."

"I won't miss any ultrasounds," he promised as he snaked his arms around her back, pulling her body to his. "Or parenting classes. I won't miss anything, AJ."

"I believe you," she said with a smile.

"Are you hungry?" Evan asked as he pulled his arms free from her. "I'll give you a tour of the house later on if you'd like."

"Can we stay like this a little longer? It's been so long since I've been with you like this."

He nodded as his arms circled around her waist. Alex rested her ear against his hard chest, and she heard his strong heartbeats. It felt so right to be with him again. To be in his arms. To hear his heartbeat as if it were calling her name.

"AJ," Evan whispered as his palm cupped the back of her head, holding her tight.

"Yes?"

"I love you," he murmured into her hair after he pressed a kiss to the top of her head. "So much. I love you so much, AJ. I also love this baby so much."

Smiling, she tilted her chin up to see him. "I named him or her Little Atom."

His eyes gleamed with recognition. "Little Atom ... you mumbled that name to me."

"I did."

Evan's brown eyes flared with emotion as he said, "I already love Little Atom so much."

It was the first time he had ever called their son or daughter by that name.

The name AJ had chosen because the first time she had ever seen their child, she couldn't see it until the doctor in Zürich had pointed out her baby to her.

Their baby was small.

The size of an atom.

It was their atom.

"And I know Little Atom loves you, too."

A large, proud grin consumed his face. "Well, can we feed you and my child now?"

Alex laughed. "Okay. That sounds good to me."

And it was.

Everything Evan Gilmore offered her tonight sounded good.

Especially the part where his life would be spent next to hers.

Evan had made her dinner. The roast chicken he cooked in the newly installed oven was her favorite meal. Her mother would approve of this large, bright, and spacious kitchen with a lot of storage space. While sitting at the dinner table and eating, Evan had updated her on his trip to LA. He had even met up with his old college roommate, Milos, and told him that he and Alex were expecting a child. Milos was currently working at Google in their coding department. Then he asked her to update him on her time at the Rodahawe Institute. He asked how all her friends were, and she told him they all missed her.

Evan insisted she tell him about her formula, but within a few minutes, she had lost him in her explanation. She had laughed, told him that it was okay that he didn't understand, and kissed him on the lips. After they washed the dishes, he showed her the two living rooms on the first story and the patio outside. They watched the snow fall for a while as Evan slung an arm around her, bringing her close to feel his body warmth against her.

They talked about what they wanted to do to the house and the life they'd live together. He asked when they could share the news of the pregnancy, and Alex said the safest time to tell her parents and his brother was after the twelve-week mark. Evan didn't mention telling his parents, and Alex didn't press. She knew they had a strained relationship. If he was happy with just her parents, then she would be, too.

Now, they stood in an empty room as he stared at her, waiting. He asked her to guess what this room would be used for, and Alex couldn't come up with anything.

"I have nothing," she stated as she spun around to find her boyfriend leaning against the wall by the window.

He grinned. "Seriously?"

Alex shrugged her shoulders. "I seriously don't know what plans you have for this room, Evan. If you say it's a playroom for our baby, I might hurt you. The nursery is big enough."

Evan pushed off the wall and sauntered to her. He pressed his palms to her shoulders and turned her. "You see that wall?"

"Yeah," she said, skeptically.

His thumb rubbed her shoulder blades. "I'm thinking bookcases."

"Okay?"

"And in front of the bookcases, I'm thinking a desk."

She glanced over her shoulder to eye him. "A desk?"

He nodded. "And behind us, on that wall ..."

Alex spun around, his hands falling away from her. "On that wall?"

"Your bachelor ..." His smiled deepened. "And your Ph.D.," he added.

"What?"

"This is your office, AJ."

"My ..."

He nodded once more. "This is your office. You need the space for your Ph.D. I've scheduled carpenters next week to build your bookcases. Then we can go shopping for your desk and everything you might need."

"So this is my office? *My* office?"

He laughed. "AJ, when you weren't at the institute, you worked at the kitchen table or on our bed. You deserve an office where you can work comfortably. We can even get those big whiteboards for your formulas."

She looked at him in awe. While she was in Zürich being upset and hurt by his decision to return to the US, Evan was busy setting up their future in Cambridge. Alex just happened to come home earlier than he had planned. For Alex, she had spent six months too long in Switzerland without him. The only reason she stayed after Sebastian's birth was because she was so close to perfecting her formula. She had responsibilities she couldn't walk away from—no matter how much it killed her not to stay with him.

"I love you," she said truthfully as she stepped closer, pressed a palm to his solid chest, and settled her hand on his neck. "After everything, I'm still in love with you."

His hands settled on her hips. "I'm still—and will always be—in love with you, AJ."

She looked deep in his light brown eyes and smiled as she brought his lips to hers. The moment their lips met in a kiss, her heart burst with the warmth of familiarity and love.

He felt like home as his lips fluttered over hers. It was as if he was welcoming her home. It wasn't like the soft peck on her bed. No, this was so much more. This was him kissing her as if she were the love of his life and not just the woman carrying his child.

His mouth whispered unvoiced promises of their life together, and her heart believed in each kiss. With each stroke of his hands up the side of her body, her heart fell in love with his touch the way she had always loved his touch.

He was careful, precise as his arms wrapped around her.

"I want to be with you," she murmured against his lips.

Evan's fingertips dug into her flesh as he pulled her back, panting. Alex's breathing was as erratic. The beats of her heart called his name, wanting, needing him.

"Are you sure?" he asked, his voice was barely a whisper over the sound of their breathing.

Sliding her palm up his chest to settle on his nape, she nodded. "I'm sure."

His eyes flashed. It wasn't lust she saw but adoration and love, and then it happened so quickly. Before Alex knew it,

Evan led her out of her office and into their bedroom. After he had flicked on the light and closed the door behind them, Evan reached up and cupped her face. He dragged his thumb along her bottom lip.

"This should be more romantic and perfect," he murmured, unable to hide his disappointment. "With candles and in a room that has painted walls. In a room that already smells like you. In sheets you picked out. It should be—"

Alex shook her head. "Hey," she whispered, her fingers curling around his wrists. "We're where we should be. We've had romantic. We've had slow. We've had rushed, and we've had heartache, Evan. Right now, it's just us. Doesn't matter about the paint on the wall or whether I picked out those sheets. I just want to be with you. Like I've always wanted to be with you. Because I choose you and this moment over anything else."

Evan's thumb brushed the corner of her mouth as his eyes gleamed at her. "And I'd choose you in a heartbeat. With my last breath of air. I'd choose you with the very last day. Just like you chose me on the very first ... when you chose me to be your best friend. When you chose me to be the first person to know you. And not just intimately, but the real you. The Alexandra who lets me—and only me—call her AJ." He took a deep breath and expelled it seconds later, whispering, "My AJ."

And then Evan Gilmore stole her breath away when he kissed her and returned the beats of her heart that she had been missing for months.

He kissed her slow.

So slow that it was torture.

And so slow that it was perfect as he walked her back to

the bed until the mattress hit the back of her knees.

Alex hands left his wrists and found the button of his shirt. Fumbling between ridding him of his shirt and his kisses, Alex finally managed to peel the material from him and let it fall to the floor. He was more tone, more defined than she last remembered. His manual work on the house showed on his body. He was more man than the boy she had grown up with.

The boy she had loved.

Through every moment in their lives.

All through college.

Even after he left her in Zürich, she had still loved him.

And as her eyes found his, she knew she'd loved him for all of time.

Through every turbulent moment and euphoric milestone life threw their way.

"I love you, AJ," he declared as he grasped the hem of her dress and pulled it up and over her head, leaving her in the pale peach lingerie set she had chosen. It wasn't skimpy or scandalous.

It was lace.

Delicate.

A set she knew he would love.

His eyes roamed her body and landed on her stomach. He had never seen her small naked bump before. She was sure it was strange to see. Just as Alex was about to cover her stomach with her arms, Evan got on his knees and pressed his warm palms on her bump. Alex flinched in surprise at the unexpected contact of his skin on hers.

"Evan," she breathed.

He said nothing as he concentrated on her stomach, his

fingers caressing her skin. Alex watched as a soft smile slowly crossed his lips. "AJ …"

"Yes, Evan?"

He tilted his chin back so that he could look at her. "This bump … this bump suits you. I've never seen anything more perfect. I can't wait to meet him or her in your next ultrasound." Then he glanced back down, and said, "Hello, Little Atom, it's me, your daddy. I'm your daddy."

And just like that, Alex fell in love with him all over again.

Because this moment meant more to her than the Rodahawe Institute.

Meant more to her than her Ph.D.

Meant more to her than MIT.

And meant more to her than Evan making love to her.

Because this was true intimacy.

The father of her child staking his claim, letting their child know that he or she had a father waiting for them.

Alex covered his palms with her own as she fought back her tears of unbelievable happiness.

"And this is your mummy, and she's going to keep you nice and snug for a while until we can meet you and love you. And in case you were wondering, we do. We love you, Little Atom," Evan said before he pressed a kiss to her stomach.

Alex gave up the fight. She let her tears fall at the most beautiful moment she had ever experienced with Evan.

"I want to stay like this," Alex said.

"You don't want to …?"

She shook her head. "I just want you to hold me and talk to him or her."

Evan got up from his knees and kissed her forehead. "I

want that, too."

And for the rest of the night, they laid in bed.

Just talking.

Just her, Evan, and Little Atom.

Alex lay on the table as her boyfriend gripped her hand. The nurse who escorted them to the ultrasound room smiled as she glanced down at the clipboard.

"The doctor won't be too much longer. I'll give you both a minute," she said before she slipped out of the room, leaving them alone.

Glancing over, she noticed Evan chewing his bottom lip. "Hey," she said as she held his other hand. "Are you okay?"

He released his lip and nodded. Since their first date nine weeks ago, Alex and Evan had spent a lot of time together. Her small bump had grown, but since it was still winter in Massachusetts and the snow permitted layers, her parents had no suspicions. When her mother and father were at work, Alex would occasionally bring her little brother to her house and look after him. She hadn't officially moved in just yet, but the house was starting to look like a home. The morning after her date with Evan, he drove her home and told her parents that they were together again after they had spent the night talking about their future. It was quite possibly the most intimate night of her life, and they hadn't even made love. Instead, Evan settled his palm on her stomach and promised her and their child his devotion and love.

Of course, her parents were happy that they were together. They apologized for keeping the house a secret from her, but she didn't mind. The only problem Alex had was not knowing how much Evan paid for the house. She knew Cambridge wasn't cheap. And when she had attempted to pay her share, he refused. Apparently, the money from selling the family home to his older brother had paid for it without having to get a mortgage. He also had enough left over to renovate and furnish the house. That, and he assured her that they were good with money since he had started his job at Fenway Park a month ago.

In the end, Alex was too tired each day to argue with him. She knew that what was his was hers and vice versa. Just as it had been back in Switzerland. In a few more months, the house would be complete, and they'd both move in.

"I'm okay," Evan finally said. "I'm just …"

"Nervous?"

He nodded. "Is it okay to be nervous? I mean … We've been calling him or her Little Atom for months."

Alex laughed. "You can continue to call him or her Little Atom. It doesn't change. Our love for our child doesn't change. It just means we know what kind of clothes to get and what color to paint the nursery. Nothing else changes."

"Nothing changes," he agreed. "All I want is for our baby to be healthy."

"I do, too," she said with a smile on her lips and a full heart.

A knock on the door had her turning her head away to find Dr. Livingston entering the room with a big smile on her face.

"Alex, Evan," she said with so much happiness in her voice as she approached them. "I'm so sorry I haven't been available for the past two months. I took time off to go to

Chicago to see my daughter. I'm sure Dr. Kent was helpful."

"That's okay, Dr. Livingston. And Dr. Kent was wonderful," Alex said, praising Dr. Livingston's associate while she was on leave.

"How is Claudia?" Evan asked sincerely.

Their doctor smiled. "She's really good. So before I perform the ultrasound, I just have to say that I am very happy to see you two together *and* expecting a child."

Evan squeezed her hand. "We're hoping for that reaction from everyone once we tell them."

"A lot of people still don't know that we're together or that we've been together since college so ... it'll be a surprise," Alex added.

"I think it'll be a nice surprise. How about we see how baby Gilmore is doing?"

Alex's smile widened. "Yes, please."

"Okay. Alex, I'll just get you to lift your shirt."

"Evan," she said as she turned her attention back to him.

His brows furrowed. "Yeah?"

"I need my hands back."

His lips made an O as he let go of her hands so that Alex could lift her shirt. The moment it was up, exposing her baby bump, he grasped her hand once more.

"Okay, you're just going to feel the cold gel and then we can see how everything is," the doctor said before Alex flinched at the cool sensation covering her stomach. Turning her head, she gazed at the screen, waiting for the familiar shape of her child.

Then she heard it. The heartbeat. As strong as ever.

And then she saw it. The prominent shape that had her

heart clenching.

"There's the baby's head," the doctor said, pointing at the screen. Alex could just see the hint of a smile on the doctor's face. "And the hands. The baby is looking good."

"And he or she is healthy?" Evan asked.

The doctor nodded. "I'll just take some measurements. But the baby's growing as expected. Now, there's nothing on your file about gender reveal. Would you like to know the gender?"

Alex's lips splayed into a smile. "We'd like to know the baby's gender."

"Okay then," Dr. Livingston said as she moved the scanner, and her smile stretched wider. Then she turned her focus away from the screen and to them. "Congratulations, Evan and Alex. You're going to be parents to a beautiful daughter."

"A girl?" Alex breathed.

"A girl," Dr. Livingston confirmed. Then she reached for the computer and pressed some keys before she put the scanner down on the table next to them. "I'll give you both a minute and then come back."

"Thank you, Dr. Livingston," Evan said as she left the room.

Once the door clicked close, Alex reached over and grasped the white towel from the table next to the bed. As she brought it closer to her stomach, Evan took over, wiping the gel from her skin. She took in the soft features of his face, wondering if he was happy to know that their Little Atom was their daughter.

Daughter.

We're having a daughter.

"Evan," she said in a small voice. He stopped his wiping

and tilted his chin to face her. "Little Atom is a girl."

Her boyfriend stared at her for a moment and then set the towel down. She couldn't read his face. It was his poker face, keeping his true emotions from her. He let out a breath of air and leaned over, settling his palm on her cheek. "We're having a daughter."

The happiness in his voice had her chest filling with warmth. "We're having a daughter."

His eyes shone with unshed tears. "Can we please tell your parents now?"

A laugh escaped her. "We'll just have to pick up some things first, and then we can tell them. But we also have to tell your brother."

Evan's eyes widened as if it only now had sunk in. "Holy crap. Kyle is going to be an uncle."

"And you're going to be a father."

"Yeah," Evan breathed as he pressed his forehead to hers and kissed the tip of her nose. "The father to our beautiful daughter."

At that very moment, her life had never been more perfect.

An hour after she and Evan had left the clinic and went into the city to purchase some essential baby reveal items, her boyfriend parked his car outside her parents' house. It was strange that she suddenly felt nervous. She had absolutely no idea how her parents would take the news that she was pregnant. It wasn't as if she was a teenager. Alex was an accomplished research physicist about to commence her Ph.D. at MIT. And Evan was part of the operations team at Fenway Park. They had a house and good finances.

"There's nothing to worry about, AJ," Evan said in the driver's seat.

Alex took her eyes from the house and directed a tight smile at him. "I know. My parents will be okay. I'm just freaking out because some of the staff at the bakery now know before my mother."

"Don't worry. None of them would tell your parents. They love you. They would never do that to you or your parents," her boyfriend assured.

Alex picked up one of the boxes on her lap and handed it to Evan. "Promise me that whatever happens you won't be upset with my parents if they're not as happy as you want them to be."

His brows met in confusion. "Why wouldn't they be happy?"

Alex sighed. "My Ph.D. I haven't even figured that out with my advisor or the faculty. She's due the first week of fall semester."

"You're going to take maternity leave?"

"If they'll let me, I'll start in the spring. I don't know, though. I'll have to ask."

Evan leaned forward and pressed a chaste kiss on her lips. "I promised your father I wouldn't let you give up on MIT. Our daughter won't either. You'll get your Ph.D., AJ."

"I know," Alex said as she pulled back and reached for the door handle. "Let's go tell my parents they're going to be grandparents."

Once she stepped out of Evan's car, she pushed the door

closed behind her as Evan rounded the car to be by her side. His fingers laced with hers as they walked toward her house. In a couple of months, she would pack away her childhood bedroom and move to Cambridge with Evan. Soon, the house she grew up in and had memories in would be in the past.

As they climbed the steps, her heart tremored in her chest as she played out every worst-case scenario in her head. She didn't want Evan to know that she was scared that her parents would be disappointed in her. But she knew deep down that her parents would be excited.

Evan released her hand and grasped the door handle. Then he turned to face her. "We're in this together. No matter what, okay?"

The way his eyes softened, she knew he'd be by her side. She nodded. "No matter what."

He pushed the door and held it open for her. Alex wiped the bottom of her boots on the welcome mat and stepped inside. She didn't bother taking off her coat. All she had was a shirt on underneath. If she walked into the house with her coat off, her secret would be blown.

"Mum, Dad, I'm home!" Alex called out as she spun around and found her boyfriend closing the door. He kept his coat on as he nodded at her in reassurance.

"We're in the kitchen, my love!" her mother replied in a raised voice.

Alex let out an anxious breath and made her way toward the kitchen with Evan right next to her. When they entered the kitchen, she noticed her father holding her baby brother as her mother stirred whatever made the kitchen smell good on the stove.

"Hey, you two," her mother greeted with a warm smile as she lowered the flame on the stove and turned to face Evan and Alex by the island counter. "How was furniture shopping? Did you find a desk for your office, Alexandra?"

She shook her head as she set the small box down. "Ah, no. Um, listen, can we talk to you both?"

Her parents looked at each other skeptically as Evan set down the box he was holding. "Is everything okay?" her father asked.

Alex inhaled a deep breath and felt Evan lace his fingers with hers. "Everything's okay. Actually, better than okay. But we don't know how you'll take this. Just know that Evan and I are happy. We're really happy. And we just want you both to be as happy as we are."

Her mother's eyes glazed over with unshed tears. "Oh, Alexandra," she said in awe.

"We're really happy, Mr. and Mrs. Parker," Evan added.

"We can see that," her father said. "So what did you want to talk to us about?"

Alex picked up the white boxes, went around the bench, and handed her parents each a box. Then she returned to Evan's side and wrapped her arm around his. "Open it."

She watched as her parents set the boxes down and flipped the lid open to take in the cupcake with a pacifier placed on the icing. And on the inside of the box Evan had stuck the ultrasound picture to greet her parents.

Her mother gasped

Her father's eyes widened.

They were silent.

Too silent for her liking.

Evan cleared his throat, and said, "We found out the gender today. Alexandra thought it would be a good idea to surprise you both with the gender inside the cupcake."

Alex watched as her father stepped closer to her mother and handed Sebastian over to her. Then he made his way around the kitchen bench.

His emotionless face was proof that he might be disappointed in her.

Her father didn't approve.

Then he stood next to her, and Alex turned to face her father. "You're not disappointed, are you?"

"That you're pregnant?"

She nodded. "Yes."

He cupped her cheeks in his palms and shook his head. "I'm not." Then he pressed his lips to her forehead. "So you're really pregnant?"

She smiled at the way his green eyes softened. "I'm really pregnant, Dad. You're going to be a grandfather."

A tear ran down his cheek. "And Evan ...?"

"I'm the father," her boyfriend said behind her.

"I'm so happy," her mother said, getting her attention. She was rocking the almost five-month-old in her arms as she stared at the ultrasound. "Nolan, come over here and find out if we're having a granddaughter or a grandson." Then she smiled down at Sebastian. "You're going to be an uncle, Sebbie."

Her father left her side to join her mother. Evan slung an arm around her shoulder and kissed her temple. "They're happy."

She nodded as she reached up and cleared her cheeks of her tears. "*I'm* happy."

Alex and Evan watched as her father picked up the

cupcake from the box and removed the pacifier from on top of the icing. Then he broke the cupcake apart to find the pink filling and showed it to her mother.

"Our little girl is having her own little girl," her father said, his voice cracking.

I'm carrying Evan's little girl.

My parents' little girl, too.

Her mother and father gushed over the pink filling and the ultrasound, showing her little brother as Alex rested the side of her face against her boyfriend's arm.

"Evan?"

"Yeah, Alexandra?"

She gazed up at him, loving his soft smile and the adoration in his eyes. "Can we tell Kyle next?"

He grinned at her. "We should tell Kyle next."

Her heart leaped in her chest. "I love you, Evan."

"Eight protons," he whispered as he pressed a kiss on her lips. Then he pressed a palm to her stomach and added, "Eight neutrons, Little Atom."

"We need to celebrate!" her mother announced.

And just like that, any fear she had about her parents being disappointed simply faded away.

Her life found its perfection.

Its rightness.

Everything was where it was meant to be.

With the love of her life.

With her daughter.

And with her family.

No amount of love had mattered more than right now.

95

Am

americium

EVAN

Senior year of college

E van watched intently as his girlfriend knotted his cardinal colored tie. AJ had landed in San Francisco two days ago, and her parents and his brother flew in yesterday for his graduation. Kyle's girlfriend, Angie, had landed this morning. Evan didn't mind that she was late due to a speaking engagement. In fact, he was surprised she made the effort to attend his college graduation at all because she wasn't obligated to come. He was just her boyfriend's brother, but it meant a lot to Evan that she wasn't just supporting him but also Kyle. The sweet smile on AJ's face had him grinning. He couldn't think of a better send-off than graduating as the championship winning captain of the Stanford men's baseball team. But it was made better when he flew to Duke and watched his girlfriend graduate over two weeks ago and promised to go to Zürich with her.

The weeks he had spent being cold and distant from her had been torture. He shouldn't have blamed her for applying to become a research assistant with the world's leading physicist. Evan knew it meant another year away from his girlfriend. Another year of distance. Another year of not feeling like he was truly hers. He had almost missed her graduation because of his stubbornness and stupidity. It was his roommate, Milos, who talked some sense into him—telling Evan that if he didn't go to North Carolina to see her graduate, he'd lose her for good. And Milos was right. He would have lost AJ for good. It was stupid that he even thought of them spending another year apart when he could go with her.

Returning to Massachusetts might have been the original plan, but it wasn't home without her. He had several job offers and an opportunity to be drafted to the Major League with the Red Sox, his brother's team.

But he didn't want any of it.

Evan Gilmore just wanted a life with Alexandra Parker.

And that meant following her to Zürich, Switzerland.

In the two weeks since he watched her graduate, she had reached out to the Rodahawe Institute to accept the offer, and AJ and Evan began to plan their life together in Switzerland. The Rodahawe Institute had even offered to help Evan with his visa papers if it guaranteed AJ's employment.

Massachusetts could wait.

AJ deserved the very best—especially after he stood in the way of her MIT dreams for so many years.

It's her turn.

"There," she said as she adjusted the perfectly knotted tie in place. "Now, you're ready to graduate."

Evan covered her hands with his, splaying them flat on his chest. "Thank you for being here today, AJ."

She smiled that flawless, beautiful smile that always softened her dazzling emerald eyes. How he never saw just how stunning and breathtaking she was during high school, he'd never know. It kept him up some nights wondering how he could have missed her.

Missed her love.

Missed the way her eyes glittered brighter when she was happy.

Missed the way her smile always brought warmth to his chest.

But now he was finally hers.

And it had always been her even when he was oblivious to his love for her.

It would always be Alexandra Parker.

Now until forever.

"Why are you smiling at me like that?" AJ asked as she tilted her head at him.

She has no idea how much I love her.

"I'm just happy," he answered as he squeezed her left hand.

The very hand he wanted to hold when he got down on one knee.

His future always included her.

A life with her.

A life with her as his wife.

He had planned to propose before she started her Ph.D., but now that she would be a research assistant at the Rodahawe Institute, Evan would wait. He didn't want her to worry about an engagement and a wedding while she worked with one of her heroes.

It was about her being Alexandra Parker, research assistant to Dr. Rodahawe.

And not Alexandra Parker, engaged to Evan Gilmore—if she said yes.

But just as he had done while she had dated someone else,

Evan would wait. When it was the right moment in their lives and in her career, then he would ask her to spend the rest of her life with him.

His girlfriend's brow arched. "Are you sure that's all?"

He nodded. "I'm sure."

A knock on Evan's bedroom door had them turning. His girlfriend's father opened the door, then stepped inside the room. "Alexandra, your mother would like a hand with some of the food."

AJ pulled her hands away from Evan and nodded. "Sure thing, Dad."

Just as she made her way to her father, Mr. Parker asked, "Evan, can I speak with you?"

"Sure, Mr. Parker," Evan said as he watched AJ glance from him to her father. He saw her confusion. Hell, he was just as confused as she. But as she slipped out of his room, her father closed the door behind her.

Then he approached Evan and set a hand to his shoulder. "I'm very proud of you, son."

Son.

Mr. Parker had no idea the power of the word "son" from his lips had over Evan. If he wanted to make anyone other than his girlfriend proud, it was his girlfriend's parents. The very couple who had raised him and supported him when he had no one else.

"Thank you, Mr. P," Evan said gratefully.

"Listen, I've been thinking about your graduation present and—"

Evan shook his head. "You shouldn't have bought me anything."

Mr. Parker smiled. "It's not something you can buy, Evan. But you have to promise me that you'll be grateful and appreciate this present. I never gave it to Landon, but I am giving it to you because well, I see a little of myself in you. And when I watched you take in my daughter graduating from Duke, I just knew. Just as I knew with my wife."

"Knew?"

His girlfriend's father nodded his head. "I'm giving you my assurance."

"Your assurance?"

"If I know you—and I know you, Evan—someday you'll ask me for my blessing to ask my daughter to marry you."

Evan's eyes widened.

Mr. Parker's green eyes softened the way his daughter's had—but not as light. "When that day comes, just know that you have my assurance. My assurance that I'm going to listen to you promise me that you'll take care of her, just as her grandfather listened to me ask him for his blessing to marry her mother. And know that if you continue to make my daughter happy, you will have my blessing when the time comes."

Evan was in shock. Unsure of what to say.

"I knew I wanted to marry her mother before I was even well and truly in love with her. I'm not forcing you to pop the question today or tomorrow or even before you both leave for Zürich at the end of summer. I'm just saying that you never have to worry about me thinking you're not good enough for my daughter. You are, Evan. You're more than good enough because her heart chose you." Mr. Parker smiled and squeezed Evan's shoulder. "That's my gift to you. The assurance that I'll listen, and the knowledge that I will give you my blessing someday."

"Thank you, Mr. Parker," Evan finally said around the lump in his throat. "I appreciate it. You have no idea how much this means to me. Besides your daughter and your family's love and kindness, this is the greatest gift you've ever given me."

Mr. Parker pressed his lips into a smile and removed his palm from Evan's shoulder. "You're welcome. I'm just happy that you and Alexandra have finally found your way. Now, come on. Kyle will be over soon. Then we can watch you graduate from Stanford."

"A lot of eyes will be on us today," Evan mumbled.

"There will be."

He nodded. "Yeah, Kyle is an attraction."

Mr. Parker let out a soft laugh. "I don't think so, son. I think all eyes will be on the very Gilmore who captained the Cardinals to their first NCAA championship in years. It's all about you today, Evan."

His chest filled with warmth. For years, the spotlight had always been on Kyle, but today, it would be on him. And from the pride that flashed in Mr. Parker's eyes, Evan knew he had made him proud.

"Evan!" AJ called out from the kitchen. "Kyle and Angie are here!"

"We better get out there," Mr. Parker suggested.

"You're right," he agreed as they left Evan's bedroom and entered the living room where his roommate was sitting on the couch with a plate of cupcakes on his lap. Evan noticed Milos's parents were in the kitchen with Mrs. Parker. "Got enough cupcakes there, Milos?"

Milos set the cupcake in his hand on the plate and

swallowed down the bite he had just taken. "I'm going to miss Mrs. Parker's baking now that I'm no longer your roommate."

"I will send you a box every week, Milos," Mrs. Parker announced from the kitchen as Milos's parents joined their son in the living room.

Mr. Parker chuckled as he walked past Evan and to the kitchen. All the things Evan needed had already been shipped back to Brookline. The rest, he was leaving behind with Milos who would continue to live in the apartment after getting an internship with a respectable IT company.

"Evan," his brother called.

He craned his neck to find Kyle standing next to Angie in the kitchen with AJ and her parents. Because of AJ, he was able to mend his strained relationship with his older brother. And seeing them all together in his kitchen, Evan knew that this was the family he'd love and be grateful for.

Evan's parents weren't here, but Mr. and Mrs. Parker had taken their places a long time ago, so it only made sense that they would be present to witness him graduate from Stanford, Mr. Parker's alma mater. Evan approached his older brother and shook the hand held out to him. Then he pressed a kiss to Angie's cheek.

"Thank you both for being here today."

Kyle grinned. Evan wasn't used to the genuine pride that gleamed in his older brother's eyes, but Kyle had told him numerous times how proud he was of Evan throughout the years. "I'm proud of you, little brother. You're the first of us to graduate from college."

"Yeah, but you're the successful professional baseball player. And it's not like you're not doing online college."

Kyle chuckled. "Just a few more years and I'll be done with my online degree. As much as I have loved being with the Red Sox since I finished high school, I would have loved to have gone to college and experienced it all. But that's not what's important. How long are you and Alexi going to stay in Massachusetts?"

"Pretty much all of summer," Evan replied as AJ stepped next to him.

"We're going a little earlier so we can settle in before I start my position as Dr. Rodahawe's research assistant," AJ added.

"I'm so jealous that you're both going to be living in Europe for a year," Angie said with wanderlust sparkling in her eyes.

"Angie, could you help me get some of these appetizers on the table?" AJ's mother asked.

"Sure thing, Clara."

One by one, the guests left the kitchen with the appetizer trays until just he and AJ remained. Then his girlfriend stepped in front of him and turned to face him, wrapping her arms around him. "I'm so proud of you," she whispered with a smile on her face.

"Are you kidding? AJ, if anyone here is proud, it's me of you."

She rolled her eyes at him. "This isn't my graduation. It's *yours.*"

"I won't be able to see you from the stage," he said with disappointment in his voice.

"That's okay. I'll be the one looking at you." Then she bit her lip. "Are you sure you still want to come to Zürich? Freelance work for my dad's clients won't be the same as the offers you received from the firms in Boston."

Evan placed his palms on her hips. "My visa's been approved, AJ. There's no way I'm missing a year of my life without you in it. I've done that, and it was hell. I want you and Zürich. Those firms and companies in Boston were fine, but that's the thing. They were just fine. They didn't feel right. Not in the same way as Switzerland feels right."

"I love you," she breathed, staring into his eyes.

"Eight protons," he said, glancing down to see her atom necklace clasped around her neck. "Eight neutrons. I love you, AJ."

And he meant it.

With every inch of him did he mean it.

Because his life was always better with Alexandra Parker in it.

The very woman who would watch him graduate from Stanford.

And the very woman he'd someday ask to marry him.

The woman he'd watch as the Zürich sunlight touched her skin each morning when he woke up with her by his side.

Summer after senior year of college

E van Gilmore wasn't sure how it happened, but it had. He fell even more in love with his girlfriend during their perfect summer.

All summer, they spent their time together. They had even picked out an apartment in Zürich close to the Rodahawe Institute. The studio apartment that came with the research assistantship offered little room, and Evan had suggested that they find a place together. Just as AJ was about to bring up the topic of money, he shook his head and kissed her troubles away. Evan had more than enough guilt money from his parents. They had sent him money for his graduation and under the transaction details was a short message from them: *Happy graduation, Evan.*

It was more than he had ever expected from them. And like the other times, Evan sent an email to his lawyer to contact his parents and say thank you on his behalf. It was more than they deserved after years of neglect. The people he loved had watched him graduate with his business degree from Stanford. He might not have been drafted to the Major League—to the disappointment of a lot of Red Sox, Stanford, and baseball fans—but he was happy. He would be doing freelance work while his girlfriend lived her dreams. Some might say he was sacrificing his career for AJ's, but no one really knew the sacrifices AJ had already made for him to go to Stanford. It was about her dreams and not his.

His only dream, as it had always been, was a life with her.

And by playing professional baseball, he'd only thrust her back in the limelight she had always hated. Not playing in the Major League kept her safe and gave her the private life she always deserved the most.

Evan was truly happy.

And as he watched his girlfriend hug her mother, he knew that he had made the right decision in turning down

402

the management and marketing job offers to follow her to Switzerland. He would have never been truly happy knowing that she had given up a once-in-a-lifetime opportunity because of his selfishness.

Mrs. Parker stepped back and wiped away her tears. "I can't believe you two are going to Switzerland." Then she turned and smiled at him. "Thank you, Evan, for going with her."

He stepped forward and wrapped his arms around the woman who had supported him through everything. The woman who gave him love so freely and fiercely when she didn't have to. "Thank you, Mrs. Parker." He pulled back. "For everything. My life, your daughter, your love. Thank you."

"You turned out amazing, but it wasn't just us. It was you, too," Mrs. Parker explained.

He smiled his appreciation as he watched AJ hug her father. When their embrace ended, Mr. Parker turned his attention to Evan. "You take care of her, all right? She's my only daughter."

"Dad," AJ whined.

"I promise, Mr. Parker. I'll take care of Alexandra."

"You better, or I'll be on the first flight over there to kick your ass," his brother, Kyle, said as he approached them and stood next to AJ's mother. "Sorry I'm late. Meeting with the manager. Angie sends her apologies for not being here today. The charity still has her in Houston."

"That's okay," Evan said as he stepped forward and wrapped his arms around his brother. They may not have seen eye to eye for a long time, but they were still brothers. Kyle was the only relative Evan cherished. Ever since college, Evan felt as if he finally had a brother.

"Seriously, take care of her," Kyle said once their embraced ended.

"I will," he promised.

His brother smiled. "And take care of yourself. If you need anything, just call me."

"I will."

He squinted at Evan. "I mean it, Evan. Pride aside, I will send you money. I'll always be here for you. I know I wasn't for a long time, but I am now."

"I know," Evan assured. "And I'm always here for you. Any day or time."

Kyle nodded as he turned his attention to AJ. "And you ..." He stepped in front of her and cradled her jaw in his palms as unshed tears gleamed his eyes. It used to bother Evan that Kyle loved her, but as time passed, Evan accepted that AJ was a positive influence in his brother's life. While Angie set him free to be his own person, AJ had kept him grounded until he met his girlfriend. "You take care of my brother."

AJ let out a soft laugh. "I'll take care of Evan."

"Good." Kyle hugged her tight before he let her go. Then he smiled at them both. "This feels right. You and Evan. This was always right."

"You take care of yourself, Kyle. We'll be back in time for Thanksgiving," AJ announced.

"You two better get going. You still need to get through TSA and find your gate," AJ's father pointed out.

AJ and Evan exchanged one last embrace with her parents and his brother. When they pulled away, AJ said, "I love you all. We'll call once we've landed."

Then they said goodbye to their family.

The family they loved so much who had tears in their eyes and smiles on their face.

Their family who would wait for their return.

Taking his girlfriend's hand in his, Evan led them toward the TSA line. He heard AJ let out a sigh and glanced over to see her brushing away tears with her free hand.

"Are you okay?"

She nodded before she craned her neck and smiled at him. "I'm okay. I've said goodbye to my parents and Kyle every year before I left for Duke, but this time, it just felt so different. It felt like a real goodbye. We're going to be in a different country, miles and miles away. I've never been this far away from home for such a long time."

Evan squeezed AJ's hand and kissed the top of her head. "I know. But you're not alone."

"And I have you to thank for that. Thank you for being a part of this journey with me."

"You're welcome," he said once they arrived at the TSA line. "You ready, AJ?"

He watched her inhale a deep breath and release it. "I'm ready."

Evan and AJ had landed in Zürich just after midnight. By the time they had passed through customs and reached their apartment, they were exhausted. A lot of the bedding and the mattress had already been delivered and brought into their apartment by their landlord. The only thing they were missing was a bedframe, but it would arrive in a few days. So as his girlfriend showered, Evan made the bed for her. When she stepped out of the bathroom, he saw the tiredness in her eyes and helped her into bed. Then he kissed her forehead and went to the bathroom. After he finished showering, he returned to the bedroom to find AJ already asleep. So Evan slipped into their makeshift bed, kissed her good night, and fell asleep. They slept for almost nine hours.

This morning, after they had showered together, they ate a late breakfast at a café near their apartment on their way to the institute. As they stood in the reception of the Rodahawe Institute, he watched his girlfriend take it all in. Her eyes were the widest he'd ever seen them. She was in complete awe of the fact she was standing in the very institute where so many of the journal articles she had read during the summer had been written and researched.

"Alexandra?" a man with a British accent asked.

Evan whipped his attention to find a man in a white lab coat standing by the reception desk. He glanced over at Evan and then smiled at AJ.

"Hi," AJ said with a bubbly voice as she approached him. "That's me. But please call me Alex."

The Brit's smile widened as he held out his hand. "Nice to finally meet you. I'm Brandon. I'm on Vincent's team."

AJ shook his hand and then let it go. "It's so nice to meet you, Brandon." She glanced over her shoulder at Evan and waved him over. "And this is my boyfriend, Evan."

Brandon's blue eyes clouded with surprise as Evan stepped closer and held out his hand. "Nice to meet you, Brandon."

"Nice to meet you, too, Evan." Then he pulled out a

visitor's pass from his coat pocket and handed it to AJ. "I'm sorry I don't have one for you, Evan, but it's okay. I'll get you one when we see Vincent since he approves the passes. Alex, if you'll wear yours, then I'll show you both around."

"Thank you," AJ said as she attached the pass clip to her blouse pocket. She reached over and grasped Evan's hand, threading her fingers with his.

"Well, let's do a quick tour and see if Vincent is out of his meeting, shall we?"

AJ nodded. "Lead the way."

As they followed Brandon, he filled them in on the historical facts about the institute. When they reached the classical mechanics wing of the Rodahawe Institute, AJ inhaled sharply as they walked through the doors that Brandon had to swipe a card to open. She had released Evan's hand and stepped inside the large laboratory. It was the size of a small warehouse with equipment that appeared to be worth millions of dollars. But that wasn't what stunned him. It was the sight of his girlfriend taking in the lab. She was so beautiful when she was in awe. When she was so moved she was speechless.

"I've only ever seen videos and pictures, and they don't do the classical mechanics lab justice," AJ said, bewildered. "It's so incredible."

Brandon laughed. "It definitely does take your breath away the first time you see this place. Ah, Vincent! Your research assistant is here."

AJ stilled, her eyes flashing with sudden nerves as she took in the doctor who walked toward them. "Oh, my God," she breathed.

Dr. Rodahawe smiled. The doctor was tall and had dark

brown hair and eyes. He wore a light purple tie with his white business shirt. Several pens poked out of his shirt pocket. He was in his late thirties, a fact AJ told Evan numerous times, but to Evan, he just looked like another college science professor. But he knew the achievements of this man. His girlfriend had told him some impressive facts. He had been nominated for the Nobel Prize several times before winning it for the first time last year. He was likened to some of the very greats. He was also AJ's idol. And that kind and warm smile on his face was enough for Evan to know that his girlfriend would be working with someone who wasn't cold. The man had gentle eyes, and Evan believed he wouldn't break her in order to teach her.

"Ah, Alexandra, it's so nice to finally have you here. I'm Vincent Rodahawe."

AJ's lips parted as she blinked up at him. She was speechless. Finally, she said, "It's an honor to meet you, Dr. Rodahawe," and shook his hand.

The doctor glanced over at Evan who was waiting on the sidelines, allowing his girlfriend to take her time and take in her new workplace and co-workers. "And you must be the boyfriend who convinced her to change her mind. I must thank you for that. The moment I read Miss Parker's application, recommendations, and saw her video, I knew she would be perfect for the position."

Evan closed the distance and nodded at AJ's new boss. "There's no need to thank me, Dr. Rodahawe. Alexandra has been a longtime admirer."

The doctor's dark eyes glimmered. "Well, I am an admirer of hers. Alexandra, we'll just get your papers. Why don't you

THE DISSOLUTION OF UNREQUITED

go over to your work station and see if it's to your liking? It's just the desk by the window with the small welcome balloon. We won't be too long."

When Brandon and Dr. Rodahawe walked away, AJ led Evan to her new desk. The window wasn't just a window. It was an entire wall of glass panels with a view of the lake. If he thought the view from their apartment of the lake was stunning, he was wrong. The view from her desk topped it completely. Evan glanced down at the balloon and smiled, happy that his girlfriend had such a warm welcoming at her new job.

"Evan," AJ said, getting his attention.

He craned his neck to find the appreciation flash in her eyes. Her smile was gone, but she wasn't upset. She appeared grateful. "Yeah, AJ?"

Her lips formed a small, honest smile. "Thank you for this. I don't even have the words to express how thankful I am and how much I love you. Because I do. I could have never experienced this, and I would have been okay. But experiencing this with you, my heart feels so full right now."

And that sweet smile of hers took him back.

To all the times that smile made her green eyes softened.

To all the times he watched her experience life so purely.

And Evan knew that he had made the right decision in following her.

Because he didn't know it, but this—seeing her this happy—was his biggest dream come true.

Evan bent down and kissed her forehead. Then he looked down at her, and whispered, "I'd follow you here if I had to make the choice again. I'd follow you anywhere, Alexandra.

409

Anywhere and forever."

And that was the truth.

Six months before AJ's Boston return

A lot had happened in over a year.

But a lot had also stayed the same.

His love for his girlfriend had strengthened, flourished even.

He had never felt so right than when he woke up each morning to find her lying next to him. To watch her be so tired but still so happy with her job made him happy. He was often lonely during the day when he worked from home, but at night, when she came home, and on the weekends, those were the moments he cherished the most.

Zürich wasn't so bad. Evan had even come to love and appreciate the Swiss city. The lake was his favorite part. After he ate breakfast and walked or taken a cab to the institute to drop off his girlfriend, he'd run as far as he could around the lake. The lake was so large that he would never make it all the way around, but he always ran as if he might someday. Things back home had continued without them. His brother was still going strong with Angie, and from the sounds of it, Savannah missed them and Zürich after she had visited for a week during the summer.

But the biggest change back home was when they had

found out that AJ's mother was pregnant. It had come as a shock to not only AJ but also her parents. They had been told by doctors that they wouldn't be able to conceive after AJ. The fact that Mrs. Parker would have a baby boy had stunned them all. AJ was excited; she had always wanted a sibling. Her parents had assumed she'd be upset, that she'd think they were replacing her, but AJ had assured them she was excited and happy. In four months, they would return for the Christmas holidays and hopefully be home in time for AJ's brother's birth.

As for AJ, she excelled at being Dr. Rodahawe's research assistant. She was surprised when she actually assisted him in his research and catalogued his findings on the first day. She strongly believed that she would be making him coffee, but she was wrong. A few months ago, she had noticed a mistake in his formula and had pointed it out to him. That had resulted in Dr. Rodahawe entrusting her to create a new equation that could further assist his research on velocity. It also meant longer nights away from Evan, but he didn't mind. She was doing what she loved. Evan—like most things in the past year—had adapted to fit in his girlfriend's career.

And tonight was another one of those things.

It was Brandon's birthday. They were at a bar celebrating with the rest of the research team. Evan didn't have many friends in Zürich. His girlfriend's friends and co-workers were his friends. Well, except for Brandon. The Brit didn't like Evan so much. Sure, Brandon was friendly, but Evan wasn't stupid or blind. He knew that Brandon found AJ attractive. Who didn't? It wasn't at all surprising to him, but he did nothing. He knew AJ loved him and chose him. Evan wasn't afraid that some Brit with a science degree would steal his girl away.

"Here you are," the bartender with the thick Swiss accent said as he handed Evan his Heineken and AJ's vodka and Sprite. He spun around to find his girlfriend on the other end of the dance floor with Julia, one of the scientists from the classical mechanics department.

Evan took in his girlfriend. AJ had worn a tight black long-sleeve dress with a pair of heeled boots. Her hair was down in her natural curls, and the large dip in the front of her dress showed off her cleavage. Evan knew he was a lucky man to have such a beautiful girlfriend, but it wasn't just AJ's physical features that made her beautiful to him.

It was her heart.

Her mind.

Her thoughts.

Her kindness.

Her intelligence.

Her devotion.

Her love for him.

She was everything to him.

"You can't ever take your eyes from her," Dr. Rodahawe stated as he leaned on the bar next to Evan.

Evan swung his gaze to find the doctor staring at AJ. "She's the love of my life, Dr. Rodahawe."

The doctor smiled. "I don't doubt that at all. And I can see it in her eyes that you're the love of her life, too. That's why I understand why she declined my offer."

What offer?

Evan winced, confused at the news of an offer presented to his girlfriend. "I'm sorry, what?"

He faced Evan, a tight smile on his face. "I can see that

she didn't tell you. Evan, Alexandra is one of the most gifted physicists I've ever had the pleasure of knowing and working with, and I know she will do very well in her career. I offered her a three-year contract to continue to work at the institute. More money and more time to work on her own research. But she declined my offer."

"She did?"

The doctor nodded. "She did."

Evan shook his head in disbelief. "She loves the institute. Why would she say no?"

"Oh, Evan." He sighed. "Alexandra might love science, but she's in love with you. Her love for you is far greater than her love for science. She knows that you're not truly happy here in Zürich, and she wants to go home with you. You've both stayed far longer than her initial assistantship. She told me that your dreams are next once she finishes here."

AJ gave up three years with the best research institute for me.

Evan glanced over to find her still talking to Julia. "I can't believe she did that for me." Then he returned his focus on AJ's mentor. "She loves it here in Zürich."

Dr. Rodahawe set his palm on Evan's shoulder. "Science isn't going to love her back, Evan. Not many of us get to go home to someone we love after hours of research. She has that with you."

He nodded, understanding what the doctor was saying. "Thank you. I better get her drink to her before the ice waters it down. I'll see you in a bit."

"Sure thing, Evan."

And just as he was about to step toward AJ, Evan halted and then smiled at Vincent Rodahawe. "Thank you for telling me."

"Of course," Dr. Rodahawe said before Evan left the bar and made his way to AJ.

"And one vodka and Sprite for my beautiful girlfriend. I'm sorry it took so long. Dr. Rodahawe could not stop singing your praises, AJ."

His girlfriend's cheeks tinted in a lovely pink. "Oh, stop it. He did not, Evan," she downplayed as she took her beverage from him.

"He does not stop talking about you, Alex," Julia added as she brushed her auburn braid over her shoulder. "In all my years at the institute, no one has ever had quite the impact as you. No intern or assistant has ever had the intellect to challenge him. You shouldn't be embarrassed. You're incredible, Alex. Okay, I'll leave you both. I'm going to go see if there are any of those mini burgers I love." And before they could even say bye to Julia, she was already gone.

Evan set his beer on the table next to them and pressed his cold hands on her cheeks, causing her to flinch and laugh at the coolness. He stared into those eyes he loved so much.

She had kept the offer from him, but he understood why. At the end of the day, it was her decision.

Why would you give up three years at the Rodahawe Institute for me, AJ?

He wanted to ask her.

But it would cause an unnecessary fight.

She had made her decision.

She had chosen him.

And as his thumb brushed along her cheekbone, he had chosen her. "I love you."

AJ smiled. "I love you, too." Then she reached over and

set her glass down on the table. "Can we go home now? We've stayed long past the mandatory stuff. I'd really like to go home and be with you."

"Be with me?" he asked, coy.

That smile turned into a seductive grin as she leaned in close, and whispered, "I need you, Evan. I need you to make love to me."

And before she could further seduce him with her whispers, he kissed her hard and deep. Just like he intended to make love to her tonight.

Because unlike AJ and her love for science, Evan had nothing he loved more or as close to his love for the woman who kissed him with as much urgency and love as him.

And her kisses, they were love letters from her heart, and he treasured them entirely.

Just her.

He would only ever love her.

96

Cm

curium

EVAN

Now

I t had been a day since Evan and AJ told her parents
they were expecting a daughter. Mrs. Parker's idea of a
celebration was a home-cooked meal together. And as Evan sat
at the table with his girlfriend and his daughter's grandparents,
he had never felt more content in his life.

He felt truly a part of their family.

Not just as Alexandra's best friend or boyfriend.

But as the father of Alexandra's child.

They had spoken briefly about their plans, and her mother
had already promised some of Sebastian's old clothes to them.
His girlfriend laughed and nodded along. Her mother wanted to
plan the baby shower with Savannah, and AJ's only request was it
not just be about her but also about Evan. They were going to do
a joint baby shower to celebrate with all their friends and family.
She wanted as much love celebrating their daughter's arrival into
the world as possible. Now that they had told AJ's parents, she
was happier. It was as if the secrecy of their baby had weighed
her down. She was close to her parents, and he knew keeping
it a secret had taken its toll on her. They still had the rest of
her family to tell, but they would be video-chatting with them
since they all lived in Australia and New York.

Today, they would tell the last important person in their lives.

Today, they would tell his brother.

Evan was nervous. As much as he now loved and respected his brother, he still worried about his reaction. Still wondered if Kyle harbored any feelings toward AJ. He knew Kyle loved Angie, but from what he was last told, things weren't as perfect as they had once been. The past few weeks were hard for Kyle with Angie traveling back and forth from the US to Zimbabwe for aide work. They apparently fought more, and Kyle had become more distant around Evan. AJ told him it was just a rough patch and that Kyle and Angie would get through it together. They just needed time.

"Are you okay?" AJ asked as her hand on his arm squeezed.

He turned away from his brother and some of the pitchers warming up at Fenway Park. It was just after three p.m., and the park tours had ended early for today's game. When he had asked AJ how she wanted to tell Kyle, she smiled and told him before today's game at Fenway. So that their daughter's uncle had an even more special connection with his niece.

"I'm okay. Just nervous," he admitted.

AJ smiled at him. "We don't have to do it today if you're not ready."

He shook his head and glanced at the bag he held. His girlfriend had spent most of the morning getting Kyle's baby reveal gift. She had even managed to get some of the players in on the reveal, too. "No. I want it to be today. Why do you want it to be today?"

"Well," she said, as she let go of his arm and stepped in front of him. AJ smiled as she adjusted his red tie. Now that he worked at Fenway, he had traded his casual clothes for suits and ties. "Do you remember the day we sat in the bleachers and got caught on the jumbo screen?"

He nodded. "I remember."

AJ inhaled a deep breath and released it with a small smile on her lips. "Do you also remember how mad and hurt Kyle was?"

Evan remembered that day. It was the day his brother called AJ stupid for listening to him. It was also the day he drove AJ to New York, and she promised she'd always pick him over his brother. "He was mad at me, AJ."

"Well, do you remember the team the Red Sox played that day?"

He would never forget.

"The Rockies ..." he breathed.

His girlfriend cupped his jaw, her thumb brushing against his skin. "It's been years since Kyle last played a series against them. Today, I want to replace that memory of his last game against the Rockies with a new one. With him finding out he's going to be an uncle before the game against them today."

His heart stretched.

He loved how much she cared for others.

Adored every inch of that generous heart of hers.

He hoped to God their daughter was like Alexandra.

"I love you," he whispered.

"I love you, too," she said in a small voice as she got on her toes and kissed him soft and sweet. Then she dropped her hands from his jaw and took the bag from him. She turned and glanced over at Adrian Whitaker, the manager of the Red Sox.

He was smiling at them and then nodded. It was the sign

they had been waiting for. Cameras around the park had been turned off. The media were ordered to set up later than usual. This moment was theirs and the Red Sox. AJ wasn't ready to share it with the world just yet and neither was Evan. This was about ensuring that their daughter was loved by those important to AJ and Evan before they let the world love her, too.

"You ready?" Evan asked as he stepped next to her and grasped her hand.

With an assuring nod, AJ squeezed his hand, and said, "I'm ready."

They walked around the park and headed toward where his brother, Kyle, was throwing the ball to one of the pitchers. His brother had a smile on his face as his teammates threw the ball back and forth. Once AJ and Evan made it past first base, he glanced over his shoulders to find several of the Red Sox players with hands behind their backs, ready to play their part. He turned his head and concentrated on calming his fast heartbeats. He had no reason to worry. Evan and his brother had been good and solid for years.

Evan just wanted Kyle to be as happy and excited as he was.

He wanted Kyle to love the daughter Evan would raise with AJ.

When they reached his brother, he caught the ball from Waller and noticed him and AJ. He raised his hand at his teammate, indicating they were taking a break. Kyle turned and smiled at them.

"Hey," he said as one of the equipment staff ran up to him and took his glove and ball from him. Then they were left alone. "It's still so weird to see you in a suit at Fenway, Evan."

AJ released Evan's hand with a laugh.

Evan rolled his eyes. "Whatever."

Kyle grinned at AJ. "Alexi always dresses the part. I can't believe this is your first home game. It was too bad you were too sick for our last home series."

"I'm so sorry about that. I promise, I won't miss any more," AJ said. She had to miss the series against Tampa Bay because of morning sickness. She had felt so awful when she had to stay at home and watch it in bed.

"It's okay, Alexi. I expect you cheering today," Kyle said.

"I will be," AJ confirmed and peeked over at Evan. Her eyes shone bright with questions.

Are you sure you're ready?

If you are, now?

Evan cleared his throat and straightened his spine. He was ready. More than ready. He was ready to share this part of his life with his brother. "Kyle, AJ and I got you something."

His brother's brows furrowed. "You did?"

AJ nodded, her smile stretching as she presented the Red Sox captain with the white gift bag. "We did."

Evan peeked over his shoulder to find Kyle's teammates making their way toward them. He even noticed Mick, the social media manager, with a camera, no doubt capturing this private moment Fenway Park was about to host.

"Why are you two being so weird?" Kyle asked, humor echoing in his voice as he stuck a hand into the bag.

AJ hugged Evan's arm and kissed his cheek.

He looked down at her and smiled.

It didn't matter what happened. As long as he had her and his daughter, nothing would matter more in his life.

Evan lifted his chin as Kyle removed the white Red Sox bodysuit with the navy sleeves. Kyle dropped the bag and held the bodysuit in his hands. His eyes widened as he read out loud, "I'm not worried. My uncle's the captain of the Red Sox."

"Turn it around," AJ urged.

Kyle turned the bodysuit over as tears washed over his eyes. "Gilmore. Thirteen." His tears rolled down his cheeks as he lifted his chin. His glanced at Evan and then at AJ. "Really?"

Evan nodded. "Really," he confirmed as AJ unwound her arms from his.

"I'm going to be an uncle?" he breathed in bewilderment.

"You are," AJ said, her voice cracked with emotion.

Then Kyle advanced toward Evan and wrapped his arms around him, sobbing into his shoulder. "Thank you," his brother cried. Then he pulled back as Evan blinked his own tears free. "I'm going to be an uncle."

Evan laughed. "You are."

Kyle looked at the baby bodysuit in his hand and then at AJ. "You're really pregnant with my niece or nephew right now?"

AJ stepped forward and hugged Kyle for a long moment. When she pulled away, she announced, "I'm pregnant with your niece."

Kyle's brown eyes softened. It appeared to be unconditional love that shone bright. "I'm going to have a niece."

"Congratulations, Uncle Kyle!" was shouted around them as streamer poppers exploded, coating them with red, white, and navy streamers. Kyle's teammates and some of the Red Sox staff joined them as camera shutters went off, capturing this moment.

Evan watched as the other players pulled his girlfriend away to hug her and congratulate her on her pregnancy. She was carrying a future Red Sox fan, and they all knew it. He smiled, seeing the love they had for his girlfriend. The Red Sox had always been her family through every up and down.

And he knew that this team and this city would love his daughter too.

He was sure of it.

He looked at his brother who was still staring at his surname and number on the back of the onesie.

"You'll be her favorite player," Evan said, knowing how true it would be. "She's going to love you."

Kyle nodded as he looked up at Evan. "I hope I'm a good uncle."

Evan laughed. "You will be. I hope I'm a good father."

It was as if it suddenly hit his brother. "Holy shit. You're going to be a father."

"Yeah. I know. It's crazy. I'm so glad we told you this way. AJ wanted to replace your old memories against the Rockies with a new one. So when you think of the Rockies, it won't be of us sitting with their fans. It'll be of you finding out you're going to be an uncle."

He looked over at Evan's girlfriend. "She really is something special. She's going to make a great mom, Ev."

Evan looked at AJ, his heart wanting to burst at the smile on her face, the happiness in her eyes, and the contentment in each hug she gave. He couldn't wait for every day of the rest of his life with her. "She really is."

"Have you told her parents?"

"We did. We told Mr. and Mrs. Parker yesterday."

Kyle closed the distance and set his palms on Evan's shoulders. "Evan?" He stilled at the way Kyle's brows met with concern. "I think you should tell our parents."

It was a thought he'd contemplated for weeks now, but he didn't want to burden AJ with it. She had never once pressured him to reconcile with his parents. For years, he was happy without them, but recently, he thought of AJ. Thought of her growing up without her other grandmother's love or acknowledgment. AJ had always handled it with more maturity than her grandmother, but he knew it still hurt her knowing that her mother's mother didn't want anything to do with her. Evan had concluded he didn't want his daughter to grow up with that same feeling.

And it meant putting aside his pride.

For my daughter.

If they didn't want to be in his daughter's life, then so be it. But he had to give them a chance so that he knew he at least tried.

He pressed his lips into a tight line. "I haven't spoken to them in years."

"Me either. I'm still angry with them for what they did to us. I was old enough to take care of myself. I was drafted right away. But you, Ev, you were still a kid. What they did to you, never making you feel loved, that wasn't right. If you want them in your daughter's life, I will respect that, and I'll put my pride aside. I won't forgive them, but I'll learn to be civil. She's going to be my niece, and I will always protect her. I won't ever let them hurt her."

The protectiveness in Kyle's voice was all that Evan had

wanted to hear growing up. But hearing it toward his daughter and her happiness meant so much more. "Thank you, Kyle. That means everything to me. I'll think about talking to them. For now, let's celebrate with AJ before your big game. You sure you're gonna be okay to play with the news we just told you?"

Kyle's grin widened. "Are you kidding? I'm playing to win for my niece. Today's game and every game for the rest of my life. After all, her uncle is the captain of the Red Sox."

Evan laughed.

Yeah, his daughter was going to be so loved by her uncle.

He was as sure as the way AJ looked at him with love.

True and right.

It had been almost two months since AJ and Evan had told their families that they were expecting a daughter. Two months since Kyle had cried before his game against the Rockies. It didn't take long for the people of Boston and the Red Sox fans to learn that their captain was going to be an uncle. Their baby's gender was even a guessing game. But to keep some aspects of their pregnancy private, they kept the gender from the public. AJ didn't mind being back in the spotlight, but she didn't go out looking for it. As for Evan, he concentrated on work. His role in operations at Fenway Park was not easy. He had to ensure that the business side of Fenway Park ran smoothly. Now that he'd held the position for four months, he felt more comfortable in his job and even enjoyed it.

Being related to the long-serving Red Sox captain came

with perks. So long as Evan was happy at Fenway Park, Kyle Gilmore was happy. And when Evan asked for a few days off to take care of some family business, it was granted. He was worried since Mondays were one of the busiest days of the week, but they still let him take a few days off.

Family business.

His family was his girlfriend, his girlfriend's family, and his brother. They were his family. But this particular family business involved him leaving Boston for a few days.

It meant flying to Chicago of all places.

Evan closed the trunk of AJ's car and walked around it to find her cradling her baby bump. He set his suitcase down and pressed his palms to her cheeks.

"If anything happens, like you don't feel well, call me right away, and I'll take the first flight out. Also call your mother until I can get home," he instructed.

AJ let out a laugh. "Evan, I'm six months pregnant. I'm not about to give birth while you're away."

"I mean it, AJ. Anything, you call me."

"You're only going to be gone until Wednesday. You won't miss a lot."

He rolled his eyes at her. "I'm serious."

She laughed once again. "I know you're serious. I'll call if she kicks or moves even a fraction while you're in Chicago."

She.

He loved it when AJ said *she* or *their daughter*.

It made his heart swell and fill with warmth that he had come to love so much.

"Have a safe flight, okay?"

He nodded. "As soon as I finish talking to my parents, I'll come home."

"Evan, you don't have to talk to them if you don't want to."

He dropped a hand from her face and pressed it against the swell of her stomach. "AJ, I'm doing it for her and for you."

"For me?" she asked once he lifted his chin so that his eyes met hers.

"I don't ever want our daughter to feel the way you have when it comes to your grandmother. Sure, I might not ever get along with my parents, but I know that if I tell them they can be in her life, they will want that. It's not about me; it's about her. I don't want her to feel what you did growing up when Will, Lori, and Reese used to speak about your grandmother," he explained.

Her hands reached up and pressed on his chest. "You're really doing this for her?"

Evan nodded. "She's my daughter, AJ. I want everything figured out before she's here with us. I want to at least know where my parents stand in her life."

"You're amazing. I know this is uncomfortable for you. Just know that I appreciate what you're doing, and she would, too," AJ said as she got on her toes and pressed her lips to his in a chaste kiss. "Just come home safely, okay?"

"I will," he promised as his hands reached up and steadied her face. Evan kissed her forehead and looked down at her. "I love you, AJ."

"I love you, too," she whispered before he pulled away and grasped the handle of his suitcase.

He kissed her once more, and promised, "I'll call you tonight. Drive home safely, all right?" His girlfriend nodded as Evan set his palms on her stomach. "Daddy will be home in a few days. Don't be too hard on Mummy, okay, Little Atom?"

Then he smiled at AJ before he entered Logan International Airport, ready to finally see his parents after all these years.

Evan was surprised when the cab pulled up at an apartment tower in South Loop. He had always assumed his parents had bought a mansion outside of Chicago, but he had been wrong. After he had checked in at the hotel, he left his suitcase in his room and got in a cab to see his parents. His cab driver said that many business executives lived in South Loop's luxury high rise apartments, so he understood why they chose this part of town to call home. Evan would have been fine without knowing where his parents lived, but he was doing this for his daughter. So that his daughter would never experience what AJ had with her own grandmother.

"Mr. Gilmore," the man at the front desk said, getting Evan's attention.

"Yes."

"Mrs. Gilmore and Mr. Gilmore are aware that you are here."

Evan nodded. "And will they see me?"

The man behind the desk stood and pointed behind him. "Yes, Mr. Gilmore. Just take the elevator behind you and use this key card to access the top floor. They are waiting for you."

Taking the plastic card from the employee, Evan spun around and made his way to the elevator. Once he pressed the button on the wall and the doors opened, he stepped inside and swiped the key card on the panel. Then he pressed the top floor number and waited as the elevator ascended to his desired floor. The soft melody from the elevator's speakers didn't settle his nerves. At that moment, he was numb. He wasn't sure how to feel. He was confronting his absent parents. It wasn't to mend his bridges.

But for my daughter.

When the elevator opened, the sight of a grand foyer welcomed him. Evan stepped off the elevator and took in the apartment. It was luxurious and everything he expected of his parents. But unlike the family home in Brookline, this apartment in Chicago had warmth and personalization. It had the remnants of a family. And as he took in the picture frames on the table by the wall, he was shocked to find pictures of him and Kyle. His parents had never truly cared about him. They did love Kyle but never Evan. But when they left Brookline, they left both sons.

"Evan," he heard a woman say.

He took his eyes from the photographs to find his mother in the foyer. She seemed softer in her features. Every time he thought of her, he always remembered her hard features—the lines on her face and the coldness in her eyes—but in front of him wasn't that woman. Nor was the guilt in her light brown eyes.

"Susan," Evan said. The term 'mom' had never fit her. She had never been motherly to him. It was all for show for his brother's baseball career.

A tight smile strained her lips. "I didn't know you'd be in town."

Evan turned to face her properly. "I got time off work. I had to come see you and Christopher. We need to talk."

"Your father is in the living room. Follow me," she said before she led him out of the foyer, down a hallway, and into the living room.

And just like the rest of the house, it was stylish and grand. Leather seats and oil paintings on the wall. The summer sun brought light through the large windows and made the apartment feel even larger. Evan had planned to give himself tonight to think through what he wanted to say and see his parents tomorrow, then return to Boston by Wednesday morning. But after reading his girlfriend's text message about how their daughter had kicked in her stomach, he wanted to return to Massachusetts as soon as possible.

"Christopher, Evan is here," Susan alerted.

His father glanced up from his laptop, his eyes wide with surprise to see him. Christopher looked like an older version of Kyle with the same brown hair and light brown eyes. He set the laptop on the coffee table and stood. "I can't believe you're actually here in Chicago."

"I asked Lucas for your address. He told me that you both allowed him to give it to me or Kyle should we ever ask for it. We need to talk," Evan announced.

Susan nodded. "Would you like a drink?"

Evan shook his head as he walked toward the armchair next to where Christopher had just sat. "No, thank you. I'm fine."

"Okay," she said as she and Christopher sat down next to each other on the leather couch. "How are you, Evan?"

He winced, surprised that she sounded so genuine. "I'm okay."

His father stared at him and then glanced at his mother. They nodded at each other before he asked, "Do you need money?"

Of course, that's what they would ask.

"No, I don't need your money. That's not why I'm here."

Susan leaned closer and revealed the picture that sat on the side table behind her, causing his nostrils to flare. "Okay. What can we do for you?"

"Where did you get that?" he demanded.

"Get what?" Christopher asked.

Evan pointed at the framed picture of him and Kyle at Evan's Stanford graduation. "Where did you get that picture of me and Kyle?"

His mother glanced over her shoulder, reached over, and grasped it. When she turned, she gazed at the picture, her thumb brushing against the glass. "Clara sent it."

Mrs. Parker?

"She did?"

Susan nodded and then lifted her chin, her eyes glazed over with unshed tears. "She's been more your mother than I have ever been even though I never asked her to, Evan. Sometimes, I get a letter with some pictures from her. That one is my favorite. You graduated from Stanford."

"That was over two years ago."

"It was," she said, setting the frame back on the table. "So what brings you to Illinois?"

Evan inhaled a deep breath and exhaled it shortly later. "It's been tense between us for years. I get it. I'm the son who kept you in Brookline when you both wanted to travel and work. For so long, I've felt so much resentment toward you both. But I have to admit, I'm tired. I hate going through lawyers when I have to thank you for things like giving me the deed to the house when I turned eighteen. But we can't continue this. We either settle it or cut ties."

His mother gasped, and his father covered her hand with his. It was oddly nice to see that even though they never truly loved their children, they still loved each other.

"Evan, we never meant to hurt you or Kyle. We were starting a business. And yeah, your mother and I fought, but leaving Massachusetts was what saved our marriage. Noel and Clara took you in and gave you what we couldn't. And they shouldn't have needed to do that. We're so sorry," his father said. From the sympathy in his voice and eyes, it was evident he meant it.

"And we couldn't bring you to Illinois with us. Kyle had baseball, and you had Alexandra," his mother explained.

Alexandra.

He had Alexandra.

He had always had Alexandra.

Evan would have never joined his parents in Chicago if it meant that he had to leave her behind. Even when they were just best friends, he wouldn't have done that to her. He cared and loved her too much to be without her.

"That's who we have to talk about." Suddenly, nerves succumbed him. They shouldn't have, but they did. "I'd like to talk about Alexandra with you."

"You want to talk about your best friend with us?" his father asked, confused.

Evan nodded. "Actually, Alexandra isn't just my best friend ..."

His mother's brows furrowed. "What happened? You didn't go to Stanford together."

"No, we didn't. She went to Duke. We've been through a

lot together." He paused and smiled at the thought. They really had been through a lot together, and they had come out of it stronger. His heart made a strong beat as he revealed, "She's actually the love of my life."

His mother's concern faded away as glee consumed her face. "Evan, that's great. I always knew you both had a special connection."

"We're together," he added.

"Together?" Christopher said, skeptical. "Her father's okay with you two being together? I know Noel and—"

"Noel knows," Evan said, interrupting him. "We've been together since junior year of college. We even lived in Switzerland for over a year together. I'm here because of her."

Evan rubbed his lips together to give himself a second. A single second to decide if he wanted his parents in his daughter's life. He didn't know them, but then again, he had never given them a chance, so he would be the bigger person. "I'm here because when Alexandra was growing up, she had to watch and hear her cousins spend time with her grandmother. Because of her mother's strained relationship with her own mother, Alexandra never got to meet her grandmother. It doesn't hurt her the way it used to, but I know she's a little upset by her grandmother's refusal to meet her. Though she has never come out and admitted it, in Alexandra's mind, she doesn't think she's good enough in her grandmother's eyes."

"I … I don't understand, Evan," Susan uttered.

He inhaled a deep breath and released it slowly, ready to reveal the truth to his surprising visit to Chicago. "I'm here today to mend bridges because I don't ever want *my* daughter to feel the way Alexandra did when her grandmother ignored her."

His parents' eyes widened in shock.

"Your daughter?" his father breathed.

Evan nodded. "Alexandra and I are expecting a girl in September. And we can continue whatever this tense relationship is, but I'd like you both—if that's something you'd want—to be part of her life. You don't have to talk to me, but it would mean the world to Alexandra if you gave our daughter the chance to be a part of her life."

"You're going to be a father?" his mother asked in awe.

"I am," Evan confirmed as he stood and pulled his wallet from his back jeans pocket. He flipped it open and removed AJ's latest ultrasound. Then he handed it to his mother. "You can keep it. I have more at home."

His mother unfolded the ultrasound and stared at it as his father asked, "Are you and Alexandra living in the house together?"

Evan shook his head. "I sold the house to Kyle. Alexandra and I live in Cambridge, close to MIT where she is going for her Ph.D."

"Wow," his father uttered. "I always wondered why you gave up the chance at Major League baseball."

Smiling, Evan proudly said, "I gave it up for her. I followed her to Switzerland so she could work and learn at the best science institute in the world. I also gave it up for me. Kyle's the professional baseball player. Not me. It would have hurt Alexandra more to be thrust back into the limelight. I would much rather work at Fenway Park than play there."

Susan got up from the couch, stepped forward, and bent her knees so that her eyes were on him. Then she pressed her hands on his knees. "Evan, I have been an absent mother, and I know that. I will never stop being sorry for that. All the moments I missed, I got photographs of, and I knew I'd never get to be a part of your life. But if I can be a part of my grandchild's life, I will."

Evan's lips splayed into a small smile. "It's going to take time to make up for everything. Not with just me but with Kyle, too. But this is a start. I know Alexandra will like that you want to be a part of our daughter's life."

"I want to. I want to be in not only my granddaughter's life but in my sons' lives, too." Then she stood and glanced over her shoulder. "We both do, don't we, Christopher?"

His father got up from the couch. "Yes." He stepped closer and stood next to Susan. "We were neglectful parents who allowed a wonderful couple to raise our children. We owe Noel and Clara so much for raising you and Kyle right. And to know that you fell in love with their daughter ... It feels right. And if you'll let us, we'd like to be in all of your lives."

Evan stood. "I can't speak for Kyle, but we can try."

His mother squealed. "I've been waiting for this moment for years. How long are you in Chicago for? We can go—"

"I have to get home to Alexandra. I hope you understand," Evan said, interrupting his mother.

"Of course. You need to be with the woman carrying your child," Christopher said. "Can you stay for dinner?"

"We can have dinner before I leave," Evan said, his chest feeling light.

He had gotten rid of the bitterness that had held him back all these years.

For his daughter, he'd face the very worst to give her the very best.

It was almost two a.m. when Evan inserted the key into the lock and twisted the handle. After he entered the house he owned with his girlfriend, he pulled the key out and closed the door behind him. Ensuring the front door was locked, Evan set his suitcase by the door and headed up the staircase to his bedroom. Once he reached his bedroom door, he gently pushed it open and snuck inside to find AJ still asleep on his side of the bed with her phone on her chest and the lamp still on. After he had dinner with his parents, he had FaceTimed AJ and they'd spoken briefly of his parents' involvement in their lives before she had fallen asleep. He didn't tell her that he managed to get on a late flight out of Chicago and was coming home early.

Evan walked over to his side of the bed and picked up AJ's phone from her chest. He set it down on the nightstand and switched off the lamp. Making his way around the bed, he reached AJ's side and kicked off his shoes. Evan reached down and peeled off his socks, then removed his jeans and shirt, leaving him in just his boxer briefs. Pulling the thin blanket back, he slipped into bed, wrapping his arm over AJ. She turned slightly, snuggling into his chest. Evan dug his arm under her so that he could hold her properly.

"Evan?" she mumbled as she tilted her head back. The moonlight that crept through the break in the window shades gave him enough light to see the love in her green eyes.

"It's me," he whispered, smiling down at her.

She set her hand on his hip. "You're not supposed to be home until Wednesday."

His palms rubbed her lower back. "I missed you too much."

AJ hummed as he rolled onto his back, pressing her cheek to his chest. She snuggled against him and let out a contented sigh. "Welcome home."

Evan closed his eyes and let out his own contented sigh, loving how perfect his girlfriend felt in his arms. "My home will always be you and Little Atom."

^{97}Bk

berkelium

ALEX

Six months before Alex's Boston return

Alex: I am so sorry I missed dinner. I'm so, so, so sorry, Evan. I know I promised I'd actually be home in time to sit and have dinner with you, but I lost track of time. I swear, I'll be home early tomorrow. I'm on my way to the apartment now. I just picked up three cakes from that store you like for every hour I'm late. I'm so sorry, Evan. I'll be there soon. I love you.

    "*Merci vilmal*," Alex thanked her elderly neighbor who held the elevator for her.

"Ah, very good, Alexandra. And you're very welcome. *Sächzä?*" he asked as his finger hovered over the panel. No doubt seeing her struggle with the boxed cakes in her hands.

"*Sächzä.*" Sixteen.

When the elevators closed, he said, "Your Swiss German is getting better. Soon we'll be talking in sentences. How is your *Früünd?*" Boyfriend.

Alex smiled. "Evan is good. I bought home some of his favorite cakes because I'm late coming home."

"Long day at the institute?"

439

She nodded. "Too many long days. Hopefully, once I finish this small formula that will help break down the bigger component of my actual formula, I can come home on time." The elevator came to a stop at Mr. Impfeld's floor. "I'm sure he doesn't mind."

I hope not.

But Alex hadn't voiced that out loud. Ever since Brandon's birthday party last week, Evan had been acting strange. When they had come home from the party, they had made love, and it was amazing. The next morning, as she was getting ready for work, she saw the guilt in his eyes. Guilt that she didn't quite understand. Maybe it was because he had caused her to arrive later at the institute than she had originally planned. However, waking up in her boyfriend's arms was perfect and worth being late. But throughout the week, Evan didn't seem like himself. And it didn't help that she saw him late or not at all when she came home from spending all day working on her equation.

"You two have a good night. *Bis spöter*, Alexandra," Mr. Impfeld said.

"*Bis spöter*, Mr. Impfeld." *See you later.*

Then the doors closed, and the elevator resumed its journey to her floor. Alex hadn't heard from Evan all day, and she knew he must be mad at her. They had been in Zürich for over the intended year, and she knew he wanted to go home. He had bit his tongue and stayed longer in Switzerland without a single argument. That was why she had turned down Dr. Rodahawe's offer for three more years of employment. She wouldn't be a research assistant. She'd be a researcher working on her own research. It would have been the first step toward her own discoveries and dreams of being published in journals. But she had turned it down because she loved Evan Gilmore more than her career.

She had the experience of working with the finest physicist and mentor, but it was time she returned to the States. It was time to support Evan's dreams and follow her initial desires of MIT. The elevator came to a stop, waking Alex from her wandering thoughts. She hated the look of disappointment on Dr. Rodahawe's face when she turned down the offer, but she hated coming home to see the hurt on Evan's face more. To feel his pain. She couldn't take it anymore. They needed to go home.

Alex exited the elevator and made her way down the hall and to her apartment. She pulled her keys out of her jacket pocket and juggled the boxed cakes with one hand. Once she unlocked the door, she pulled the key out and stepped into her apartment, kicking the door shut behind her.

Alex's brows furrowed as she took in her dark apartment. She headed down the hall and made her way into the kitchen. Carefully, she set the boxed cakes and keys on the counter. Then she headed over to the light switch and flicked it on, causing the kitchen to illuminate. Shoving her hands into her jacket pockets, she realized he must have fallen asleep and headed to their bedroom. Alex saw light coming from the open bedroom door. She stepped in the room to find her boyfriend sitting on their bed, staring at his hands.

"Evan," she said, worried and unable to see his face.

He didn't say anything.

Alex stepped closer until she was able to get on her knees in front of him. She looked up at him. "I'm so sorry I'm late.

I didn't mean to be so late."

Evan sighed as he lifted his chin and stared at her. His heartbroken eyes searched her face, trying to find answers to questions she had no idea he had. "AJ ..."

It was the way he said her name.

The pain in his voice.

She suddenly felt sick as her eyes stung with tears. "I'm sorry, Evan."

He reached up and covered her cheek with his palm. "I love you."

"I love you, too," she whispered as she wrapped her fingers around his wrist, wanting to hold him to her.

"And I'm so proud of you." His thumb gently brushed her cheek. "I've tried, AJ. All week, I've tried."

"Tried what? Talk to me," she begged.

Her boyfriend sighed. "I can't let you do it."

Confused, her brows met. "Do what? Evan, you're not making sense."

"AJ, I can't let you say no to three more years at the institute," he explained.

Her heart stopped as her lips parted. "You ..."

He nodded. Pride and sadness gleamed his light brown eyes. The perfect backdrop for his heartbreak.

Heartbreak she was now understanding.

"Evan, whatever you're thinking—"

He stopped her as he cradled her cheeks, holding her in place. "Do you love working with Dr. Rodahawe?"

"You know I do, Evan," she answered in a small, truthful voice.

"And do you want to be a physicist?"

Her throat tightened at his question. He knew the answer. They both knew the answer. Everyone knew the answer. "It's my biggest dream." Her thumb brushed against the pulse on his wrist.

Evan pressed his lips together and nodded. "You belong here, Alexandra."

"Evan."

"I don't belong here," he stated. His voice strong with conviction.

Her eyelids fluttered. "You're unhappy. I'm so sorry I've made you unhappy."

Shaking his head, he pressed his forehead to hers. "Unhappy is the last thing you make me, Alexandra. *I* make you unhappy." He pulled back. His eyes firmly on hers. "You come home, and I see the guilt in your eyes because of me. Because you hate disappointing me. You only disappoint me when I hurt you. And I hurt you by holding you back. By making you turn away from opportunities your career needs."

"You do no such thing," she cried.

He brushed away the tears that stained her cheeks. "I do. I hurt you by preventing you from achieving your dreams."

"Evan, please stop. That's not it. I should have told you about Dr. Rodahawe's offer, but I don't want it. We both agreed we'd go home after my formula. I'm close. I'm so close and then—"

"I know you want to stay. You have so much to achieve here, and I can't hold you back. I can't let you hurt your future."

She shook her head. "You're my future, Evan."

A small smile curved at his lips. "And I'll be waiting for

you in Massachusetts."

Alex clenched her eyes shut. She knew what he was doing. What he was giving her. Three years at the Rodahawe Institute could change her life. She could discover her own theory. Alex could get published. But an opportunity like the one Dr. Rodahawe presented her came with consequences.

And Alex knew the moment he offered it to her that she could lose Evan. As she had suspected, he wanted her to stay and he would leave. That was why she said no. Because she didn't want Evan to ever think he didn't matter.

She chose Evan.

And he was choosing her career.

A promise he had made to her a long time ago.

He wasn't letting her give up on her dreams, but he was breaking her heart.

"You're on the cusp of greatness, Alexandra. I know it. You've sacrificed enough for me. You have. I couldn't live with myself if you went back to Massachusetts. Stay here and continue to make me proud."

A sob escaped her. He was saying goodbye to her. She knew it. "Don't say goodbye to me. Don't. Please don't. Just give me a month. I'll finish the formula, and we'll go home. Together."

"It's not that easy, Alexandra. You and I both know you need more than a month. You need these three years. This is your love and your career. You can have both here in Zürich. You can have both."

Alex pulled away from his touch. "No, I won't. Not if you leave."

He grasped her hands in his. "Just for a little while."

She didn't believe him. "We were supposed to go home.

We were supposed to live your dreams next, Evan."

"And we will. My dreams are for you to achieve everything you ever wanted to in physics. Please, stay. Stay here and make me so proud of you. This, you working toward your dream with the best physicists in the world, is my dream. Let me stop hurting you."

"You can't stop if you leave."

Evan squeezed her hands. "I would hurt you more if you didn't take this opportunity. I'm not saying goodbye, AJ. I'll be waiting for you when you're finished achieving everything you wanted here. I won't stop loving you. I'll just stop holding you back. Three years. Let me give you these three years."

Three years.

Three years to make my mark in physics.

Three years away from him.

Alex stood, pulled her hands from Evan's, and then straddled his lap. She captured his jaw in her palms as he held her hips. "Three years?" she whispered.

He nodded. "Three years."

God, it hurt to see the love in his eyes, knowing they were essentially saying goodbye.

"And you'll continue to love me?"

"I will."

Her heart clenched at his vow. "And what if I meet someone here? What if—"

"You love him?" Evan asked as tears slowly dragged down his cheeks.

"Yes," Alex answered. "What if he supports me and loves me?"

Evan squeezed her waist. "Then I'll make sure he's good

enough for you."

He was doing it again.

Choosing what he thought she wanted over what she actually needed.

Alex leaned forward, her lips close to his. "Would you let me have him?"

"Yes," he whispered.

She loved him.

So much that there would never be another man for her.

There was no denying she wanted to stay, but she also wanted Evan to as well. But she knew he wouldn't. He was so stubborn. So headstrong about fulfilling promises he made her.

Alex stared at him through her lashes. "What if he's you, Evan Gilmore?"

Evan wrapped his arms around her back and pulled her close to his body, causing a small gasp to pass her lips. "I'm yours forever, Alexandra. Always. And I'll give you my word. I love you by supporting your dreams. That's how I love you. Stay here. Then, when you're finished and you're ready to come home, I'll be waiting for you."

She believed his promise. Believed it as much as it hurt her. "Will you fall in love with someone else?"

"No," he answered without a hint of hesitation. "I'll be too busy still being helplessly in love with you."

"I have one request," she said.

He swallowed hard, his Adam's apple bobbing. "Anything."

"Don't leave me in the middle of the night. Let me go to the airport with you. But don't you dare leave me without saying goodbye," she cried as her tears returned.

Evan reached up and wiped her tears away. "I promised I

would never say goodbye. I won't leave without seeing you. I promise, I'll hold you all night."

Her heart found a small ounce of relief from her pain.

All night.

They had one night left. And come morning, he would leave her. So she would cherish him. All night, she would.

"Don't say goodbye," she repeated. "Instead, make love to me."

She wanted him to mask his goodbye with his love.

His lips softly found hers, and she tasted his sadness and her heartbreak.

"I love you, AJ," he mumbled as she moved her hands into his hair, holding him tight. Refusing to let him go. Not now. Not ever. Her heart, body, and soul refused.

"I love you," she panted as she pushed him onto his back.

Evan's chest heaved. "Eight protons—"

She pressed her fingers to his lips, silencing him. "At the airport, if you still love me fiercely and truly after tonight, finish that declaration then."

His lip twitched against her finger. Then he grasped her wrist and moved her hand from his face. "I promise," he murmured before his lips founds hers, kissing her.

Cherishing her.

Loving her ...

All night.

Until the following morning when Evan Gilmore broke her heart.

Woke her with a kiss.

And told her to stay in bed.

He broke his promise as he slipped out the door, never

finishing the declaration he vowed to say to her.

He never said he loved her as he left.

Utterly destroying her.

Three months before Alex's Boston return

I t had been three months since Evan left her.
It hadn't taken long for everyone at the institute to realize what happened.

Alex threw herself into her research. There was no point in rushing home since he wasn't there anymore. Some days, she couldn't even bring herself to sleep in the bed they had shared for over a year. Plagued with heartbreak and her newfound anger, she slept on the couch or even in the break room at the institute when she didn't want to leave.

She missed him.

She still loved him.

He had messaged her when he had landed back in Boston.

He had messaged her for her birthday.

He had called her several times, but Alex never answered.

Evan Gilmore left her that morning without the reassurance of his love as he had promised. He didn't wake her properly so she could accompany him to the airport. He knew she would have fought him. She wouldn't have let him get on that plane.

Supporting her dreams meant breaking her heart.

She understood his choices, but they weren't the choices

she wanted him to make.

A few months after he returned to the US, her mother told her that he was moving on with his life and that had only broken her heart more. That belief that he would wait for her was tarnished.

In theory, Alex should have moved on, but she couldn't.

Evan Gilmore was her forever.

But forever wasn't today.

Or tomorrow.

Forever seemed forever away.

As if it would never be a reality.

"So how did I do?" Brandon, one of Dr. Rodahawe's researchers, asked.

Alex smiled as she handed him the bottle of water. Brandon had just finished his introduction to classical mechanics and quantum physics speech at Oxford University. Alex was surprised when Dr. Rodahawe had invited her to attend the seminar in England. It had always been a dream of hers to visit some of the best universities in the world. And truthfully, she needed the week away from Zürich, the lab, and her empty apartment. England allowed her to pretend she wasn't walking around with a broken heart.

"You were amazing, Brandon. You got the crowd so engaged."

Brandon grinned as he uncapped the bottle. "After the break, Vincent will take over. Trust me, if you thought the crowd was engaged before? Get ready to be blown away."

Alex laughed. "Oh, I'm ready."

A throat cleared behind her, and she spun around to find Lynette Earman, an Oxford physics professor and their guide, with a smile on her face. "Well done, Brandon. You made us very proud."

"Thank you, Professor Earman."

"Alex, there's a gentleman here who would like to see you. Asked for you personally," the professor informed. "Please follow me."

"Umm, sure," she said and then glanced over at Brandon. "I'll be back. If Dr. Rodahawe needs me, tell him I won't be long."

"All right," Brandon said.

Then Alex followed Professor Earman through the mass of people who were making their way to Brandon to ask him questions and out of the lecture hall. Once out, the professor pointed at the man sitting on the stone bench.

Alex froze, realizing who it was.

"I'll give you some privacy," Lynette said before she retreated into the building.

Alex made her way toward him as he stared out at the campus. "Landon?"

He tilted his head at her and smiled. Years had passed since she last saw him at Duke, but he still smiled so flawlessly. "Massachusetts," he breathed with adoration in his voice.

Unable to help herself, she walked over to him and hugged him the moment he stood. As her college ex-boyfriend wrapped his arms around her, she inhaled his familiar, clean smell. Then she pulled away, shaking her head in disbelief.

"What are you doing here at Oxford?"

His blue eyes gleamed at her. "I got called up for the national team in a friendly game against Serbia. So I'm here for some press and PR before I fly out to Belgrade."

"And you knew I was here?"

"I keep tabs. I heard Dr. Rodahawe would be in Oxford, and I thought maybe you would have joined him since you were his research assistant," Landon explained.

"Alexandra!" she heard Dr. Rodahawe call out.

She glanced over her shoulder to find her mentor waving at her. "I'll be there in two seconds," she yelled. Then she returned her focus to Landon. "I'm sorry. I have to go. Work."

He nodded. "Okay. But do you think I can see you while you're here in the UK? How about dinner?"

Her eyes widened in shock that he had just asked her out. Alex's lips parted, breath escaping her and causing her lungs to squeeze as hard as her heart had.

"Sure," she found herself saying. Her heart halted as if it had ceased to beat. Ceased to continue.

Evan.

They weren't together anymore.

He left her.

But she still felt guilty.

"I'm staying at the Malmaison Oxford Castle. Just ask for me at the front desk at seven."

Landon grinned, his eyes twinkling with hope she hated to see. But she couldn't help herself. Maybe because she knew Landon and knew she felt no love. That she just needed someone outside of the institute to talk to.

Her ex-boyfriend leaned down and pressed his lips to her cheek, causing her skin to heat at the contact. Then he pulled back, the hope never leaving his eyes. "I'll see you tonight."

Alex nodded and spun around, needing space away from him and the terrible decision she just made. When she reached

Dr. Rodahawe, who was staring at Landon behind her, he let out a displeased sound and looked at her.

"Ex-boyfriend of yours?"

"Yeah," she said and pressed her lips into a tight line. "The very ex-boyfriend who broke my heart and inspired me to apply to be your research assistant. He's also the ex-boyfriend who broke up with me and put me back on Evan's path. So yeah, he's an ex-boyfriend." She reached up and wiped her tears away that fell at the mention of Evan. "But he's not an ex-boyfriend I want or am still in love with."

Dr. Rodahawe slung an arm around her shoulder and pulled her close to his side. "If it makes you feel better, you can take the stage for me."

Alex laughed. "No, Dr. Rodahawe. No, that wouldn't make me feel better. But it definitely made me laugh."

"And I have missed your laughter, Alexandra. It's nice to hear it again."

It was strange, but Alex thought so, too.

Maybe tonight won't be so bad.

It's not cheating.

Alex replayed those three words as she got ready for her dinner with her ex-boyfriend, Landon Carmichael.

She wasn't in the wrong.

Evan had ended them three months ago.

It wasn't even an official date. It was two people catching up. Two former lovers who would sit opposite each other. So why had she put so much effort in her appearance?

Alex let out a sigh as she stepped out of the elevator. She should have canceled, but she didn't have Landon's new number. Just as she was about to make her way toward reception, her phone vibrated in her purse and caused her to stop and retrieve it. When she glanced at her screen, she unlocked it to find her best friend had messaged her back.

Savannah: Alex, it's not cheating. Evan broke up with you three months ago. He left without a proper goodbye. I'm not Landon's biggest fan, and I will never forget how rough he was with you at that party during sophomore year, but maybe he's right. I hate that I just said that. But maybe you two both being in England is a sign? You don't have to do anything. You don't owe him anything. It's just dinner.

Alex: You're right. It's just dinner. That I completely dressed up for. God, I'm such an idiot.

Savannah: Breathe, Alex. It's okay to want to be seen as beautiful by a member of the opposite sex.

Alex: Savannah, I need you to know that I'm still so in love with Evan, and I feel terrible right now.

Savannah: You're going to catch up with an old friend. But you don't have to go. And I know you still love Evan. I don't think you'll ever stop loving him. He's your one. And sometimes you can't ever forget the one. Good luck tonight. Remember, you don't owe Landon Carmichael anything.

Alex: Thanks, Sav. I really needed that. I'll Skype you later tonight. I love and miss you.

Savannah: Okay. I want to know everything. And I love and miss you, too, Alex.

Satisfied with the advice given to her by her best friend, Alex locked her phone and shoved it back inside her purse. She inhaled a deep breath to calm her nerves and then proceeded toward reception, ready to have dinner with Landon Carmichael.

Once she stopped at reception, she found him waiting for her. Her thoughts of a casual dinner between them were thrown quickly out the window. Landon had dressed up, too, in a white dress shirt free of wrinkles and a light blue tie. His black slacks appeared tailored, and his leather shoes had a shine to them.

She smiled at his effort as she stood in front of him. "Hey," she greeted.

"Wow," Landon breathed. "You look beautiful, Alex."

Hardly, but her heart fluttered at his compliment. The dark red dress that hugged her body had been a last-minute addition in her suitcase. She hadn't even thought about going out on a date. She just assumed there might be a time when she'd have to dress up for an occasion with Dr. Rodahawe. Never in her wildest dreams did she ever think she'd see Landon again.

Not in the US and definitely not in the UK.

"Thank you," she said, hating that she could feel her warm cheeks. "I like your tie."

He glanced down at the tie and then grinned at her. "Duke blue."

"Of course," she said with humor in her voice.

"So you wanna get out of here? I got us a reservation at a Mediterranean restaurant not too far away. I remember Mediterranean was always one of your favorites."

Alex nodded, ignoring the annoying flutter in her chest. They were old memories, and they meant nothing. They couldn't. "Sure, let's go."

"Won't be long," their waiter said as he took the menu from Landon after he had ordered. Alex had opted for the seafood pasta, hoping it was as good as the pasta she was used to having in North Carolina. It surprised her that after all these years, Landon still remembered that she loved Mediterranean food.

The restaurant they were sitting at had been awarded a Michelin star. She wondered if her mother knew the chef. Alex's mother was known throughout the industry, and Alex often wondered if they knew she was the daughter of one of the finest dessert chefs in the world. But she doubted it. The ambiance of the Anatolia was stunning. It wasn't bright. The lights were dim and gave that intimate and romantic feel. No doubt this restaurant had hosted many dates and anniversaries.

"You're quiet," Landon noted as he set his hands on the table, staring at her.

Alex produced a tight smile. "I've had a long day of seminars at Oxford. And will have another long day tomorrow."

"But you like it, right?"

"I do," she said with an honest smile. "I love my job. My

job took me to England, so I can't complain."

Landon leaned closer to her. "Then why do you look sad?"

She flinched. "Sad?"

He nodded. "I know you, Alex. I know when you're upset. You try to hide it, but there's always a glint in your eyes you can't hide behind."

Her heart sank.

She did feel sad.

She had everything, yet she still had that horrible pressure in her chest. The same pressure that had found its roots in her heart since Evan left.

Alex exhaled a heavy breath. "You seem to always come back in my life when I'm at my lowest." She swallowed the lump in her throat. "Why?"

Landon's lips parted as he stared at her. "I don't know. But it's fate, right?"

"First at Duke on my graduation day and now here at Oxford. You've always come into my life when I least expected it. I met you when I didn't expect to meet you at Duke."

Her ex-boyfriend smiled as he reached over and grasped her hand. "Can I ask you a question?"

She nodded, not trusting her voice at that moment. Scared she'd tell him lies or honest truths she had kept hidden away.

It was confusing.

So confusing.

She shouldn't have agreed to have dinner with him. Alex knew where her heart was and that was in Massachusetts. But she couldn't deny that Landon Carmichael had always been there for her at her very lowest, and today was no exception.

"If I had never broken us up, would we still be together?"

His voice was a whisper, full of fear and hope.

She had thought about that question after she had seen him at her college graduation and they sat on their bench together. But that question had been long forgotten the moment she saw Evan waiting for her.

A million emotions and memories collided.

She had loved him.

Truly loved him until he had broken them. They were good together, and they had always been good and right. Until it wasn't.

"I love Evan, Landon," she said as a tear rolled down her face. "I'll always love Evan."

"But?"

Alex glanced away from his pleading blue eyes and stared at the happy couple to her right. She gazed in envy at how they looked at each other with love in their eyes. She'd known it for years when she had looked into Evan's. She had even known it when she looked into Landon's.

"That question isn't fair, Landon." Alex turned her attention back to him. "It's not fair because I don't know. I don't have an answer for you. I think deep in my heart I would have found a way to him. When I'm with Evan, I'm home. I'm where I need to be."

"But if I hadn't broken up with you …"

"Landon," she breathed as she pulled her hand away from him. "Don't do that to yourself. We broke up for a reason. You went to Phoenix, and now you're with the Spurs. I'm at the Rodahawe Institute. I'm where I need to be, and you're where you need to be."

He blinked at her several times as if he were taking in

what she just said. "But—"

"It doesn't matter, Landon. Not anymore."

"But you and he aren't together. That's what you said on the way to the restaurant. We can ..." His voice trailed off. The hesitation flashed bright in his eyes.

His insinuation stunned Alex.

There couldn't be a *we*.

Not when her heart still mourned Evan.

"Landon, we can't. It would never work. I'm here in Europe, and you're back in the US. It would never work."

He let out a sigh as he grabbed her hand again. "It would never work now or ever?"

It was a loaded question.

He wanted hope for them.

Alex licked her dry lips. "It would never work now ..."

Or ever.

But she couldn't get herself to say it out loud.

Determination flared in his eyes as a smile spread across his lips. "I can work with it not working now. How about if we talk when you come home? We can try again. San Antonio isn't that far from Boston. I can fly and see you. We can make it work."

Just as Alex was about to tell him that she couldn't promise him that, their waiter returned and set their plates down, interrupting them. And as she watched Landon pick up his knife and fork, she knew he had taken her silence as acquiescence.

That someday might work for them.

Alex didn't have the heart to take that away from him.

After dinner, Landon and Alex walked around Oxford and talked. They didn't talk about promising to make it work when she returned to America. Instead, they talked about his upcoming game against Serbia and how her formula was going. She told him that she was going to be a big sister next month, and he was stunned. The same expression she had on her face when her mother and father had told her the news. Once the cold night air became unbearable, they took a cab back to her hotel, and he walked her to her room.

"Here," Landon said as he pulled out a piece of paper from his pocket and handed it to her. "It's my new number. I wrote it down while you were in the bathroom."

Alex glanced down to see the digits scribbled on the paper. "Oh, thank you. My number's changed."

"I figured it would," he said with a sheepish smile on his face. "When my number changed, I called you. I got your voice mail and just listened to your voice. I thought about leaving a message, but I chickened out. You know it's been you ever since I met you."

Her breath caught in her throat as Landon stepped closer to her, Alex pressing her back to her hotel room door. He was close. Too close for comfort. Too close for Alex's emotions to grip her heart. "Landon," she whispered.

"It's only been you I've loved since I met you." He ducked his head, his lips inching closer to hers.

Alex held her breath in suspense.

His eyelids hooded as he raised a palm to cup the side of her face.

Then he pressed his forehead to hers. "I still love you, Alex. I've never stopped."

"But I have," she whispered, her voice tight. She hated the way he clenched his eyes shut in pain.

But it was the truth.

She had stopped.

Stopped the moment Evan rescued her from Blue Jay's when she had returned to Boston.

"I still love him, Landon. He has my whole heart. It's been three months, and I still love him," she said as he pulled his head back.

"Then I'll wait," he promised.

She believed the hope that sparkled in his eyes. "I don't know when I'll be home. Dr. Rodahawe offered me a three-year contract with the institute. It's a long time," she pointed out.

"I know," Landon said before he pressed his lips to her cheek. Then he straightened his spine and smiled at her. "Good night, Massachusetts."

Relief poured into her chest that he didn't kiss her on her lips. The last kiss she had ever tasted and felt was Evan's, and she didn't want Landon to kiss it away.

Opening her clutch, she pulled out her room key and smiled at him. "Thank you for dinner. I'll text you so you have my Swiss number. Goodbye, Connecticut."

Because a goodbye was final, and good night held promises of a new day.

98

Cf

californium

ALEX

Now

A lex sat nervously in her seat.
It was strange.

For the first time in years, she didn't look at MIT as a stranger with dreams and desires to learn in such a prestigious institute. This time, she sat in the admissions office, waiting to hear word about starting her Ph.D. in the spring. But after weeks of back and forth emails, the dean of admissions had asked her to the college to talk. She had been excited to talk about finally being an MIT student, but that excitement fizzled the moment she met the dean and sat in his office.

For the past twenty minutes, she sat in silence as she watched the man in his mid-forties behind the desk read her file. He'd let a hum, a grunt, and even an ah. But nothing that indicated whether she could start her Ph.D. later than first anticipated.

It didn't help that her boyfriend, Evan Gilmore, was waiting at his office at Fenway Park for her. She had pleaded with him not to come with her to MIT because she could handle it on her own. Dean Carey was definitely surprised the moment he walked out of his office to see her large baby bump. Just over six months pregnant, she was definitely showing. Alex hadn't exactly been upfront about her pregnancy with the college. All of Boston knew, so she just assumed MIT would, too.

"Miss Parker," the dean of admissions said as he closed her file. "You are an ideal student, and MIT would be honored to have you attend." He paused. Anxiety now coated her heart. "But unfortunately, there is no way we can allow you to start in the spring. Massachusetts Institute of Technology's physics department starts their Ph.D. program at the start of the school year, which is September."

Alex's heart dropped. "Dean Carey, I'm due the second week of September."

Sorrow swept his face. "I know this must be hard for you, but there's just no way. To hold your place in the Ph.D. program, you'd have to start in September with the rest of the physics postgraduate students."

"There's a high probability my water will break in the middle of class. There's no other way without losing my place at MIT? I've worked so hard to get into this school. I've wanted MIT for as long as I can remember."

"I'm sorry, Miss Parker. You will have to apply for the next school year. Your funding will be reallocated, and you will have to reapply for grants next year."

Alex shook her head in disbelief. "I thought Ph.D. students could take a leave of absence when they're pregnant."

He nodded. "Yes, but if you had already *started* your Ph.D. with MIT. You're due as the fall semester starts. It puts you, your advisor, the department, and the classes you'd TA for in quite a limbo. You must understand that it's in your best interest to start next fall."

"Which is fine," Alex said, "but my place here at MIT isn't

guaranteed. You said I'd have to apply again. I have applied, and I was admitted. I had recommendations. I worked with a Nobel Prize winning physicist. I'm sorry, but why do I have to reapply when other colleges allow their students to defer their studies?" Heat rose in her chest as her eyes stung.

Oh, God.

Don't cry, Alex.

It seemed her hormones were all over the place. For weeks, she found herself upset more often. But this time, she was devastated and on the brink of erupting in tears.

MIT was her dream.

And now that she had it, it was being ripped from her.

"Miss Parker, this is MIT. We're the number one ranked university for a reason. We want to make sure that when you come back to us, you are devoted and determined. That is why we ask you to resubmit your application."

Alex let out a shaky breath as she blinked her tears back. "I'm sorry to get emotional about this, but MIT has been my dream since I saw Professor Yates speak at the Smithsonian when I was a little girl. I've wanted MIT for so long ..."

But maybe MIT isn't the dream.

It's always been my dream to be a physicist.

She sat there, staring at Dean Carey.

Maybe it was a sign that she and MIT weren't meant to be.

"I recommend you take the year off, Miss Parker, and spend time with your child. I can assure that if we were to receive your application again, you would be accepted. We just have to follow protocol, and unfortunately, that doesn't help you."

Slowly getting up from the uncomfortable chair, she held

out her hand to him. "I understand, Dean Carey." She set her free palm on her stomach as the dean shook her hand. "Thank you so much for your time."

He nodded and then released her hand. "You are exactly who MIT looks for in a student, Miss Parker. Please, I urge you to apply for next year."

She made no promises as she smiled and made her way out of his office, feeling lost but somehow liberated knowing that MIT was unattainable. As she opened the door, she realized that MIT was never the dream. She had been inspired by a man who had passion for science and not the educational institution he lectured at.

The dream was and had always been to be a physicist.

Just like Duke ended up being her dream after she had lost MIT.

Evan: AJ, do you want me to leave Fenway to pick you up? Is your meeting with the dean of admissions over? How did it go?

Alex stared at her boyfriend's text message and frowned. She hated that she'd disappoint him with the news. Hated the idea of telling him that all his hard work and sacrifices were for nothing. She wouldn't be able to start her Ph.D. this school year. In fact, Alex wasn't even sure if she'd reapply. Dean Carey had been right about one thing. She would spend the year she was supposed to be doing her Ph.D. raising her daughter.

That was her plan.

It had always been the plan.

Her Ph.D. could wait so she could welcome and love her Little Atom.

Alex: Hey. How's work? Don't worry about picking me up at MIT. I took a cab. I'm not home right now, but I will be soon. I just needed to go somewhere to think.

Evan: Are you okay? AJ, I can come pick you up.

Alex: I know you can, but I'm fine. The meeting didn't go our way. They revoked my Ph.D. admission, and I'll have to reapply for the next school year. And before you go insane, it's okay. My Ph.D. isn't important right now. Our daughter is. And even if I started in the spring, she'd only be four months, Evan. That's too soon. I'll call you when I'm done thinking. I love you.

Evan: I can't believe they revoked your admission. That's not right. Call me when you're ready. I love you, too, AJ.

Satisfied that Evan at least sounded calm in his text messages, she slid her phone into her purse. Then she knocked on the classroom door, relieved that the hallway of her old high school was air conditioned. It was the middle of summer, and it was hot. So hot that Alex wore a thin floral maxi dress. It wasn't too casual, but fancy enough for her appointment with the dean of admission at MIT. Alex turned the door handle and opened the door, stepping into the old classroom where she had spent so much of her time in high school.

"Alex?" Mr. Miller, her former physics teacher, asked as he got up from the barstool he sat on. "Oh my goodness, look at you."

"Hello, Mr. Miller. The lady at the office said you were on lunch and would be in your classroom. I thought I'd come visit," she said, closing the door behind her. And on instinct, she pressed her palm to her stomach. She was a lot heavier now that she was inching to the seventh month mark. But her third trimester consisted of being more tired than nauseated. At least all her food cravings outweighed the terrible morning sickness of her first and second trimester.

Mr. Miller walked toward her and carefully led her to the barstool he had been sitting on. "I'll go grab one of the kids' seat." Seconds later, he pulled a chair close to hers as they sat at his desk. "You have that glow."

Alex let out a small laugh as she set her purse on his desk. "I get that a lot. How are you? How's summer school going?"

"It's good. I have a lot of bright kids this year but they are not applied. Mainly some of the upcoming athletes who failed tests," Mr. Miller said. "I can't believe you're pregnant."

"Yeah," she breathed as she cradled her stomach. "Mum said she accidentally told you."

"She didn't mean to tell me. I was ordering a batch of cupcakes and we were talking about how proud we were of you. She was just so excited."

She brushed her hair away from her face and smiled. "No, don't be sorry. We slowly told everyone. But being home means being back in the Red Sox spotlight, so we've tried to be careful."

His brow arched, a smirk on his face. Her high school

teacher knew, but he just wanted her to confirm it. *"We?"*

Laughing, she glanced down at her baby bump and then back at her favorite teacher. In her years since she had graduated from high school, so many brilliant academics had taught Alex—Dr. Rodahawe included—but Mr. Miller was still the man who inspired her to continue and embrace her love of physics.

"Yes," she confirmed. "Evan and I are having a girl."

"Wow," he breathed in awe. "You and Evan Gilmore."

Alex smiled, unable to help the flutter in her chest. "Yeah, me and Evan Gilmore. If you had told me when I was a senior that we'd end up together, live in Zürich for a year, and then have a baby together, I would have never believed you."

"I'm so happy for you, Alex. I always thought you two would end up together. It's just meant to be. So how was working with Dr. Rodahawe?" He straightened his spine, curiosity blazing in his eyes.

"Amazing. He offered me a three-year contract with the institute, but I turned it down before I even found out I was pregnant. I learned a lot in Switzerland. I also learned that in the end, I love Evan so much more than science. He gives me purpose and a sense of home. And well, I'm very happy with my life." Content filled her voice as it did her heart.

She was happy.

She had been since she and Evan got back together.

"That's great," her former teacher said with a smile. "So what's next for you?"

Alex bit her lip as her thumbs caressed her stomach. She tilted her head and then released her lip. "Well, I finished my velocity formula before I left Switzerland over four months ago. It's a new formula that calculates maximum velocity in airplane engines. It also calculates breaking point tension in engines. So the point before an aircraft can stall during high speed. My formula works in conjunction with Dr. Rodahawe's. And that's it right now."

"That's all?"

She sighed. "I actually just came from MIT. I got accepted into the Ph.D. program, but with my due date being the start of the fall semester, there's no way I can start this year or even in the spring. They're reallocating my funding and have asked that I apply for the next fall semester."

Mr. Miller's eyes widened in shock as his jaw dropped. "What?"

"Yeah, they recommended I take a year off since I'm going to be a new mum. I understand why; it's just frustrating. I don't know why I thought MIT would ..." Alex let out a short laugh. "I don't know why I thought they'd treat me like I won a Nobel Prize. I'm sure if I had, they might have let me."

"You could contest it," he stated.

"I know," Alex agreed. "But in a way, they're right. Even if they allowed me to start in the spring, my daughter would only be four months old, and it's way too soon. I'll just apply for the next school year."

His brows furrowed as his lips pursed. Then he inhaled a deep breath and said, "Why don't you try another college? I know a lot of colleges would want you. There's always Harvard."

"Harvard?"

He nodded. "You got into Harvard for your undergrad. There's also Boston University and Northeastern—assuming you'd like to stay in Massachusetts."

She had options.

She had always had options outside of MIT.

And they were great options.

"I did get into Harvard. Do you think if I applied, I'd get in?"

His lips stretched into a wider grin. "I do."

"Harvard is an Ivy League school. Second in ranking behind MIT in physics," she mumbled, mulling over her options.

"I really think you would get into Harvard, but you have time to make up your mind. And I feel like I should give you full disclosure."

"Full disclosure?" she asked, raising her brow at him.

Mr. Miller pressed his lips into a tight line before he said, "I think you'd get in because I know what kind of student you are, Alex. I know how hard working and dedicated you are. I know just what kind of recommendations you come with and what you strive to achieve. I might not be dean of admissions, but as of September, I will be one of the physics professors at Harvard University."

"Are you serious?" Alex blurted out, in shock.

He laughed. "I got the job before summer but have stayed to finish up with my summer classes. The professor I'm taking over for got a job offer at the Smithsonian. He recommended me, so I interviewed with Harvard. My old colleague at MIT actually was my recommendation. So if you do consider Harvard, Alex, I would love to be your Ph.D. advisor. No pressure, of course. But if MIT is still your dream, I say go for it."

"Congratulations, Mr.—sorry, *Professor*. That's incredible. I am so proud of you."

He blushed. "Not as proud as I am of you, Alex. You were my highlight of my high school teaching career. Not only did you get into five of the eight Ivy League schools, but you also followed your heart and pursued science, and it took you all the way to Switzerland. I think you should let your love of science guide you. You'll get into your Ph.D. Any school you choose would be lucky to have you."

"And Harvard and its students are lucky to have you, Professor Miller."

It was after three, and an hour since Alex had left Mr. Miller's classroom. In a few months, he would leave behind his position as a high school physics teacher and become a professor at one of the most prestigious universities in the world.

Harvard was an option.

But for Alex, her plans for further education were put on hold.

And as she sat on the bleachers of her high school's baseball field, she smiled. Motherhood was what she wanted. With Mr. Miller, she felt a sense of guilt in her heart. She didn't want her career to dictate her life. She didn't want her daughter to suffer because she wanted a Ph.D. Not in the way Evan had suffered when his parents chose their careers and Chicago over him and Kyle.

Alex would follow her parents' footsteps. Her mother put her restaurant and bakery dreams on hold the moment Alex was born. And she would do the same for Little Atom.

"AJ?"

She turned her head away from the ballpark to find her boyfriend climbing up the bleachers. Her heart fluttered in her chest, knowing he had rushed to see her after she called him. He turned and made his way down her row, sitting next to her. Alex wrapped her arms around his arm and rested the side of her face on his shoulder. "Hey, how was work?"

He hummed as his palm settled on her thigh. "Good. They want to test out a new season ticket holder card program. It could do well with fans, but I suggested we hold off until next season. At least then we can fix the bugs. How was your afternoon with Mr. Miller? Are you okay with what happened at MIT?"

"I'm okay with what happened. It's protocol, so I understand. It would be hard to go straight into my Ph.D. with a newborn. Plus, it would make being a TA difficult." She took her eyes from the home plate and glanced up at her boyfriend. "Mr. Miller is actually going to be Professor Miller of Harvard University come September."

He gawked at her. "No way!"

Alex laughed. "Yeah. He is. He said he'd be honored to be my advisor if I should decide Harvard was for me rather than MIT."

"You love Mr. Miller. He's always supported your love of science."

"He has," she said with a smile. "And you have, too." Then she craned her neck and looked back out at the ballpark. "I used to sit here and watch you practice and play. Even in the snow."

Evan squeezed her thigh gently. "You were always my biggest supporter."

"I always will be," she said in a small voice as she lifted her chin to see those beautiful light brown eyes. "During senior year, I was sitting here in the snow watching you. Hunter came and sat next to me. Do you remember that day?"

He nodded. "We picked up all the baseballs together."

"We did. He sat here with me and asked me when I'd tell you that I was in love with you."

"He did?" Evan's face paled with disbelief.

Alex nodded. "Yeah. I asked him not to tell you. I was scared for you to know because I didn't want to lose you. Because you were my best friend first."

His hand left her thigh and reached up and thumbed away her tears. "I was scared to admit that I loved you, too, AJ. I was stupid. I was scared of how I felt about you. Sometimes, when I wake up and see you, I'm scared I'll lose you again. It makes me thankful when you hold me, and I'm reminded that I still have you after all these years—after everything."

Untangling her arms from around his, she reached up and pressed her palms to his jaw, steadying his face. "I couldn't imagine the rest of my life without you. I wouldn't have spent three years away from you. I won't ever."

"I know," he whispered with a glint in his eyes.

Alex brought his face closer to hers and pressed her lips to his in a chaste kiss. "We better go home before we have dinner with my parents and Seb."

"Speaking of parents. Mine want to fly in from Chicago for the birth. They wanted to know if it was okay with you and Kyle."

"Are you okay with it?" she asked as she dropped her hands from his face.

Evan made a small nod. "They've kept in touch since I left

Illinois. But it's about you and Kyle. They want to be in our daughter's life, AJ. Kyle would like to see them. If you're not comfortable, it can just be me and him."

She shook her head. "It's fine with me as long as it's okay with you."

"You're amazing. Oh, and Susan wants to know if we had any names in mind for Little Atom."

Alex smiled. It was a topic they always glanced over. They didn't want to put pressure on her name, but Alex knew her daughter's name.

Had known it for some time.

"I have an idea of some. You?"

"I know her surname will be Gilmore."

Laughing, Alex reached over and picked up her purse from next to her just as Evan stood from the bleachers. Then he held out his hand and helped her up with such ease. Whenever Alex had to get herself up, it took some effort and energy.

"What if we hyphenated her last name? She can be a Parker-Gilmore," Alex suggested as she slung her purse strap on her shoulder.

She had expected to offend Evan with that suggestion. Instead, he grasped her hand, lacing his fingers with hers. "If that's what you want, she can be a Parker-Gilmore."

He said it with so much softness and adoration that her heart melted.

She loved this man.

So much.

It had always been his love she wanted, needed, adored the most.

"She's a Gilmore," she clarified. "Just like her daddy."

99

Es

einsteinium

ALEX

Two months before Alex's Boston return

"Thank you," Alex said, handing her cab driver the cash she had taken out of the machine at the airport. She had almost hailed a cab outside of Logan International Airport when she had realized that she only had Swiss franc and no American currency.

"Hey, congratulations on the baby brother, and welcome home, Little Miss Red Sox."

Alex flinched. It had been a long time since she had heard her Red Sox nickname. It had been stupid of her to think it had faded away while she was in Switzerland. That Angie had taken all the unwanted and unwarranted spotlight from Alex. But she was wrong.

"Thanks," Alex said as she slid out of the cab, dragging her suitcase from the seat with her. When she closed the cab door behind her, she rushed toward the entrance, the glass automatic doors widening for her. She bolted to the reception desk jet-lagged, tired, and out of breath.

The woman at the desk lifted her chin the moment Alex leaned against it. "My mother. She's in labor and—"

"AJ." His voice had cut her off, awakening her heart's beats and tearing away the wounds she had wrongly stitched up.

477

Stitches tore away, love bleeding her heart.

She still loved him.

So in love with his voice that always sounded like home.

Letting out a small breath of tortured air from her toxic lungs, she turned and faced him. Faced the supposed love of her life who had ended them with a final night. Who had left her in their Zürich apartment so she could pursue her dreams. But at that moment, she didn't care.

For now, she'd mentally forgive and forget so she could be with her family. Her mother was giving birth. There was no way her problems with Evan mattered right now.

"Evan," she said in a small voice, "is she okay?"

Suddenly—and to her surprise—he wrapped his arms tightly around her, causing her to still. It had been so long, too long, and it felt so right to be in his arms. To hear and feel his heartbeats against his chest. He even smelled right.

God, she missed him.

Four months later and she still missed him like crazy. But this was a stolen moment that wasn't theirs for the taking.

Evan's arms fell away from her. "Come on. Let's sit. Your dad is with her."

She didn't say anything.

Afraid words would turn into declarations.

She should be mad at him and hate him for leaving her, but Alex was just too damn tired.

Too goddamn in love with Evan Gilmore to resent him.

So instead, she followed him and found safety from her heart in her mind's solitude. When she set her suitcase on the ground, she sat down, sighed, and faced him. He was staring at her, eyeing her for a reaction.

She gave him none.

Not for him, but for herself.

"How was your flight?" he asked.

Alex hated the small talk.

Hated that she knew it was easy to talk to him.

But the gentleness and plea for forgiveness in his eyes had her warming from her desire to be cold to him.

Brushing her hair behind her ear, she sighed. "*Flights.* I had to fly to Dublin, which was fine, but then the weather turned bad, and they canceled all the flights because of the snow. I was stuck in Dublin for over eight hours, but it doesn't matter anymore. I'm glad I'm finally here."

As she took in his perfect, beautiful smile, she found herself smiling. He was so beautiful in her eyes. She didn't doubt that others found him just as beautiful, too.

Evan Gilmore was and will always be her everything.

He was quiet, and she didn't say a word, letting him have his silence. Then he grasped her hand, sending shivers up her arm to consume her heart. "I'm just happy you're here."

Me, too.

But why did you have to leave me?

The thought had her smile fading as her heart filled with grief. It was supposed to be a joyous day, but seeing her ex-boyfriend made her sad. And according to her mother, he was happy and had been around when Alex wasn't. For that, she'd show him her gratitude.

"Thank you for being here while I was in Zürich."

He squeezed her hand. It was the perfect amount of pressure to comfort her and make her aware that he was there with her. "Of course. Your mother is, and always will be, family to me."

479

Alex's heart clenched tightly in her chest, making it hard for her to breathe.

He's not here for me.

The thought had her glancing down at their hands and then back at him. Her heart ached. A pressure built in her chest, and she knew it was because she still loved him, and that love was only hers to hold at night.

As she looked into those light browns that used to have forever in them, she said, "I don't think we should be holding hands, Evan."

Because it's too hard.

Because you're here to support my mother.

Because you're not here for me.

"I know we shouldn't." His voice was tight, filled with emotions he was trying to hide. "But I can't think of a reason that makes sense except for the fact that I miss you. A lot. I've missed you a lot, AJ."

Her eyelids fluttered. Breathlessly, she whispered, "Evan."

Her heart immediately fell in love with make-believe lies and promises she told herself.

Promises of a life they were supposed to have lived together.

But her hopeful heart just added to her pain.

"Hey, AJ?"

Alex tilted her head at him in confusion. "Yeah?"

"You did it."

"Did what?" Her brows met with confusion.

Evan laughed as he squeezed her hand. "You're in a hospital without looking like you're going to throw up right now."

Blinking, she scanned the waiting room. Her jaw dropped in disbelief. *He's right.* "I guess I was just so worried about my mum that I forgot. But now I'm totally aware of the smell and ..."

Oh, God.

The smell suddenly hit her hard, but Alex swallowed hard as Evan's eyes frantically searched her face. "I shouldn't have said anything. I'm just proud of you since this is the first time you've been in a hospital and haven't run out in a panic. Are you okay? Are you going to be sick?"

Her heart picked up at his concern.

Even after all this time, he still cared for her.

She saw it on his face.

"I'm fine." She inhaled a deep breath and then slowly exhaled, hoping it would calm her. "You're right. This is the first time I haven't run out of a hospital. I want to be here. I have to be here to support my parents. I'll be okay. So have you just been waiting here?"

Evan nodded. "Yeah. But while we wait, catch me up. How's Dr. Rodahawe and everyone? How's your research and your formula going?"

Unable to stop the fire in her chest and needing to touch him, to *feel* him, Alex reached up and pressed her palm softly against his cheek. That spark she felt made its way to her chest and reminded her of all the moments they had shared together. Moments she still replayed when she was alone with her thoughts. "Zürich isn't the same since you left." Alex had to pause and bite her lip to stop the intimate truths from being revealed. "Evan, I miss you a lot, but we shouldn't hold hands."

She knew it was wrong. He had broken up with her. Alex had cried long after he left her, so she had to end it. But as she tried to release her hand from his, he tightened his grip on her and shook his head.

"I was your boyfriend for three years, Alexandra. Not holding your hand while you're right here next to me doesn't feel right. I shouldn't have left Zürich. I shouldn't have left you." He inhaled a deep, shaky breath. "I—"

Her father burst into the waiting room, and said, "Evan, I have a son." He turned his head slightly and noticed that she had made it back home in time. The tears that ran down his face had her eyes stinging. "Alexandra, you're here. You have a brother, my love."

Alex pulled her hand free from Evan's and stood from the chair. "Can I see him?"

"Of course."

She smiled, excited that she was about to meet her baby brother for the very first time. Just as she was about to take a step, she glanced over her shoulder to find Evan staring at her vacant chair. She couldn't do it without him. He belonged with her in that moment. Like he had always belonged with her.

"You coming?" she asked with a smile.

Evan's gaze met hers. "Can I?"

Nodding, she held her hand out for him to take. "Like you said, you were my boyfriend for three years, but you have been a part of our family for much longer. You can't miss this."

He stood, grabbed her suitcase and purse, and placed his hand in hers. Alex bit the inside of her cheek, hoping the inch of pain would distract her from the fact that his touch was home.

That *he* was home.

That he was her heart, and she had been without it for so long.

A newborn's cry after midnight was excruciating.

Alex's little brother had been crying on and off since ten p.m.

Her mother had cracked Alex's bedroom door open just a bit and apologized for her brother's cries, but it wasn't her mother's fault that Alex couldn't sleep through them. It also didn't help that Alex had an early morning flight back to Zürich. She didn't want to go back to Switzerland so soon, but Dr. Rodahawe had put her on an assignment that required her back if she intended to return to the US in time for the Christmas holidays in several weeks' time. Four days wasn't long enough. Not when it came to being with her family.

But it was too long with Evan.

To be in the same room.

To see his smiles.

To long for him.

Four days was just too long when it came to Evan Gilmore.

So Alex got out of bed, stepped into her slippers, and contemplated how she would get some sleep. Her brother's cries seemed to echo through the large house. When she glanced over at her window, she knew that if she were to go to him, he'd help her. It was stupid, but she did want to see him before she left.

Maybe they could talk until she was so tired that sleep found her.

Her heart longed to talk to him.

To touch him.

To hold him.

To never let him go.

But their lives were different now.

Had been since he left.

Alex made her way to the door and grasped the handle. She paused for a moment, her mind and heart at war with her decision to see him.

This might be my last time.

The thought had her turning around. She went over to her nightstand and grasped her phone. She let out a sigh, unlocked her phone and texted her mother just in case she checked up on her through the night.

Alex: Hey, Mum. Please don't worry, but I have to see Evan one more time before I leave.

Satisfied that she wouldn't worry her mother, Alex returned to her bedroom door, grasped the handle and pulled the door open. There was nothing her heart wanted more and nothing that could sway its desires. She exited her room and closed the door gently behind her, scared she might wake her brother after her mother had put him to sleep. Tiptoeing down the hall and then the stairs, Alex walked over to the hallway hooks and removed her coat. She threaded her arms through and buttoned it up in hopes of shielding her from the cold winter winds and snow. Reaching over, she picked up her keys from the table and shoved them and her phone in her pocket. Alex glanced over her shoulder to ensure her parents hadn't awoken before she left the house and headed toward Evan's.

She knew it was a bad idea. But she was heavily jet-lagged

and lacked sleep. Her rationality only led her to Evan. Because when she returned to Zürich, she wouldn't be returning. Alex had accepted Dr. Rodahawe's offer after months of stalling. After months of hoping Evan would return to her. It was time she moved on with her life.

Telling her heart to be kind to her soul, she climbed the short steps to his door. Alex curled her fingers to form a fist and knocked gently on his door. She waited but heard nothing. Frowning, she attempted once more and was greeted with the very same response. Just as she was about to take a step back and return home, the porch light illuminated above her. The door opened, and she came face to face with her ex-boyfriend's surprised expression. He hadn't expected to see her at his doorstep so late. And truthfully, she hadn't either.

"Alexandra." His voice was full of concern as his brows met. No doubt he was cautious of her appearance. "It's late. Are you okay? Is Seb okay?"

Flames consumed her heart at the way his voice had softened when he asked about her brother's welfare. She was happy he cared so much for her family.

Alex smiled before she nodded. "It's stupid me being here. But …" She exhaled, realizing how stupid it was for her to be at his doorstep. "I have a flight back to Zürich in the morning, and I love Seb, but he keeps crying every two hours. And that would be okay but Dr. Rodahawe has me on assignment as soon as I land. I'm so sorry, but can I sleep on your couch tonight?"

"Wait." He appeared confused. "You just got here."

"Yeah, four days ago."

He shook his head. Disbelief washed all over his face.

"And you're already leaving?"

She chewed her bottom lip. "Yeah. They need me back at the institute. Plus, I'm almost done with my formula."

And to her surprise, he asked, "Can't you stay?"

Her eyes widened. He had never asked her to stay with him before. Evan had left her. It was the only question she had ever truly wanted to hear from him.

"I can't, Evan. I can't stay," she said in a tiny voice.

"So this is your last night?"

Alex nodded.

She saw it.

The heartbreak bright in his eyes.

It gave her a small ounce of hope that he still loved her.

Cared for her the way he had when they were together.

Evan stepped forward and cupped her face in his palms. "I love you," he whispered. "I still love you. Please say you love me, too."

Yes.

It had been all she had ever wanted.

A million times yes.

Her eyes filled with unshed tears. "I do love you, Evan."

It was as if her declaration of love had been all he needed to break the tension as his lips collided with hers. It was perfection in his sweet touch. It was life he breathed into her as she threaded her fingers through his hair.

She was hot.

Needy.

She wanted forever with him.

Only ever him.

He walked them back into his house, kissing her relentlessly.

As if time was never a concept that had worked against them.

And time had always been their enemy that she would fight against.

Just for tonight, she kissed him with everything she had in her. To prove to him that he shouldn't have left. That they were forever.

Don't you see, Evan?

I'm your soul mate.

"Evan," she moaned, kicking the door closed and keeping the cold air away.

"Stay," he begged, pressing her body against the hard door, causing her to gasp. "Please, God, please stay."

His hands disappeared from her face and grasped her coat, ripping it open. Alex helped him take it off and dropped it on the floor. Then she grasped the end of his T-shirt and lifted it off him, showcasing the very chest she missed sleeping on. The T-shirt then joined her coat on the floor by the door as he pulled his lips away, panting and staring into her eyes.

She loved this man so much.

She was sure she'd love him forever.

Alex felt it in the very depths of her chest.

"Please, Alexandra. Please stay with me," he begged with so much emotion in his voice that she had to touch him.

To somehow reassure him with her touch.

Reaching up, she cupped his face, gently brushing her thumb across his cheek. "Just tonight, Evan. I can only stay for tonight."

Evan slipped his hand under her tank top and grasped her hip, pressing her body against him. "Just tonight," he agreed in a tight voice and pressed his forehead against hers. "But just know that I'll still love you after tonight."

Alex nodded as she stepped out of her slippers, and Evan pulled away. Grasping her hand, he led her upstairs, leaving the months they had spent apart behind them just like their clothing. It took them seconds to make it to his room. And once they were inside, he closed the door and slowly undressed her.

He kissed her naked breasts.

His hands roamed her hips and held her in place as he licked from hip to the very edge of her panties. Then his fingers grasped each side of her underwear and peeled them down her legs. The lace caressing her skin as they fell to the floor. Alex threaded her fingers into his hair as he kissed her mound, causing her to moan.

"Evan," she whispered.

The light coming from the window allowed her to see him in all his beauty as he dragged his tongue across where she ached the most.

"Oh," she moaned as she threw her head back.

It had been so long since he touched her.

Pleased her.

"Evan," she managed to breathe out. She tugged at his hair, and he stood. "Make love to me."

He nodded. Alex grasped the tops of his jeans and unbuttoned them. She couldn't look away from his pleading brown eyes. She saw that same question in his eyes. He wanted her to stay, but she couldn't. She had committed to three more years in Switzerland.

"Get on the bed, Alexandra," he instructed.

Licking her lips, she made her way to the very bed she had

spent so many nights in. The same bed he had made love to her so freely and honestly in. The very bed that would house their final touches and goodbyes.

Alex climbed onto his bed and waited, watching as he pushed his jeans and underwear down his hips and stepped out of them. Evan joined her in bed, covering her body with his. Alex widened her thighs to let him press his hips to hers. Their contact had them both sighing in pleasure.

He brushed her hair back. "You're so beautiful."

Alex pressed her fingers to his jaw. "I've missed you so much, Evan."

"I've missed you, too. So much. It's pained me to be here without you."

Blinking her tears away, she dropped her hand and reached between them, grasping his hardness in her palm. She felt him throb as she stroked him.

Up and down.

Her thumb rubbed the tip, and he shuddered. "Alexandra," he groaned, voice full of desire and desperation.

She guided him to her entrance, feeling him there. Where she wanted him. Her heart raced as she felt him flex his hips, slowly entering her. Her lips parted as that pinch of his intrusion caused her discomfort. He stretched her. He kissed her. He inched farther into her until he was to the hilt. Until she was completely full.

"Evan." She sighed as he opened his eyes, staring at her.

"AJ." He breathed. "My AJ."

Her heart wept.

His AJ.

She was only ever his AJ.

"Make love to me," she pleaded. "Slow. God, please I want you to make love to me. Like we have forever in this one night. Like you never left me."

He dropped his face into the curve of her neck and nodded. He turned his head, his lips finding her skin.

He kissed her once.

Twice.

Three times before he pulled out of her.

Evan whispered, "I'll love you long after tonight. I'll love you forever," before he slowly pushed himself inside her, filling her once again.

She felt his love through his touch.

His kiss.

His thrusts.

His whispers of love.

In the very way he made love to her.

Evan Gilmore did what he promised. He made love to her all night as if they had forever waiting to kiss them both with the morning sun.

And before she drifted to sleep, he breathed the very words he owed her, "Eight neutrons."

Alex watched him sleep.

He was so peaceful.

Beautiful.

Last night was perfect. She felt his love in ways she had never felt before, but it was full of sadness rather than hope.

It was goodbye, and he knew it. She saw it in his eyes each time his hips met hers, in the way his eyes pleaded for her to stay. As she slipped her tank top over her head and corrected it around her stomach, she stared at him once more, hating that he would wake up alone.

But she had a flight to catch.

She had to leave.

Taking one last look of him, Alex pulled her hair free from her top and made her way out of his room. Once she was downstairs, she put on her slippers, picked up her coat, and made her way out of Evan's house. The snowfall was light as she trod across the driveways and up the porch steps. She dug her hand into her coat pocket and pulled out her keys. Once she inserted it and unlocked the front door, she walked inside and closed the door behind her.

Her eyes stung as her heart cried. Tears escaped her. And as Alex made her way toward the staircase, she brushed them away to find her mother at the very top, waiting for her.

"Oh, Alexandra," her mother said, the sadness bright in her tired brown eyes.

Alex attempted a smile. "I'm going to shower and get ready for my flight."

She didn't need to confirm to her mother that she had spent the night in her ex-boyfriend's bed, feeling his touch and his love for her.

But it was quite clear she knew.

All Alex could do was wash Evan Gilmore from her skin.

As reluctant as she was, his touch had to leave her for the very last time.

After a scalding hot shower masked her tears, Alex sat down with her parents at the table and had a farewell breakfast together. She wouldn't be home until Christmas. And she knew they were sad she couldn't stay longer. For them to actually be a family.

Her father frowned. "Are you sure you don't want me to put your suitcase in the cab for you?"

Alex shook her head. "No, it's okay, Dad. I've got it."

Her mother handed Sebastian to Alex's father. "Do you really have to go back, Alexandra? You were barely home. You usually stay longer."

A pang of guilt erupted in her chest. "I wish I could, Mum, but Seb wasn't supposed to be born for a few weeks. I'm lucky the institute let me leave." Alex stepped closer to her mother. "I'll be home again soon," she promised as she wiped her mother's tears away.

"Hey, Evan," her father said, alerting her that Evan was behind her.

She hated that she left him this morning. All she wanted to do was stay for just a minute longer. But she knew if she had, a minute would turn into an hour, and an hour would turn into the whole morning, ensuring she missed her flight.

Turning around, she finally smiled and saw the hurt in his eyes. "Hey," she said in a soft voice. The loud sound of the cab's horn got her attention. She glanced over to find her driver waving her over. "I better get going. Traffic to Logan is gonna be insane." Alex bent down and kissed her little brother. "I'll see you soon, Seb. Don't grow too much while I'm away."

She smiled at her father who asked, "Christmas?"

Alex nodded in agreement. "Christmas." She swung her focus to Evan's direction and stepped closer to him. She pressed a palm to his cheek, loving the feeling of his skin against her hand. "I love you, Evan. And I don't think I ever told you enough how much I loved you being my boyfriend. How much I appreciated you coming to Zürich for a year to be with me. I don't know when I'll be home again. I took the job."

He froze, his eyes wide in shock. "Three more years in Zürich ...?"

"Yeah," she confirmed. "Three more years in Zürich at the institute. I won't be an assistant anymore but a researcher."

Evan was silent as he stared at her. The horn from the cab sounded again. It rang loud with annoyance. She knew she wouldn't get much from him. She gave him news he probably didn't want to hear.

Three more years in Switzerland was the indefinite end of them.

Getting on her toes, she pressed her lips to his. "I'll still love you after I leave." Then she pulled away and smiled at her parents and the little boy in her father's arms. "I'll call you both once I land in Zürich. I love you all."

Alex refused to sneak a peek at Evan for fear she'd change her mind and stay. To tell him that nothing else mattered. But she couldn't. They both had lives away from each other, and Alex was about to start hers the moment she landed. She would no longer be a research assistant but a researcher herself.

A researcher at one of the finest institutions in the world.

She was living and experiencing her dreams.

The dreams she and Evan had fought so hard for.

Walking down the steps and then the path, she wheeled her suitcase behind her as the driver got out of the cab, lifted the trunk, and put her suitcase inside. She smiled her appreciation and made her way to the back seat. Pulling the door open, she slipped inside and closed the door behind her.

"Where to, miss?" the driver asked.

"Logan International Airport, please," she replied as she buckled her belt in place.

As the cab pulled away from the curb, temptation became a rash on her skin. An irritation she wanted to itch. She wanted to turn around and see him. To see if he was watching her drive away and out of his life.

"Excuse me, sir," Alex said, staring at the driver's headrest rather than him.

"Yeah, miss?"

Alex wet her lips. "In your mirror, are you able to see if he's watching the cab drive away?"

He was silent. Then he let out a breath, and said, "He is."

Her heart ached.

Evan was still watching the cab long after she said goodbye.

Then the driver glanced over at her and smiled. "Your boyfriend's still there."

My boyfriend ...

If only it were true.

¹⁰⁰**Fm**

fermium

EVAN

Now

Two weeks.

In two weeks, his daughter would be born.

For the past three months, Evan and AJ attended their remaining birthing and parenting classes and ensured that everything was in order to welcome their daughter into the world. His girlfriend, Alexandra Parker, had spent the past few weeks making sure the hospital bag and their baby's nursery was perfect. Now it was a waiting game and attending to his girlfriend's every request. A lot of them consisted of food runs and massaging her aches. But Evan loved it. He'd loved their entire journey through her pregnancy.

Every ultrasound was amazing.

Every class was a brand-new experience.

They were as prepared as they could be.

Evan bent down and brushed Alexandra's hair from her face. "Baby," he whispered, his thumb caressing her cheek. "AJ?"

"Hmm," she mumbled.

"I'm going to work."

That had her opening her eyes. It was slow. She was still half asleep. But the sleepy smile on her face was utter beauty. "Morning."

He bent down and pressed his lips to hers in a long and unrushed kiss. Smiling against her lips, he pulled away, hating that he couldn't stay. He'd much rather stay in bed with her. "I have to go." He set his hands on the edge of the mattress.

AJ shifted closer, pressing her lips to his pinky. "I know. I'm going to help Mum at the bakery this afternoon. Do you want to have dinner in the city after you finish work?"

"Are you sure you should be helping around the bakery? AJ, you're nine months pregnant."

She rolled her eyes and then sat up, letting out a groan. He knew she wasn't particularly comfortable. She always complained about the aches and talked about how she couldn't wait to give birth. "I'll be fine. I'll be serving. And Mum will make sure I don't do anything that requires too much work. And don't worry, she's driving. Your driving ban is still in effect."

"Baby, that was a self-imposed ban." Evan stood, then bent down and kissed her forehead. "I'll call you when I leave work, and I'll pick you up, okay?"

"Okay." She pressed her fingertips to his jaw, steadying his face. His girlfriend smiled before she kissed him deeply. He let out a groan when she began to pull away, causing her to laugh. "Go to work."

"But—"

She shook her head and lowered her hands. "Go to work. I'll see you later."

"I love you."

She hummed. To Evan, it was the sound of contentment that reached his ears. "I love you, too, Evan. Have a good day."

"You, too," he said as he stood straight and picked up his briefcase. "Don't work too hard, okay? Take care of yourself."

AJ tilted her head and then curled her finger at him in a *come-hither* motion.

Evan bent down and watched as she gripped his tie in her hands and adjusted the knot to perfection. "There. Now you're really ready."

"Thank you," he said. He kissed her one last time and left for work.

As he walked out of their bedroom, he smiled, loving how good his life truly was.

"I never imagined I'd see you behind a desk," Evan heard a familiar voice say. He had been working on department expense reports for most of the morning in hopes of finishing so he could have dinner with his girlfriend without bringing home work. He glanced up from his laptop to find his high school best friend and college rival at his office door.

Evan grinned. "You'll start rumors if you're photographed at Fenway, you know."

Hunter Jamison, starting batter for the Los Angeles Dodgers, shrugged. "Dodgers fans know I'm a Red Sox fan. They'll deal with it. I signed a new contract, so they know I'm committed to life in LA."

"Well, come in," Evan said, watching Hunter stroll into the office and take the seat in front of him. "So what are you doing back in Boston?"

"Mom's birthday," Hunter said. "You have a pretty sweet view of the ballpark."

Evan laughed as he closed his laptop. "Perks of being the brother of the Red Sox captain. Trust me, if Kyle weren't my brother, I would not have this office."

Hunter nodded. "You ever miss playing?"

"Sometimes," Evan admitted. "But I couldn't imagine playing professionally. I sometimes go to the batting cages on my days off, but they're rare, and it's only when I really miss the game. AJ comes with me and watches."

"Ah, Alexandra Parker," Hunter said with a smile. "You lucky son of a bitch."

Evan smiled. Not smug but grateful. He was so grateful for the life he had with her. "I couldn't agree more."

"How are you both?"

"We're good. The house is officially done. We had to wait to do the garden. We weren't sure how we were going to do it until we hired a landscaper."

Disbelief shone in Hunter's light green eyes. "You have a house and a pregnant girlfriend. You're living the life. How is Alex?"

"She's good, man. Really good."

"That's great, Ev," he said. "So ..."

Evan leaned back into his leather chair. "So?"

The glint in Hunter's eyes had Evan raising his brow. "When are you going to marry her? You have a house. You're the father of her unborn child. Do you want to marry the love of your life? The girl who used to sit on the bleachers and wait for you. The girl who watched you take another girl to homecoming and prom. The girl who has been in love with you for forever."

He let out a small laugh. "When am I going to marry AJ?"

"Yes!" Hunter exaggerated the agitation in his voice, throwing his hands in the air. "It's all any of our friends have been talking about since the baby shower."

"Like who?"

Hunter squinted at him. "Like *everyone*—especially Carter and Jordan. They need more married friends to hang out with. I'm sure Jordan's tired of hanging out with all the Patriots wives."

Evan shook his head. "Well, I have to ask her first."

His best friend's mouth dropped. "You haven't asked her yet? I'd have asked Alex to marry me the moment she said she loved me. What are you doing, Gilmore?"

Evan sat up straight and stared at Hunter. He knew Hunter was teasing him, but the envy was thick in his voice. "I want AJ to know that I want to marry her because I love her and not because she's pregnant."

"Seriously, that sounds like an excuse. What are you waiting for?"

"I'm waiting for our daughter to make it perfect."

"So you're going to ask?"

A soft smile splayed on his lips. "Honestly, I've been wanting to ask her to marry me since our senior year of college. The moment she came back, I knew I was going to ask. But right now, it doesn't feel perfect. Something is missing, and I know it's our daughter."

"You've gone soft," Hunter teased with a smirk on his face.

"I've lost her too many times, Hunter. I'm keeping her for good." Evan folded his arms over his chest. "So besides your interest in my and AJ's relationship, how is everything with you?"

Hunter shrugged a shoulder. "I haven't met the love of my life."

Something was off about Hunter. Normally, he'd say something tacky about the perks of single life, but Evan was intrigued. "But you've met someone?"

"I've known someone for a while."

"And ...?"

A displeased expression consumed Hunter's face. "Let's just say if you knew, you'd be disappointed." He sighed. "And it's not your ex, Molly, either. It's just ... you know what? It's nothing. She's nothing. Single life is great."

And there it was.

Hunter couldn't deny it.

He was troubled by love.

Or at the very least, lust.

"I bet it is," Evan said, not missing that life one single bit. "Hey, why don't you come over for dinner tomorrow if you're still in town? AJ would be happy to see you."

"Are you sure?"

"I'm sure. She'd be upset if she knew you were in town and you didn't see her ..." Evan paused the moment his phone vibrated on his desk. He smiled when he saw her name. "Speaking of AJ, she's calling. I'll just tell her now."

"Sure," Hunter said.

Evan picked up his phone and answered AJ's call, pressing his phone to his ear. "Hey, AJ."

"Evan," she sounded out of breath.

His heart dipped as concern washed over him. "Baby, are you okay?"

"Uh-huh," she groaned.

"AJ, you don't sound okay."

She inhaled a deep breath. "Are you busy?"

"I'm just with Hunter."

"Oh," she whispered. "That's nice. Tell him I said hi."

Evan glanced over at Hunter who had his wide eyes focused on him. "I will. Now, AJ, what's going on?"

She was quiet and then he heard her shuffled footsteps. "Evan ...?"

"I'm right here, baby."

"Are you sure you're not busy?"

Then she let out a groan that had Evan jumping from his chair and pulling open the desk drawer to get his car keys and wallet out. If she told him she needed ice cream, he'd rush out and get it for her. "I'm sure."

She was silent once again, and then she uttered the words Evan would never forget. "Evan, my water broke."

Her water ...

"Broke?" he breathed out. "Your water broke?"

"Yes, and oh, my God, it's everywhere."

"Are you okay?"

AJ let out a small laugh. "I had this nightmare that as soon as my water broke, I'd have these awful contractions. But nothing. Maybe a little pressure." Her laughter faded. "Evan?"

"Yeah, baby?" he asked as he shoved his wallet in his pocket.

"Can you please come home?"

It was Evan's turn to laugh. "I'm on my way. I won't be too long. I'm going to keep you on the line, okay? You keep talking to me."

"Okay."

Evan lowered his phone and gave Hunter a smile. "Hunt, I'm sorry, I—"

"Go," his best friend encouraged. "Alex needs you."

"Thanks, man. We'll all have dinner soon."

Hunter grinned as he got up from his chair. "Gilmore, go be with your girlfriend. You're about to become a father. You can worry about dinner another time. And let me be the first to say congratulations. I bet you anything she's going to be as beautiful as her mother."

"Thanks, Hunter. I'll keep you updated," Evan said as he stepped away from his desk and tightened his grip around his car keys. As he and Hunter exited his office, he found his newly hired college graduate assistant at her desk. "Nina."

"Yes, Mr. Gilmore?"

He smiled at her. "My girlfriend's water broke. Could you tell Mr. Schmidt that I had to take her to the hospital?"

"Of course. And congratulations, Mr. Gilmore. Please tell Miss Parker the very same."

"Thanks, Nina." As he and Hunter headed out of Fenway Park, Evan returned his phone to his ear. "AJ, you still with me?"

"I'm still here."

He breathed out a sigh of relief. "Baby, I'll be there soon," he promised.

Fifteen minutes later, Evan pushed his front door open and rushed into the house he shared with his girlfriend.

"AJ!" he yelled out.

"I'm in the kitchen." It was a small shout.

Evan ran down the hall and into the kitchen to find her sitting on the floor next to the puddle, cradling her stomach.

"I felt some pressure and had to sit."

Stepping over the puddle, he bent down and pressed his lips to her forehead. "Are you okay?"

She nodded. "Just pressure. I haven't had any contractions just yet. But I think we should go to the hospital."

He nodded as he grasped her hands in his. "We should definitely go to the hospital." Then he helped her to her feet. "You're two weeks early."

"I know. But I think she's ready to meet her daddy."

His chest tightened. "I'm so ready to meet our Little Atom."

"Me, too. Come on. We need to get the hospital bag and get to the hospital. Then we can call our parents and Kyle."

Wrapping his arm around her, he helped her over the puddle and walked her to the staircase. "I'll grab the bag. Stay here."

"Okay," she said.

Evan climbed the stairs and ran down the hall to his baby's nursery. When he stepped inside, he took in the room.

For months, it had been almost perfect. They had a crib and a changing table. The walls were painted a soft gray. The stained-glass panels hung on the wall. The planets mobile hovered over the crib. It was just missing one last addition.

Their daughter.

And as Evan took in the room, he knew it would be perfect once they welcomed her home.

Almost twelve hours.

That was how long Alexandra was in labor.

For the first four hours after she was admitted into the hospital, she had been calm. But that pressure she had felt quickly became contractions. And each hour that passed, they seemed to become stronger. There was nothing Evan could do but sit by her side and hold her hand when she wanted to.

The longer she was in labor, the more pain she was in, refusing his touch.

But by the ninth hour, she had begun to cry, and Evan held her.

And at the eleventh hour, Dr. Livingston announced that Alexandra was ten centimeters dilated and ready to push.

"You're almost there, Alex," Dr. Livingston said. "Keep pushing and breathing."

His girlfriend's grip tightened around his hand, and Evan bent down and kissed her temple. "You've got this, AJ. You've got this. I'm so proud of you."

"I can't, Evan," she sobbed. "I can't push anymore."

"Just one more," he pleaded with her. "One more, baby."

She gulped down some air and nodded, blinking her tears away. The sweat dotted her forehead, and her face was red. "Okay."

"Are you ready to push again?" Dr. Livingston asked.

"Yes," AJ answered in a weak voice.

"Okay, deep breath in for me, Alex," the doctor instructed.

His girlfriend inhaled a deep breath. "As you exhale, I want you to push, okay?"

AJ nodded.

"And push!"

"Ahh!" AJ cried as she strangled Evan's hand once more.

"Good, Alex," the doctor praised. "A few more and I think we'll meet your beautiful daughter."

Evan squeezed her hand, reached up and brushed the drenched strands of hair from her sweaty face. "One more, baby."

AJ groaned as she breathed in quick breaths. Then she nodded and inhaled deeply before she said, "Okay, I'm ready to go again."

"Okay, and push!" Dr. Livingston encouraged.

The next few minutes were a blur. He concentrated on his girlfriend as she pushed. Her face contorted in agony, sweat, tiredness, and determination. And Evan thought she had never looked more beautiful than at this moment.

Then he heard the most perfect small wail he had ever heard.

The very first sound their daughter had ever made.

Md

mendelevium

ALEX

One month before Alex's Boston return

A lex had made a lot of mistakes in her life but had few regrets.

Her biggest regret had been returning to Zürich after she had spent the night with Evan Gilmore.

The moment she arrived back in Switzerland, she felt wrong.

It felt as if pieces of her were missing.

Alex knew why, but she also had obligations.

She had promised the Rodahawe Institute three more years, but most of all, she had promised Dr. Rodahawe a completed formula. Since she landed, she had spent all her time on it while fantasizing about home.

She gave herself two months.

Two months to finalize the formula as much as she could before she left Zürich for good. If she didn't finish, she'd work on it from her bedroom back in Massachusetts. She had purchased her ticket home two weeks ago and spent the past two weeks working and rewriting the letter in her hands. Alex glanced down at it one more time and exhaled a heavy breath. Then she formed a fist and tapped on the glass wall.

Dr. Rodahawe stopped what he was writing on the board and spun around. He smiled the moment he saw her and set his marker on his desk. "Ah, Alexandra. What can I do for you?"

She stepped into his office and then stood in front of his desk. "I have some good news," she announced.

Surprise and excitement dazzled his eyes. "Oh, please share."

"I got accepted into MIT," she revealed. "I got the letter yesterday."

"That's amazing, Alexandra. I knew you'd get in."

Her heart warmed at his belief in her. "All because of your recommendation."

Pride brightened his face. "I'm so proud of you—*Oh.*" His lips spread across his face, and she saw the bittersweet emotions in his smile. "You're leaving us."

Alex reached out and handed him her resignation letter. "I am," she said with sorrow in her voice. "I have learned so much here at the Rodahawe Institute and from you, Dr. Rodahawe. You have inspired me to go forward with my academic goals. I appreciate everything you and everyone at this institute have done for me. But after almost two years here, I think it's time I go home."

"You love him more than science," Dr. Rodahawe said.

She knew who he meant by *him*, and she nodded. "I do. And I should have chased after him when he left. If it's okay with you, I'd like to stay for another month to finish all my obligations here. That should give you enough time to find someone to take over my position. I am so thankful for everything you have done and taught me, Dr. Rodahawe."

"And I am so thankful to you, too. You have been an honor to teach and mentor. You remind me every day of why I became a physicist. To inspire and teach those who love physics just as much as I do." Then the doctor walked around his desk and wrapped his arms around her. "I am very proud of you, Alexandra."

"Thank you."

He pulled her back, and said, "You will always have a home here at the Rodahawe Institute. Whenever you'd like to return—even to just visit—you are always welcome. You will always be family—Evan, too."

"Thank you," she said, holding back her tears.

She would always be thankful for her time, experience, and every person she had met at the Rodahawe Institute, but it was time for Alex to return home.

Two weeks before Alex's Boston return

A lex sat in the waiting room of the health center near her Zürich apartment, anxiously waiting for her name to be called out to see her doctor. It was the same health center she visited when she had the flu a few months ago. Alex knew very well that her blood tests would confirm what she already suspected.

"Miss Parker," Dr. Amsler called out. The handsome doctor was tall and blond with blue eyes. The kind of man you'd find modeling in perfume advertisements instead of treating patients.

She got up from the chair where she had been sitting for

the past half an hour and followed the doctor into the room. Once they were inside, she sat on another chair and watched him take his seat in front of her.

"*Guete Morge*, Alexandra." *Good morning.*

"*Guete Morge*, Dr. Amsler," she said in a soft voice.

He smiled. Her doctor knew her Swiss German wasn't very good and only knew the basics and understood some phrases. But to hold a conversation was out of her league. "You look lovely today. How are you feeling?"

Her smile faded as anxiety washed over her. "Okay. I've been thinking about the results."

He reached over and picked up a folder. "Well, I have the results. Are you ready?"

She inhaled a deep breath. After she exhaled the air from her lungs, she nodded. "I'm as ready as I can be."

"All right," he said as he opened the file. His eyes scanned the page, and then he lifted his chin. "Your blood results came back."

"And?"

His lips pressed into a tight smile. "They came back positive."

Although she had expected the results, it still surprised her.

"*Positive?*"

He nodded. "Congratulations, Alexandra. You're pregnant."

Pregnant.

She swallowed the lump in her throat. Alex was pregnant.

It didn't take much for her to put the math together.

She was six weeks pregnant.

Six weeks ago, she had been with Evan Gilmore. She hadn't been with anyone else since him. It had only been him since they got together during the end of their sophomore year of college. Six weeks ago, they'd had unprotected sex. Alex wasn't on birth control. She hadn't thought of it when she was with Evan. She had stopped taking the pill and was about to move onto a different form of birth control. Her night with Evan had been spontaneous and unexpected.

It resulted in them creating a life.

"If you'd like, we can perform an ultrasound and see how the baby is doing?"

Alex blinked at Dr. Amsler in disbelief. "You can?"

He nodded as he stood. "I can. With how early you are, it will have to be a transvaginal ultrasound. I promise, you don't have to worry. It won't be dangerous."

"Okay. I'd like to have an ultrasound." Then she stood and followed the doctor out of his office and into an examination room.

He opened a drawer by the table, pulled out a paper gown, and set it on the table. "I'll give you a few moments."

After she nodded, the doctor left her alone in the examination room. With shaky hands, she unbuttoned her jeans as she stepped out of her flats. Alex shimmed out of her jeans, folded them and set them on a chair. Then she removed her underwear and covered them with her jeans. Exhaling, she grabbed the paper gown and put it on. Once it covered her, Alex grasped the sheet on the table, climbed onto it and set her feet on the stirrups. As she covered her lower half with the sheet, the doctor knocked and then opened the door.

"Everything okay, Alexandra?"

"Yes, Dr. Amsler. I'm ready." She watched as he entered the room, closed the door behind him and headed over to the machine. He turned it on before he smiled at her. Once he put on some gloves and sat between her legs, Alex kept her eyes on the screen. She heard a wrapper crinkle and inhaled a sharp breath.

"I'm just putting a condom over the probe. Then I'll put some lubricating gel on it." A few moments later, Dr. Amsler said, "You're going to feel a little bit of pressure."

"Okay," Alex said, then she felt the pressure he warned her about. It was uncomfortable but manageable as Dr. Amsler conducted the ultrasound.

She was in awe to think that she had life growing inside her. In the next eight months, her stomach would swell. Her baby would grow.

Their baby would grow.

Evan's baby will grow.

She smiled at the thought of their child being half Evan. Her heart fluttered at the thought of him holding their child. But then her chest tightened. She had no idea if Evan wanted to be a father. When she had planned her return home, she had no idea she was pregnant.

But now, it felt as if everything was falling into place. Right now, she'd experience her very first ultrasound. Later, she'd think of Evan and how she'd tell him that she was pregnant with his child.

"And there is your baby, Alexandra."

"Where?" Anxiety crawled up her throat as she searched the screen for her child.

From the corner of her eye, she noticed the smile on his

face. "It's okay. Most new mothers don't see their baby either. That dot right there on the screen. Do you see where it's different from the rest of the screen?"

She nodded. "I see that."

"That's the baby."

"He or she is so small," she said in bewilderment.

He let out a small laugh as he removed the transducer from her and set it on the table. "He or she is. Would you like a copy of the ultrasound?"

"Yes, please."

The doctor stood from his chair, removing and disposing of the condom from the probe and his gloves before he handed her a towel. On instinct, Alex closed her legs and sat up. Moments later, Dr. Amsler handed her a printed picture, and she glanced down at it.

"I'll give you a minute," he said, and he stepped out of the room.

She smiled as she took in the small little dot. It reminded her of atoms. The little dot was her Little Atom.

She dropped the towel next to her and pressed her hand on her stomach. "Hello, Little Atom," she breathed as she peeked down at her stomach and then back at the picture. "I'm your mum, and I hope I'm a really good mum."

Tears slipped down her face. The sudden swell of love in her chest was so new, so different from anything she had ever felt before. It was unconditional and perfect.

She would love her child no matter what.

Then Alex reached up and pressed her fingertips to the necklace Evan Gilmore had given her for Christmas all those years ago.

"I promise you'll see your daddy soon," she said in a small voice.

Alex had two weeks.

Two weeks to prepare herself to see Evan Gilmore and tell him that they were expecting a child. For a moment, she was terrified. But it disappeared when she remembered just what a good, loving man Evan Gilmore was.

He might have broken her heart, but he would love his child wholeheartedly until his very last breath.

Alex was sure of that.

1:02 am
time of birth

EVAN

Now

He was a father.

Alexandra was a mother.

They had a daughter.

Evan swung his focus in the direction of the small cries to find Dr. Livingston handing his and AJ's daughter to the delivery nurse who held out a sheet. He glanced back at AJ to find her still crying. He wrapped his arm around her and let her sob. Evan knew it was out of relief because she had endured the very worst pain possible.

"I am so proud of you, AJ," he whispered.

"Evan, would you like to cut the umbilical cord?" Dr. Livingston asked.

He nodded and then reluctantly pulled away from his girlfriend. He stepped toward the end of the bed, and his eyes found his daughter for the very first time.

Even though blood and mucus covered her, she was perfect and small.

Ten fingers and ten toes.

She was still crying, and Evan thought her cries were perfect.

A nurse handed him the scissors, and he cut just where he was instructed. Then the nurse took his baby away, and Evan handed the scissors back to Dr. Livingston who smiled at him.

"Congratulations, Evan, you're now a father. You should be proud of Alexandra. It wasn't easy for her," Dr. Livingston said. "We'll look over your daughter, and then we'll bring her right back. Go to your girlfriend."

"Thank you, Dr. Livingston," Evan said with so much appreciation.

The doctor smiled, and Evan returned to AJ's side. She was staring at the nurses as they attended to their daughter. Evan grasped her hand and linked his fingers with hers. She faced him and directed her small smile his way.

"How did she look?" she asked, her voice full of concern.

"Perfect," he assured as he squeezed her hand. "You did amazing. I'm so proud of you."

"Oh, God. That was …"

He leaned forward and kissed her on the lips. "I know. Don't think I don't appreciate everything you did today. You brought our beautiful daughter into this world."

"And here she is," the delivery nurse said as she stood by AJ's side. "Would you like to meet your mama, Little Gilmore?" AJ whipped her head around and sat herself up at little more. "I think your parents really want to meet you." Then she lowered the baby girl into AJ's arms.

He heard a flash and knew that the other nurse had taken photos. One of the nurses had taken over for Evan when he abandoned photography duty.

"Oh my, God," AJ breathed as tears ran down her face once she finally held their daughter.

Reaching into his pocket, Evan pulled out his phone and turned on the camera. He snapped a picture of his girlfriend holding their daughter for the very first time, wanting to keep this moment forever. Then he set his phone down on the table next to the bed and gazed over at the two most important loves of his life.

His girlfriend.

And his daughter.

Evan had everything he had ever wanted right in front of him.

He heard more shutter sounds capturing their moments, and he was thankful for the nurse who took their photos.

"Does she have a name?" Dr. Livingston asked once she returned to the end of the bed.

His girlfriend glanced up from their sleeping daughter and up at him. A silent question burned bright in her eyes. She had asked him about names months ago. She had suggested one name, and it was perfect the moment she said it. AJ had told him that they could always change it if he wasn't comfortable with it, but it was their daughter's name the moment it left AJ's lips.

He nodded at her, giving her the permission she did not need. The wide smile on her face was priceless. Evan gently caressed his daughter's soft cheek with his index finger. He had never been so overwhelmed with love before.

Never fell in love with anyone as fast as he had for his daughter.

He watched Alexandra's eyes fall to the baby in her arms. "She does." She looked up at Evan and smiled. "Her name is Miller Clara Louise Gilmore."

"That's beautiful," Dr. Livingston said.

Evan couldn't agree more.

"Do you want to hold her?" the love of his life asked.

"Yes," he breathed.

It was a careful exchange, but when he had his daughter in his arms, he broke into tears. Miller had the smallest nose and the chubbiest cheeks. Her hair was on the darker side, so she definitely got it from her mother. He wondered what color eyes she had. He prayed she had her mother's eyes. Those beautiful emerald eyes he was hopeless for.

"Miller, you are so beautiful. The everything in my life I needed." Then he looked over at AJ to find her crying. "Thank you," he whispered as he bent his knees and kissed his girlfriend. "Thank you for the most precious gift you could have ever given me. I love her. I love her so much. And I love you so, so much, Alexandra."

"I love you so much, Evan," she said wholeheartedly. He lowered his arms a little more so that she could see their daughter. "Miller, you're perfect."

Miller.

Miller Gilmore.

Miller Clara Louise Gilmore.

His heart clenched at his daughter's name from his daughter's mother's lips.

It was perfection.

"Alexandra," he said, getting her attention.

"Yes?" Her large emerald eyes gleamed at him.

He smiled. "I love her name."

"I do, too. Thank you for agreeing."

Evan laughed. "Her name was Miller the moment you told me you wanted to name her after the most influential academic you've ever met. I know he will love it."

"Evan," Dr. Livingston said. He craned his neck in her direction. "We'd like to check on Alex for a little bit."

"Of course," he said, handing Miller back to her mother. "Keep your *mum* company, Miller."

AJ laughed. "You said *mum*."

"Yeah. She's half Australian, after all. I'll go let our families know. I'll come back soon." Then he kissed her lips and pressed his forehead to hers. "Eight protons ..."

"Eight neutrons," AJ whispered back.

After Evan left the delivery room, he walked down the hall and found his parents, his brother, his brother's girlfriend, and AJ's parents and brother in the waiting room. Once Evan stepped through the doors, they all rose from their chairs, staring at him.

Mr. Parker was the first to rush over to him. "Is she okay? Are they both okay?"

Evan took in the very man who had raised him. The man who took him in and made him feel worthy as a man and a son. Evan owed this man everything. He owed his daughter's grandfather everything.

Evan blinked back his tears just as Mrs. Parker approached them, carrying nine-month-old Sebastian in her arms. He stared at them both, in awe that his daughter would have the very best grandparents. In awe of the family that would love her. Because of how early Alexandra had given birth, the rest of her family would be arriving from Australia later in the day. AJ's best friend, Savannah, was on her way from Vermont to visit.

"How are Alexandra and the baby?" Mrs. Parker asked.

He nodded at them both and brushed his tears away. "Alexandra is getting looked at by Dr. Livingston. The baby ..." He paused, getting emotional as he thought about how perfect she was. "She's beautiful. She's so perfect."

Mrs. Parker cried as she rocked Sebastian. "You're an uncle, Sebastian."

"Evan," his older brother, Kyle, said as he approached him along with their parents and Angie. "How are they?"

His eyes scanned his and AJ's family. He knew their daughter would have a lot of love surrounding her, and the thought had Evan smiling. "Alexandra and the baby are both fine. I know it's late, but thank you all for being here. I appreciate it, and I know Alexandra does, too."

"What did you name her?" Angie asked. It had been a rough few months for Kyle and Angie. Evan knew that his brother had kept a lot from him because Kyle didn't wanted to make his problems Evan's with the pregnancy. Once everything settled, Evan was determined to spend time with his brother and see if he was okay.

Evan let out a breath. "Her name is Miller," he said and received many awws from their families. Then he glanced at Mrs. Parker, and continued, "Miller Clara Louise Gilmore."

"Clara Louise?" AJ's mother asked, her voice cracked with emotion.

He nodded. "Alexandra wanted to name her after the most important people in her life. Miller's middle name is a testament to you, and to Mr. Parker since Louise is his mother's name."

"And *Miller*?" his mother, Susan, asked.

Evan had called his parents and AJ's parents after she had been admitted into the hospital. Then he called Kyle, Angie, and Savannah. Unfortunately, with how early AJ was giving birth, Savannah wasn't able to reschedule her important meeting with some of her clients. Though she had missed the birth, she was still on her way. His parents had taken the first flight out of Chicago to Boston.

When he called Mrs. Parker to tell her that her daughter's water broke, she asked where her water broke, and Evan replied in their kitchen. Later in the hospital, she told Evan that she used her key to the house and cleaned up their kitchen floor so they wouldn't have to worry about it when they returned home. Evan hadn't even thought to clean it up. He had just wanted to get his girlfriend to Massachusetts General Hospital.

"Named after the very man who taught her to appreciate her love for science," Evan revealed. Then he turned and smiled at Kyle. "I know we've had years when we couldn't stand each other, but since college, you've been there for me. And I'm so proud Miller has you for an uncle."

Kyle's brown eyes widened, tears streaming down his face as he stepped forward and wrapped his arms around Evan. "I'm so proud of you," Kyle whispered as they embraced. Then he pulled back and smiled.

"Be proud of Alexandra. You should have seen her."

"I'm so proud of both of you," Kyle said. "You're a father now, Ev."

Father.

I'm a father.

He nodded. "I am. And my daughter has the most

wonderful mother."

"Evan?"

He spun around to find Dr. Livingston standing by the waiting room doors. "Dr. Livingston. Is Alexandra okay? Is Miller all right?"

The doctor didn't say anything for a moment, and his heart kicked into overdrive, consumed with fear and concern.

AJ has to be okay.

Miller has to be okay.

My family has to be okay.

She smiled as she nodded. "You'll make a great father, Evan. They're both healthy. Alex is asking for you."

He sighed in relief. Evan spun around and faced their families. "I'll go check on her. Once she says she's ready, I'll come get you all, and you can meet our daughter."

"Okay," Mr. Parker said before Evan spun around and followed the doctor back to the delivery room.

When they reached the room, Dr. Livingston faced him. The serious expression on her face had him tensing. "It's not uncommon for a new mother to cry excessively after birth. It was tough on Alex, but she was amazing. Just comfort her like you have been and she'll be fine. Miller is healthy, but Alex will need a lot of rest. The nurse will be by later, but for now, Evan, just be with your beautiful family."

"Thank you, Dr. Livingston," he said before he entered the room to AJ holding Miller in her arms. Upon reaching her, he bent down and kissed the top of his girlfriend's head.

She gazed up at him, tears rolling down her cheeks. "Can you sit with us?"

He nodded and sat on the tiny remaining space on her bed.

"Are you okay?" Evan asked as he slung an arm around her, AJ resting her head against his shoulder.

"Yes," she said, eyes falling back to their daughter. "I'm happy. She's so tiny."

"What did the nurse say about you and Miller?"

AJ tilted her head back. "We're both good. There was some concern about my blood pressure, but I'm sure it's nothing. She's going to come back later and show us how to change her diaper and everything we need to know." Then her smile deepened. "You said Miller."

"That's her name."

"I know," AJ said as she glanced down at their daughter. "But she'll still always be Little Atom, too."

Evan reached up and brushed his daughter's soft cheek. "I haven't messaged Sav yet since she's probably still driving. I'll message her soon. I told our parents, Kyle, and Angie of Miller's birth. They're all waiting. Your grandparents should be here in the morning, and so should Alex and Keira with the girls before Lori goes to college."

"Seriously? I can't believe they're coming. Lori is starting her freshman year at LSU. They should concentrate on traveling to Louisiana and moving her into her dorm."

"They all want to meet our daughter."

Alexandra let out a soft contented sigh. "We have a daughter."

"Yeah," he agreed.

"You don't mind if we just sit like this for a little while longer? I don't want to let her go just yet." A small laugh escaped him as his girlfriend moved closer to him, and asked, "Do you want to hold her?"

"Can I?"

AJ laughed. "You're her father, Evan." Carefully, his girlfriend handed him their daughter and shifted across the bed, giving him more room.

He adjusted his position on AJ's bed for comfort and took in their sleeping daughter. She hadn't opened her eyes around him just yet. "Do you know what color eyes she has?"

"The nurse said they're gray, but we'll know what color when she's about nine months. Dr. Livingston said it's hard to tell," AJ answered as she leaned her head back against his shoulder. "I think she might have green eyes."

Evan tilted his chin to look down at her. "I desperately want her to have your eyes."

His girlfriend wrapped her arms around his, staring at their little girl. "Thank you."

He flinched, careful not to harm Miller. "*You're* saying thank you to *me*? AJ, you were in labor for twelve hours. I should be thanking you profusely."

"Thank you ..." she said, unwrapping an arm from around him and gently brushing Miller's soft hair. "For being her father." Then she kissed their baby's forehead and glanced up at him. "And for loving her the moment you saw her."

"I loved her the moment you told me you were pregnant, AJ."

She sat upright and nodded. "I know you did. You just fell deeper in love with her with every ultrasound and kick. But you loved her unconditionally as her father the moment you saw her after she was born."

"I love her," Evan said, staring at his daughter. "I didn't think I could ever love anyone like this." He glanced up at his girlfriend. "But you, AJ, I love you entirely. You gave me the most beautiful daughter. I love you so much."

Tears skimmed her cheeks as they fell. "And I love you, Evan Gilmore." Her focus dropped to the baby in his arms as she let out a soft sound. "And I love you, Miller Gilmore. Mummy and Daddy love you so much."

Evan lifted his daughter a fraction higher and pressed his lips softly to her forehead. "We love you so much, Miller. Are you ready to meet your grandparents, uncles, and aunt?"

Miller moved her head as her lips parted.

AJ laughed. "I think she'll be ready."

"Would you like me to get your parents first?"

She nodded. "If that's okay."

"All right. But let's just stay like this for a little longer."

Evan and AJ had spent the past twenty minutes staring at their daughter. He had handed Miller over to her mother before he got off the bed and fetched AJ's parents and little brother. She had wanted to see her parents first before Evan's, which was understandable. His parents had made the effort to be there for them, and they would always be his daughter's grandparents, but Noel and Clara Parker had a bigger role in Evan's life.

"Just in this room," he said to her parents once they reached AJ's room.

Clara held Sebastian to her body as she and Noel entered the room.

"Hey," AJ whispered to her parents as Evan followed

them inside.

"Alexandra," her mother said in awe.

Evan rounded the bed until he was on the other side of his girlfriend's hospital bed.

Her father bent down and kissed the top of her head. "She's beautiful, Alexandra."

She smiled, proud of the little girl in her arms. "Do you want to hold your granddaughter, Dad?"

Tears gleamed Noel's eyes. "Can I?"

Evan grinned. He had never seen AJ's father this emotional in his entire life.

"Miller," AJ whispered, "are you ready to meet your grandfather?"

Noel bent down and held his arms open, taking his granddaughter from his daughter. "Hello, Miller," Noel said in awe as he stood straight. He gently rocked Miller, his eyes focused on the newborn.

Reaching into his pocket, Evan took out his phone and snapped pictures of AJ's father with Miller. It was such a sweet moment, and he knew Noel would want a picture of it. Then he set his phone on the table next to AJ's bed and sat down next to her.

AJ turned her head away from her father with her daughter and smiled at him. "Hi."

"Hi," he whispered before his hands settled on the nape of her neck. "I love you, and I don't think I can say it enough." Then he pressed his lips to hers, not caring that her parents were right there.

She kissed him back.

Softly.

But full of love.

A kiss that only she could make.

And when she pulled back, only two words wanted to escape him as he stared into those beautiful green eyes of hers.

Marry me.

God, it was all he wanted to say.

But he bit his lip, not wanting her to think his proposal was a spur-of-the-moment decision. That her giving birth was the reason he wanted to marry her. He'd wanted to ask her for years.

But he had to remain silent.

Soon, he would ask her.

And as he stared into those eyes he saw forever in, he knew that when he finally did ask her to marry him, her answer would be yes.

Official statement from the Boston Red Sox:

The Boston Red Sox would like to congratulate Fenway Park operations associate Evan Gilmore and his girlfriend, Alexandra Parker, on the birth of their beautiful daughter, Miller Clara Louise Gilmore.

We would also like to congratulate our captain, Kyle Gilmore, on becoming an uncle to baby Miller.

With warm arms, we welcome baby Miller to the Red Sox family.

Official statement from Kyle Gilmore:

I would like to congratulate my brother, Evan, and his girlfriend, Alexandra, on the birth of the most beautiful little girl I have ever seen. Thank you both for bringing my perfect, beautiful niece whom I already love so greatly into the world.

Miller, thank you for coming into my life.

You are a light I love and will always love you.

Love,

Uncle Kyle

[Image of Kyle Gilmore holding Miller Gilmore]

Official statement from
Evan Gilmore and Alexandra Parker:

On behalf of my girlfriend, Alexandra, and I, we would like to express our gratitude to the Red Sox fans and the people of Massachusetts for congratulating us on the birth of our daughter, Miller. We are truly in awe of how amazing this state has been to us.

We would also like to say that we are not in need of diapers, toys, or any other essential items. Thank you so much for your generosity, but we have more than we need. If you have bought gifts, we please ask that you donate them to children's charities, your local hospitals, and women's shelters. Please find below links of approved charities that we support.

[Link 1]

[Link 2]

[Link 3]

Your donation and generosity will help them all tremendously.

To the people of Massachusetts, our daughter will grow up loving this amazing state just like her parents.

Thank you.

Evan Gilmore & Alexandra Parker.

To: Ester

From: Alex

Subject: My daughter

Dear Ester,

How are you? I am so sorry I am replying to your email so late and that my last one was so brief. Thank you so much for all your tips in the leadup to the birth of my daughter, Miller Clara Louise Gilmore.

She was born September 2nd at 1:02 a.m., and she is the most perfect little girl I have ever seen.

I named her after the most influential academic in my career who inspired me and encouraged my love for science, my high school physics teacher.

Evan is also doing great. He says hi, too.

I've been in hospital for four days due to some minor complications, but I'm fine. Today, we're finally taking Miller home.

I've attached some photos of her for you to see.

Please let me know when you're in Boston next. I'd love to have you come over for dinner.

Take care of yourself.

Love,

Alex.

To: Alex

From: Vincent

Subject: Congratulations, Alexandra.

Alexandra,

Congratulations on the birth of your beautiful daughter.

From everyone here at the Rodahawe Institute, we'd like to wish you the very best.

I know you will make a great mother, Alexandra. You and Evan will make amazing parents.

Please bring Miller with you to Zürich when she's old enough to fly.

I would love to meet her.

Also, I have attached a copy of my upcoming results and have credited you as a contributor to the research. If it had not been for you and your formula, I would have not progressed with my research. It has been submitted to several journals and academics for peer review. I believe your report will impress more than enough to be published in journals.

I wish you the very best.

Your friend,

Vincent Rodahawe.

Landon: Congratulations, Massachusetts. You are going to be an amazing mother. Your daughter is beautiful. Please extend my congratulations to her father. I am so proud of you, Alex.

103

Lr

lawrencium

ALEX

Now

"Okay, Miller," Alex said as she unbuckled her daughter from the car seat. "Are you ready to see your home for the very first time?"

Her daughter moved her arms, eyes wide open. Alex's heart melted at the sight of the mittens on her daughter's hands. Mittens Alex's grandmother had made for Miller. It had been four days since Alex had given birth, and she was finally allowed to take her daughter home. Her high blood pressure during and after childbirth meant Alex was in the hospital for much longer than planned. The doctors had also wanted to make sure her daughter was healthy after having been born two weeks early.

The hospital wasn't so bad. Her family had visited every single day. Alex's best friend, Savannah, had visited her the day of Miller's birth but had to drive back to Vermont hours later. Savannah had cried when she met Miller for the first time and cried even harder when she had to leave to get home for her half day of work. But Savannah would be back in Boston to spend the weekend with her, Evan, and Miller. The only person who had yet to meet her daughter was her cousin Will who was currently away on business. Though he did see

Miller in a video call Evan had with him the day after Miller was born.

Alex picked up her daughter and held her in her arms. "Don't worry, Daddy isn't too far away. You look very pretty in the outfit Grandma Clara picked out for you."

"All right," Evan said once he returned to her side. "The door's unlocked, and the bags are inside. Have you got her?"

"I do," Alex said as she carefully turned. "Do you want to walk her into the house?"

Evan flinched. "You want me to?"

"Well, yeah. You're her father, and that is the home she's going to grow up in. My mother said that when I was a baby, my dad was the first to walk me through my childhood home's doors. She said it was a way of him promising me that in his house, I would always be loved and safe. I want her to feel that." Alex stepped forward and handed him their daughter. "I want you to promise her the world like you did with me a long time ago."

"I will," Evan said as he stepped away from his car, and Alex closed the door. They walked toward the path that led to the steps.

Alex pulled out her phone from her jacket pocket and turned on the video. Pointing it on Evan, she recorded her boyfriend climbing the steps and pausing outside the front door. Alex heard him whisper before he used his free hand to push the door open. Then Evan entered the house, paused again, and then turned around. A smile wide on his face as he realized she was recording this moment.

Alex continued to record as she slowly climbed the steps, feeling the pressure and soreness in the lower half of her body.

She was still recovering from giving birth, and Dr. Livingston said it would take some time before she felt like herself again. Her movements were slow and concentrated, but she finally made it up the steps unassisted. She stepped into the house and closed the door behind her before she stopped in front of her boyfriend. Alex lowered the phone to capture video of their daughter before she held the camera up at Evan.

"Welcome home, Miller," Evan said, warming Alex's heart.

Then Alex turned off the camera and shoved her phone into her pocket. "I can't believe she's finally home," she said in awe as she took in her sleeping daughter.

"Should we put her in her crib?"

"Yeah. I fed her before we left the hospital so she should be okay for a little bit," Alex said as she followed Evan up the stairs, down the hall, and to their daughter's nursery.

The morning light brought different colored rays into the bedroom thanks to the stained-glass windows. They hadn't needed a feature wall. Instead, the gray walls were the perfect background for the atomic numbered stained-glass panels. They would need a new one made with the one hundred and second element to mark the time their daughter was born.

Evan walked over to the crib, Alex standing right next to him, and he gently laid Miller on the mattress. They didn't leave. Instead, they watched her sleep. Watched in awe at the life they created together. The life they'd love forever.

"Are you tired?" Evan asked in a soft voice as he held her hand in his.

She shook her head. "No. I think I want to watch her a little longer."

A low laugh escaped him, and Evan kissed her temple.

547

"We can watch her a little longer. I want to make sure the baby monitor is working properly, too."

Alex released his hand, reached up, and turned on the planets mobile that dangled above her daughter. The planets orbited around the sun as a soothing melody played. Then she turned and wrapped her arms around Evan's neck, loving the softness of his eyes and the love she saw in them.

"We need a new panel to mark her birth," AJ said as she glanced down at their sleeping daughter.

"One hundred and two. Nobelium," Evan noted.

She craned her neck and smiled at him, not at all surprised that he knew that Nobelium was the one hundred and second element. "That's right. Nobelium. It's perfect for her."

Evan reached up and brushed her hair from her face. "It is?"

"It is," she said as she unwrapped her arms around him, then turned and pressed her palms on the crib. "Nobelium was named after Alfred Nobel. He invented dynamite and was the founder of the Nobel Prizes. He was a benefactor to science and, in turn, supported many scientists, their dreams, and the future. And well, she's my Nobel Prize. My purpose." Then she turned and circled her arms back around Evan's neck. "And so are you. I'd do it all again."

He tilted his head at her. "You would?"

She nodded. "For her, I'd do it all again. And for you, I would. Because right now, in this spot, I've never been happier. I'd have waited forever for you, Evan Gilmore. And I mean that," she stated, tears running down her face. "When you kissed me on New Year's, I wanted you forever. And that hasn't changed. It won't ever change. Because each morning I wake up to you, I think back to when I didn't have you, and

I hurt all over again. Those memories hurt, but I'd rather the memory of them than the reality of having lost you. I don't want it ever again."

"Alexandra," he breathed. "I'm never going anywhere without you ever again. There's no one else I belong to than to you and Miller. You and my daughter are the loves of my life, of my entire being. And I can honestly say I have never been anything or worth much if I wasn't yours. You made me mean something when I didn't deserve to. I'm in love with you. I'll continue to keep falling in love you. Every day. Every morning and every night. Each time I wake and each time I fall asleep, it's your name, your touch, and your love my heart wants for all of time."

"My heart wants only you for all of time. Past, present and forever," she said before she pressed her lips to his in a kiss that meant every word she had just said.

Promises her heart had breathed.

That Evan Gilmore was her forever.

And their daughter was their forever and a day.

104

Rf

rutherfordium

ALEX

Three months later

" I can't believe how cute she's gotten," her best friend, Savannah Peters, said over video chat. "God, I hate that I live in Vermont while my niece gets more adorable every day."

Alex laughed as she glanced down to find Miller staring at her plush toy of Albert Einstein. Her uncle Julian had brought it with him when he first met Alex's daughter when she was just a week old. Uncle Julian found immense pride in knowing that the little Einstein was Miller's favorite toy. All of her parents' friends and their children had eventually made it to Massachusetts to meet Miller within the first two weeks of her birth. Alex, Evan, and Miller had spent more time at Alex's parents' house than their own.

But Alex didn't mind.

They were family.

One of the visitors she hadn't expected to see at her childhood home was Hunter Jamison. She appreciated his visit, of course, but she got the feeling that it wasn't just her baby who Hunter wanted to see. But with a house full of people, she couldn't pinpoint who. And in the end, she was too tired to think straight.

"Don't forget that you have to be here in a week for her baptism," Alex reminded.

Savannah sighed and pushed her blond hair from her face. "I won't forget. Alex, you're a woman of science. How do you believe in religion?"

Alex's brows furrowed. She had never had her faith questioned before. "I like to believe there's a higher power. We don't practice it, but we both believe there's more. And Evan is Catholic. But yes, even though I believe in science, I have faith in the universe, too."

"You would insult my mother," Savannah noted. Then her smile turned straight and serious. "I wouldn't miss my goddaughter's baptism. Has everyone RSVP'd?"

Reaching over with her free hand, she picked up the sheet of guests and glanced at the list, then she set it down. "Mika's coming down from Utah, and Milos from California. Mr. Miller RSVP'd a couple of days ago. He's been busy with classes at Harvard. Everyone we invited is coming. A lot of the Red Sox players, too. I took Miller to Fenway to surprise Evan at work last week, and you should have seen them all fall in love with her. Kyle was all like, 'Back away from my niece! None of you are good enough.' It was pretty adorable."

"I bet it was. I'm glad Mika and Milos are coming, too. Hey, isn't this the first time your high school physics teacher is going to meet her?"

"Yeah, I'm so excited to see his face when he meets her."

"AJ! I'm home," Evan yelled out.

"The boyfriend's home," Savannah teased.

Evan entered the kitchen, pressed a kiss to Alex's cheek and then on Miller's head before he said, "I heard that. Hey,

Sav." Evan set his briefcase on the floor and took Miller from Alex, planting kisses on their daughter's chubby cheeks. "All right, Miller. Daddy's home, so it's daddy and daughter time."

"Did you pick up Seb's present I ordered at the toy store?" Alex asked as she glanced up to find Evan smiling at their daughter.

"I did. It's in the car. They wrapped it. I'm going to change for his party. Are your parents upset that we're a little late?"

She shook her head. "No. They knew you had that important meeting with the executives. Do you want me to take her?"

"I'll lay her on the bed as I change. You and Sav finish talking. Does she need anything else to wear for the party?"

"Her headband."

Evan's eyes lit up. "Miller, let's go choose a headband for your uncle's birthday party." Then they disappeared down the hall.

Alex shook her head and returned to her laptop screen to see the large grin on her best friend's face. "What?"

"Y'all have no idea how perfect y'all are with that little girl."

She playfully rolled her eyes. "Evan's madly in love with her."

"And he's madly in love with you, too, Alex. I can see it."

She felt her cheeks blush. A few weeks ago and before her postnatal check, they had been intimate. Alex was nervous, scared she would feel different to him since giving birth. Instead, she felt his love with each kiss and touch. He was gentle with her, and it was perfect. Her fears that Evan wouldn't desire her body had been quickly squashed the minute he whispered how much he loved and wanted her.

"I know. I'd better go get ready for Sebastian's birthday party, too. So I'll see you next week?"

Savannah raised her brow. "Seriously, Alex? I'm not missing her baptism for the world. I'll see y'all next week. Give Miller a kiss for me."

"I will," Alex promised before she waved goodbye, ended the call, and then closed her laptop. She got up from the dining room chair and made her way down the hall and up the stairs. Once she reached her bedroom door, she pushed it open to find her shirtless boyfriend with their daughter on his lap, making the Einstein toy dance for their daughter.

"Evan," she said, faking the annoyance in her voice.

He stopped Einstein's dance and looked up at her. "What?"

"As cute as this is, you're getting distracted." She closed the distance and picked up Miller from Evan's lap. "Go get dressed so we can go."

"Fine." He sighed as he got up from the bed. "But the minute I'm dressed, I'm getting my daughter back from you."

Alex peeked down at Miller who now wore a pink headband with a bow. Her daughter was staring at the toy still in her father's hand. "Fine. Just get dressed."

"I will," he said. He pressed his lips to hers in a chaste kiss and then walked toward the closet.

God, she loved that man entirely.

Alex's little brother's first birthday party was a mix of cake destroying and a lot of food. Her mother had baked Sebastian his own wrecking cake and hired a photographer to take pictures. It was the cutest, messiest thing Alex had ever seen. Her brother had their parents wrapped around his little finger. A lot of the attendees at his party were neighbors, family, friends, and her parents' co-workers and employees. Kyle and Angie had made an appearance, and when they had, Evan seemed nervous. His mood had changed. His happy smile turned into one filled with anxiety. When she had asked him what was wrong, he shook his head and said nothing, but Alex didn't believe him entirely.

"Are you sure you don't need any help, Mum?" Alex asked as her mother picked up several plates.

She shook her head. "It's okay. It's getting late. Your father and I have got this."

"All right. I should get Miller home. She'll be tired." She stepped forward and kissed her mother's cheek. "I'll see you later." Alex then walked out of the kitchen to find her boyfriend holding their baby and speaking to her father. Although it was just a first birthday, Evan had dressed in a nice white dress shirt and a pair of tight dark blue dress pants. He was beautiful with their baby in his arms. She approached them and smiled. "We should get going. Miller will be tired."

Evan nodded, a usual smile on his face. The anxiety from before had left his face, and he was back to his normal self, so her worries faded away. "We have to stop by my office. I have to bring home some work that Schmidt emailed me about. Is that okay?"

"Of course, it's okay." She reached over and took Miller from Evan. "We'll see you later, Dad."

"Bye, my love," her father said before he kissed Alex's

cheek. Then he kissed Miller's head and adjusted her headband. "Bye, my tiny love."

Evan and Alex had said their goodbyes, and she had kissed her baby brother and wished him a happy birthday. She was "Al" to him, and it warmed her heart when he would reach out for her. Once they stepped out of the house after Evan had picked up their baby bag, she grabbed Evan's hand, careful not to wake Miller. "Hey, is everything okay? You weren't yourself during the party."

He nodded. "Yeah, I'm sorry. I saw Schmidt's email, and I didn't want to bring home work with us. I didn't want to disappoint you."

"Hey," she said in a soft voice. "It's okay. Work is important. You're not disappointing me, Evan. I was worried something serious was troubling you."

"I'm sorry. I promise, it's nothing serious."

Relief consumed her chest, lightening the pressure. "Let's go to Fenway so we can go home."

Fenway Park was awfully quiet as she and Evan walked toward security.

"Hey, you two," Reggie, the security guard, said. "How's your night going?"

"Good," Alex said as she tightened her grip on the car seat where Miller was sleeping. "How about you?"

Reggie shrugged. "Same old. Is this little Miller?"

"It is. But she's asleep right now."

The security guard bent his knees to look. Alex and Evan had never brought their daughter out this late, so many of the night staff at Fenway had yet to meet their daughter. "She's a cutie. You better keep an eye on her, Mr. Gilmore."

Evan groaned next to her. "Oh, please, Reggie. Let's keep her a baby for a while longer. I'm going to head over to my office to pick up the files. Do you want to wait in our seats and show Miller the view?"

"I can show her our seats. We haven't taken her there. I'll meet you there when you're ready." She smiled and walked past Reggie and her boyfriend and made her way toward the tunnel. "Let's go see our seats, Miller. Daddy won't be too long and then we can go home."

Alex made it through the tunnel and smiled at the sight of the lit ballpark. When she made her way to the railing, she saw the thin layer of snow covering the grass. Glancing down, she knew the blanket would protect her daughter from the winter temperatures. To protect Miller further, Alex set the car seat down. She took off her coat and wrapped it around Miller, happy that she'd be warm. Then she picked her back up and made her way toward the first row.

Once she reached her home seat, she sat down and set the car seat on her knees. Miller stirred, letting out soft cries. Alex pulled Evan's seat down and set the car seat on it. Then she pulled the handle back and reached inside, picking up her daughter. Ensuring the coat and blanket remained wrapped around Miller, Alex sat back in her seat. She held her daughter close to her chest and slowly swayed her until her cries softened.

Alex smiled. "Your father and I spent a lot of time here

growing up. This is also the very spot your father found out about you."

Then something bright in the corner of her eye caught her attention. Alex stood and turned, taking in the white jumbo screen.

"I think they're testing the jumbo screen, Miller."

When the white screen turned black, she expected the Red Sox logo to take over the screen. Instead, to her surprise, she saw a picture of her and Evan in the away stands wearing Colorado Rockies caps.

Alex laughed at the sight of them. It had been years since they were on the jumbo screen, and her heart warmed in her chest. She was about to sit back down when the screen changed to a different image. It was of her and Evan when they were in middle school. And then another image replaced it with one of her and Evan during their senior year of college.

For the next few minutes, she watched the screen flash different images of her and Evan throughout their lives together.

Images of them together at Duke.

Of them together at Stanford.

Of them together in Boston.

Of them during the summers and all the holidays.

With her parents.

With his brother.

With Savannah.

Even with Milos.

Of their graduations.

Of them in Zürich.

And the last image of them was of the day she had given

THE DISSOLUTION OF UNREQUITED

birth to Miller; Alex holding their daughter as Evan lovingly looked on.

Tears streamed down her cheeks. Alex and Evan had come so far through the years. The last image hadn't disappeared from the jumbo screen. It was proof that throughout all their love and pain, their daughter was the very best of them.

"Alexandra," she heard Evan say behind her.

She spun around and found him on one knee with a ring between his thumb and finger. A smile on his face when he realized she was holding their daughter.

"Evan," she said in a shaky voice.

"Alexandra." He took a deep breath and released it moments later. "I love you. With my whole heart and my entire life. With every inch of my soul. We have to stop this unrequited we've experienced for years. AJ, I love you. I am in love with you. You are the greatest love of my life. I am a better man because of you. You're the mother of my child. You have been my best friend for as long as I can remember and even longer than that. You have been my best friend, my girlfriend, always the love of my life, and now you're my daughter's mother. You gave me Miller. You gave me what I had always been missing. You gave me a family who loves me. A family I love.

"You're my soul mate. I've known it for years. When we were apart and you loved someone else, I wanted you to stay with him because I wanted you to be happy. Because that's what soul mates do. They make sure the person they care about, love the most, is happy. So I waited. I'd have waited forever for you to tell me you love me. And now we can have forever. I've wanted to ask you for years. I've had this ring for over a year. I asked your father over a year ago for his blessing, and he told me to wait three years for you. And I was waiting. Because your dreams will always be important to me. Then, you came back to my life, and we spent the most perfect night together. I felt your love, and I asked you to stay. That night we conceived our daughter, and two months later, in this very spot, you told me you were pregnant."

Oh God, Evan.

She blinked her tears away.

Evan licked his lips. "You are the only thing I got right in my life. Being with you. Loving you. You were the right thing in my life. You are my home. Be with me. Forever. Marry me. Let me be your proud husband when you complete your thesis and complete your Ph.D. Let me be your proud husband as you make your dreams a reality. Let me be the man you wake up to every morning and go to bed with every night. The husband you raise your daughter with. Let me be the husband who gets to call you his wife. I want you to be my wife. Just you. Only ever you for the rest of my life and my last breath. Because I love you. I love you so much." He inhaled a shaky breath and lifted the ring higher. "Make us a family. Have me and keep me with all the love I see in your eyes."

She lowered her left hand for him to grasp.

Evan let out a soft laugh. "Alexandra Louise Parker, will you make me complete? Will you let me make you and our daughter happy for the rest of our lives? Will you marry me?"

"Yes," she breathed out.

"Yes?"

She nodded once again. "Yes, Evan Gilmore. I'll marry you."

560

Smiling, he slid the ring onto her finger. Then he got up off his knee, cupped her cheek, and kissed her deeply, careful not to squash their daughter between them.

Alex sighed into his mouth and he pulled away, ending their kiss. Then he glanced down at their daughter. "Mummy and Daddy are getting married, Miller."

"You waited over a year to ask me to marry you?"

He nodded. "I wanted it to be perfect. I wanted Miller to be with us. And this was the very spot you made me a father when you told me you were pregnant. And when we were in the away end, you were your freest. You kissed me in Fenway Park. We have had our best moments in a crowded venue. Even better ones in an empty ballpark. Just you and me. And now with Miller."

"We're getting married," she breathed as she raised her left hand and saw the green diamond. It was beautiful. Understated. It was perfect.

"Sixteen diamonds ..." Evan said as he collected their daughter into his arms so that Alex could take in her engagement ring. "To represent eight protons and eight neutrons. To represent how much I love you." Then his cold hand cupped her cheek. "I love you so much, Alexandra Parker."

"I love you, too, Evan Gilmore," she whispered back. Then she kissed him softly before she pulled away.

"Let's go home, AJ."

She nodded.

Home.

With my daughter and my fiancé.

My true home.

105

Db

dubnium

EVAN

Two months later

"I'm nervous," his fiancée said.

Evan reached over and covered her hand with his. "Baby, you're going to get in."

Alexandra Parker attempted a smile he saw right through.

She was nervous.

He knew she was afraid of another setback.

Of another rejection.

"Miller, Mummy's going to get into her Ph.D., isn't she?"

Their daughter was sitting on his lap as she held her Einstein toy she was still in love with. She opened her mouth and closed it. Then she smiled when AJ brushed her hair back. Her phone beeped, signaling that confirmation letters would be posted on the portal.

"So which one first? MIT, Harvard, University of Massachusetts, Northeastern University, or Boston University?"

"MIT," Evan said, knowing that was her dream school.

She nodded, then she clicked on her screen. Her breath hitched. "I got into MIT."

"Mummy got into MIT!" Evan said with glee as he kissed Miller's cheek, and she giggled. MIT had been AJ's dream school for years. Knowing that she had been accepted for a second time was proof that she deserved a place at the very best. His fiancée smiled. "Okay, next is Harvard."

Unlike MIT, her Harvard admission made her incredibly nervous as she bit her lip. And he knew that Mr. Miller, the very man she had named their daughter after, was a professor at Harvard.

AJ inhaled a deep breath and then clicked on the screen. "Oh, my God!" she squealed. "I got into Harvard!" She faced Evan, her eyes gleamed with unshed tears. When she was a high school senior, her reaction to being admitted by Harvard didn't come close to this time. This time, AJ was relieved and elated. "I got into Harvard."

He leaned forward and kissed her. "I am so proud of you." He pulled back. "Check the other statuses."

She nodded. A few minutes later, she shook her head in disbelief. "I got into all of them."

"I knew you would," Evan said, incredibly proud of his fiancée. "You hear that, Miller? Mummy's going back to college!"

Evan lifted his daughter, and she giggled, kicking her legs until AJ took her in her arms from him. "I'm going to college, Miller. I'm going to make you so proud of me."

"She's already proud of you," he assured as he got up from the chair and stood by her side. Then he wrapped his arms around her. "I'm really proud of you."

AJ rested her head against his. "Thank you for being there. For supporting my dreams."

"Always, AJ. Always," he whispered.

She would be starting her Ph.D. over a year later than she had expected, but she had done it. Night after night of essay writing and filling out applications had paid off.

AJ was finally going to live her dream.

And Evan and their daughter would be there, supporting her every step of the way.

EPILOGUE I
ALEX

Seven months later

"Evan!" Alex shouted as she threaded her arms through her blazer. Once it was on, she picked up her earrings from her dresser and fastened them on. She then spun around, taking in their bedroom to make sure she had everything.

It was her first day of her Ph.D.

She was so nervous but so excited. Last week, they had celebrated their daughter's first birthday. Alex couldn't believe that her daughter was already a year old. In the past year, as she watched her daughter grow, she lived an honored life knowing that she was Miller's mother.

"There's Mummy," Evan Gilmore said as he entered their bedroom with their daughter in his arms. "Miller, doesn't Mummy look beautiful?"

Miller smiled and then let out a giggle. She wasn't much of a talker, but she understood some words and could say "mama" and "dada."

"Oh, come here, my love," Alex said as she walked up to Evan. She took in Miller's sparkling green eyes. They were like hers. And she was happy that her daughter had her eyes. But Miller had Evan's smile and nose.

Their daughter was so beautiful.

And the past year of their lives had been wonderful watching her grow.

"You're going to spend all day with Daddy until Mummy finishes at school, okay?"

Their daughter nodded. She always did when she was asked a question that ended with okay. On their first trip to New York together, they had taken their daughter—eight months at the time—to the Smithsonian. Miller's favorite exhibit had been the solar system exhibition because of all the colors and displays. After their visit, Alex couldn't wait to take her daughter back when she was a little older. Just as her father had done with her.

"And here," Evan said, picking up her briefcase and stepping toward her. "Let's get you to school. You don't want to miss your first day."

Alex laughed. "No, I don't." She kissed Miller's cheek. "Let's finish getting ready, Miller."

An hour later, Alex got out of Evan's car and stepped on the sidewalk outside of the entrance. She spun around to find him walking around the car to their back seat. He opened the door and unbuckled Miller from her car seat.

"Dada," Miller mumbled as she held her little Einstein tightly in her hands. Evan held her to the side of his body as he closed the door.

"Have you got everything?" Evan asked.

Alex glanced down and took in the leather briefcase her parents had gotten her. It had her initials monogrammed in gold stitching.

A.G.

Alexandra Gilmore.

They had married three months ago in her parents' backyard with all their family and friends watching.

Her father had walked her down the aisle while her mother walked Alex and Evan's daughter—the flower girl. Alex's little brother, Sebastian, had been the ring bearer.

It was perfect.

The most perfect wedding she could have ever imagined.

They had spent their honeymoon with their daughter in Honolulu, Hawaii. Her parents had offered to take care of Miller, but Alex and Evan had wanted her with them. They had rented a house by the water and had the most magnificent two weeks in paradise. They loved their honeymoon so much, they had plans to return during her breaks.

"I have everything," Alex said as she stepped toward him and set her palm on his cheek. "Call me if you need anything, okay?"

Her husband nodded and dipped his chin to kiss her. When he pulled back, he said, "We'll be here to pick you up. Have an amazing first day."

"I will," she promised and then she bent her knees and brushed their daughter's hair away from her beautiful face. "You have a great day with Daddy, okay, Miller?"

Her daughter pressed her cheek into Evan's chest and nodded with a smile.

"Okay, Miller. Say bye-bye to Mummy. Wish her luck on her first day at Harvard."

"Bye-bye," Miller said, waving her toy at Alex.

Her heart melted.

God, she had no idea how she could truly be away from her daughter for a whole day.

"We'll be fine," Evan assured, answering her internal question. "And you will be, too. Say hello to Professor Miller for us."

Alex smiled. "I will."

Then she stood straight. "Oh!" she said, remembering what they were forgetting. She dug her hand into her pocket and pulled out her phone. Then she stood next to Evan and held her phone in front of them and snapped a picture of her family.

Of her husband and daughter.

Then Evan grabbed her briefcase and handed their daughter to her. "Okay, we need a picture of you and Miller on your first day."

"Smile for the photo, my love." Alex pointed at the phone he had taken out of his pants pocket.

Their daughter stared at Evan as Alex smiled for the photo. Then he lowered the phone and took Miller from her. Alex kissed her husband's cheek. "I love you, Evan." And she glanced back down at her daughter. "Mummy loves you so much, Miller. Be a good girl."

"You are going to be amazing. Harvard is so lucky to have you," her husband said.

"I love you so much. I'll call you later."

Alex sat in awe as she watched her former high school teacher, and now her Ph.D. advisor and Harvard physics professor, teach the first freshman classical mechanics class.

He made it so interesting.

Professor Henry Miller was a natural when it came to teaching, and his passion for science showed in his lectures.

"Now I'd like to introduce to you all your TA for the semester, Alexandra Gilmore."

Alex got up from her seat and walked toward the podium. She smiled at her professor and then turned around, facing the large lecture theatre filled with students and their wide eyes on her.

"Just introduce yourself and tell them some things about you," Professor Miller encouraged.

Alex's heart raced in her chest as she inhaled a deep breath to calm her nerves. She released it seconds later. "Hello, everyone. My name is Alexandra Gilmore, and I am in my first year of my Ph.D. here at Harvard. I graduated from Duke University with my bachelor and spent over a year and a half as a research assistant to Dr. Rodahawe at the Rodahawe Institute in Zürich, Switzerland before I became a mum. I decided that out of all the colleges I got accepted into, Harvard was where I wanted to do my postgrad. I was born and raised in Massachusetts. If you're a local, you might know of me through my husband and his brother, who is the captain of the Boston Red Sox."

She heard, "Aw," and some gasps.

"You're being modest," Professor Miller said next to her.

Alex laughed. "I was also published in the *Science* journal and several other peer-reviewed journals alongside my mentor, Dr. Rodahawe. My velocity formula has been nominated for and won several awards and has been peer reviewed by many of the world's leading physicists. I know it seems like I've achieved a lot, and I might not look approachable, but please don't hesitate to ask me anything. I tried to keep a lot of my achievements on the down low because I wanted to seem approachable. Trust me, I'm just like all of you. I was a freshman once. And I can assure you all, you have the most amazing professor this semester. Had it not been for Professor Miller, I wouldn't have discovered Dr. Rodahawe's work and have become a published researcher."

She smiled at Professor Miller with admiration. Although Dr. Rodahawe was her mentor, Professor Miller had guided her many times throughout the years. He was always her voice of reason. He gave her relativity when her heart suffered in agony.

"Any questions before we move onto the syllabus?"

To her surprise, dozens of hands were raised.

She pointed at the hand raised closest to her. It was a male student with glasses. "Yes?"

"Hello, Alexandra. Is it true that you're rumored to be nominated for the Nobel Prize alongside Dr. Rodahawe for your research on the impact of velocity? If so, that is amazing."

Alex laughed. "Please, just call me Alex. My research with Dr. Rodahawe has been reviewed and used by many. As for the Nobel Prize, I would not have a clue. I'm just lucky to have worked with him. Great question, thank you." Then she turned her attention back to the lecture hall. "Any other questions?"

This time hands lowered because most were interested in the rumors of her Nobel Prize nomination that she had yet to hear about. Dr. Rodahawe did say he believed their research could be nominated.

She pointed at another student who asked, "Why did you pick Harvard?"

"Harvard had Professor Miller."

More hands lowered. She pointed at another student. "What is your greatest achievement, Alex?"

Alex smiled, knowing her answer. "My family. My husband and daughter are definitely my greatest achievement."

One last hand remained. "Red Sox or Yankees?"

Alex chuckled. "Oh, Red Sox, of course."

When there were no more hands, Alex turned her attention back to Professor Miller. "Now that I've introduced myself, let's get started. And before I pass you back to Professor Miller, I just wanted to welcome you all to Harvard University and to classical mechanics. You're all taking your very first steps toward your degree and careers. And let me also just say, I'm so happy to be part of that journey with you."

An applause erupted in the lecture theatre as she stepped back from the podium.

Professor Miller set his hand on her back and smiled at her. "You were great. You are going to make a great TA, Alex."

And as Alex returned to her seat and sat down, she took in the sparkle of her engagement ring and her wedding ring.

Harvard.

Her husband.

Her daughter.

Their home in Cambridge.

No matter if she was nominated for a Nobel Prize, Alexandra Gilmore was where she was meant to be.

Her life was perfect, and she couldn't wait until she saw her husband and daughter to tell them about her day and listen to theirs.

For so much of her life, Alex had known unrequited.

Then her love for Evan Gilmore had become reciprocated.

Many years later, they had reached the dissolution of unrequited and found nirvana in a life spent together with their daughter.

A daughter who Alex was doing her Ph.D. at Harvard for.

To make her daughter proud and to prove to her that dreams were always better shared with the ones you loved most and when you trusted in yourself.

When she felt her phone vibrate in her pocket, she pulled it out and unlocked it. She opened her messages to find one from her husband.

Evan: We're so proud of you and love you, AJ.

Attached to the message was a picture.

A picture of her husband and her daughter.

Her entire heart and life.

Unrequited had evolved.

It was now null in her life.

All because of Evan Gilmore.

The man who gave her their beautiful daughter.

And she couldn't wait to see him and tell him just how much she loved him.

EPILOGUE II
EVAN

"It's just you and me today, Miller," Evan Gilmore said as he glanced into the rearview mirror to see his daughter playing with her favorite toy.

His heart, as usual, filled with so much warmth when he saw her beautiful smile. Pair it with her stunning green eyes, and his daughter had him wrapped around her small finger. Evan had never known love like the one he had for his daughter. Some nights, he wondered how his parents could have ever left him the way they had. He couldn't stomach the thought of ever upsetting his little girl. But Evan was sure his parents never had a love like the one he had with his wife. He was sure they had never felt or experienced the unconditional love Noel and Clara Parker had given him and Kyle as children.

Evan knew, without a shadow of doubt, that he would never stop loving his daughter.

Never stop wanting the best for her.

Never give up on her or her dreams.

His daughter was his world.

And as she lifted her chin and smiled at him, he knew all the choices, actions, and mistakes he had made were in order to have her.

The MLB was never his future.

His future was his wife and daughter.

After he dropped his wife at college, Evan drove back to their home in Cambridge and finished getting ready for work. His boss knew he would be coming in later than usual. It was the first day of AJ's Ph.D., and the first day of his new work schedule. Evan knew he was fortunate to work at Fenway Park. His bosses were more than accommodating to make his, his wife's, and his daughter's lives easier.

His new work schedule had him working most days from home and the occasional day in his office at Fenway Park. It wasn't too hard to convince his boss for flexibility so that he could take care of his daughter while his wife taught and commenced her Ph.D. at Harvard University. Evan was sure his brother had played a big part in it.

Miller was, after all, the captain of the Red Sox's niece.

What made her happy made Kyle happy and, therefore, made the Red Sox happy.

Evan's daughter was always welcomed at Fenway Park.

"Dada," Miller said.

The warmth in his chest spread as he grinned. He wasn't wrong when he had admitted to AJ that for so long, he had always assumed her children would call him uncle. That had been before. Before he fell in love with her. Before he realized he wanted a family with her.

It was Alexandra Gilmore he wanted to raise their daughter with.

His best friend.

His wife.

His daughter's mother.

THE DISSOLUTION OF UNREQUITED

"Mummy's at Harvard today, so we're going to work together, okay?"

His daughter nodded her head. Her beautiful green eyes shimmered up at him. She took after her mother. He saw it every day he looked into her gleaming eyes. And God, was he helpless when he saw them. Evan saw a love he had never known and had always wanted staring back at him as he looked at his daughter.

He loved her.

Completely.

Unconditionally.

Evan loved her the moment he knew she existed.

He had never felt so right than when he held her in his arms for the very first time.

Unbuckling his seat belt, Evan removed his keys from the ignition and shoved them into his suit jacket pocket. He got out of his car and headed to the back passenger side. Opening the car door, he reached forward and unclipped his daughter from the car seat.

"Hold Einstein tightly, okay?" Then Evan carefully removed her from her car seat and held her to him. "Daddy's got you. Are you ready to visit Uncle Kyle?"

She nodded excitedly. "Ky. Ky!"

His brother's nickname was only one of the few words she could say. Her first word had been dada, much to his wife's dismay, wanting mama to be her first word. But her envy dissipated shortly after she kissed him and stated how mesmerized she was that he was their daughter's first word.

Evan laughed as he closed the car door and headed to the trunk of his BMW SUV. He'd traded in his old sedan for the

SUV just before his daughter's birth. Carefully juggling Miller in his arm, he opened the trunk and pulled out her diaper bag and set the strap on his shoulder. Then he grabbed his briefcase and shut the trunk, deciding to remove her stroller later. Yesterday, he had brought over her portable crib and set it up in his office. Now that his wife began her Ph.D., Evan was taking care of their daughter. Daycare was an option, but he couldn't be away from Miller just yet. He knew it was completely selfish, but his daughter owned his heart, and he wanted every minute with her.

"You want to walk for a little bit?" Evan asked as he glanced at her.

Miller nodded, and Evan laughed at her enthusiasm. Bending his knees, he carefully set his daughter down and grasped her small hand. It would take them longer to get to his office, but he didn't care. He loved watching her little legs take each step as she tried to keep herself balanced. But his daughter would never have to worry about falling because, as her father, he would always be there to catch her.

"Evan!" he heard behind him.

He glanced over his shoulder to find his brother walking toward him. "Miller, look who it is," he said as he watched his daughter release his hand and turn.

Her lips spread into a grin as her green eyes shimmered. "Ky!"

"Hey, sweet girl," Kyle said as he ran to them and swept Miller into his arms. Evan's daughter giggled before she pressed her face into Kyle's neck. "How are you?"

Miller pulled back, her smile radiating at her uncle who held her tight. "Ky."

His brother's eyes softened. "My sweet girl, did you take Mommy to school today?"

"Yes," she said in a small voice as she held her toy to her uncle.

Kyle took the toy from her and pressed Einstein's nose to Miller's. Then he glanced over at Evan. "Was your wife excited?"

My wife.

God, did his heart stretch with warmth at the statement. AJ had been his wife for three months, but he still couldn't believe it. Most mornings, he woke up in disbelief and with so much gratitude that she was asleep next to him with his ring on her finger.

As they walked toward the security entrance, he smiled. "Words can't even begin to describe how excited AJ was about her first day at Harvard. You couldn't wipe that smile from her face."

"I can just imagine," Kyle said as they stopped in front of Caesar at security. "Hey, Caes."

The security guard smiled. "Hey, Mr. Gilmores." Then he grinned at Evan's daughter. "Hello, Miss Miller. Are you joining your dad and uncle at work today?"

Miller nodded. "Yes."

Evan laughed at her smiling at her favorite security guard. He watched Caesar raise his palm and hold it out to Miller. Kyle leaned forward and helped Miller high-five the security guard as Evan reached into his pocket. He stepped closer to his daughter and set the card in her small hand. "Miller, show Caesar your ID."

She held out the ID card to Caesar who took it from her.

The security guard's face softened as he held the card up to Miller's face. "Your pass checks out, Miss Miller. You're free to explore Fenway Park." Then he handed her back the card. "She's a real cutie, Mr. Gilmore."

"Dada," Miller said, swinging her arm back and giving Evan the card.

He took his daughter's Fenway Park pass from her and returned it to his pocket. "She gets it all from her mother."

The security guard chuckled. "No doubt. You've got yourself a beautiful family, sir."

Pride swelled in his chest. He did have a beautiful family. One he loved and was so thankful for. "Thanks, Caesar. We'll see you a bit later." Then he turned and smiled down at his daughter in his brother's arms. "You want to go watch Uncle Kyle do some press?"

She tilted her head back and nodded at her uncle.

Evan laughed as Kyle set her down on her feet, and she grasped her uncle's hand. "Come on, then." He turned and began to make his way inside Fenway and toward the tunnel.

"Dada!" his daughter called out. He spun around to find her blinking at him. She held out her hand she held her toy with.

"Sorry, my love," he apologized as he went to her and kneeled in front of her. "Do you want to hold Daddy's hand, too?"

She nodded her head as she dropped her toy in Evan's waiting hand. "Yes, Dada."

Evan leaned forward and kissed her forehead. "Okay, Daddy's got you." He stood and grasped her hand. Then he glanced over at his brother staring lovingly at Evan's daughter. That love and pride in Kyle's eyes was priceless. Evan knew that his daughter would always have an uncle to love her and protect her.

They might not have always loved each other.

They might not have always agreed upon everything.

For the longest time in Evan's life, he never felt his brother's love.

It took AJ walking away and leaving him for them to find their way.

She had not only given Evan a life, love, and his daughter, but she had also given him his brother.

For that, he couldn't thank her enough.

As Kyle lifted his chin, Evan smiled, and said, "Uncle Kyle's always got you, too, Miller."

And Evan watched Kyle Gilmore, his daughter's devoted uncle, let his tears fall.

"Let's try this one," Evan suggested as he removed the jacket from the hanger on the rack. Then he bent his knees as his daughter held up her arms. He put the jacket on her and buttoned it up as Miller watched his hands intently. "What do you think? Do you like it, Miller?"

She lifted her chin and smiled before she nodded her head.

"I like it, too," he agreed, taking in the white sleeves and the red vest of the Harvard varsity jacket he put on her. "Do you think Mummy will like it?"

Miller picked up her toy from the seat next to them and grasped his hand. "Yes, Dada."

Evan stood, squeezed Miller's hand gently, and walked her toward the front of the Harvard shop on campus. When they made it to the accessories, he stopped, noticing his daughter eyeing the plush toys on the shelf. Evan scooped her up and held her to his side so she could better see the toys.

"Do you think Einstein needs a best friend?" he asked as he grabbed a Harvard dog toy from the shelf and held it to his daughter. "Everyone needs a best friend."

Your mother has me.

I have your mother.

His daughter swung her bright green eyes to focus on him as she tilted her head.

Evan laughed at the confusion on her sweet face. Then he kissed her head and looked down at her. "Do you have a best friend?"

She looked down at her toy and then at Evan. Her lips spread even wider as she said, "Dada."

Tears crept up, almost hitting him as hard as his daughter's declaration. Miller wrapped her arms around his neck, and Evan blinked his tears away. "Daddy will always be your best friend, my love," he promised. "Do you want the doggie or the bear?"

Miller turned away from his neck and glanced down at the dog in his hand and then the shelf. Then she pointed at the dog.

"Okay, doggie for Einstein, it is. Let's go pay for your jacket and doggie, and we'll head to the car. Mummy should be finished soon."

With his daughter on his side, and her new toy in his hand, he walked to the counter to a young Harvard student at the register. She smiled at Evan as he came to a stop. "Is it okay if I set her down on the counter? I didn't take the tag off the jacket and we'd like to buy it please."

The auburn hair student shook her head. "I don't mind at all."

Evan carefully set his daughter on the counter and handed her the dog plush. He grinned at the smile on her face as she made the toys kiss. He pulled out his phone, stepped back and held it up. "Miller, smile, my love. Aunty Sav and Mummy will want a picture of you in your new jacket."

His daughter smiled at him, and Evan snapped the picture. He returned his phone to his pants pocket and stepped closer to his daughter. He reached behind her, pulled the tag off the jacket and gave it to the girl behind the counter. Then Evan scooped up Miller, holding her to him. His daughter followed his lead and held her new toy to the girl who scanned the tag.

"Is she your sister?" the girl asked.

"No, she's my daughter," he replied proudly.

"Oh, she's adorable."

Evan laughed. His daughter had no idea how many compliments she had received today. Everywhere they went at Fenway, she had those who worked at the park, even some of the press who were packing up after the interviews, falling in love with her. Evan didn't worry about the press. There was a strict no-media policy when it came to his daughter. A choice the Red Sox and fans respected.

"Thank you," Evan said as he pulled his wallet from his pocket and retrieved his credit card.

"Are you an alum?" she asked as he handed her his card.

Evan shook his head. "No, my wife is a TA here at Harvard."

He watched the smile on her face fade a fraction. "Oh. Well, that's so nice that you're supporting her school." Then she handed him back his card and his receipt after she rang up his purchases. As Evan returned the receipt, his card, and his wallet to his pocket, she said, "Have a great day."

"Thank you. And you, too. Say bye, Miller."

His daughter waved her toy at the cashier before he walked out of the shop. Then he set his daughter down as she held Einstein up for him. Evan took her toy as she held his hand. Feeling his phone ring in his pocket, Evan shoved the toy between his arm as he pulled out his phone to find his wife had texted him. He unlocked it and read her message.

AJ: Hey. I've just finished my last class for the day. Professor Miller is just giving me some feedback and I'll be right out.

Evan: All good, baby. We'll see you soon.

Returning his phone to his pocket, he removed his daughter's toy from under his arm and smiled at her staring at the dog plush that had a Harvard shirt on. "Ready to go back to the car, Miller? Mummy will be there soon."

"Yes," she said, the excitement to see her mother rang in her voice. It had been some time since Miller had spent a whole day away from AJ. He knew his daughter missed her mother. She had even cried for a little bit after her nap looking for her in his office. It would take Miller some time before she was used to AJ being at school.

As they walked back toward the car, he heard how cute his daughter was from the students and faculty. Evan would laugh as strangers high-fived his daughter. Miller loved it but hated when she would drop her toy. In the end, she got too tired to walk, and he carried her toward the car. When they had almost made it, he noticed his wife walking with the man they named their daughter after.

Evan stopped and smiled, watching AJ so engrossed in her conversation with her professor and Ph.D. advisor. "Hey, Miller, look." He pointed at his wife. "There's Mummy. Do you want to go see her?"

His daughter's green eyes widened as she turned her head, noticing her mother. Evan set her down as she tightened her grip on her plush Harvard dog. Then he watched his daughter run toward her mother, yelling, "Mama!"

AJ immediately stopped and turned, a smile stretched proudly and lovingly across her face as she bent down and set her briefcase on the ground. Then she held out her arms for Miller to run into them before they wrapped around their daughter in a matter of seconds. AJ closed her eyes as she embraced Miller and whispered in her ear.

Evan stood by and took in this moment.

His wife and his daughter.

Their love was the purest thing he had ever witnessed and experienced.

Their love was what he wanted for the rest of his life.

As AJ lifted their daughter, Evan made his way toward them. He smiled at her professor and held out his hand. "Hello, Professor Miller."

"Hello, Evan," the professor said as they shook hands. "Hello, Miller. How are you?"

His daughter tilted her head. Though she was named after Henry Miller, she was still getting to know him. All Miller did was smile.

Professor Miller grinned. "Your mommy had a good first

587

day. You must be very proud of her."

Miller nodded. "Yes."

"Well, Alex, I better get back. Thank you for today. You were excellent," Professor Miller said before he smiled at AJ and Evan's daughter. "Have a good day, Miller. I'll see you next time."

"Say bye-bye, Miller," AJ said.

Miller waved her dog. "Bye. Bye."

The professor waved before he returned to the building behind them. Evan stepped closer and kissed his wife. "How was your day?" he asked as he pulled back.

AJ sighed. "Long but amazing," she replied. She looked down at their daughter. "And how was your day, my love?"

Their daughter didn't reply as she stared at the toy in her hand.

His wife took in the jacket, and her brow arched. "Evan, why is our daughter in a Harvard varsity jacket?"

Evan laughed. "She looks cute, right?"

"We're not pushing Ivy League on her, are we?"

He shook his head. "No. I thought your daughter should support her mother's school. She's very proud of you."

"Good. Because, you, Miller, are going to whatever college makes you happy. That's what I want for you, my love. I want you to be so happy. I want you to have every dream. I want you to succeed. I want you to find love and feel love. But most importantly, I want you to be you. I want you to be you, every single day of your life. Just be you, Miller Gilmore."

Just be you, Miller Gilmore.

His chest burned with the sincerity in his wife's voice.

He wanted the very same for their daughter.

AJ brushed Miller's curly brown hair back before she peppered kisses all over their daughter's face. Miller laughed with every kiss. "I missed you so much, my love," AJ whispered as Evan picked up her briefcase from the ground. "Did you have a good day with Daddy?"

Miller nodded. "Yes, Mama."

"Are you ready to go home?" Evan asked as he slipped his daughter's other toy in his wife's briefcase.

"I am." AJ set Miller down and grasped her hand.

"Dada," Miller said, getting his attention.

Evan bent down so that he was eye level with Miller. "Yes, my love?"

Miller stared into his eyes as she said, "Eight."

His heart stopped.

"Eight?" he breathed.

His daughter smiled.

Evan lifted his chin to find tears in his wife's eyes as she whispered, "Eight."

He gazed back at his daughter as he palmed her cheek. "Eight protons. Eight neutrons, Miller."

The four words he whispered to his daughter every night.

The four words his wife woke up and fell asleep to.

The four words his girls would always know to be theirs.

"Eight, Dada."

Evan brushed his tears away as he wrapped his arms around her and stood with his precious daughter in his arms. AJ stepped closer, setting her hand on Miller's shoulder.

"And what does eight protons and eight neutrons mean?" AJ asked, no doubt for their daughter to hear the true meaning of the words she heard before sleep found her.

As Evan stared into Miller's green eyes, he felt it all.

The peace.

The contentment.

The happiness.

And all the love she gave him.

"It's what I feel for you and your mother, Miller."

Then he peeked over to find the sweet smile on his wife's face. "And what is it you feel for us?"

For years, those four words were AJ's.

For years, she had his entire heart.

And for the past year, their daughter had joined his wife's place in his heart and life.

For the past year, Evan Gilmore had it all.

He had his beautiful wife and best friend.

And most importantly, he had his daughter.

The daughter who made him a better man and husband.

The daughter he would forever love and strive to be a better father for each day.

The daughter he was honored to raise with Alexandra Gilmore.

Eight protons.

Eight neutrons.

Eight.

Eight letters that spelled I love you.

Eight.

The atomic number for oxygen.

Oxygen that represented his wife and daughter.

They were the oxygen his life needed to thrive.

Alexandra and Miller Gilmore were his eight protons and eight neutrons.

So with a loving and true smile, and with pride and contentment coursing through his veins, Evan Gilmore simply said,

"Love."

THE END OF
Unrequited

THE SONGS OF UNREQUITED PLAYLIST

The Theory of Unrequited:

Say Love (3:38)

-JoJo

The Solution to Unrequited:

Hearts (3:33)

-Jessie Ware

The Results of Unrequited:

No Peace (4:43)

-Sam Smith Ft. Yebba

The Dissolution of Unrequited:

When We Say It's Forever (3.43)

-The McClymonts Ft. Ronan Keating

Listen to *The Songs of Unrequited,* AJ & Evan's entire playlist, on Spotify:
https://open.spotify.com/
playlist/35cNepwCwwrTSSPJJi57SC

"Ask yourself, how many days does it take to fall in love?"

Start at the very beginning and find out with

Noel & Clara

in

Thirty-Eight
DAYS

Read on for an excerpt.

Thirty-Eight DAYS

Book one in The *Thirty-Eight Series*.

Ask yourself, how many days does it take to fall in love?

Nolan Parker and Clara Lawrence never saw eye to eye. In fact, if you asked Clara she would tell you that Nolan hated every thing about her. They never shared any form of connection besides Alex Lawrence.

She was Alex's bratty sister and he was Alex's best friend, they never stood a chance.

Five years have passed and almost 12,000 miles have kept them separated, both living completely different lives. Unchanged perceptions and expectations should have kept them apart but when Nolan returns, the foundations of their 'relationship' is sure to change.

CHAPTER ONE
Noel

"Hey, Nolan. Did I wake you?" Alex Lawrence's hazy voice asked over the phone. Noel rubbed his eyes to see that it was ten past seven in the morning and groaned.

"Nah, what's up?" Noel replied as he climbed out of bed and opened the window to the smell of Boston in the morning. As he looked out at the grey and cloudy view of the city, he could hear his best friend sounding frustrated over the phone. Noel shook his head in an effort to properly wake up before making his way out of his bedroom and into the living room.

Noel and Alex had been best friends since they were babies. They both had the same dreams and went after their own pursuit of happiness. They worked hard at school and grew up in the suburbs of Melbourne, Australia. When Noel and Alex were accepted to Stanford University, they were the talk of the town as two Melbourne boys headed off to the States for college. Noel owed everything to Alex. If it weren't for him, then Noel would never have survived Stanford or received the promotion in Boston, which he felt Alex had deserved instead of him.

But Noel knew that Alex wouldn't call him at such an hour if it weren't important. Even at seven in the morning, Noel knew the importance of Alex's early call from the New York office. They both worked for G&MC, one of the leading accounting firms in the country. Although New York was lucrative, Noel held one of Boston's head office positions, practically Alex's boss.

"Mate, you know the Owens account?" Alex asked as the clatter of papers and erratic typing pitched higher.

"Yeah."

"IRS is looking into it, claiming fraud. G&MC's in trouble, Noel. I could be fired. I handled the account, remember?"

"Shit! That could be our asses on the line. What the hell happened?" Noel asked, utterly shocked at the circumstances his best friend was in. Having once worked in the New York office, by association, Noel would also be looked at.

"Fraud's gone back long before we picked up the account. But it doesn't look good, even for us. This account could ruin the company's reputation."

"Anything I can do?"

"Nah, I don't want to put this kind of pressure on you. You have your own problems in Boston. But listen, I do have one favour to ask," Alex asked as Noel moved towards the kitchen counter.

"Anything, Alex." For all the times Alex had come through for Noel, this was the time to be the best friend.

"Go back to Melbourne without me. Get your ass home. I know we were meant to meet up in L.A. together, but I'm going to have to stay here in New York till this gets sorted. But could you please take care of Clara? I booked flights that land back home a day earlier than she expected just to surprise her. She's going to be disappointed that I'm not there for her birthday." He could hear the desperation and pleading in Alex's voice.

"You want me to babysit your sister?" Noel blurted out.

He hadn't seen her since he and Alex had left for Stanford, almost five years back. She had been fourteen when he left Australia. And after he was gone, he never really thought much of her.

"Please, Noel, you know our folks are cruising all around the world, and she needs company right now."

"Doesn't she have a boyfriend or something?" Noel asked, hoping he could offload Clara to anyone else.

"Don't get me started on that little shit. Wait till I get my hands on that son of a bitch!" Alex was never angry, not even when Tori, his ex-girlfriend, had told him it was over. She was tired of Alex's dedication to his job rather than to her.

"What's Little Shit done for you to be angry?" Noel laughed as he settled into the barstool next to the counter. He watched as rain started to pour down on the streets below. Tomorrow he'd be on a plane back home to Melbourne.

"He cheated on Clara, that's what he did! He's been sleeping around with another girl for months. If this Owens audit hadn't come up, I'd be on that plane back to Melbourne and straight to his door to rip his balls right off!" Alex fumed.

"Shit. Sorry to hear that. Poor Clara, is she okay?" Noel hadn't even recognised the concern in his voice for her.

"She's okay. That's why I don't want to leave her alone. With her birthday coming up, she's going to be dragged through hell once she finds out I won't be there. So, what do you say? Stop by and look after Clara?"

Noel heard Alex's name being called and knew this was important to him. He sighed, knowing he would do this for his best friend.

"Fine. I'll stay at Clara's until you get back. Just make

sure this Owens account gets sorted quickly." Noel sighed heavily.

"Thanks, man. I owe you big time! I swear it'll be a week tops, only seven days with my sister," Alex replied as the sounds in the background started to pick up. "Gotta run. The meeting with Mercer is about to start. Thanks again for helping out Clara."

"No worries," Noel replied before he hung up his phone. He wasn't helping the heartbroken Clara. In reality, he was helping his best friend.

Thirty-Eight DAYS

Book one in The *Thirty-Eight Series*.

NOW AVAILABLE FOR FREE!
Grab your copy on:
Amazon | iBooks | Kobo | Barnes and Noble
Find it on Goodreads

ACKNOWLEDGMENTS

This Love (4:10)
-Taylor Swift

I have never loved a couple more than I have loved AJ and Evan. I've said goodbye to many of my characters, but saying goodbye to these two best friends who fell in love was the hardest and best goodbye. *The Dissolution of Unrequited* was the only book I have ever rewritten, torn apart, added, deleted, restructured, and poured my entire heart and soul into. I've cried, laughed, hurt, and loved over this book and their characters. It took me three long months of rewriting and editing to get to the end.

The end ...

I can't believe AJ and Evan made it to the end. I wrote the ending I felt was true to them, and for them. I always knew AJ would leave Massachusetts for Zürich. I always knew she'd find her way back to her soul mate. I wanted her to reach her dreams, and her dream was always her Ph.D., but she was able to share that dream with her husband and her daughter at Harvard.

Sometimes, dreams change, and AJ's definitely changed ... for the better.

And honestly, I feel like I'm a better author for writing this series. AJ and Evan taught me so much. They taught lessons and things I'll hold onto. I hope they did for you, too. No matter who they loved, they always loved each other more.

They were always best friends. And their story ended with them always being each other's best friend and soul mate.

But don't worry, it's not entirely goodbye forever for AJ and Evan. They'll always be here for you.

Always my first to thank, my family. Thank you for all your love and support through the five years I've been a published author. When I give up, you're all there to tell me to pick myself up. Thank you for all your belief. I love you all. And of course, to the best writing partners and dogs in the world, my little Curly and Chloe.

I couldn't have published and written this series without my own best friend, Jaycee Ford. Thank you for making sure I don't give up on myself. You are the best roommate and friend a girl could ever ask for.

To my incredible beta readers, Jennifer, Danielle, and Leeann! You input and love for this series means the world. Thank you for making their story even better.

Thank you to my incredible publicist, Veronica Adams. Veronica, you always work so hard to make sure as many people fall in love with my books as possible. I will always love you and your dedication.

My incredible editor, Jenny Sims! You work so hard. And I did not make it easy with every cliffhanger I sent your way. I especially didn't make it easy giving you 140,000 words to edit this time. But seriously, thank you for making my books so incredible. You always make them better.

The always incredible, Najla and Nada Qamber of *Qamber designs & media*. Thank you. I don't even think a thank you is enough to tell you both how much I appreciate the hard work, talent, and love that you pour into *The Science of Unrequited's* covers, teasers, and formatting. You both made an idea come to absolute life. You gave AJ and Evan a brand and a concept many now recognise. Thank you both so much.

To the incredible authors who have always supported me and this series, Veronica Larsen, Nikki Sloane, Fiona Cole (my soon-to-be food tour partner!), LJ Shen, Staci Hart, Saffron A. Kent, C.L Matthews, Kata Cuić, Hazel James, and Cynthia A. Rodriguez. And of course, to all the other incredible authors who share, comment, and like my books. I'm honoured to get to work in an industry with you amazing women.

Special thank you to Nadine, for helping me with my Swiss German! When I'm in Europe, I'll be hugging you!

To all the amazing bloggers, thank you for sharing AJ and Evan's covers, teasers, excerpts, everything. And your reviews, I read them and I'm in awe that I'm able to touch your hearts the way I do. You all write your own magic in those reviews. Thank you for all your hard work and love.

And finally, thank you to my absolute incredible and loyal readers. You have all supported me through the very beginning of my career. Five published years later, here we are. *My fifteenth book!* Thank you for all your love and support. For opening your hearts, minds, and time to my books and characters. Without you all, I would not know what an incredible honour it is to write for you all. Thank you. Thank you all sooo much. You're the absolute core of who I am.

And to you. Always YOU. Without you, I wouldn't have published this book and all of my books. So remember,

Just be you.

Until the next adventure we share together, whether it be a new series or standalone, I can't wait to experience it with you all.

Love,
Len

P.S. He did it! Evan Gilmore said *love*!

ABOUT THE AUTHOR

Len Webster is a romance-loving Melburnian with dreams of finding her version of 'The One.' But until that moment happens, she writes. Having graduated with her BBusCom from Monash University, Len is now busy writing her next romance about how a boy met a girl, and how they fell completely and hopelessly in love.

She is also not a certified explorer, but she's working on it.

CONNECT WITH LEN

Facebook, Twitter, Instagram, Goodreads: @lennwebster
BookBub @lenwebster | www.lenwebster.com

Want exclusive teasers, giveaways, excerpts, and news?
Join Len's private reader group and be part of the family!
Len Webster's Lenatics:
www.facebook.com/groups/618455798210117/

Or you can join Len's newsletter for all the need to know!
There's giveaways and all the news your might have missed.
Subscribe to Len's newsletter: http://eepurl.com/bJGWe5

Printed in Poland
by Amazon Fulfillment
Poland Sp. z o.o., Wrocław